QUANTUM LEAP

**OUT OF TIME. OUT OF BODY.
OUT OF CONTROL.**

QUANTUM LEAP

MIRROR'S EDGE

A NOVEL BY

CAROL DAVIS

with ESTHER D. REESE

**BASED ON THE UNIVERSAL TELEVISION
SERIES *QUANTUM LEAP*
CREATED BY DONALD P. BELLISARIO**

BERKLEY BOULEVARD BOOKS, NEW YORK

This is a work of fiction. Names, characters, places, and incidents are either the product of the authors' imaginations or are used fictitiously, and any resemblance to actual persons, living or dead, business establishments, events or locales is entirely coincidental.

Quantum Leap: Mirror's Edge, a novel by Carol Davis with Esther D. Reese, based on the Universal television series QUANTUM LEAP, created by Donald P. Bellisario.

QUANTUM LEAP: MIRROR'S EDGE

A Berkley Boulevard Book / published by arrangement with Universal Studios Publishing Rights, a division of Universal Studios Licensing, Inc.

PRINTING HISTORY
Berkley Boulevard edition / February 2000

The Penguin Putnam Inc. World Wide Web site address is http://www.penguinputnam.com

ISBN: 0-425-17351-8

BERKLEY BOULEVARD
Berkley Boulevard Books are published by The Berkley Publishing Group, a division of Penguin Putnam Inc., 375 Hudson Street, New York, New York 10014.
BERKLEY BOULEVARD and its logo are trademarks belonging to Penguin Putnam Inc.

PRINTED IN THE UNITED STATES OF AMERICA

10 9 8 7 6 5 4 3 2 1

For my mother

ACKNOWLEDGMENTS

Ten years of Leaping—hard to imagine. When I sat down to watch the first episode of *Quantum Leap* back in 1989, I had no idea that that show would end up having such an impact on my life. You're holding in your hands what probably is the last Leap novel, and since that's the case, I have many thanks to express . . .

To my mom and dad, for teaching me to love books, and for their unwavering support; to my brother, Brian, for his humor and his love; to Dale McRaven, Larry Gelbart, and Jeri Taylor, who encouraged me along the way; to Ginjer Buchanan, for giving me two opportunities to join the team; to Candy Camin, Lee Reider, and Mindy Peterman, for their input and advice; to the L.A. Leapers, for all the good times, and to the Leapers I've met from all around the world, for their support; to my friends Sharon and Bob, the two Beckys, Suzi, Sabine and Ralf, Claudia, and the Wohlgemuth family for cheering me on; to Stephen Collins and Barry Watson, for being the visual inspiration for Joe Powell and Kevin Maxwell (and for their kindness); to Esther, for all the ideas she contributed; to all of the people who worked on *Quantum Leap,* for giving us something so special to share; and last but not least, to Don Bellisario, whose idea for a story brought us all together and put right a good many things that had once been wrong. I owe you!

—Carol Davis

QUANTUM LEAP
MIRROR'S EDGE

CHAPTER ONE

Phone . . .

Pat Boone was crooning on the car radio (*"All oldies love songs, all Sunday long"*) as she rested her head against Sam's shoulder. Her hair was full of the stale smell of cigarette smoke from the bar they'd left almost an hour ago, but he could still find a hint of her shampoo, and her cologne. He shifted a little and let her nestle closer. She curled an arm around his and smiled at him, just a small curve of her lips, but he could see the affection behind it. "I love you," she murmured. He murmured back; whether he matched her words or not didn't seem to matter. He did love her, and would love her always.

Always.

Phone's ringing . . . somebody . . .

They reached the turnoff overlooking the shoreline a few minutes later. She scrambled out of the car before he could manage to get around to open the door for her and beckoned for Sam to follow her down the narrow path to the beach. They'd gotten here without much time to spare: the sun was only a few degrees above the horizon. She was still a few steps ahead of him when she reached the shore and turned to watch him approach. *My angel,* he thought, although that sounded stupid even to him.

"I'm sorry about the coffee," she said.

He made a face, both at the memory of the coffee and at the notion that she'd worried about it all day. "Forget it," he told her softly, curling his arms around her. "It's a talent. Not everybody makes great coffee."

"I'd like to be able to make you a cup of coffee you don't need to spit into the sink."

He hesitated, then admitted, "Maybe that's something to aim for."

She smiled and settled into his embrace. He could tell by the look on her face that the subject of that awful cup of coffee wouldn't be brought up again—and that this morning was probably the last time she'd attempt to brew him anything but tea. Both were fine with him. She was so perfect otherwise. He knew Grandpa Beckett would have commented, "No wonder she's not married, can't even make a decent cup of coffee," but that had nothing to do with her being single. She'd been engaged once before, and had realized a couple of months into it that that guy wasn't the right one.

So I am, I guess, he thought. *The right one.* And he had never wanted to be anything so badly in his whole life.

Phone!!!

She placed her hands—warm, soft, delicate hands—on either side of his head and turned it. "Look," she insisted.

"I see."

Sunset, deep blue and rose. Rose . . . "Are you telling me to stop and smell the roses?" he asked, grinning at her.

"If I have to," she said, "I can be even more lame than that. I love you."

"I love you too." *Always.*

Always . . .

Would somebody please answer the damn telephone?

Finally, somebody did, but too late. He'd lost the dream. At least it was quiet now, he thought as he lay there, eyes clamped stubbornly shut. He was very near the ocean: he could smell the salt in the breeze, hear the pounding of surf on rock. He tried letting himself sink back down into sleep, wanting to be lulled by the warmth of the sun on his skin and his clothes, by the scent of evergreen, by the soft cushions underneath him. For now, he insisted, he had no interest in where he was, when he was, or who he was. If he could just drift back into the dream, he could be with her, hold her, listen to her voice.

"Joe? It's Providence."

Sam Beckett opened his eyes and turned his head. The sun was hanging high in the sky in that direction, backlighting the woman in the doorway. He squinted. She wasn't the one in his dream.

"He's asking for a decision."

"I . . ."

She waited. That wasn't going to do her much good, Sam thought. He pushed himself into a sitting position and blinked away a sudden wash of vertigo. Now he could see her more clearly. "Can I—call him back?"

Too earnest. He sounded like a kid asking for a cookie. She frowned at him, then nodded and spoke quietly into the phone, words he couldn't quite make out, then pushed the off button.

"Are you all right?" she asked. "Is the headache any better?" He couldn't decide quickly enough whether yes or no was the better answer, and she took his lack of response as a no. "I'll push back the teleconference," she told him as if she'd decided to do that long before she approached him. "The people from InterData are probably already on their way, but I can meet with them."

"That's, um, that's great. If you can do that."

She was already moving, punching out a number on the phone as she carried it back inside. "Thanks," Sam said mildly, knowing she wouldn't hear him.

Once she was gone, he got up from the chaise longue and shook his head hard to clear it, then pulled in a couple of deep lungfuls of the cool, salt-tinged air. *Providence wants a decision. That's a good one. Okay, I decide . . . I decide . . .*

I want you back.

He looked around as if he thought he'd find her standing in a corner of the terrace, gazing thoughtfully off into the distance, soft wisps of her hair fluttering in the breeze. *The girl of my dreams,* he thought, his shoulders drooping as something worse than the vertigo swept through him and filled him so completely it felt like a living being itself. "But you're gone, aren't you?" he murmured, not sure how he knew that or why he felt compelled to say it aloud.

I'd give my left arm just to curl up and go back to sleep for a couple hours and be with you. To not have to figure out who she means or what they want. Providence. What Providence wants.

Nothing answered him except the sound of the waves. Slowly, he walked to the end of the terrace and leaned against the waist-high wall that surrounded it. The water, aluminum white under the afternoon sun, stretched off toward infinity, unmarked by anything but the insignificant ripple of waves. It was the Pacific, and again, he was unsure how he knew that.

You love the Pacific—that's why this house is here. You love taking your shoes off and walking along the edge, even when the water's cold. Especially when the water's cold, because it makes you laugh.

He wanted to cry.

"You're falling apart, Beckett," he told himself, squaring his shoulders and stepping away from the wall to dispute that diagnosis. "That's a luxury you can't afford. You're here for a reason. Something that needs to be done."

Though apparently, it didn't need to be done right now. The woman with the phone hadn't come back. She'd accepted his lack of response as if it were something that happened a lot, something she would wait out because she had to. But Providence would still need an answer, eventually. The people who wanted to teleconference would too, more than likely. Maybe they could have one now—if he could get her to explain what the question was.

Of course, first he had to find her.

She'd left him through a narrow door in the center of a wall constructed almost entirely of dark-tinted glass. Sam turned his back to the ocean and walked in that direction until he was close enough to the glass that it stopped being a mirror and became transparent.

Inside was a room that impressed him probably more than it should have, because he could tell even from this limited perspective that this was one humdinger of a house. His, more than likely. He smiled then, because "humdinger" was Grandpa Beck-

4

ett's word. Grandpa, who'd put a lot of stock in women's culinary talents. Then he stuck out a hand, pushed the door open, and entered the house. His house. The home of the guy he'd seen reflected in the dark glass.

Because he'd been taught to close doors (against insects, or dust, or loss of heat or air-conditioning, or to protect his work from interruption) he closed this one. The silence that produced was startling and absolute.

It's like . . . then.

Sam's breath caught in his throat. No surf, no wind in the trees, no music, no voices, no hum of machinery. Being in this room was like being profoundly deaf.

Just like the moment of the Leap.

No sound, no light, no sense of the cool metal beneath his bare feet, of the Fermi suit surrounding his body. Nothing but the bitter taste of apprehension in his mouth, for a second, then even that was gone. The fear of that moment came back and Sam closed his eyes, testing it. He didn't realize he was holding his breath—when he opened his eyes again, air flooded into his lungs. He'd been without air long enough to make himself dizzy, and he stumbled. The bed was the nearest place to sit down and he aimed for it, collapsing onto it as if he'd been thrown there. Voices began to ring in his head.

"Sam. Why do you do things like that? You should know you'll only make yourself sick. You'd think you were no older than Katie."

"I was making her laugh, Mom."

"And I suppose it would make her laugh even more if you got sick to your stomach all over the rug. Stop this, now. Use a little common sense. You're supposed to be a good example to the baby."

"But I made her laugh."

"A good reason to be proud of yourself. I swear, Sam Beckett."

SamBeckettSamBeckettSam

He shuddered hard, thinking, *Voices. All the nut jobs say they hear voices. You're really losing it! Pull yourself together. You've got something to accomplish here.* Instead, he huddled on the bed, curled almost into a fetal position until he realized how silly that was. He wasn't sick, and had no reason to be frightened. He'd Leaped how many times now? A hundred? Two

5

hundred? He forced himself to relax a little, stretching out his legs, easing onto his back. His right shoulder found a sudden patch of warmth, where the sun had warmed the bed, he supposed. The sensation was comforting, and he let his eyes drift shut again, blocking out a room that seemed as big as the whole ground floor of his parents' house, a room whose furnishings had cost more than that whole house had been worth when the bank took it away from his parents.

The patch of warmth grew larger. A heating element inside the bed, Sam decided, triggered by his weight.

"Come back to me."

What? He lifted his head and scanned the room, rapidly, end to end. No one there. He could see all of it from where he lay: the grouping of comfortable chairs around the stone fireplace, the oak wardrobe that had to hold enough to clothe a family of six, the trio of oil paintings (all seascapes), the flat TV with a screen bigger than a door, the round table placed close to the glass wall, providing a place to eat that would be almost outdoors when the weather outside was bad. The lights in the bathroom were out, but he could see enough of that room, too, to know there was no one inside. Not the woman with the phone, not Al, not someone playing a trick on him. He was alone.

But the voice had been very real. Real enough to seduce him into closing his eyes, to fold his hands almost as if he were praying. To think, *Don't leave me.*

He fell asleep, soothed by the warmth of the bed, and again he dreamed of her.

The woman who had answered the phone came looking for him at the end of the afternoon. She didn't have to disturb him this time; he'd been up, awake, for maybe twenty minutes, going through the bedroom and then the bathroom, feeling more and more like a curious child as he opened drawers and cabinet doors and stepped into a shower stall with doors of etched, leaded glass, big enough to accommodate a dozen people. One of the cabinet drawers was filled with carefully rolled pairs of socks, arranged according to color, and the drawer beneath it held crisply folded cotton boxer shorts, also in a variety of colors. Sam was counting the socks when the woman found him, and, stubbornly, refused to look embarrassed or sheepish when he was caught. After all, this was his house. And they were his socks.

"So," he said mildly, "is Providence okay with waiting?"

"Yes, of course."

Sam took a long look at her expression, which was so bland it told him nothing. Most people would blink, or shuffle their feet, or look away from the kind of scrutiny he was giving her. She didn't twitch a whisker, which made him think she was used to being stared at. Why, or by whom, he didn't know. She was probably close to forty, attractive, but not stunning; her dark hair was pulled back into a ponytail and she'd opted for only a light touch of makeup. And she wasn't a clotheshorse—she was wearing khaki slacks and a navy-blue short-sleeved blouse that didn't quite fit her, as if they'd been chosen for someone else.

"I told them you'd be in touch tomorrow," she went on. "They're fine with that. It's still very early. But you know how Peter is."

"Sure."

"The people from InterData left their proposal materials. It's an enormous package. I can weed through it later on if you like. I know they're figuring on you looking at the whole thing, but there's probably two pounds of paper there."

"Great," Sam said. "Weed away."

"The E-mail is sorted. There's nothing that needs your attention today. I know it bothers your eyes if you try to focus on the screen." She took a closer look, studying his eyes. "Unless the headache is gone? Do you feel better?"

"I'm okay."

"Would you like me to call Dr. Platt? He's waiting to hear how the medication worked."

"Sure. Tell him—" *Tell him I think I know who I am, but I don't have a clue who you are, or who he is, or what medication he prescribed. Tell him*—Sam smiled absently to himself—*Beckett is my name and winging it is my game.*"—I feel pretty good."

"I'm glad. Then—should I call Providence back? I'm afraid if Peter's gotten to them, they're going to twitch all night. I really don't know if he's the right man for the job, Joe. He's so nervous."

Sam shook his head. "No. Let them wait. You told them I'd call tomorrow." *They have to be okay with that, don't they? They're waiting, or he's waiting, or it's waiting, because I said they had to. And I . . .* He realized something then, something that made him want to break into a big, ridiculous grin, because it

7

was something he had never experienced before. He considered several ways to ask the question, and decided on one that seemed the most—*What's the secret word, Gramps?*—highfalutin'. "What's my net worth?" he inquired idly, as if he were asking what the temperature was outside. As if it were something he asked several times a day.

"You're still number four, Joe."

"Four?"

"The fourth wealthiest man in the country."

"That's a lot of money." He stood there, looking at the woman's poker face, and wanted to sing, softly, to the tune of an old advertising jingle, *I've got money/Clean up to my armpits*. The leaded-glass shower doors were in his peripheral vision, as was the marble Jacuzzi tub—like the wardrobe and the shower, it was big enough to accommodate an entire family. The thing needed enough water to freak out an army of environmentalists—who could have fit in there too, slouching back with martinis in hand to watch a video or two on the TV mounted into the wall. Or maybe make a few calls on the multiline phone. Or just stare vacantly out through the—yes, another one—glass wall at the sky and the evergreens.

"What time is dinner?" he asked.

That, oddly, surprised her more than the money question. "Whenever you're hungry."

Of course. "Ten minutes?"

She nodded. "I'll tell Marie." Then she left Sam alone in his colossal, dome-ceilinged bathroom with his drawer of coordinated socks. And his television, which more than likely would offer the day's news on a dozen different channels. Sam seized the remote from the marble edge of the tub and pointed it at the TV, which obligingly blinked on and showed him the earnest face of Tom Brokaw.

"June fifteenth, 1999," a voice said behind him.

"Your birthday," Sam said without turning.

"Yeah. But don't remind me. It was a while ago. It's not that here. Not June any more."

"What is it?"

"Never mind."

The only reflection in the mirror over the sink was that of the fourth wealthiest man in the country. Sam turned to smile at the hologram of his best friend, Al Calavicci, then to grimace at Al's suit, made of a fabric Sam would have earmarked for the costume designer of a big-budget science-fiction movie. The thing shimmered in a full spectrum of colors. Sam sighed and shook his head. "You're a live special effect."

"Like it?" Al asked happily. "I got it yesterday."

"Christmas present?"

Al's expression flickered. "Uh . . . no."

"Uh, yes," Sam sighed. "It's Christmastime there, isn't it? Why don't you just give up and admit it? You get that same look every time I land anywhere near December twenty-fifth. It's Christmas, I'm missing it, just like I've missed how many others? Just let it go. If Verbena's going to put me on suicide watch because of this, she needs other ways to occupy her time."

Al's head tipped slightly to one side, listening to something, or someone, Sam couldn't hear. Al had completely lost the joviality he'd been wearing a minute ago, and his shoulders seemed to draw in on themselves. "I know," he said, barely above a whisper, addressing someone other than Sam. "I noticed."

"You noticed what?"

"Nothing."

"You noticed that I'm—" Sam cut himself off. He rested his hands on the countertop surrounding the sink and peered at the reflection in the mirror. The man he saw there was in his early fifties, blond and handsome. Fit. Well dressed. So far beyond "making a nice living," as Grandma Beckett would have put it, that he probably didn't remember what being "well-off" had felt like, if he'd ever been far enough down the ladder to be simply well-off. The fourth richest guy in the country. A mover and a shaker, with the power to profoundly affect other people's lives as simply as those other people would blow their noses.

Sam had spent a long time studying that reflection before the woman with the phone found him counting rolled-up socks. It was a face people liked, he'd decided. A face that looked good on magazine covers: none of them were clear in his mind, but Sam remembered this face with mastheads dangling above it. He'd smiled experimentally, over and over, as if he were posing for a photographer, and knew that yes, this was a face people were drawn to. A movie-star face, but one with some years worn into it.

When he let the smiles fade, he knew this was the face of someone who was painfully and irreparably alone.

And owned eighty-four pairs of neatly rolled socks.

"What's the matter?" Al asked him.

Sam lifted his left hand and showed Al the narrow gold band on the third finger. "Where is she?"

"Dead."

"Recently?"

"Nah. Twenty or twenty-five years ago, something like that. You're a widower."

"You mean *he* is."

"You, he, whatever."

"She's not here. You're sure she's not here."

"She's dead, Sam."

"Huh," Sam said ruefully, then turned his back on the mirror and moved toward the door to the bedroom.

"Where're you going?" Al protested. "I've got . . ."

Sam shook his head. "Dinner. I told her I wanted to eat in ten minutes. Which is true. I'm famished."

"So you'll be a couple minutes late. They can keep it warm for you." When Sam continued to move, Al tried to block him, blustering loudly when he failed. "Sam! You know it's tougher to have a conversation with other people around. What's bugging you?"

"Nothing."

"Let me just tell you what we know, then you can go chow down."

Sam reached up and ran a hand through his hair. He considered the suggestion for a moment before he shook his head again. "You know," he said quietly, "I really don't care what you know."

And he walked away, leaving his best friend sputtering in the doorway of the bathroom with Tom Brokaw talking somberly behind him.

CHAPTER TWO

"Sam!"

With the handlink howling in protest, Al slammed in the co-ordinates that would beat Sam to wherever it was he thought he was going. A second later, the Observer found himself downstairs, in what he supposed its owner referred to as his living room. *"Living" room, my ass,* he thought. No one did any living in this room—it was strictly for show, designed to tell you what the owner wanted you to think about him—which was something Al anticipated in the moment before the hologram coalesced around him. He'd read enough articles about and seen enough interviews with the fourth richest guy in the country to have done a pretty accurate sketch of this room without ever seeing it. Though come to think of it, maybe he *had* seen this room before, in one of the copies of *Architectural Digest* Verbena Beeks liked to flip through during her downtime.

Sam emerged from the foyer a moment later. He didn't seem surprised to see the Observer. In fact, Sam wasn't interested in him at all, Al realized. He was looking for something else.

"Sam?"

"Where are the pictures?" Sam asked, prowling the room, scanning the walls, his fingertips straying over the objets d'art placed with precise casualness on priceless antique, inlaid tabletops.

"Pictures?" Al repeated helplessly.

"Photos," Sam elaborated. "Mom, Dad, Aunt Sylvia, Uncle Bill . . ."

Not looking for something, Al realized: Sam was looking for some*one*. "Look around, Sam. Guys who live in museums like this don't have snapshots of the kinfolk—they have Art." Al waved a cigar at a Hunter-Wasser original dominating one corner of the room.

"Even millionaires have families."

"Try 'gazillionaire.' You're loaded this Leap, pal. You're—"

"Joe Powell. I know. I recognized the reflection. Fourth richest man in America," Sam answered with a smugness he regretted almost immediately.

"Kick in the butt, ain't it?" the Observer asked, whacking the handlink into submission to take advantage of Sam's possibly momentary attention. "Joseph Easton Powell the Third. Business mogul and philanthropist. Everybody's favorite Horatio Alger story for the twenty-first century. Family was big stuff back in the railroad days, lost it all by the time Black Friday hit, and he got it all back, plus some. And somethin' else." Al glanced around furtively as if he thought they were being watched. And of course they were: Ziggy wouldn't miss a nanosecond of this. "Catch this, buddy. You're the Sexiest Man in the World." Grinning, he displayed the cover of the magazine he'd pulled from the voluminous pocket of his shimmering jacket.

"Not me," Sam replied firmly. "Him."

"You, him, same difference. You're him and he's you, until you do whatever the ol' Master Planner sent you here to do and"—Al gestured—"Leap on out."

"Which is?"

"Didn't I just say 'whatever'? We don't have specifics, Sam. It's way too early for specifics."

"Well, color me surprised."

"But—"

Sam gestured to cut him off. "You're keeping me from dinner. Do you know something other than stuff I've already figured out for myself, or not?" When Al hesitated, he prodded, "Tell Ziggy . . ."

"Ah. Ziggy. About Ziggy . . ."

"There's *another* problem with Ziggy?"

"It's not her fault, Sam," Al protested. "She was researching this Leap and got caught in some, uh, binary difficulties."

"Binary difficulties? Ziggy isn't limited by binary code."

"No, but the computers she talks to are. She's having a little trouble getting the information she needs from the ones that think it's 0001 B.C.E. Until she gets that, she refuses to make any calculations."

"Terrific."

"We can figure this out, Sam. We've done it before without Ziggy's help."

For a moment, Al was certain Sam was going to blow his cork. Then the moment passed, expelled by a resigned sigh from Sam. "I Leaped in in the middle of a dream, Al. His dream. About her. It's like the time I Leaped into that cop, and had the memory flashes. I think Powell and I are psycho-synergizing."

"Kinda early to make that assumption, isn't it? How do you know it wasn't your dream?"

"Because it wasn't. It was about her. His wife."

"How do you know that?"

"I know. I was reliving things he experienced. His memories, his emotions, all about her. Then I heard the phone ringing. There was a woman in the doorway, holding the phone. She woke me up."

"With a kiss?" Al brightened.

Sam shot him a disapproving look. "I think she lives here. Dark hair, late thirties. Who is she?"

Al whacked the handlink. "Has to be Barbara Maxwell. 'Max' to her friends and associates. She's Powell's personal assistant. Keeps him fed, on time, informed. The woman behind the man."

"She said someone called me—called Powell. A . . . Providence?"

"Ah." Al tortured the handlink again. "Not 'a Providence'— Providence, Rhode Island. There's a movement afoot to draft

Powell to run for president and it's headquartered there." Al chuckled. "Rhode Island. Figures."

"Does he know about that?"

"Of course he knows. They always know. It's not like being picked Queen for a Day."

"So does he? Run for president?"

Al shrugged. "He hasn't said one way or the other. There's a lot of speculation in the media that he's gonna announce it at a big millennium charity bash he's throwing on New Year's Eve, but nobody knows for sure other than him, and whoever's in his inner circle. She might know. The girl Friday. Max."

"That's an outdated, sexist term, Al."

"Political correctness is gonna kill me." Al sighed.

"What *do* we know for sure?"

"Ah . . ." Al was spared an honest answer by the arrival of Barbara Maxwell, whose soft-soled shoes had made her approach unnoticeable until she was actually in the room. Al, who had had people sneak up on him far too many times, shuddered and clutched the handlink hard enough to make it shriek. "That's her? Gee, Sam. With that outfit, I woulda thought she was a counselor for a bunch of rotten twelve-year-olds at Camp Gottalottabucks."

"Dinner's ready, Joe," she announced quietly.

"Be right there," Sam told her.

She retreated without another word, Al trailing her as far as the three gleaming mahogany steps leading out of the sunken living room. "Okay, so she's not gonna make any of the best-dressed lists. But hey, Sam: your secretary's got great legs. And a very cute . . ."

Sam glared and Al held up a mollifying hand, using it as a small shield from his best friend's frustration. "She's wearing pants," Sam said softly. "How can you tell anything about her legs?"

"Educated guess." Al stared off in the direction she'd taken, as if some image of her still lingered there. "Many, many years of—"

"Al."

"Have your dinner. I'll go and tell Ziggy she's gotta learn to be flexible."

"Tell her to find alternate sources of information."

"Sure. I'll just tell Ziggy that, and she'll listen to me, like

14

she's supposed to." Sam raised a brow. "Eat," Al told him. "I'll be back later."

"Well, Bingo, that was the easy part."

He was talking to himself again. Beeks was gonna have a field day.

Taking a long drag on his favorite vice, Al closed his eyes for a moment and fortified himself for the crisis waiting on the other side of the Imaging Chamber door. As with Powell's living room, he knew what he was going to see before he saw it. They'd be waiting for him out there, the whole bunch of them—Verbena, Gooshie, Donna, David. A bunch of faces that would make the Grinch look like a party boy, and all because of one guy. It was a good thing Tina was away for the holidays, because he hated her to see him wither under the scrutiny of people who were supposed to be his subordinates. How was it possible, he wondered, that one guy could create such a monumental pain not only in Al's backside but in pretty much every other square inch of his body?

Then he reminded himself that the one guy's last name was Beckett.

No one said anything when he strode down the ramp into the Control Room. Not a peep. Not a "How's Sam?" or even a "Merry Christmas." They didn't have to; Donna Alessi-Beckett's face spelled it all out, chapter and verse.

"He's here," Al moaned, a glorious statement of the obvious.

"He's got clearance to be on the grounds," Sam's wife reminded him.

"And you couldn't get somebody to revoke it?"

"He'd be on the phone in a heartbeat to get it reinstated. We already tried. He said he can go over higher heads than you can."

"The SOB wants to one-up me?"

Before he could anticipate the move, she reached out and plucked the cigar from his mouth, rolled it around in her fingers for a moment as if she intended to smoke it herself, then passed it on to a techie who quickly disappeared with it. "Smoke-free environment, Al," she pointed out, then went on, "Tom's chairman of the House committee. They're brand-new and they're gung-ho. We can't keep him out. He's trying to do his job."

"Well, is he out or is he in?"

"He's upstairs in Reception."

"Then keep him there. Keep him waiting until I can think of somebody to call," Al ordered, staring off in the direction the techie had taken and mourning the loss of his stogie, the third one that had been swiped from him this week. "Stall him. Hell's bells, if there's one thing we've learned how to do in the last five years, it's stall." Ignoring the skeptical look that he earned from Donna, he addressed the kaleidoscope of lights that was Sam's supercomputer-brainchild-brat. "Ziggy, baby, you got anything for me? Tell me you got something for me."

"I told you before you entered the Imaging Chamber, Admiral: my data is incomplete."

"That was ten minutes ago. Your daddy's eating his shorts, precious. If you don't give me something by the time I get back here, I promise you a whole new series of sensory input to study."

"Threats will not produce results," Ziggy said loftily.

"But promises will," Al countered. And, he mused, after five marriages and seven collapsed engagements, he ought to know. Flinging the handlink to Gooshie, he headed out of Control to the one place in the complex he thought he might find some of the answers to Sam's questions.

Verbena Beeks was in the corridor outside the Waiting Room, arms folded across her chest, the toe of one faux-alligator shoe tapping idly against the tile floor. Her attention was fixed on a spot where the ceiling met the top of the wall and her gaze was a little unfocused, as if she'd been hypnotized.

"Well?" Al demanded.

She peered at him for a moment before she said anything. "How's Sam?"

"Cranky."

"How so?"

"I dunno. Just off his feed. Something's put a bug up the kid's butt. And *he* doesn't have people swiping his cigars. He's looking for pictures."

"Of whom?"

"Family." Al tipped his head toward the Waiting Room door. "How's *he* doing?"

"A typical response to the Leap. Disoriented, worried, a little scared, a little blustery. After I managed to convince him that no, he really cannot have access to a telephone, he asked me if he'd been kidnapped by the CIA."

16

"Paranoid?"

"Not unreasonably so, given the current political climate."

Al nodded, stroking his chin. Verbena waited for him to reply, but instead, he leaned against one of the corridor's mirror-smooth walls and felt around in his pockets for a fresh cigar. He'd spent a few minutes watching their Visitor over the Waiting Room monitors before heading for the Imaging Chamber, interested at first in getting a "live" glimpse of the man who'd gotten more media attention in the past few months than Harrison Ford, Tom Cruise, and Arnold Schwarzenegger combined. He was forced to squeeze out of the monitor room when it began to fill with female staff members. All of *them* wanted a peek at the Sexiest Man in the World, even if they knew that because of the Aura, the man they'd see over the row of six color monitors would look like Sam Beckett. Only to Al, because of his neuron link with Ziggy, did the Visitor actually look like Joseph Powell.

Sexiest Man in the World, Al snorted. Well, let the ladies have their fun. He'd done his own share of celebrity gazing a couple months ago when Elvis popped in. The King of Rock and Roll, in his prime—now, *that* had been a hoot. Al basked in the memory of those few days for a moment. *Kinda wish He was more like a good screenwriter. He just doesn't get the value of a good laugh. A little comic relief.*

"You're worried," Verbena suggested.

"No kidding."

"Could you fill me in, please? Since I'm the one primarily responsible for the Visitor's care and well-being?"

Al turned and looked at the Waiting Room door as if he could see through it. He'd done a fast, silent round of thank-yous to Whoever was in charge of all this when Sam failed to notice that he was glossing over Joseph Easton Powell the Third's interest in the presidency of the United States. There was *speculation* Powell intended to announce his candidacy at the kick-ass New Year's Eve party he'd be hosting at . . . "Mount Olympus"? Yeah, that should win the Understatement of the Decade sweepstakes. The incumbent had used up his two terms (with some ass-kicking going on there too, in both directions) so the Oval Office was going to be up for grabs next November. There were a few "experts" still yammering about the chances of a certain woman senator, and those of the son of a former chief executive who was well liked by all the voters in his home state, but the yammering was being drowned out by what had begun as a murmur back around Martin Luther King Day. *Joe Powell. Joe Powell's going to run. Joe Powell Joe Powell JoePowellJoePowell JoePowell . . .*

Powell had made it very clear he wasn't a party man. The powers-that-be of both the Democratic and Republican parties were sweating bullets. Let them yammer; they knew which end was up. If Powell ran, Powell would win, and Powell was beholden to no one. Politically speaking.

"This is not a good thing," Al said.

"What isn't?"

"Having the next president of the United States sitting in there stewing in his own juices. You're treating him good, aren't you?"

"Al. I treat all the Visitors 'good.' "

"How PO'ed is he about the phone thing?"

"No more so than anyone else we've had in there. I told him his business interests were being taken care of."

"And he bought that."

"Of course not."

"It's not good, Beeks. Having him in there."

The Project psychiatrist caught her superior by the sleeve and tugged him down the corridor, not far enough from the marine guards posted outside the Waiting Room to be out of earshot, but enough to make a demonstration of the need for a little privacy. "I wondered why you spent so much time watching him over the monitors without actually going in to see him. You don't like him, do you?"

"Since when does that butter the bread on a different side?"

"You tell me."

Al was silent for what seemed like an hour. Then he gestured with his head and walked farther down the corridor with Beeks treading quietly alongside. When he finally stopped, they were far enough away from the Waiting Room that the two marines would have no chance of overhearing him. "Powell started the 'Un-Tour' six months ago. Sam's sitting right at the beginning of the preamble to a race for the presidency. You're not a mushroom, Beeks. You tell me how big of a problem it is for Sam Beckett to be able to change the life of a guy who more than likely is going to be the most powerful man in the world thirteen months from now."

"A man you don't like. A man you don't think should be the president."

"It doesn't matter whether I like him or not. Yeah, okay, if my ego was a lot bigger I'd be standing here rubbing my hands together, going, 'Go for it, Sam, sink this guy.' Everybody we've had here up till now has been small potatoes. This is a bad thing. Where something Sam does could affect the presidency."

Verbena thought that over for a moment. "Maybe we should trust that God will sort it all out. In the meantime, I think you should go in there and talk to him, just as you've done with all the other Visitors. Do your job—the one Sam wanted you to do, and the one you volunteered for. You've handled everyone else perfectly well. But go easy this time. You're right: this is an important man, and a very intelligent one. If you try to get too much information out of him, he might clam up." The corner of her lip twitched. "Or bullshit you."

Al blinked at her. "What?"

"You heard me."

"Thought I did. You're spending too much time in this hole in the ground, Beeksie."

"Says the pot." Verbena smiled. When Al turned and took a step toward the Waiting Room door, her expression changed suddenly and she grasped his arm to hold him back. "Al?" she said, her voice full of concern. "What are you not telling me?"

"What? Nothing."

"What's happening with Sam?"

"Nothing." He frowned down at the slender fingers curled around his biceps and heaved a grumbling sigh. "Nothing. He says he Leaped in in the middle of a dream. Thinks he dreamed about Powell's wife. Or Powell was dreaming about Powell's wife. Whatever."

"And . . . ?"

"He's got that look in his eye. Like he's gonna obsess about it."

"Why?"

"I don't know. I don't know."

"That's who he wants pictures of."

"Yeah. That's what he said."

She let go of Al and began to gnaw thoughtfully on the tip of her neatly manicured thumbnail. "I was talking with David while you were in the Imaging Chamber. We're both concerned about

19

Sam. His attitude has changed so much these last few months. You've said so yourself: he doesn't rest much, and he doesn't have the same sense of satisfaction when things turn out all right. It's not good for him, to lose the sense that he's accomplishing something."

"What, you mean he's not having fun? Who the hell ever said this was supposed to be fun?"

"We're concerned about Donna too. Sam has never Leaped this close to the present before. When Gooshie told her the date of the Leap—"

"Her hopes are up. I don't blame her."

"We don't know if it means anything at all. Gooshie says it's probably completely arbitrary, and I have to agree with him. Remember, back in the beginning, we thought Sam's Leaping forward in time meant he was getting closer to home. There's been no pattern to it, not once in five years. No predictable movement in any direction."

"I don't want to knock her down, if she wants to hope. You want somebody to wreck things for her, you do it."

"We all want to hope, Al."

"Now tell me something I don't know."

"I can talk to Donna. I can talk to everyone here. But I can't help Sam. He used to have a sense of anticipation at the beginning of each new Leap. It meant a great deal to him, being able to change things for the better. I could be wrong—I'm getting everything secondhand, through you, and through Ziggy. But I'm concerned about him."

Al cut her off. "What do you want me to do, give him a month off? Maybe you forgot: I'm not the one who's Leaping him around."

She reached out to touch him again. "Help him, Al. Boost his spirits."

The Observer's eyes widened. "What the Christ do you think I've been trying to do for five years?"

"He's got no one else to turn to."

"You're the one who's singing gloom and doom. Don't think that way. And don't tell Donna what you're thinking." He peeled her fingers away from his arm, squeezed them for an instant, then let her hand drop. She let it dangle as if it no longer belonged to her, then tucked both hands into her armpits and hugged herself.

"Go talk to Powell. Maybe he can give us something to help put Sam's mind at ease." Before Al could reply, she turned sharply on one heel and hurried off down the corridor.

Don't tell Donna? he thought as he returned to the Waiting Room door, absentmindedly returning the salutes of the two kids standing guard. Like that was going to work. He and Beeks might keep their silence, and Frick and Frack here at the door probably would, but the walls had ears in this place. So did the floors, and the ceiling, and the doors, and the sprinkler heads.

"Ziggy," he said sharply.

"Yes, Admiral," the computer cooed, the voice seeming to come from everywhere and nowhere.

"Keep your trap shut."

"Of course, Admiral."

"Huh," he snorted.

After a quick retinal scan confirmed his identity, the four-inch-thick door slid upward in its track. Inside, sitting quietly on the examining table in the middle of the room, was the latest in a frighteningly long line of Visitors: the Sexiest Man in the World. The fourth wealthiest man in the country. The next president of the country? Al denied himself the right to shudder and instead offered Powell a noncommittal smile.

Powell glanced at him, then at the door.

"How's it going?" Al asked.

Powell ignored him and slid down from the exam table. He began to pace the room, slowly at first, then more determinedly, stalking the space much as Sam had stalked Powell's living room moments before. Scared? Nervous? Ziggy could probably offer up a nice neat percentage—something like, 28.6 percent of the Visitors did this dance, looking for a way out, an explanation, or just a way to keep moving and avoid facing the fact that they were frightened out of their wits.

"Who are you?" Powell asked.

"You can call me Al," the Admiral answered, resisting the urge to hum.

"Where am I?"

"You're in the Waiting Room." This was an old routine, set up almost five years before, after Sam's first few Leaps. The truth, even tiny drabs of it, helped put the Visitors at ease. Some of them asked, the Waiting Room for what? To where? Some of them didn't bother. Some of them were too consumed by the

21

tap-dancing, pants-wetting heebie-jeebies to remember how to form words.

"The doctor told me that much. *Where?* What am I waiting for?"

Yep, that was on the list of "been here, heard that." "What can you remember about getting here?" Al asked.

"I . . ." Confusion etched the man's features. "I'm not sure."

"Any chance you were asleep?"

"Yes. I think you're right. I must have been asleep." Powell stopped in front of the benign pastel abstract bolted to a wall that, unlike those in the rest of the Project, had been painted a soothing blue. "Dreaming." He blinked at Al. "Am I dreaming?"

"Could be," Al said. "You got a name?"

"Joe."

"Nice to meet you, Joe. You smoke?"

Powell looked at the cigar Al was lighting. "I do when they're Cubans."

Bagged. The Cubans were contraband as hell, but Al justified his possession of them as spoils of a cold war, spoils he'd more than earned. Sam had always maintained that that was a morally shaky argument, but what did the kid know about it? He didn't know a fine cigar from a table leg.

Joe Powell did, taking the slim bundle of fragrant leaves from Al at the same time that he patted at nonexistent pockets for a knife to trim it with. When his hand met the fabric of the Fermi suit, he was instantly disgruntled—and a little embarrassed.

"Was this"—Powell indicated the skintight garment—"really necessary?"

" 'Fraid so," Al answered amiably, producing from a trouser pocket a cigar cutter whose design rendered it reasonably unfit for homicidal mayhem and handing it to Powell.

"Why?"

"We're monitoring your vital signs."

"With this . . . leotard?" Powell lifted his right arm, then his left. The sensors that lay against his skin were hard to spot from the outside, but he zeroed in on them almost immediately and smiled absently, appreciatively. "I'm not connected to anything. It monitors and transmits the data? Where's the receiver?"

"Nearby."

Powell smiled again, then seemed to lose his equilibrium and sat down. It took a gesture from Al to prompt him to prepare the cigar and put it in his mouth. Al lit it for him and watched Powell puff the cigar into life.

"What were you dreaming about, Joe?"

He thought hard. Letting a long wisp of smoke trail from between his lips, he looked steadily at Al. "I don't remember."

"Don't worry about it, then."

Expensive Cuban smoke collected around Powell's head for a moment before the room's ventilation system kicked into high gear and sucked it up to the ceiling and out. "How long am I going to be here?" he asked hesitantly, looking at his bare feet, the end of the bed, the row of tiny ceiling vents, anywhere but at Al.

"Could be awhile."

"Could I have some water?"

"Sure."

"Thank you."

Al nodded and gestured at the cigar. "Enjoy that. The next face you see is probably gonna tell you it's bad for your health, and her health, and the ozone, and baby seals, and every other damn thing she can think of, but don't let her wrestle that little gem away from you." Powell nodded, still not looking at him, and Al stepped toward the door. "Open," he said to nobody in particular. He wasn't concerned about Powell trying to rush him in a bid for freedom; anyone other than him trying to cross the threshold going out would get a jolt of electricity courtesy of Ziggy that would knock him on his very wealthy butt.

Think of that, Al mused. *The whole country wants you, and we've got you. Betcha Diane Sawyer would like to be locked up in this room right now, face-to-face with . . .*

Something made him glance back over his shoulder.

Powell was watching him, smoking, smiling absently, like a guy leaning on the railing of a cruise ship drifting through the Aegean Sea. A nanosecond after their eyes connected, Powell looked away.

Al trotted through the doorway and zoomed on past the guards as the door settled back down its track and locked. Beeks, back from wherever she'd disappeared to, was huddled with the marines and tried dashing after him, but he outpaced her easily.

"What is it?" Verbena called after him. "Al?"

It had lasted only a second, but five years of playing this game had taught Al to spot things that came and went so fast, their only effect ought to be subliminal. Always, always, the Visitors showed up magnafoozled. Scared, worried, nervous, catatonic, gibbering, peeing their drawers, hiding under the bed, confused, puzzled, angry. Always! Every last fricking time.

It had lasted only a second, but Al had seen it.

Joe Powell wasn't magnafoozled. Those lights were on, and *everybody* was home. Powell was exactly where he was used to being: in the driver's seat.

"Nothing," Al said, and kept running.

CHAPTER
THREE

The dining-room table was three times as old as Sam; it was also as long as a Greyhound bus and weighed almost as much. Two places had been set: one at the head of the table, and one beside it. Serving dishes oozing wisps of fragrant steam sat on hot pads on the breakfront.

That all made sense. So, in a way, did the laptop, the cellular phone, and the stack of manila file folders beside what had to be Barbara Maxwell's place.

No one had asked what Sam wanted to eat. The answer would have been several helpings of his mother's fried chicken, biscuits and gravy, with homemade cobbler à la mode for dessert, all washed down by a couple of cold glasses of milk. Maybe, he thought as he settled into the chair at the head of the table, someone had asked Joe Powell that morning what he thought he'd like for dinner. Or maybe whoever was on duty at the stove simply prepared something and hoped Powell would like it.

"Max" sat beside him and arranged a linen napkin over the lap of her khaki slacks.

"Smells good," Sam offered.

A gray-haired woman no bigger than a ten-year-old child popped through a doorway behind Sam, juggling a china soup tureen she deposited on the breakfront with a loud gasp of relief. Sam's first instinct was to scramble out of his chair to help her, but he had managed to do nothing more than shift his weight before the door swung open again and a man was there to slide a hand under the little woman's elbow.

"Good Jesus, Marie, use the cart," the man said with exasperation.

Even drawn up to her full height, Marie came no farther up than the middle of the man's chest. She faced him sternly anyway, fists on her hips, ignoring the tendril of hair that flopped down onto her cheek. "I am not so old," she announced, with a French accent broad enough to drive an army convoy through. That said, she stalked past him, back into the room she had come from, leaving the man to shake his head and stare at the soup tureen.

"If she dropped that bastard," he groaned, "we'd have soup from here to Carmel."

"I'll talk to her," Max said, her attention not on the tureen or the man standing guard over it but on the pile of folders, which she seemed to be sorting by order of importance.

"That's a waste of air."

Sam, sitting down, found himself nose to chest with the man and had to tip his head back to consider anything farther north. He grinned nervously for a second, then dropped his head and pretended to be fascinated by the basket of warm rolls sitting a few inches from his plate. "Maybe the, uh, cart is a good idea," he murmured. "I'm sure that thing is heavy."

Even without looking he could tell the man was staring.

This is your house, he reminded himself. *These people work for you. At least I think they do. They're not relatives—they don't look anything like him. You. Powell. So don't waffle, tell them what you want.* "Tell her to use the cart," he said.

The man began to uncover serving dishes, releasing the aromas from inside. Okay, the meal wasn't a Thelma Beckett Special, but whatever it was would certainly do in a pinch. Sam sat fussing with his napkin, then with a roll and a butter knife, as the man plucked his plate out from in front of him, arranged it with food, and deposited it back in its original spot. *Is he gonna cut my meat for me?* Sam wondered, and grinned absently again. Instead, the man filled Max's plate, then a third plate that seemed to have come out of nowhere. Sam watched him out of the corner of his eye. He was easily six-foot-four, and his blue-black hair, gleaming in the light of the crystal chandelier, topped a body that was almost pure muscle. Sam knew who he was without asking: Powell's bodyguard.

And nursemaid, judging by his actions. When Sam's water glass had dropped below half-full, the man refilled it, his dinner plate balanced on his left hand. When Sam's napkin slipped off his lap onto the floor, the man retrieved it. To Sam's relief, he replaced it with a clean one that he handed to his employer rather than attempt to deploy it.

"Thanks," Sam murmured.

The word came out only halfway. A memory, fuzzy at first, pushed its way into his mind as he took another bite of fillet of sole. Himself, crouched on the floor, holding out something white. White cloth. White . . . undershorts.

The owner of the shorts was standing an arm's length away. Scowling. Naked. Waiting for Sam to dress him.

The bite of fillet lodged in Sam's throat. He began to cough and choke, and pounded himself violently on the chest until it broke loose, waving away the man, who had ditched his plate and was ready to help.

If he does the Heimlich on me, he's gonna crush me like a piece of rotten fruit.

"Joe?" Max said.

"Okay," Sam choked. Suddenly little Marie was there too, and Sam felt like a vaudeville act. A bad vaudeville act. "Finish your dinner," he wheezed.

"Are you all right, Joe?" Max asked.

He gulped down some water, nodding up and down, up and down, like the fuzzy toy German shepherd old Doc Crosnoff had kept in the back window of his Chrysler. "I'm fine," he was able to say after a minute. "Please, just finish your dinner. It just went down the wrong pipe."

But nobody moved. Marie stood there looking at him until he asked with a small sigh, "What?"

27

"I make such a terrible meal."

Sam began, "No, I'm sorry, it's—"

The man cut him off. "Don't start, Marie. Every Tuesday, we get this? You're making my head pound." Marie glowered at him until he commanded, "Marie, we get two hundred channels on the damn satellite. Pick one of them."

"Marie, don't be difficult," Max added quietly.

Finally, after a murmuring of French that seemed to come from the other end of the room, as if Marie were a ventriloquist, the tiny woman spun on her heel and left. The murmuring lingered in the air like smoke. Sam's French was more than good enough to tell him that none of it was anything complimentary.

"What does she want?" he asked, puzzled.

"Rescue 911," Max replied.

"What?"

The man retrieved his plate and resumed eating. "The TV show. She said it's Tuesday, she's supposed to watch *Rescue 911*. She's like the damn Rain Man, screaming to Tom Cruise about having to watch Judge Wapner. I tell you, boss, we could find you another chef in two days. You'd be saving me from a massive brain hemorrhage if we could just send that little monster packing back to San Francisco."

"Dove," Max said mildly, "we get two hundred channels. Go watch one of them."

He grunted loudly at what seemed to be a private joke. The look they exchanged seemed to be private too, and lasted only a second. Long enough, though. Sam returned—cautiously—to his fillet, with two more bits of information: the big man's name was Dove, and he was sleeping with Barbara Maxwell.

"It's not being rerun?" Sam asked.

"Who the hell knows?" Dove replied. "Who the hell cares?"

Sam grabbed a roll and tore it in half. "I do. She's part of my staff. If she's happy, she'll do a better job. That show has to be syndicated on some channel. If it's not, get her some videotapes. Arrange for her to ride along with some EMTs. Arrange for her to meet William Shatner. Whatever she wants."

Max and Dove blinked at him, then at each other.

"Make her happy," Sam said. "If she's unhappy, she's going to make other people unhappy."

"Whatever," Dove murmured.

After the main course had been cleared away, Dove disappeared, leaving Sam alone with Max and her computer and her file folders and a plate of chocolate-chip cookies. She watched him play with the cookies for a moment, indulging him, he thought. He'd been allowed to enjoy his dinner without having to make any decisions other than how fast to chew, though the files had sat there like the proverbial other shoe, waiting to drop.

"Harmony," he said. "Harmony is a good thing."

She seemed not to have heard him. "I have copies of the final press releases from Nirvana and the list of VIPs for the opening events. They're fully booked through September, with occupancy averaging eighty-four percent through mid-November and back up to full capacity over the holidays. No one balked at the price increases for New Year's, and the tickets for 'Millennium Eve at Nirvana' are sold out. Oh, and the changes to the penthouse were completed yesterday."

"Changes?"

"To the layout."

"Of Nirvana."

"Yes."

"That wouldn't be anywhere near Providence, would it?"

Max put her hand over her mouth, pretending to stifle an entirely natural cough, then took a long drink of water. "It's in Las Vegas, Joe, unless they've moved it and didn't tell me."

"Just a . . . little joke."

The smile she gave him looked more like a tic. "We leave here Friday morning. I've scheduled the jet for ten o'clock. We'll be on the property by eleven. The reception begins at noon and the awards luncheon at one."

"And I'm speaking at this luncheon for how long?" Sam guessed.

Another gulp of water. "Three minutes."

"How many words is that?"

With a frown, she pulled a sheet of paper out of the top folder. "Five hundred and six."

Sam reached over and took the paper away from her. "Why don't you just ask me the question?"

"Question?" she echoed feebly.

Variations of it ran through his mind. "What's the matter? Don't you feel well? Is there a problem? Why do you keep ask-

29

ing things you already know? Why don't you let us run Marie out of town on a rail? Go ahead, pick one." Sam let out a long sigh, broke a cookie in half, and stuck one of the halves in his mouth. "I want to be honest," he said around the mouthful. "Is that okay?"

"Yes, Joe."

"I hate Las Vegas. Do I have to go to Las Vegas?"

"Yes, Joe."

"Even though I hate it. Even though I'm saying I don't want to."

Max sucked her lower lip. "Yes, Joe."

"I would rather go anywhere in the world than Las Vegas. Including Furnace Creek in Death Valley."

"Well—we *could* open the hotel from somewhere else, but we'd have to arrange for a remote feed. And it would seem a little—"

Sam cut her off. "I was just making a little . . ."

"Joke?"

"Joke." He shoved the other half of the cookie into his mouth and chewed it rapidly, washing it down with a swallow of the milk he had insisted Dove bring to him a few minutes ago, wondering if he was going to have to explain "joke" to his very off-balanced assistant.

How many years? he wondered. *How many people have I played this game with?* It had to be more than "hundreds"; maybe it was more like "thousands," but that idea scared him. Max was as adept at poker faces as anyone he had ever met, but he looked harder and found body language, a lack of words, a wisp of something in her eyes. Somehow, he had managed to produce banter that, while it had thrown her off-kilter, she was trying to enjoy.

"It's going to be fine," she told him. "Exactly what you had in mind to get the precampaign under way."

"There are always glitches."

"Well, yes, but the people we've had do the advance work are the best there is."

"So you're not worried."

"I'm always worried. That's why you hired me."

Sam wiped the oil and crumbs from the cookie off his fingers with his napkin and left the napkin beside his plate. "Do we have anything else scheduled for tonight?"

"No. I moved it all. I didn't think the migraine would be gone. Dr. Platt must have come up with a miracle cure. He was very pleased, by the way. You've never gotten over a headache this quickly."

"Why don't you go to bed? Sounds like you've had a long day."

"At seven-thirty?"

Clearly, the real Powell was not an early-to-bed, late-to-rise kind of guy, and expected Max and her phone and her paraphernalia to be at his side until he finally was ready to retire. It made sense, Sam supposed; you didn't build multibillion-dollar conglomerates by spending a lot of time unconscious—and it seemed to him that all the high-powered types he'd ever known had been night owls. He'd met a lot of them, back in the early days of the Project, when he and Al spent every waking moment of their own trying to woo private funding. Had Joe Powell been on their dance card? He wove his fingers together and rested his chin on them, thinking, prowling back through his memory of those days.

"I'll stay out of your way, then," Max offered.

She was already on her feet, though moving slowly enough to tell him she was puzzled by his instructions and expected him to change his mind. Sam broke out of his reverie, frowning at first, then nodding. "Thanks. I just need a little time to think some things over. As long as the rest of the world thinks I'm out of commission, I might as well take advantage of the respite."

"I'll be up. If you need me."

Sam smiled at her and held her eyes for a moment. "I won't need you."

"I—thank you, Joe."

"No problem," he said.

CHAPTER
FOUR

Eleven minutes after she'd gotten off the elevator at Level One, Donna Maria Frances Wojehowicz Alessi-Beckett was still standing on the wrong side of the reception-room door, searching for inspiration.

This is ridiculous. He's your brother-in-law, not a blind date. You've spent vacations at his house! You've seen him sound asleep, with drool running down his chin. Just open the door, go out there, and talk to him. Say whatever it takes to make him happy, tell him you'll meet him in town for dinner. Make him happy, and send him away.

You've dealt with Weitzman. You can deal with this.

She could. Of course she could. She was used to lying about her husband's whereabouts. Hell, she had it down pat. She'd done it so many times, to so many people, she'd almost started to believe, herself, that Sam was downstairs, so consumed by the work he would not walk away from that he'd forgotten what day it was. What year. What lifetime.

Whose lifetime.

But Tom—Tom was different. Lying to Tom reminded her of all the lies she'd been told by her father, all the promises he'd made to her that had become lies when his duty called. Tom Beckett and her father were cut from the same bolt of cloth, from the bright eyes and the square jaw to the ironed underwear she was certain lurked under the straightforward cut of Tom's tailored-in-America suits. It made her feel like her mother must have felt, trying to explain to her daughter why Daddy wasn't there to take her to the movies, or to teach her how to drive, or tuck her in and kiss her when she crawled into bed. It made her remember how much she'd come to hate her mother for lying to her. Worse, it made her understand why her mother had finally left her father. Tell too many lies, and you forget why the truth ever mattered in the first place.

Then again, the truth was often overrated. Especially when the truth was that her husband, the man she loved enough to lie for, the man who'd promised he'd be with her forever, had left her. Without a kiss goodbye.

Shaking the thought away, she squared her shoulders and keyed in the security code for the reception-room door.

Tom turned to look at the door as she entered, his usual smile conspicuously absent. He took a moment to tuck away the cell phone he'd been using, then said, "Donna," his voice telling her absolutely nothing.

"Tom!" she answered, her cheekbones aching with enthusiasm. "This is an unexpected pleasure."

"Unexpected. So no one told you I've been here for almost two hours."

"I'm sorry, Tom. We're all so busy."

He began to stand, using his height to push into her personal space and avoiding their customary hug and kiss on the cheek. "So you didn't know about the Committee audit."

"We did. But we expected a carload of CPAs."

"They'll be here. The Monday after New Year's."

She backed off a step, trying to keep herself out of the heat of his displeasure. "You're making quite a name for yourself on the Hill," she said brightly, forcing the issue of space by making herself comfortable at one end of the large couch stationed strategically across from one of Ziggy's sensors. "That was a terrific piece they did on you on *Dateline*. Calling you the new Bobby Kennedy? That's very flattering."

Tom had tracked her across the room with his eyes, the shadow of a smile on his lips. "How did Sam like the story?"

"He hasn't actually seen it. We taped it for when he has a chance to watch it. He's been really busy over the last few months."

"With what?" He paused. "Does he know I'm here?"

"I'm sorry. No, he doesn't. He's in the middle of something I really can't pull him away from. But if you don't want to settle down to work right away, I can break away for a couple of hours. Would you like to have dinner? There's a great new Italian place in town. Garlic bread that melts in your mouth."

"It's been almost five years, D. Since I've seen him. Since anybody in the family has seen him."

"I—I know it has. But you know how he gets when he's focused on something. If anything, you know him better than I do. He won't leave his work, Tom. Not until it's finished."

"Finished," Tom echoed. Ignoring the discomfort in her voice, Tom pressed on, the shadow he'd been wearing slowly becoming a smile that didn't reach his eyes. "Where is he, Donna?"

"Downstairs."

"Where? What room?"

"I can't tell you anything about the layout of the Project, Tom. It's classified. And your security clearance isn't high enough for me to tell you anything more than you already know." The words were out of her mouth before she remembered what most of them composed: Sam's rule. The one that had caused so much grief for them both. She'd laughed the first time Sam said it aloud, telling him it sounded like a line from an old sitcom. *If you don't know, I'm certainly not going to tell you.*

"Right. Classified." Tom laughed softly, the smile disappearing. "When are they going to admit he's dead?"

"What?"

"Dead. Not living. Deceased. Crossed off the tax rolls."

Donna shook her head slowly. "Sam's not dead, Tom."

"Right. He's working. He's lost track of time. That's why my brother the doctor didn't show up during the whole time Mom was in the hospital after her stroke, so scared from all those years of watching malpractice exposés on television that she was convinced she wasn't going to wake up in the morning." He paused, not expecting her to respond. He was unsurprised when she didn't. "He was so busy he couldn't 'break away' for the funeral when Jeffrey died."

Donna's nails bit into the palms of her hands. It took all the strength she could muster to keep meeting Tom's eyes. "He wanted to be there," she said, trying not to let her voice tremble. "You can't doubt that, Tom. But he has," she stumbled on, fishing for words that turned out to be the polar opposite of what she had told Katie Bonnick, "responsibilities to the Project. How many times did you have to sacrifice your family obligations to a higher need when you were in the navy?"

"Sam's a civilian."

"Working for the—"

Tom's hand jabbed through the air. "He doesn't have any higher duty to this Project, or to his country, or to anyone or anything, than to his family. It was his nephew's funeral, for God's sake! Do you know what it did to my sister that he couldn't bother to show up? To my mother? Do you have any idea how much that hurt them?"

"Yes. I do, Tom. I was there."

"Right. You were there. And he wasn't. Like it was some state funeral where you examine the protocol and decide that sending a representative is good enough? It was his nephew, Donna! His sister's baby!" He began to bite off his words one at a time, forgetting how much Donna had shared Katie's grief. "He would have been there—if he was still alive."

"Sam *is* alive," Donna insisted, wondering for a crazy moment which one of them she was trying to convince.

"Then why didn't he come?"

"Tom, it was months ago."

"So that makes it water under the bridge? I'm sorry: not to me. Not to my family. I've tried to be all right with it all these years, Donna. I've tried telling myself, he's made his own choices. He started separating himself from the family a long time ago. But this is too much. You want to know how much fun Christmas was at Katie's this year? We all went, me and Linda and the kids, to be there for Katie and Jim and help them get through the holidays. This time, even Sam's representative didn't come. Well, let me describe it for you, Sam's rep. My sister looks like the living dead. Jim put us on a military transport back to San Diego on Christmas Day because Katie couldn't stand looking at us anymore. It was a lovely holiday. I'm sorry you missed it."

Tears had welled up in Donna's eyes. "I'm sorry, Tom. I'm truly sorry. I wish I could do something to help."

Tom's voice became suddenly, strangely gentle. "When was the last time you saw him?" The question made Donna look away, at the couch cushions, the wall, the hands she'd clasped over her knee. "How long?" Tom insisted. "Weeks? Months?" His voice sharpened again. "How many years?"

"He's alive," she repeated.

"According to who? Calavicci? Is that who's forcing all this crap? All the pretense, the excuses? For what? To keep the Project going? That's what it's got to boil down to: take away this Project, and Calavicci has no career. Take away Sam Beckett, 'the next Einstein,' and Al Calavicci is nothing but a pathetic drunk. A loser who should have been court-martialed years ago." Her eyes jammed shut, Donna felt the couch shift as Tom sat down beside her. She opened her eyes when she felt his hand cover hers. "He's not going to let you tell the truth. He can't afford to."

She shook her head. "It's not like that."

"I know what's going on here. I've seen it before. So has everyone with a television. They expose this kind of stuff on those news-magazine shows, too. All the money being poured into what they say is Sam's research, but with no results to show in five years. It's a front, Donna. A way to fund more Iran-Contras without those messy middlemen." He leaned closer, his face lit with passion. He looked so much like Sam it made her tears spill over. As she swiped them away with the heel of her hand, he demanded, "How many more years are you going to let them keep hurting you? And everyone else Sam loved? How much longer are you going to help them hide the truth?"

Pulling away from him, Donna fled across the room and leaned against one of the row of vending machines, keeping her back to him. "You don't understand," she said as soon as she knew her voice would sound steady.

"But I *do*. I used to work for these people, remember?" She heard him walking, felt his hands land on her shoulders. "Now they work for me, and with me. I can help you, Donna. I can make this stop, for all of us."

36

"I have to go," she said, pulling against his grip.

"Donna."

"I have to go," she repeated, breaking his hold and turning to face him. "I have a job to do. Your brother's counting on me to do it."

"Just remember what I said."

"Sam's alive."

"Then tell me. When was the last time you saw him?"

"This morning," Donna replied. "I saw him early this morning." Tom's teeth slid across his lower lip. There was a lot written in his expression, and she was sure none of it was anything he didn't want her to see. He was impressed by, and hurt by, the quality of the lie he thought she'd just spoken. But she'd learned a long time ago: lie with the truth. She *had* seen Sam that morning. At least, she'd seen Sam's aura, wrapped around their Visitor. But she had *seen Sam.*

Tom let her get the door open before he spoke again. "Tell the admiral—" He cut himself off and pulled in a long, steady breath. "Remind Admiral Calavicci that I've been on the Hill longer than he's been buried in this pit in the ground. Tell him that 'the new Bobby Kennedy' has a lot of friends, and some of them owe me a favor. Tell him some of those friends like him even less than I do, and if his ass isn't up here in ten minutes, he's going to welcome in the new millennium out of the navy, and out of a job."

Thump, thump, thump. Donna listened to the rhythm her footsteps made in the corridor. It kept her focused, kept her from running back to Tom and telling him everything she knew, everything she feared, everything she'd kept inside for so long. So long she'd forgotten why it all had to be a secret, why she had to be so damned alone. *Too* long.

A bright flash from the corner of her eye told her she'd found what she'd been looking for.

"Al!"

Her voice had a strident quality that made the muscle in Al's left cheek jump like a frog in a high-school science experiment. Hiding the twitch with his cigar, he gave her a welcoming smile. "So how'd it go with Big Brother?"

"Al," she repeated, either not getting his joke or not agreeing with it. Neither of them was surprised by the way her voice trembled. "He's not here for Committee work. He's looking for Sam. He doesn't believe me anymore."

"Honey, he's never believed either one of us, ever. He's just finally decided to stop being a good soldier."

"He wants to talk to you. Right now. He's not going to wait any longer. And he's not going to go away."

"Yeah, I figured that."

Donna stared at him, amazed by his calm, something he'd shown none of since Joe Powell's arrival in the Waiting Room several hours ago. He was placid enough to have been strolling on a beach in the horrible red-and-yellow Bermuda shorts he'd worn the last time they all visited Hawaii. Centered enough to be somebody other than who he was. If he'd been anybody other than who he was, she would have suspected that Beeks had tranquilized him.

"You're going to talk to him?" she ventured.

"You just said he's not gonna go away unless I do. Probably won't, even then."

"We could have Security take him off the property. Back to the base."

"And he'd find a way to get back here, if he had to dig a tunnel over here from White Sands with a teaspoon. He's a Beckett. Wouldn't understand the word 'quit' if it was right in front of him in neon letters fifty feet high."

"Al?" Donna said. "Are you all right?"

"Splendiferous," Al told her. Then he smiled and patted her on the cheek as if she were five years old and the dearest thing in his life. She understood, then, and stepped away from him. He was a couple of steps on his way to the elevator when Donna called his name.

"Be careful," she warned.

"Thirty seconds, you son of a bitch," Tom Beckett murmured, watching the seconds tick away on his father's Timex watch. Thirty seconds—before he did what? Break out of a secure room at a top-secret government installation? He'd be dead before he reached the elevator. It'd be easy to cover up: *Tragic helicopter crash in the New Mexico desert ends the life and career of a promising young politician. Film at eleven.*

The second hand swept past his deadline. God damn Calavicci.

He was in charge while Tom was on his turf and they both knew it.

But this wasn't going to remain Calavicci's turf for long. "Remember the mission," he counseled himself, grinding his jaws together but finding patience again in the memory of why he'd come here in the first place.

Two minutes and fifty-three seconds after his deadline had passed, the door to his comfortable holding cell opened and Rear Admiral Albert Calavicci walked in, wearing a jacket that looked like it had been made from upholstery stolen from a third-class Louisiana bordello.

"Admiral," Tom said, letting his voice rise just enough to make the rank a question.

"Congressman," Calavicci answered, his voice carefully neutral.

"I want to speak to my brother."

"Sam's not available."

"Because Sam's dead."

People kinda like that theory, Al acknowledged silently. He remembered the first time he'd met Tom Beckett, standing in the rain in D.C. while Sam ran his fingers along one name among the thousands engraved on a long black wall. Things hadn't changed much since then; they were still strangers linked by the needs and ambitions of Sam Beckett. "Bullshit," was his answer to both Tom and the theory.

Tom laughed without humor, sliding his hands into his pockets to hide his fists. "Prove it. Take me to him."

"I can't."

"Because I don't have clearance to go below Level Two? If I thought that was really the roadblock, I'd get clearance. You can't, because you can't show me what's down there." He jabbed a finger toward the polished floor. "It's not what's supposed to be down there, is it?"

"Depends. What's it supposed to be?"

"Come on, Calavicci. You think I haven't figured out what's going on? Sam travels the country for half a dozen years, bleating to anybody who'll listen about that cockamamie notion of his that a man can travel in time. Whether it's doable or whether it's not, it's something that's going to attract attention from the wrong kind of people. So to quiet him down, the United States government says, 'Okay, Sam, here's a blank check. Take a few billion and build yourself a time machine. Just keep your trap shut about it.' We both know it doesn't work that way. There is no free lunch. You've got to earn toys from Uncle Sam. He doesn't give them away. Not to shut somebody up or for any other reason."

Al smoked his cigar and said nothing, leaving the blanks for Tom to fill.

"What did you turn the thing into? Another 'defense system,' maybe?" Tom shrugged. "It doesn't matter. Whatever it really is, I'm sure you would have been able to convince Sam that no one would ever be hurt. He'd believe you. He'd have to, if he wanted the money to build his time machine."

"And without Sam's coattails to ride on, I'd be washed up, busted. Just an old drunk living off his pension and his past. You're a broken record, Beckett. I've heard it before." Al took a drag on his cigar, letting the smoke trail out to curl into Tom's face.

Tom didn't flinch. "It's over, Admiral. But for Donna's sake, for my family's sake, I'd rather do this the easy way. Create an accident, do the paperwork, give me the body, and go quietly into that good night."

"That'd work. If there was a body to give you."

"Find one. You've got until Friday—I've got somewhere I have to be. If you don't give me what I want, I promise you, I'm gonna burn your whole life down around your ears."

Tom hadn't expected Al to take the threat seriously, and Al didn't. Instead, Al asked, "Why now? You looking to start the new millennium with all your problems solved?"

"Something like that."

"Good luck, then."

Walking crisply past Al, Tom stopped just inside the reception-room door and rested his hand on the knob. Turning to look back at the admiral, he added in a tone that was almost pleasant, "I'm leaving now. But I'll be back."

Al gave him a ferocious smile and a promise of his own. "We'll be here."

CHAPTER
FIVE

He opened everything—drawers, cupboards, closets. With a glass of orange juice in his right hand, in between sips Sam looked at racks of gleaming copper-bottomed pots and pans, multiple sets of Haviland china, trays of silver cutlery whose handles all bore the entwined initials "JP," canned goods in long rows. Bins of fresh fruit and vegetables. All of it carefully arranged and spotless, as if it had been set up for a magazine photo shoot. Exactly when Marie had cleaned up after dinner, he didn't know. He'd heard no sound of activity in the kitchen after Dove had dismissed her from the dining room, and she wasn't around now. Neither was anyone else, which was exactly what he'd wanted.

Shaking his head, Sam leaned against the butcher-block-topped island in the center of the room and sipped his juice.

Twenty years, Al had said. The woman whose ring Powell still wore had been gone for twenty years or more, which meant she'd died when he was what? Thirty? Yet he still wore the ring.

And he still dreamed of her.

Many of the rooms he'd looked into had doors to the outside, opening onto a narrow terrace that ran all the way around the house. The kitchen was no exception. In one corner, between a functional flagstone fireplace and a tier of shelving that displayed rows of the bright copper cookware, were double doors covered with sheer, pale yellow curtains. To the right of the doors was one of a ubiquitous set of keypads for the security system. Sam's hand strayed toward the pad, and in the depths of his memory he heard a woman's voice say, *"Good evening, Dr. Beckett."*

"Ziggy," he murmured. He hadn't heard her voice (at least, as far as he recalled) in almost five years, but it became clear in his mind now, as dismayed, offended, and officious as it had been that night. *"I really must advise against this, Dr. Beckett."*

He pressed his thumb to the small red window beneath the keys, then popped his index finger up and touched the key at the left-hand end of the middle row. An instant later he heard a soft click: the door locks disengaging.

"If you persist in following this course of action, I feel I must notify Admiral Calavicci."

Sam twisted the knob and pushed the door open. Cool night air, scented with salt and pine, surrounded him and made him pull in a deep breath. Down below, waves swooshed against the rocks. He peered hard into the night but could see nothing; there was almost no moon and the light from the kitchen bathed an area that went no farther than the edge of the terrace. The breeze brushed against his face, cool and then, just for an instant, warm.

From very far away, he thought he could hear music, but it was gone before he could decide whether it was real or not. Six notes. He reproduced them one at a time as soft exhales. Da-dum. Da-dum. Da-dum.

"No pictures," he said. "Not a single picture anywhere. Nothing with her name on it. No sign that she was ever a part of his life. Just the ring."

And the dreams.

Something rustled near the edge of the deck. A mouse, or the wind teasing old leaves. He almost didn't bother to look, then did, and found a curious pair of amber eyes watching him. "Hello, kitty," he offered, crouching and extending a hand. The cat, its curiosity firmly piqued, ambled onto the terrace and sniffed his skin, then rubbed itself against his ankle. Smiling absently, Sam sat on the stone and let the cat rub its way around his body, finally settling contentedly in his lap. When Sam began to scratch behind its ears, the cat let out a few notes of purr, then a loud, unmistakable squeak.

"Where'd you wander in from?" Sam asked as his fingers found a delicate collar around the animal's neck. He had to lean close to read the simple brass tag attached to the collar, which bore only the word TONTO. "Tonto, huh? Well, when you go home, tell the Lone Ranger he needs to put his phone number on here."

The animal squeaked again as if it were agreeing with him, then climbed down from Sam's lap and padded off into the darkness.

Alone again, Sam sat listening to the surf. Every wave seemed to carry a voice from long ago. One of them was his own. *"I know you don't agree with me. I don't have a lot of choices. I do this, or I lose everything I've worked for."*

"That is not a foregone conclusion."

"Foregone enough. Run the initializing sequence. Begin on my mark."

"Dr. Beckett . . ."

"Mark."

Joe Powell had built himself a very elegant cocoon, Sam mused. He'd looked into eleven different rooms, all on the ground floor, and was sure there were as many more he hadn't seen. The flooring alone had probably cost more than anyone named Beckett had ever earned in a lifetime. He and Al had visited scores of places like this, places that were more properly called mansions than houses, hoping to charm the owners out of checks bearing a lot of zeroes. Most of the time, they'd left empty-handed.

Most of those places had had the same lack of warmth Sam found here. The rooms, the furnishings, the bric-a-brac were all too perfect, too *chosen,* as if they were part of a movie set. Every piece chosen by a decorator, and none of it a gift or a souvenir of a special moment. None of the cushions had small stains concealed by strategically placed throw pillows. None of the wood was marked by scratches from a cat's claws. There were no jackets tossed on arms of chairs, no schoolbooks left abandoned in the living room, no tiny dust bunnies in hard-to-reach corners,

43

no thin spots in the varnish on the floors made by years of foot traffic, no sudden blasts of rock music from upstairs, no trace in the air of last Tuesday's tuna casserole that no amount of air freshener would eliminate.

How far Powell's mansion was from the nearest town, he couldn't guess, but it might as well have been inside a dome on Mars. *Does anybody laugh here?* Sam wondered. *Turn the stereo up loud enough that it vibrates the walls? Do they sing? Shout at each other?* He was badly tempted to go into the sunken living room, to the polished baby grand that was the room's center-piece, and pound out the most ferocious piece of music he could remember. That would certainly get the attention of Powell's two flunkies—break them away from whatever they were doing with each other. Or trying to do, with the fear of being summoned hanging over both of them. It would bring them running so they could stand there gaping at him, trying to figure out what had possessed him.

You should.

Tom would do it—his brother, whose love of mischief had always eclipsed Sam's. Tom would rattle the bars of this gilded cage good and loud, and shock Max and Dove out of their obe-dient stupor. The more Sam considered the idea, and the closer he got to the bottom of his glass of juice, the better he liked it. Grinning, he slipped back into the house, abandoned his glass in the sink, padded down the hall, through the foyer, and down the steps into the living room. "Look, Al," he whispered. "I'm gonna blow my cover." He flexed his fingers and stepped toward the piano. "Great Balls of Fire" seemed like a good opening number.

Then he heard the sound. Or thought he did. Music again, very faint, those half-dozen first notes followed by a few more. He cocked his head, listening, straining to pick it up again. He fol-lowed it back through the foyer, down another hall, and up a short flight of stairs. As he reached the top he heard another sound, coming from the living room: the Imaging Chamber door. A moment later, Al popped in beside him.

"Sam," the Observer protested. "You need to light someplace. What're you doing, roaming around in the middle of the night?"

"I heard something."

"A good something or a bad something?"

Sam pressed a finger to his lips to silence his friend. They listened together for a few seconds, then Al's eyes widened in fascination.

"Who is that?" Al squeaked.

Sam hushed him again, although even if Al shouted, no one in the house would hear him except Sam. "I didn't mean that. It was something else. Music. And who do you think it is?" he asked. "There are only four people living here, and one of them is standing in front of you."

"Three," Al corrected him.

"What?"

"There's only three people living here. You, the camp counselor, and Powell's hired muscle. Gregory something-o-vich. Goes by Dove."

"I know. I met him. There's four. A cook, Marie."

"She doesn't live here," Al said firmly. His face filled with something very much like glee, the Observer was moving steadily toward a closed door at the end of the hall. The sounds coming from behind it were unmistakable in nature and growing louder, even through the heavy oak of the door. Growing flustered, Sam began to move in the opposite direction, back toward the stairs. He beckoned fiercely to Al, who waved him off.

"Al," Sam insisted.

"Wow," the Observer breathed. "I wish Tina would make noises like that. Sounds like the counselor is really enjoying herself."

"Al!"

"Would never have thought she had it in her."

"Albert."

Sam had reached the bottom of the steps when Al finally consented to use the handlink to relocate himself and join his partner. The scientist led the way into Powell's living room and sat down wearily on one of the cream-colored couches.

"Makes sense to me," Al offered cheerfully. "They live here, they're on call all the time, can't really go out and try to set up a romance with anybody else. Use what's handy, I always say. He's kinda big and hunky, she's got a pretty cute little bod, if you overlook the tacky duds, so what the hey."

"What about Powell?" Sam asked.

"What about him? What, you mean a threesome?"

Sam groaned, "No, I don't mean a threesome. You told me

45

he was widowed twenty or twenty-five years ago. Does he see someone? Is there a girlfriend?"

"Nope."

"No one?"

Al waggled his head. "You told me not to confirm stuff you already know. You know that thing, 'No man is an island'? This guy's an island. According to the tabloids, he squires the occasional model or movie starlet or society babe, but that's it. He's a grieving widower. Lost his true love many years ago and never got over it. I think that's romantic."

"I think it's unhealthy."

"It's not like he's holed up in here picking lint out of his navel, Sam. The guy runs a multibillion-dollar corporation—Powell Technologies International. They've got a finger in almost every pie there is. Computers, cars, real-estate development, consumer-product manufacturing, modeling agencies, film production, electronics, and a bunch of charitable stuff. He travels between two hundred and fifty and three hundred days a year, mostly to go to meetings. PTI has offices in seventeen different countries. His schedule is action-packed from sunup to sundown. This is one very bright, savvy, aggressive guy."

Sam slouched back against the cushions and pushed a hand through his hair. "Where'd you get all that?"

"The company's annual report."

"So it's his official biography."

"Yeah. What did you want, gossip? I can get that too, by the truckload. The sleaze-oids think he's got a secret life."

Sam asked mildly, "Secret life? Is there a cave under the house?"

It took Al a moment to get the joke, and even then he didn't laugh. "I don't know why it's so quiet here now. From what I read, the place oughta be jumping. He's not home much, but when he is, people come to him. Did you find his office? There was a picture of it in the report. Talk about state-of-the-art. Gooshie's been making whimpering noises all afternoon over the computer Powell has on his desk. It's hooked up with a super-computer they're developing at some thinktank in Marin County."

"Why would that upset Gooshie? Gooshie has Ziggy."

"Nobody has Ziggy right now."

"Still? I need to know why I'm here! I told you—"

"Yeah, I know what you told me. And like I said, we figured it out without her. Here's the deal." Al looked longingly at the couch for a moment, then adopted as casual a pose as he could while still standing up. "It's that Y2K thing."

"Ziggy's safeguarded against Y2K systems failures. She knows that. It was one of the first things I integrated into her programming. There's an automatic communication break if she tries to interface with any system that's not Y2K compatible. She knows that," Sam groaned. "She's not in any danger."

"You know that and I know that. But all we can get out of her is 'Y2K, Y2K,' like she's some big Patsy Wetsy Chatterbox doll. Pull the string and she says 'Y2K.' She keeps telling us the end of the world is coming. Everything's gonna crash, and we'll be back to making fire by rubbing two sticks together."

"She's a computer, Al."

"I know that."

"Then why do you let her manipulate you?"

"I'm not letting her do nothin'," Al groused.

"I hired the most intelligent, capable people in the world to staff the Project, and all of you are letting yourselves be manipulated by an artificial intelligence? She's a machine, Al."

"She's a big machine."

"I don't *believe* you," Sam moaned.

"It's no big deal anyway, right? Brokaw said it's all under control, and if you can't believe Tom Brokaw, who can you believe?" Sam's eyes widened. Quickly, Al went on, "Why *is* it so quiet here?"

"Powell was sick this afternoon, before I Leaped in. He had a migraine."

"Yeah? He doesn't have it now."

"She's a machine," Sam persisted. "She's not in charge of the Project, you are. I don't *believe* you people."

Al ignored him and remarked, "Gotta tell Beeks. Leaping cures migraines. Maybe we can market that."

"Al."

"Everything's fine."

"You need to get Ziggy back on track." When Al accepted that with a grin and a nod, Sam peered suspiciously at him. "What are you not telling me? And don't say 'nothing.' You're trying very hard to hide a very creeped-out expression. Talk to me, Al."

47

Al looked away, fiddling with his cigar, adjusting his jacket.

"You used to talk to me. I'm your partner, remember? We built the Project together. Stop trying to distract me and tell me what's wrong."

"Ah, Sam . . ."

Sam watched his partner wrestle with the decision of what to tell him, how much to tell him. He bit back his frustration, not wanting the conversation to end with Al reminding him yet again that he was only following The Rules—the ones Sam had written down a hundred lifetimes ago, when Leaping was still just a theory. *The Leaper must not be told anything he does not already know.*

"We've got company from Washington," Al confessed. "It's getting close to number-crunching time and they're counting the paper clips again. The same old crapola," he insisted with a big grin. "Nothing for you to think twice about. The world's coming to an end and the bureaucrats are counting thumbtacks. It's just a bunch of little Nazi number crunchers."

"And?" Sam coaxed.

"And, nothing much. The one in charge is one of those real earnest guys who wants to keep everything on the straight and narrow. No spending big piles of dough where it doesn't need to be spent. Nosy as hell. A real pain in the ass. Trying to sniff out stuff that'll make him a senator."

Sam frowned. "The funding is in danger again?"

"It's in danger all the time, Sam. I'm not gonna let it go too far. Like I said, he's a pain in the ass, but I can handle it."

"And Powell is fine."

"He's not keen on the Fermi suit. He wants a phone. Nothing much."

You're lying to me, Sam thought. "Did he get out? Like Stiles? He gave the guards the slip?"

"I gotta go," Al said.

"No you don't. Stand here and talk to me."

"Yeah I do. Powell's in the Waiting Room, safe as a baby in his mommy's arms. He wants a phone is all."

"Did you ask him about the dream?"

Al nodded. "He thinks he might've been dreaming. He isn't sure. And if he was, he doesn't know what it was about."

"I feel like she should be here, Al."

"Who?"

Again, Sam held up the hand bearing the gold wedding band. All Al tossed him in return was a shrug and a mild expression that seemed to say he agreed. Or sympathized. Or was agreeing to be sympathetic. It definitely said he didn't want to explore the topic of Powell's absent wife. "I feel like he's banished her. There aren't any pictures, no mementos of trips they made together, nothing to remember her by. I've searched half the house. You'd think there'd be a wedding picture, or something. I know it sounds peculiar, but it feels wrong to me that she's not here."

"Got a few ex-wives I'd like to banish," Al quipped. "But they keep coming back."

"God, or Fate, or Whoever," Sam sighed, "must be into reading the tabloids. Look at the people I've Leaped into, or near, lately—Marilyn Monroe, Elvis, Oswald, now Powell. It's like whoever wants to write a tell-all bestseller and is using me to do the research."

Al asked skeptically, "Powell hasn't been a public figure for that long. You remember reading about him?"

"I think so. Yes. Sure."

"You gotta *be* him, Sam."

"I think I know the drill," Sam replied, eyes narrowed, watching and misinterpreting Al's peculiar expression as the Observer began to pace back and forth near the foot of the steps. "Don't worry: I won't mess up any of his business dealings. I'll stall a little. Unless," he continued bemusedly, "I'm here to make some kind of a big decision he wouldn't have made on his own. Which is hard to imagine. I also remember you telling me until you were blue in the face that I had no grasp of large sums of money. 'If it's too much to fit in your wallet,' you said, 'you don't get it.' "

"It's an abstraction," Al mumbled. "Like the number of stars in the universe."

Sam corrected him quickly. "The number of stars in the galaxy, the number of galaxies in the universe."

"What?"

"That's what I told you. When we had that conversation about money."

"We did?"

"Yes, we did. Don't you remember?"

"Ooooh," Al moaned.

"What's the matter?"

49

"Not a thing. Not a damn thing."

Sam pushed himself up off the sofa, strode across the Oriental carpet, and stuck his face close to the Observer's. "Either the color balance of the holographic projector is off, or you're green."

"Just a tiny touch of botulism. It's nothin'. Everything's fine. Ziggy and her Y2K blues—it's contagious. There's a couple people on staff who keep asking if we've got enough food and water for everybody if the rest of the world goes flooey. I don't feel so good, Sam. Gonna go kill the chef. There was something hinky about that fish we had for dinner."

"The Vampire? That chef?"

"What?" Al squeaked.

"Jamie L'Estat," Sam prodded. "You call him 'The Vampire.' Creator of Meltdown Chili." He turned around in a circle, like a dog preparing to lie down for a nap, the fingers of his right hand flickering the air. "Red hair, but he's lost most of it. He's missing part of one earlobe. Wears black all the time. Has a boyfriend named René?"

Al groped the surface of the handlink frantically until he found the keys that would prompt the Door to open. "I gotta go," he insisted. "It's late. Go get some sleep. I'll talk to you, I don't know, later."

An instant later, he was gone.

"Al," Sam said with a heavy sigh. "You didn't tell me what I'm here to do."

"Outta my way!"

Beeks, slender as she was, blocked Al's path as effectively as a cement wall. He tried to duck around her, but she planted herself in front of him, reached out to seize a castered chair from one of the workstations, and thrust it close to him. "Sit," she commanded him. "Put your head between your knees."

"And then what? Puke on my shoes?"

"Calm down, Admiral."

He shook his head fiercely and scowled at Gooshie, who dropped his head and pretended to be fascinated by the keyboard on Ziggy's main console. Pushing the chair aside, Al grabbed Verbena by the arm and dragged her with him out of Control and into a blessedly empty corridor. "My office," he said, tugging her toward the elevator. "Or yours. I don't care. But somewhere we can lock the door and there's not a million people pretending they're not listening. It's bad," he went on as he jabbed the elevator call button. "It's bad, and it's gonna get big-time worse."

"How so?"

The car arrived almost immediately and Al dragged the psychiatrist into it. As soon as the doors had closed, he snapped, "What planet are you on? I'm not posing a hypothetical situation here."

"What did you find out about Powell?"

Al blinked, struggling to find the page Beeks was on. "Powell?"

The inside of the elevator had no reflective surfaces, but Al knew even without one that he was not only green, but every color that could be found on top of a deluxe pizza. When the doors opened again, he took off down the main corridor of Level Eight at a dead run, brought himself to such an abrupt halt in front of his office that his heels left skid marks on the floor, slammed his access code into the keypad beside the door, and took refuge inside. Beeks, a few steps behind him, closed the door gently, poured him a cup of greasy-looking coffee, and watched him pour it down his throat, knowing he wasn't tasting any of it.

"You want to give me the option," he said when the cup was empty, "I'll tell you, I don't give a flying rat's ass about Joe Powell. Sam's asking questions about the Vampire."

That took a couple of seconds to sink in. Then Verbena murmured, "Oh, dear."

When she didn't seem inclined to say anything more, Al sank onto his well-worn leather couch and huddled in the corner, clutching the coffee mug. "He remembered Elk Ridge right from the get-go. His mom and dad, and Katie. Remembering Tom didn't take a whole lot longer. But as close as he's ever gotten to our 'now' is remembering MIT. He was missing pretty much all of the last twenty years." Al's eyes strayed around the room, taking in everything but Verbena's face. "He didn't realize he was doing it, but he was sitting there twisting Powell's wedding ring. Like this." He demonstrated, turning his navy ring around and around on his finger, using his thumb as a lever. "Started asking me, where's the wife? Where's pictures of the wife? How come it seems like she's supposed to be here?"

"Oh, my."

"Would you quit that? You graduated summa cum laude from shrink school and all you can come up with is 'oh, my'? I could get that much out of Arnold."

Verbena sat at the other end of the couch and looked at her shoes. "You could probably get more out of Arnold, right now."

"He remembers a conversation he had a couple weeks before we Leaped. He remembers the Vampire. Described him for me. And he's doing that thing with the ring." Al's head drooped forward, as if it had suddenly become too much weight for his neck to support. "You're the shrink. You tell me what it's gonna do to him if he remembers."

"Nothing good," she murmured.

"It's gonna tear him apart. He hasn't remembered squat up till now. He doesn't even remember finding Donna at college and tweaking things around so she'd marry him. He thinks he's alone." Al moaned softly. "He asked me one time, only a couple months into it. 'Am I married?' And I told him no. Maybe he remembers *that*."

Verbena nodded. She and Al had gone over this ground a dozen times. But that was her modus operandi sometimes, she thought. *Go over it until it makes sense.* "They could communicate with each other, through you. Maybe that would help."

"Help? Him realizing what a cheesy thing he did, putting her back into his life and then walking out on her?" He lifted his head enough to peer at her. "This isn't good. This can't be good."

"I know."

"So what do we do?"

"We help Sam do what he needs to do, so he can Leap out."

"Before he remembers."

Verbena nodded slowly. "Before he remembers."

CHAPTER SIX

"I can't make a bowl of oatmeal?" Sam asked.

Dove glanced past the man he thought was his employer, at the digital clock set into the reflective black backsplash of the stove. Five-twelve, it read—judging by Dove's expression, not a time at which Joe Powell was accustomed to puttering around his massive kitchen making breakfast, if indeed he ever did that at all.

"I thought I'd get things going. The calendar's pretty full, starting at seven o'clock. Meetings, phone calls. Some of the people on the East Coast are in their offices already. I thought we could get a jump on a few things, instead of waiting until almost lunchtime their time. I figured I'd need a good breakfast to get me started. Most important meal of the day, you know. There's plenty here, if you want some," Sam offered.

One of Dove's bushy eyebrows slid up his forehead. "No,

thanks, boss," he said after a moment. "I'm not an oatmeal kind of a guy." *And neither are you,* he didn't bother to say.

Sam ignored the implication, spooned a hearty serving of the cereal into a bowl, and sat down at the table with it and the mug of coffee he had poured a few minutes before. There was a great deal of freedom involved in being rich enough to do anything you damn well pleased, he thought, even if doing it earned you—well, this. He gestured at the blue-and-yellow cushioned chair across from his and watched as Dove perched on it.

"Relax," Sam said.

"I'm relaxed, boss."

"You're looking at me as if you're afraid I'm ten seconds away from a seizure. Or that I've completely lost my mind and I'm going to start spouting lines from Dr. Seuss. I woke up, I was hungry, I made some oatmeal."

"That's, uh, great. But you just had to call—"

"At five o'clock in the morning?"

"Anytime, boss. Anytime you want something, you just pick up the intercom."

"I'm not an invalid."

"Didn't say you were."

Watching Dove out of the corner of one eye, Sam left the table, poured coffee into a second mug, and held it out to the bodyguard. Dove accepted the mug as if it were a hand grenade and set it down on the table. Smiling, Sam brought a carton of milk and the sugar bowl to the table, pushed them toward Dove, then returned to his chair and his breakfast. "Max is sleeping in?" he asked as he resumed eating.

"Sleeping . . . ? She's in the shower." Dove frowned, then changed his mind. "She's probably out of the shower by now."

"What's her position on oatmeal?"

"You got me."

"Marie hasn't gone back to San Francisco, has she? I had an idea I wanted to talk to her about."

Surrendering to the temptation of the steaming mug sitting in front of him, Dove took a long swig of the black coffee and let it burn its way down his throat. "Why would she leave? It's her life's work to kill every last bit of patience I got in me."

"She's a very good cook."

"She makes my brain bleed, boss."

Sam sipped his coffee and shrugged. "I'd offer to fire her,

54

except you enjoy bickering with her as much as she does." Dove didn't bother to disagree with that, which made Sam smile again. The bowl of oatmeal was almost gone when Sam asked, "Have you noticed a cat hanging around outside the house? Yellow tom, with a tag that says Tonto. We should try to find the owner."

"Closest house is almost three miles from here."

"Then leave some food out for him, and bring him inside the next time he shows up. If he's roaming around out there, he's going to get hurt."

"That's not gonna go over big with Marie. Livestock in the kitchen."

Sam polished off his coffee and pushed out of his chair, intending to carry his dishes to the sink. "Then give him his own room."

"Give a room to the cat."

"We have enough extra rooms."

"It's a cat, boss."

Sam was about to press his point when he noticed Max coming down the narrow hall from the foyer. There were worry lines around her eyes, as if she hadn't slept well, and her hair was still damp from the shower. She'd chosen a more feminine outfit than yesterday's, a white pleated skirt and dark blue sweater, and had a gold locket around her neck. It made her look several years younger than she had yesterday, and a lot less anal-retentive.

"You look nice," Sam told her.

"Thank you, Joe." She would have returned the compliment, except that Sam was still wearing Joe Powell's pajamas and robe.

"Boss made his own breakfast," Dove pointed out, with an undercurrent in his voice that seemed to imply that that event had been Max's fault, or Marie's, or someone's.

"I like to cook," Sam said.

Then, to the astonishment of Powell's two employees, he made them sit facing each other at the glass-topped table, where neither of them said a word as he cooked and then served them griddle cakes and scrambled eggs, coffee, and juice. They both ate slowly, as if they thought there was something fatally wrong with the food, and each kept an eye on him as he loaded the dirty pans into the sink and washed them. Just to drive them to the brink of their disbelief, he whistled as he worked.

"Well?" he asked when they had finally finished their meals.

"It's good, Joe," Max said, clearly humoring him.

"Can one of you pick us up a couple of pints of blueberries? Can I get those before lunch? I'd go, but I don't know where the market is."

"Why?" Dove asked. "You gonna make muffins?" Sam nodded at him cheerfully, wiping his damp hands on a dish towel he'd found tucked away under the sink. "Hurt me," Dove murmured. "I didn't know you knew where the kitchen was." He recovered quickly, though, and said in a business-as-usual tone, "I can get 'em. I've gotta take the sedan down to the dealership so they can look at the alarm. I'll be back in plenty of time before those people get here. Stewart's on duty out in the shack if you need something while I'm gone."

"People?" Sam asked.

Max told him, "From the Committee, Joe. The couple you picked to spearhead the campaign in the western states. They drove up from San Diego last night. They're staying at the Barfield Inn."

He apparently was supposed to know where *that* was, but he chose to focus on something else: the Committee. Sam shook his head, remembering a row of humorless people in dark suits standing alongside a pair of black limousines, staring at him through dark-lensed sunglasses, as if they hadn't yet decided whether they were facing a firing squad or he was. One by one, they filed past and peered into a hole in the New Mexico desert as if they were viewing a corpse. It was a very deep hole in the desert. Sam had felt very much like jumping into it so that he wouldn't have to feign politeness to all those faces whose eyes he couldn't see.

"Do I have time to change?" Sam wanted to know.

"Five hours."

"Oh. Good." Sam's good cheer came back. "I'll be down in a few minutes. Then we can get started on those phone calls back east."

"Then you slept well?"

"Like a baby. With dreams. Nice dreams. Headache's gone. I feel like a million bucks." He grinned. "I feel like several billion bucks."

They watched him leave. The moment he was out of sight, Dove shook his head, hard, like a dog shaking off water. "Sweet mother," he mumbled, then looked at Max as if he thought she

56

knew something he didn't. "What dimension did we wake up in?"

"It's good."

Beeks smiled. People were different; her grandmother had told her that years ago, only she'd used the word "folks." "Folks're different, Verbena Mae, and not just in looks." But, she mused, most of them had the same reaction to that first cup of coffee in the morning. The glimmer of anticipation, the pause, taking in a deep lungful of the rich aroma, the sigh after the first long sip. Powell was true to form, holding the cup in both hands, even closing his eyes for a moment and letting his whole body savor the drink.

"Special blend," she told him. "You seem to feel better."

"Better?"

"Calmer than you were when you arrived here."

"I've had a chance to get used to my surroundings. Such as they are." He was quiet until he'd finished half of what the big insulated paper cup contained. Then he settled back a little, fingers still curled around the cup, soaking in its warmth. "I think you women must be delighted with your revenge," he began.

"Revenge for what?"

"For, oh, how many things? Panty hose? High-heeled shoes? Tight skirts? Everything painful and constricting invented by men to make you look good." The corner of Powell's mouth curled up as he said that last word, and his gaze dropped to the coffee cup. Beeks was still in his peripheral vision, though, and he saw her smile again.

"Actually, the Fermi suit was developed by a man."

"Hard to imagine."

"Strange but true," Beeks said. "I apologize for the discomfort. But it allows you freedom of movement that you wouldn't have if we used electrodes with wires."

Powell took another sip. "Freedom of movement? From there to there to there." He measured off the limited dimensions of the Waiting Room with a gesture of one hand. "Would you tell me one thing?"

"If I can."

"Am I all right?"

"Yes, Mr. Powell. You're in excellent health."

57

"Then why all the concern about my heart rate, my skin temperature? My, what else? Perspiration levels?"

"We want to make sure you stay all right, for as long as you're with us."

"And how long will that be?"

"Not very long, really. It varies. But not very long."

"It varies? Then there are other people here? You've had others take part in this experiment?"

"Yes."

He paused, then asked her bluntly, eyes fixed on hers, "Did they survive?"

There was a note of uncertainty in his voice she hadn't heard before now. Coming from this man, this very capable, brilliant, insightful man, it made her uneasy. "Of course they did," she told him, hoping she hadn't hesitated long enough to reinforce his concern. "You're not in any danger here. I promise you that."

"Why is it so important that I not leave this room?"

"Because it's more difficult to monitor you. It's very important that we observe you carefully."

"Every moment."

"Yes."

Powell ran the fingertips of one hand against the waxed surface of the paper cup. "You don't have my permission to do this," he ventured. "And no one else has the authority to give permission on my behalf for something like this."

"Someone very high up gave us permission. I'm afraid that's all I can tell you."

"So whether I object or not, I'm trapped here."

Verbena shook her head. "Don't think of it in that sense. I wish I could explain, but I'd like you to think of it as, you're taking part in an important experiment that has resulted, and I hope will continue to result, in an enormous benefit for a lot of people. You're doing good by being here, Mr. Powell. I hope you'll accept that."

"It doesn't seem like I have much choice."

"Would you like some more coffee? Some breakfast?"

"Are there cameras in the bathroom?"

"No. We draw the line there. But the sensors would tell us if you were suddenly taken ill in there and needed help." She smiled. "Or if you were trying to knock a hole in the wall in an effort to get out."

Powell grimaced. "With what? My head?"

"Let me bring you some breakfast."

"And a newspaper?"

"I'm sorry, no." Beeks got up from her chair and took the now empty coffee cup out of Powell's hand. "But if you wouldn't mind, I'd like to run some tests. They're very simple. Answering some multiple-choice questions."

Powell thought it over, then shrugged. "I suppose so. I've finished counting everything in here that there is to count. I considered contemplating my navel, but I can't see it." He waited for her to reach the door before he spoke again. "Doctor?"

"Yes, Mr. Powell?"

"Am I dying?"

"Open," Verbena said quietly, then answered his question. "You're in perfect health."

"That's what I thought," Powell murmured.

A soft scraping noise roused Al from fitful sleep. He forced open one eye and saw, a few inches from his face, a ceramic coffee mug with the word FLAMINGO lettered on it in hot pink. Wisps of steam were rising above the cup, carrying the aroma of strong black coffee. Al grunted out the same noise he would have emitted if someone had punched him in the gut, then tried to lift his head off the table. Three tries later he succeeded. His neck felt as if someone had torqued his head completely around several times.

"God help me," he muttered.

Somehow, he wrenched himself back away from the table until he was sitting more or less upright. When he was relatively sure he was able to remain upright, without flopping off the chair onto the carpet, he seized the mug and gulped half of its contents as if he were competing in a chugalug contest at Silvio's. Good coffee. Navy coffee, strong enough to strip the chrome off a truck bumper. He blessed whoever had put it next to his head seven times and finished the cup.

"Better?" asked a voice.

His head refused to turn, so he shifted his body until he could see who had spoken. The bringer of coffee was a few steps away, sitting in one of the library's half-dozen comfortable armchairs, examining a big, hard-bound book.

"You're a saint, kid," Al said.

David Allen smiled and tipped the book shut, his index finger marking his place. "Kid" was a little off the mark, but not by much; he'd only hit thirty a few months ago and still looked sixteen. Sam had plucked him out of Massachusetts while the ink on his doctoral degree was still wet. If he'd been left alone, Al had told him a while back, he probably could have matched Sam's six degrees and a Nobel. "Higher learning as a poker match," David had quipped. "I like it." He probably could have done Sam one better, Al had thought a while later: the younger man, who bore more than a passing resemblance to comedian Chris Rock, had spent two summers doing stand-up in small clubs around Boston. The bigger his audience, the happier he was. Sam, on the other hand, would stand in front of an audience to say anything that was not written down on index cards only when he was drunk. And woefully, even shit-faced, Sam was not funny.

"Funny thing," David mused. "You've got a whole complex full of intelligent people here, and nobody ever sets foot in the library."

"Why would they?" Al mumbled. "They've got the Internet."

"Maybe Sister scares them off."

David waggled a thumb at the far wall, where an enormous oil portrait of Sister Rose Bernard, the elderly nun who had taught Al Calavicci to read, stood guard over the Project library. Al took a long look at the picture, sighed, and slumped in his chair as if his bones had liquified. Straightening up again took effort he did not think he could put together. "Davey," he managed to say after a minute, "why the hell did you ever let him rope you into this?"

"This? Years' worth of work on something I can't tell anybody about?"

"Huh," Al said.

"Oh, hey, I love anonymity. I love living in a big hole in the ground like a prairie dog. I love being the bridesmaid at a never-ending wedding. Yessir, I love it to tears. Best gig I've ever had."

Yessir, that was why the kid got laughs. Al stared into the depths of the Flamingo mug he was pretty sure was his, pilfered out of his office by somebody who theoretically shouldn't have had access to either the office or the mug, and tried to wish more coffee into existence. The sullen look that had crept onto Allen's face made Al's face twitch. *Bridesmaid,* he thought.

They'd sat around a conference table about seventeen lifetimes ago, himself and Sam and Donna and Davey and half a dozen other people.

"Whadda we even need a list for?" Al had complained.

Sam had plopped his yellow legal pad down onto the tabletop and peered at his partner from twenty feet away. "What?"

Instantly, Al knew he'd said the wrong thing. "Make a list," he said quickly.

"I can't make all the Leaps myself," Sam told him sternly. "We don't know yet how much stress Leaping is going to place on the human body."

"I already know."

"You do."

"My ass has turned to stone. How long have we been in this room? A year? Make a list. Swell, go ahead, make a list. And leave me off of it."

"Al, you said you wanted to—" Donna began.

"I changed my mind."

"Sam's taking all the risk," David pointed out. "He takes the first Leap, and if he comes back in one piece, we know everything works. Look at it this way, Admiral: you climbed into a space capsule on top of a million pounds of high explosive and let somebody light a match. How scary is this compared to that?"

"I wanted to see the moon," Al grumbled.

"Yeah, but with this, you could do more. You could meet Elvis."

Sam's eyes widened a little. "This is not . . ."

David leaned forward, sliding his hands across the polished wood of the conference table. "Saaaam," he crooned. "You sit there in that butt-ugly suit and tell me one human being to another that you do not want to meet Elvis Presley."

"That's not the purpose of this Project," Sam said stubbornly. "Meeting celebrities."

"Put David on the list," Al demanded. "Number two."

"I thought you wanted to be number two."

"I changed my mind."

He hadn't exactly unchanged it, Al thought now, mourning over the barren emptiness of his Flamingo mug. If they'd stuck with the program, Sam would have gone on a little jaunt into the past for a few hours, maybe a couple of days, would have come back in one piece to a lot of shrieking and backslapping and confetti throwing, and after all the debriefing had been done and duly filed with the Committee, Davey would have suited up and gone second. Al, who had lost enough sleep that winter to decide that a trip from his desk to the john was too taxing to undertake (Arnold the janitor had caught him one night gazing contemplatively into his wastebasket), let alone Leaping, had agreed to be third. Under duress, he'd told Sam. They could add that to the list of descriptives that followed his name in the Project dossier: career naval officer. Astronaut. Golden Gloves champion three years running. And Third Under Duress.

"You'll get your chance, kid," he told David.

"Something's screwed into the ground this time, isn't it?" David asked him somberly. "You usually don't hide in here unless Weitzman's in town."

"I'm not hiding." David's face tilted. Al squinted at him blearily. "Yeah, things are screwed. And getting screwier."

"They might be getting better."

"You think so."

"Sure. Me and the Magic Pencil did some calculations." Grinning, David pulled a blue plastic mechanical pencil out of his pocket and gestured with it. "Here's the thing. Sam's never Leaped any further forward than 1991. Right?"

"Right."

"He's bounced back and forth between 1955 and 1991. Mostly between 1955 and the early eighties."

"Okay."

"But all of a sudden, here he is, only six months behind us. I've got the calculations downstairs if you want to see." He didn't wait for Al to reply one way or another; instead, he leaned toward the admiral and kept talking, rapid-fire, growing more enthusiastic about what he was saying as it went on. "I figure, and the math backs me up, that all it would take is a little 'oomph' from the Big Kahuna, and bingo. Sam's back where he belongs."

"Look at where Sam's been lately. Did you forget about the Civil War?"

"A glitch," David said stubbornly.

"The way it looks to me," Al sighed, "is more like, all bets are off. We can't predict nothin'."

"So you want me to keep this to myself."

"I'd order you to, but you wouldn't listen to me."

"A little hope would be good, Al. To keep us all going."

"You build up hope, then you squash it. What does that accomplish?" The admiral paused, drumming lightly on the table-top with his fingertips. "I know you want your shot. You'll get it. Maybe sooner, maybe later. Right now, try to just roll with it."

Art lovers had given works by the Old Masters less scrutiny than David gave Albert Calavicci then. "Is everything all right?" he ventured.

"Everything's fine."

"Sam's all right?"

"Sam," Al said, "is just peachy-reachy."

"And you wish you were."

"Kid." Al sighed. "Get me some more coffee."

He approached Verbena Beeks's office with her summons echoing in his mind. "I have something interesting to show you, Admiral." Interesting, as in, *the times we are living in have gone to hell in a handbasket, so get your butt down here. Please. If you could. Thank you very much.*

As if he needed more hell in his handbasket.

The door slid open at his prompt, revealing the subtly lit, pine-paneled oasis Beeks had created in the midst of their government-sterile underground universe. She was waiting for him behind her desk, holding a plain manila folder, her face tense despite the soothing subliminal sounds of ocean waves that hovered just within his hearing. With a sigh, he eased into one of her visitors' chairs and held out a hand for the folder.

"Okay, Beeksie, lay it on me."

"Did you get any sleep?"

"I put on my footie pajamas, grabbed my teddy bear, and got a full eight minutes of uninterrupted bliss." Al stretched out his legs and tapped the toe of one shoe against the front of Beeks's blond wood desk. There was no point in telling her to cut to the chase. Almost five years of this, he thought. Five years of her selling no wine before its time. There were too damn many chairs like this in the world, in his life—set up by people who told you to show up faster than if your keister was on fire, then made you sit and mull over the Meaning of Life until they decided they were ready to grab a bucket and douse the blaze.

After what seemed as long as Lent had gone by, he tossed her a big plastic grin and agreed, "Okay, Alex. I'll take 'Crisis du Jour' for a thousand."

"Joe Powell."

"Do I die of shock now, or later?"

Beeks leaned forward and handed him the folder. "Since Ziggy is still having a problem reaching any concrete conclusions about our guest, I decided to do a little digging myself. Seeing as how the ability to do that *is* what you pay me the big bucks for. Those"—she nodded at the folder he hadn't opened—"are the results of his Minnesota Multiphasic Personality Inventories."

Al blinked. "You ran an MMPI on him?"

Verbena pursed her lips, picked up a mug decorated with pink roses, and peered into its depths. "One and Two, and a few other tests to double-check my findings."

"On a guy who's so far above reproach that the Christian right could mount him on the wall and use him as the Star of Bethlehem in their next Christmas pageant." The absence of expression on Verbena's face piqued his curiosity. "So what's his deep, dark secret? He's a pervert?"

"Something much more dangerous than that. He's an idealist. He's also a very accomplished liar."

"An excellent character trait for the next president of the United States." Opening the folder, Al flipped through the test sheets, their answers neatly penciled within the ovals provided for the multiple-choice questions. "A liar? I bet this guy's never colored outside the lines in his life." Looking up from the papers, he got back to her point. "What's he lying about?"

"You'd like me to pretend you don't already know."

"Just say it."

"He knows how we expect him to behave. He's tailoring his responses to us based on how we've approached him: gently, like he ought to be confused, disoriented."

"Well, dammit, he ought to be!" Crushing the folder closed in his fist, Al used it to beat ineffectually at the arm of his chair. "He ought to think he's been kidnapped by Alpha Centaurians. Or that the right-wing conspiracy decided to brainwash him into becoming a TV preacher with big hair and white suits. Or white hair and big suits. Or . . . or . . ." He sputtered into silence as if he'd run out of gas. Verbena didn't respond, just folded her hands on her desk and waited, watching him. "But he doesn't, does he?" Al admitted with a long sigh.

Beeks shook her head. "He's malingering. Faking his symptoms."

"Maybe he could fake mine, and I could get out of here."

"Joe Powell is lucid and alert. He knows where he's been and where he wants to go. He's experienced absolutely no break in continuity." Reaching out again, she took the crumpled folder away from Al and put it on the desk between them. "He's telling us what we want to hear. And he's trying to find out why we want to hear it."

"Did he know what the tests were?"

"I'm sure he did."

"Maybe he manipulated his answers."

"I asked him to be honest."

"An honest liar." Al was silent for a long time, head propped on the palm of one hand. He thought Verbena's ocean-waves tape had ended, but no, it was still playing. She liked the thing, but it made him badly want to pee. "Do we know why he's different? Brain chemistry? Experience? Any clue at all why Powell is the one-in-a-bazillion exception to the one rule that never changes in this whole mess?"

"Nothing physical that I've been able to find."

"What about special training? Martial arts, something like that?"

"Martial arts?"

"Mental discipline," Al said through his teeth.

"I could make a guess. The destination date being so close to our present. Powell being asleep when the Leap happened. Some kind of resonance between Sam's brain waves and Powell's. I don't know what the answer is. Not yet, at least. All I do know is, Powell isn't Swiss-cheesed." Beeks took a sip of her coffee. "And that you knew already. Why didn't you tell me?"

"Denial? Yeah, let's go for 'denial.' "

She reached down to release one of the controls on her chair and rocked gently back and forth in it a few times, then said, "Ziggy? I'm sorry to interrupt your multitasking, but we could really use your advice."

The room was silent except for the rhythmic sloshing of water on a pebbled beach. Then a voice responded. At first, it seemed to be coming out of the tape player, then from somewhere in the middle of the brains of the two people who sat frowning at each other. "Eighty-four-point-seven percent of my available capacity is in use, Doctor. I would appreciate any effort you might make to—I believe the colloquialism is 'make it snappy.' "

"The Visitor isn't Swiss-cheesed."

"I have been monitoring your conversation." Ziggy sniffed. "You seem to have arrived at a variety of reasonable possibilities before you interrupted my concentration."

"I'd like your opinion."

"Very well." The computer sighed. "Although a number of humans are performing the same function, and redundancy is a luxury I certainly cannot afford at this time, I have not overridden my original instructions regarding observation of the Visitor."

"Go on."

"I have examined Mr. Powell's test responses, his personal background, and his family history, and have correlated them with my extensive databanks concerning Dr. Beckett. I do have a theory, although I am loath to admit my findings are not as conclusive as they might be, had the humans who programmed my fellow computers had the intelligence and foresight to realize that—"

"Some of them did," Beeks offered.

"—attempting to conserve available memory by employing two digits rather than four would result in a massive—"

"Just give us the theory, for crying out loud!" Al barked.

Ziggy maintained an insulted silence for a moment, then replied, "I see absolutely no need for a continued stream of abuse, Admiral Calavicci. Responsibility for the failings of humans does not lie in my lap, particularly with regard to their lack of foresight in—"

"You don't have a lap," Verbena sighed.

"I was employing an idiom."

"We know the problem isn't your fault, Ziggy. Humans are notorious for their lack of foresight."

"I'm glad you're aware of that, Doctor. By the way, may I remind both of you that it would be unwise to board an aircraft on New Year's Eve."

Al raised the other eyebrow, put his hand over his mouth, and muttered into his palm. Ziggy might have been able to interpret the mumbling; Verbena was not, though parts of it sounded remarkably like, "Gonna put a gun in my mouth."

"I believe Dr. Beckett may be a tanist."

"A guy who stuffs dead animals?" Al snorted.

66

The supercomputer sniffed loudly. "A tanist," she explained with noticeable disdain, "is a substitute king."

"The king is dead, long live the king," Verbena mused.

"I believe Dr. Beckett has Leaped into Mr. Powell to spare him from being killed."

"You agreed with Gooshie that Sam's there to save Max," Al complained.

"That was my theory seven hours, four minutes, and eleven seconds ago. I like this one better."

"So he's not there for Max. He's there to save Powell. When? In the accident? Powell didn't die in the accident."

Verbena shook her head slowly and turned in her chair to switch off the tape player. Left in place of the liquid whisper of waves on sand was a soft tinkling noise like distant wind chimes: New Age Ziggy. When she turned back to face Al, Beeks looked distinctly uncomfortable. "I think Ziggy believes Sam is there to die in Powell's place."

Al's stomach dropped a foot, then filled with ice. "What the hell are you talking about?"

"Human sacrifice," Ziggy offered helpfully.

The admiral wobbled his head from side to side, trying to dismiss memories of B-movie scenes of scantily clad maidens being hurled from great heights into the waiting depths of a sinister jungle lake. "What?" he squeaked.

"The data indicate that it is an ancient and highly honored tradition in a number of human cultures."

"In parts of Western Europe," Beeks picked up, a note of chagrin seeping through her professionalism, "they did have an unfortunate tradition of killing their kings, either in response to special crises like droughts or volcanoes, or on certain important calendar dates, like the turning of the millennium. A less-than-devout king could substitute a tanist—someone who would assume his rank, name, and power temporarily, in order to make the sacrifice legitimate."

Al squeezed his eyes shut. Verbena's expression didn't do anything for the churning in his stomach, and Ziggy didn't have a face for him to look at, though he knew the computer's sensors could "see" his face all too well. "And once that sucker's been buried in the cornfield, it's business as usual for the real king."

"The sacrifice of the king is usually considered a fertility rit-

67

ual," Ziggy went on, "the potency of the male ensuring the re-generation of the life cycle."

"The Sexiest Man in the World," Al muttered, feeling a dull ache begin at the base of his skull. "Jesus, Ziggy."

"There is a thirty-two-point-four-percent possibility that my hypothesis is correct."

Al sank lower and lower into the chair, until he was in danger of sliding right off the front of the seat. "You can't be serious."

"I am not in the habit of offering red herrings, Admiral Calavicci. You asked for my theory, and I gave it to you."

"What if I don't like it? I like the Max theory better."

"Irrelevant. May I return to work now?"

No one offered permission, but silence dropped over Beeks's office again. As before, there was a soft, rhythmic background noise, but this time it was Al's wincing. "She's gotta be kidding," he muttered.

"I suppose it's a valid theory," Verbena ventured.

"Human sacrifice? We're not in the twelfth century," Al said to no one in particular. "Nobody believes in that kind of stuff anymore."

"I think you'd be surprised by how many people do believe in 'that kind of stuff.' And there are special circumstances. A lot of ordinarily very sensible people are terrified of the millennium. They're convinced of the possibility of Armageddon. That the world might come to an end within the next few years."

"According to a recent nationwide poll," Ziggy chipped in, "seventy-one percent of—"

"Then they were yanking somebody's dick!" Al shrieked.

Verbena got out of her chair, poured a glass of water, and pressed it into Al's hand, remaining by his side until he had given in and swallowed a few sips. "She's blown her microchips," he grumbled, holding the glass close to his chest when Verbena offered to take it back. "What's next? She's gonna tell us Powell set this whole thing up? That he's a wizard or something?"

"I have insufficient data to draw a conclusion regarding Mr. Powell's intentions," Ziggy announced.

"I thought you were going back to work," Verbena said. She waited a moment, and when no further comment from the supercomputer arrived, she told Al gently, "She's yanking your chain. She wants to be left alone to solve her Y2K problems."

"Human *sacrifice*?"

She circled the desk and settled back into her chair. "Don't think of it in those terms. We've talked a number of times about what might happen if Sam were killed during a Leap. Whether the Visitor would return to his own time, or whether he or she would remain here, in our present. I don't know, Al. I suppose it's a valid possibility that Whoever is running the show thinks Joe Powell's life is more valuable than Sam's."

"It's not," Al said firmly.

"I don't know that Sam would agree."

"Yeah, well, nobody asked Sam." The coffee David had brought to wake him, which had tasted like nectar going down, churned in Al's stomach as if his gut were a rotating salad bowl. "In less than an hour, I've gone from 'Sam's never Leaped so close to the present, so maybe he's coming home' to 'he's gonna die in Joe Powell's place.' I can't buy that. Why let him remember who he is, if he's going to die?"

"He's always remembered who he is, Al."

She was holding something back. "Say it," Al told her.

"You're not going to like it."

"I haven't liked much of anything for almost five years. Say it."

"It could be that Sam is reestablishing his memories and his sense of self in order to prepare for—"

"His life is flashing in front of his eyes? Is that what you're saying?"

"I think it's possible."

"Uh-uh. No chance. Not as long as I'm running the show here. Sam not coming back is not on the list of options. Never. No chance. No possibility." Al flicked his hand hard from left to right several times, as if he were crossing items off on a blackboard. "Zero. Zip. Zilch. We're gonna forget you even thought about it." His head tipped back slightly and he addressed the ceiling. "Ziggy. Gimme the odds that Sam is remembering his life because he's getting ready to Leap home. And you tell me 'insufficient data,' I'm gonna take a magnet to your central processor."

Ziggy purred, "That would leave me with two possible responses. I can say nothing, or I can lie."

Al slammed a hand into his pocket, jerked out the handlink and hurled it across the room. It bounced off the side of Verbena's mahogany bookcase, falling to whir quietly on the floor.

69

"I assume that felt good," Ziggy crooned.

"Al," Verbena said softly, "ruining those handlinks is tough on the budget."

"Screw the budget," Al crabbed. "Screw Ziggy, screw the Committee, and screw the goddamn rules." The toe of his shoe began to thump rhythmically against the front of Verbena's desk, hard enough to make the pencils in her black acrylic pencil cup bounce against one another. "You said it yourself," he told Beeks. "The last bunch of Leaps have been tough on him. He's wearing down. He can't keep doing this forever. Whoever's running the show has to see that."

Verbena picked up one of the pencils and toyed with it. "There's the other perspective, too: God doesn't give us a burden we can't handle. Sam's always risen to the occasion. I don't know, Al. You know in my heart I would love to agree with you. I want Sam to come home to us as much as anyone. He was a good friend. A dear friend."

"You wanna keep this job, you won't let 'was' come outta your mouth again."

"Al."

"Might I suggest a mild sedative?" Ziggy offered. "Your vital signs are straying into the unhealthy range, Admiral. Dear friend. Honey."

Al and Verbena both gaped at the ceiling. "What did she just say?" Al squeaked.

"I'm concerned with your well-being."

Al pushed himself up out of the chair, shuddered hard, then collected himself and stepped toward the door.

"Where are you going?" Verbena asked.

"Waiting Room. To grill the only person in this crazy place who seems to have his head on straight." Al snatched the door open but stood holding on to the knob for a moment. "And I'm sticking with what I said. Human sacrifice, my rosy-pink backside."

CHAPTER SEVEN

The man liked to be comfortable, which was certainly in his favor. Soft cotton slacks, a sweater, thick socks, shoes flexible enough to roll into a ball. Sam shrugged his shoulders inside Powell's sweater and settled deeper into the sofa cushions. He'd dragged over a couple of throw pillows to lean against and idly flicked at the corner of one with his thumb as he paged through the sheaf of papers Max had given him. Max, sitting nearby, had the phone propped between her shoulder and her ear and was tapping notes into the laptop.

"A whistle-stop tour," he commented after she'd hung up, understanding that the itinerary outlined on the top sheet had been prepared with Powell's approval, if it had not been his concept to begin with. "Something that went over very well with the American people from the time railroads began to connect the country. A chance for them to see who they were voting for, to accept him as a living, breathing human being and not as a name and a badly reproduced picture in the newspaper. Something that became largely unnecessary with the advent of television. But that's not true," he went on, knowing that Max had probably heard all of this before. "They still want to *see* the candidate. Talk to him. Touch him."

"With limitations, of course."

Max was stifling a smile. Sam smiled back at her, fleetingly, then returned his gaze to the papers. He wasn't Joe Powell, but he and Powell had a shared experience. Well, he thought as if he were quibbling with Al, not an experience they'd both taken part in, but two similar experiences. Two similar embarrassing experiences. For all he knew, the same woman had approached them both.

She'd been someone's wife, or girlfriend. Or a member of someone's staff; that part didn't matter much. She was lovely, dressed in a beige linen suit, with a voice that was low and sexy and warm, soft hands. *"Dr. Beckett. You have a lot of very interesting ideas."*

"You think so?"

"Oh yes." Al's eyes would have dropped immediately to her cleavage. Sam, the brand-new recipient of a Nobel Prize, refused to stoop to that kind of—normal human male behavior. He smiled, admiring the flecks of gold in her dark eyes. There was a glass of champagne in her left hand, and suddenly she moved closer to him, to avoid being bumped by someone who would make her spill the drink. To his amazement, her right hand drifted down to his crotch and began to caress him as she went on talking in a perfectly normal tone of voice.

"Limited touching," he said to Max. "Absolutely."

He could feel the heat in his face and knew he was blushing. Max either hadn't noticed or was pretending not to; her attention was fixed on the laptop she'd set up on the coffee table. Before either of them could say anything more, the phone rang again. It had rung, on the average, every three minutes since seven o'clock this morning. Max reached for it, but Sam gestured her away and answered it himself. "Joe Powell," he said into the mouthpiece.

"Joe," an enthusiastic voice said at the other end. "Are we on for Sunday?"

"Absolutely."

"It's a beauty, Joe."

"Thanks," Sam said.

"Gonna turn the whole town around."

"That's what I like. Turning things around."

"You're a pisser, Joe," said the voice. "See you Sunday."

The owner of the voice hung up without waiting for a good-bye. Smiling crookedly, Sam pushed the off button, and the phone promptly rang again. "Powell," Sam said.

This voice had almost five minutes' worth of information for him. About thirty seconds into it, Sam realized that the voice was talking about a proposal to acquire a cable television channel whose revised programming would center around subjects taught in junior high school: geography, American and European history, basic science, English grammar, and literature. The Education Channel, it would be called, a sort of round-the-clock *Sesame Street* for older kids, and for adults too ashamed of their educational shortcomings to consider enrolling in night classes.

"I like it," Sam said when the voice stopped to take a breath. "Here's Max. She'll make an appointment for you." Max dutifully took the phone, talked to the voice for a minute as she consulted her calendar, and scribbled a note as she hung up. "I like it," Sam told her.

"I thought it was the financing that was your concern."

"We can work the money out. Can't we?"

Max shrugged and put the phone down. "I imagine so, if everything else suits you."

Her fingers had barely left the instrument when it rang again. She answered, her face coloring rapidly when she discovered who was on the other end. After a murmured request for indulgence from Sam, which he granted with a nod, she took the phone into the foyer and spoke quietly, but not so quietly that he couldn't pick up some of what she was saying.

"No, Mom. Yes, I understand. All right, yes, it does bother me that he's upset, but I'm two hundred miles away. What do you want me to do? No, I can't talk to him right now. I'm working. Mom, I'm working. No, I can't. I'm sorry you feel that way."

The flush of embarrassment had faded by the time she returned to the living room. Finding the equilibrium she'd had a couple of minutes ago took longer.

"Is everything all right?" Sam asked.

"Yes. I'm sorry about that. They know not to call in the middle of the day."

"It was your mother?"

"Yes."

"It's not a problem."

Max opened her mouth to reply, then changed her mind and shook her head, smiling self-consciously. The look told Sam that she badly wanted the subject to be closed. To show her that it was, he reached for one of the files.

They could hear a door opening and closing somewhere nearby. A minute later, Dove walked into the living room carrying an enormous cardboard tube. "Here's the blueprints," he told Sam, though he really seemed to be addressing Max.

"Was it Randi again?" she asked.

"Oh yeah. No bra again, and no panties this time either, from the way she kept twitching her leg so her skirt would ride up."

Sam stared at the bodyguard, fascinated. "Randi?"

"Chip's gofer. She thinks I'm gonna let her in the house because I can see nipples."

The idea of her lover being flashed by another woman didn't seem to bother Max. "I thought Chip was going to bring these out himself," she commented as she carried the huge roll to a table near the windows. She carefully moved the urn that decorated the table to the floor, then slid a collection of blueprints out of their protective tube onto the table and spread them out. "What's he done to change them now, without telling us?"

Sam moved to the table and looked over her shoulder. The top sheet was labeled DELTA COURT.

"Fax machine in the shack is down," Dove said. "Stewie's gonna call for service unless you tell him not to."

"Did he jiggle it?"

"Don't know."

"For God's sake." Max sighed.

Sam leaned closer to the blueprints, tracing a line with his forefinger. "There's not enough free space here." Before Max could respond, he told her, "I know he's trying to maximize the square footage. But it's going to damage the aesthetics. He can't cram all these kiosks into the lobby. You'll have people bumping into each other, like some sort of street bazaar in Bombay." Then he stopped, aware that he was repeating almost verbatim a disagreement Al had had with the designers of the Project complex.

"Tell him to stop thinking 'more bang for the buck.' People don't like noise and clutter." Guessing, he added, "Didn't I tell him that before?"

Chuckling softly to himself, Dove left the room. As his footsteps faded away, Max said, "He's a hard man to persuade."

"Most creative people are," Sam replied, not sure why he'd said that. He took a long look out the window as she rolled up the plans and pushed them back into the tube. "Do you like this view?"

Max lifted her head and considered the wide, soaring expanse of glass that made up most of the living room's western wall. It, and the high, vaulted ceiling, made the room seem as big as a convention hall, perched on the edge of the Pacific. Beyond the glass, the sun glinted off the water. Unlike yesterday, there were boats out near the horizon.

"It's stunning."

"Then I'll meet them in here. The people from the Committee. That's all right, isn't it?"

"Of course."

"Of course," Sam echoed. "Could you do something for me? When I suggest something, instead of saying 'of course,' tell me, 'That's the lamest, dumb-ass thing I've ever heard.' "

Max's hand went up to her mouth. "There's nothing wrong with meeting them in here," she said between her fingers.

"I could make lunch for them."

"You could."

"What do you think? Tuna sandwiches and some of those cookies?"

"Joe . . ."

"Say it," Sam prompted.

Max hesitated, then blurted, "That's a really dumb-ass idea. You have a cook who can make them something nicer than tuna sandwiches."

"Maybe they like tuna."

"I'll have Marie grill tuna steaks, then."

"Maybe they like tuna with mayonnaise. And stop what you're doing before you bite your lower lip off."

She looked as if she wanted to clutch the cardboard tube to her chest and use it as a shield. She must have stopped breathing for a moment, because her face grew slightly purple around the edges. Then, finally, she loosened her teeth from around her lip and stopped fighting her instincts. Both hands were quivering when she started to laugh. She went on laughing until tears dribbled down her cheeks. "If you want to," she gasped out when her laughter began to die down. "I'll help you."

"Deal," Sam said.

They returned to the couch, and Sam returned to Max the handful of papers he'd been studying. She tucked them neatly into the appropriate folder, then began to sort through what was left, not quite acknowledging that her employer was still nearby. Something in the way she avoided looking up told Sam there was more she wanted to say, but that she was unsure whether to voice it. "Penny for your thoughts," he coaxed.

She smiled and pulled in a deep breath. "I was thinking . . ."

"It's all right to say it."

"That it's so nice to see you open up."

"I have to be in the right frame of mind for this trip, don't I?"

"Yes, yes, of—" Max cut herself off. "You've got a very high approval rating, but the public doesn't really know you other than through interviews. If you're going to meet them face-to-face, they're really going to respond to you, the more you smile and put them at ease. If you seem comfortable in your own skin."

Little do they know, Sam thought. "That works both ways."

She didn't need an explanation. "I'm sorry."

"It wasn't a criticism. How long have we worked together?"

"Two years."

"Then I think you can relax." *Easy does it with that,* he cautioned himself. *She's going to think you're making a pass. And Dove is way too big for you to mess with his woman.* "But not too much lightheartedness. For either of us."

"They don't want to think you're the class clown."

"I don't think anyone's ever accused me of being that," Sam sighed. "Listen—why don't you take a break and call your mother back? It didn't sound like you settled whatever she's worried about. Take as much time as you need."

Max glanced at her watch. "She doesn't expect me to call back. Thank you, Joe, but no. I should send those faxes. See if I can catch Rolly before he leaves for lunch. That way we can get a response in a few minutes instead of a couple of hours." She hesitated, then said, "Or tomorrow, if he decides to go straight from lunch to the track again."

"Go ahead," Sam agreed.

"It'll only take a minute."

"Take your time. Oh—you said you have a file on these people from San Diego?" Max nodded and handed him one of her collection of folders, a thick one with a rubber band around it. "I'd like to take a look at it, and refresh my memory," Sam explained. "Can you catch the phone for a few minutes? I could use a break. A little quiet time before they get here."

He smiled again at Max as she left the living room, wondering how much of her wary behavior yesterday had come out of respect for Joe Powell, and how much out of fear. *She's glad I "lightened up." So he's not like that. She probably never knows what he's thinking. Whether she's done something to displease him, or whether he's just stewing about something that has nothing to do with her. So is that why you sent me here now? To take this trip in his place, meet the public, and leave them with something other than the question "What's he hiding?"*

He flipped open the manila folder Max had given him and looked down at the top sheet that lay inside.

Then he looked at it again.

"Oh, boy," he murmured.

CHAPTER
EIGHT

Al was a few steps away from the elevator when it chimed its arrival. *Perfect timing,* he thought, not realizing until an instant later that he hadn't summoned the car. The doors slid open, revealing Gooshie, who, if he was not dead last on Al's list of People I'd Like to See Right Now, was perilously close to the bottom.

"Admiral," Gooshie said breathlessly, fogging the area around the elevator with fumes that had to be deadlier than nerve gas.

"Uh," Al said.

"Dr. Beeks asked me to remind you that you left the Imaging Chamber somewhat, well, completely prematurely last night. Before you provided Dr. Beckett with the necessary information regarding his mission. She thinks, and Ziggy wholeheartedly agrees, that if you allow Dr. Beckett to continue this Leap without knowing what his mission is, it could jeopardize his chances for success."

Al grimaced at the programmer. "You couldn't just say, 'Go tell Sam what he's there to do'?"

"I thought I did."

"Ziggy agrees?"

"Very emphatically."

"You mean, when you finally got her attention, she said something along the lines of 'Yeah, yeah, yeah, whatever'?"

"Well . . ." Gooshie demurred.

"Which mission am I supposed to tell him about? The Max thing?"

Gooshie peered at his superior, his brow deeply furrowed. He obviously thought Al's last remark had been a trick question. "That is Dr. Beckett's mission, yes. Unless you know something I don't know."

"I don't know a damn thing," Al barked. "Is he awake?"

"Who? Dr. Beckett?" Pleased with himself for the way he managed to hold up under the heat of Al's withering stare, Gooshie replied, "Very much so, Admiral. For quite some time now."

"Got something I've gotta take care of first."

"Which would be?"

"None of your business."

Gooshie gnawed at his lower lip for a moment. "Begging the admiral's pardon, but I *am* here on behalf of Dr. Beeks. She asked that I remind you that avoidance, while admittedly a very popular method of dealing with a crisis, is seldom effective in the long run."

"She did, did she?"

"Yes, Admiral."

"And where is *she* right now?"

"Doing a hundred laps in the pool. Stress control." Before Al could respond, Gooshie forged ahead. "I believe now would be an ideal time to approach Dr. Beckett. Ziggy has been monitoring his whereabouts. He's alone. But given the intensity of Mr. Powell's daily schedule, he's not likely to be alone for long. He has a scheduled appointment in, let's see, about two hours."

Al grumbled, "How's Ziggy know he's got an appointment?"

"Well . . ."

Al pushed himself closer to the programmer, careful to hold his breath, and gave him a look calculated to freeze molten lava.

"She told me in confidence," Gooshie mumbled.

"She's a *computer*!"

Gooshie glanced up. The corridor was peppered with sensors, several of them close to the elevator. He had no hope that Ziggy was missing any part of this conversation; even if she happened not to be monitoring it now, she would replay the sensor records "soon," which for Ziggy meant a few seconds down the line. "She says she's intrigued by Mr. Powell. She believes he could be one of the most significant public figures of the twenty-first century, so she's, um, devoted some extraordinary effort to investigating the, um, minor details of his life. Which would include tapping into the computer system at Mount Olympus."

"And she stopped worrying about Y2K long enough to do that?"

"Well, no. One of Powell Technologies' subsidiary companies is involved in the development of supercomputers. The one in his home office is very impressive, as I understand it. Even Ziggy herself was impressed. I believe her actual purpose in investigating the minutiae regarding Mr. Powell was to, um, be able to cozy up to his computer. And talk turkey. As it were."

"His computer's not protected?"

"Well, yes, it is, but we are talking about Ziggy here, Admiral. I could explain the exact procedure she used, if you like."

"Skip it."

"She's downloaded everything, except for a cluster of files she hasn't broken the encryption for yet. I believe she's in the process of examining the various computer networks at all of the domestic offices of PTI, as well."

"And people complain about FBI wiretapping," Al sighed.

Gooshie offered him a broad smile. His hand came up out of the pocket of his lab coat holding a handlink. "I picked up the link you, shall we say, dropped in Dr. Beeks's office. Repairs should be completed within a couple of hours. Please do be careful with this one. The budget this quarter doesn't allow for another replacement." When Al did nothing but glare at him in response, the smile wobbled and then disappeared. "Then you'll go talk to Dr. Beckett?"

"Do I have a choice?"

"Probably not, Admiral."

"I have a stop to make first. Beeks knows that."

To Al's dismay, Gooshie rode the elevator with him down to Control and fell into step with him as he headed for the Waiting

Room. When he reached the door, Gooshie was still there, cling-ing to him like a white-coated shadow. Under the unblinking gaze of the two marine guards, Al counted silently to ten, then handed the computer link back to the programmer. "Hold on to that. So I don't get tempted to bludgeon somebody with it."

"Really, Admiral." Gooshie clucked. "This is a million-dollar piece of—" Al's expression cut him off in midstream. "I'll have it waiting for you."

"Good. Go warm up the Imaging Chamber."

He counted to ten again before he keyed his security code into the pad. With his fingers still resting lightly on the keys, he asked himself what he expected to find inside. That Powell had disas-sembled some of the furniture and turned it into a missile launcher? That he'd talked half of the Project staff into mobiliz-ing a rescue effort? That he'd redecorated the Waiting Room? That he'd ripped a sleeve off the Fermi suit and used it to hang himself?

Not possible. The furniture couldn't be taken apart by hand. Powell had no contact with anyone but Beeks and Calavicci. *The new Burns and Allen. Some songs, some snappy patter, a little soft shoe.* And the Fermi suit didn't rip.

What, then?

A few months ago, there'd been a boy from Tennessee inside this room. He'd had an explanation almost immediately for find-ing himself here: "Those boys must've hit me a good one. Never had a dream this clear. Do you suppose I've got brain damage? That's gonna scare Mama half to death." *The last time we had any fun around here,* Al thought mournfully. He could still hear the familiar drawl of that boy answering his question. "Presley, sir. My name's Elvis Presley."

Shaking his head, Al pressed the final key in the sequence and moved quickly through the opening, allowing the door to close only seconds after it had risen in its track.

What he saw he thought would make some funky kind of picture for *People* magazine. Over the skintight Fermi suit, Pow-ell had tied on a white cotton terrycloth robe (standard issue), and his formerly bare feet were covered with sheepskin-lined slippers (not standard issue). He was slouched back in one of the face-to-face chairs, drinking what smelled like a cup of Beeks's Brazilian Treetop Mocha Almond Cocoa Java or whatever the hell it was called and working on a jigsaw puzzle. He looked up slowly when Al entered, dropped another piece of the puzzle into place, then offered a guarded smile. "Al, isn't it?"

"How's it going, Joe?"

"Fine, I suppose. Given that I'm trapped here, unable to get any work done, unable to contact anyone who could do the work for me." He paused. In Al's imagination, the casual picture turned into an advertisement: *Joe Powell. Polite. Gracious. Madder than hell.* "Considering that I still don't know where I am, or why I'm here."

"Where do you think you are, Joe?" Al asked, looking Powell straight in the eye.

Powell held Al's gaze, his expression absolutely neutral, but when he spoke, his tone very subtly mocking. "Why don't you tell me, Al?"

"It's classified."

"I see." Powell snapped a cloudy section of blue sky into place with a precise click. "So I imagine 'why' would also be—"

"Classified."

"Try an easier question, then. Dr. Beeks. Is she good?"

Al supposed he could pretend to misunderstand the question. Come up with a quip that would undercut his friend both as a professional and a human being. He and Powell were alone, two guys shooting the breeze. What they said wouldn't leave this room. Would go no farther than the observation room next door. Or the confines of Level Ten. Or the perimeter of the complex. "Not sure how you rate that kind of thing," he said.

"Personal opinion."

"She's the best there is."

"Then maybe you could do me a favor. Maybe we could simply cut to the chase, and you can spare me your version of psychoanalysis. Dr. Beeks has that well in hand, and beyond that, it's not your gig, is it? Sit down. Go ahead, sit. Make yourself comfortable." He waited for Al to settle into the matching chair, then went on, keeping his voice low and conversational. "Dr. Beeks ran an MMPI. Both parts. I'm sure she's examined my answers long before now and has told you I'm in no need of straitjackets or inkblots or people who answer questions with questions. You," he said, leaning forward a little, "can consider my previous questions retracted, or at least revised. I don't know exactly where I am, but I can narrow it down to three or four possibilities. I have three or four possible 'why' answers too.

82

The one with the most solid lead is, you want something from me. Care to save time and tell me what it is?"

"Nope," Al said affably.

"It's not money, unless the grant application process that's worked perfectly well for the last who knows how many years has suddenly morphed into interactive theater." Powell considered his puzzle for a moment, then tapped it with a fingertip and commented, "There are pieces missing. Four, I think."

The observation made Al twitch. He would have suspected Powell was only guessing, except that Sam had always been able to pull the same trick. Four pieces missing out of a puzzle composed of three thousand. "Five," he told Powell.

"I didn't count them."

"Didn't think you did."

"I have a good eye for detail. It's one of the things that's helped me . . ."

"Buy up half the world?" Al filled in, not entirely pleased by the note of annoyance that had crept into his voice.

"I have a good memory, too, which is even more useful. People are generally pleased when you remember them. It makes them feel important. That they're of value to you." Another piece of the sky snapped together under Powell's fingers. "Eight years ago, a grant proposal landed on my desk. The usual kind," Powell added with a fleeting smile that held no amusement. "Maybe fifty pages of text with a dozen illustrations. Color photocopies of charts and graphs. A brilliant young Nobel laureate needed money to put something called 'the string theory of universal structure' into practical application. I had to read the package through several times before I understood that what the applicant wanted was to build a time machine. His name was Beckett— Dr. Samuel Beckett. The new Einstein. There was another name on that grant, as I remember. The kind of name that makes you pay attention. War hero, astronaut, Pentagon bad boy. Someone whose sterling reputation had gotten a little tarnished over the years."

"You turned it down," Al pointed out.

"You're right. And you didn't think I'd ever seen it in the first place. If you had, you wouldn't have come in here and let me see you. But anyone who works for me could have told you: if my name is on it, I've looked at it." A snowcapped mountain peak took a bite out of the blue sky forming in front of Powell.

83

"I didn't see any point in investing hundreds of thousands of dollars in a project that was going to be shut down before it ever went on-line." He paused, tapping a finger against one of the bits of glossy cardboard. "If there was a snowball's chance in hell that any of the technology Beckett was proposing actually worked, the government would never take a chance on it falling into the hands of a foreign power or hitting the open market. I thought it was a much better plan to wait a couple of years and let PTI button up some of the contracts generated by Dr. Beckett's project after Uncle Sam made it invisible."

"So you thought—"

"You know the general line of thinking among the science-fiction buffs? That warp drive probably won't be invented by someone who doesn't believe in it. I don't know what's possible. A part of me says *anything* is possible. Like the explanation for my being here."

Al suggested, "You were kidnapped."

"Out of my home? I don't think so. I was lying on the terrace outside my bedroom. In the blink of an eye I was here. That really doesn't open up very many possibilities. Sorry to spoil a popular catch-22, but I'm not going to ask if I've lost my mind, because I haven't. I'm not dreaming; I'm wide-awake. And I haven't just wakened from a coma, because there was no blow to the head. I was lying on the terrace, wide-awake, watching a seagull fly past my house. So how did I get from there to here? Let me guess: Scotty beamed me up."

They faced each other off for a minute, the billionaire and the war hero, two men who had never set eyes on each other before yesterday, but who very nearly knew more about each other than they did about themselves, thanks to the curiosity, the nosiness, and the paid investigative work of a lot of people who were strangers to them both. Above everything else, each of them knew one thing: he did not like the other one.

"You're not up," Al said. "You're down."

"Underground? That makes sense. A lot less conspicuous, and easier to protect." Powell was silent for a moment, then shook his head. Taking care not to damage any of the pieces, he swept the puzzle back into its box and pushed the box aside. "There was a lot of media interest in Dr. Beckett for a year or two. To some extent because of the Nobel. More so because he was— let's say 'interesting.' "

"Call a spade a spade. Let's say 'crackpot.'"

"I felt badly for the man. Believe me: I've been approached by enough crackpots to fill Madison Square Garden. I thought this particular crackpot was worth a second look. I had my assistant tape a couple of television shows he appeared on. He built up quite a chip on his shoulder as time went on. Then, all of a sudden, he was gone. No more interviews. No more blurbs on *Hard Copy*."

"And you knew why."

"Something made the government pay attention. I suspect that was you." Powell slid down in his chair a little and gazed up at the ceiling. "Underground. I imagine we're somewhere in the Utah-Arizona-New Mexico area. Away from population centers. Dr. Beckett's proposal mentioned something about accelerated, high-intensity radiation. So, Admiral Calavicci: I've filled in most of the holes. Why don't you take the last one? When am I?"

"Merry Christmas," Al told him.

"And where is Dr. Beckett?"

"Upstairs in his office."

Powell closed his hand and rested his chin against it. "Then it worked."

"Can't tell you that."

The billionaire said nothing as he finished sipping his coffee. "I like your methods. I wouldn't give you a grant, so instead, Dr. Beckett has switched places with me. That gives him carte blanche with my checkbook."

"Because he's sitting in your house?"

"May I borrow your ring?"

Mildly puzzled by the request, Al pulled the gold navy ring off his finger and passed it to Powell. The moment the other man took possession of it, Al realized why he wanted it. Powell turned it slowly around in his fingers, holding it close to his face, until he could see a small sliver of his reflection in the gleaming surface of the gold. "Because he's sitting in my skin," he told Al.

Verbena was waiting for him in the hallway. "He knows," Al told her.

"Which part?"

"That we know that he knows." Falling into step beside her, he went on, "Sam spelled it all out for him, chapter and verse, in the damn grant application. Eight years ago! I didn't think he even read that crap, let alone remembered all of it. 'Accelerated, high-intensity radiation.' He could probably rewrite the thing verbatim, if we gave him a pencil."

She was a lot less taken aback than he'd expected her to be. "Well, it was probably inevitable that one of the Visitors would recognize you," she ventured. "You were a very visible face for a while, Al."

"Nobody keeps track of astronauts. Or returning MIAs."

"They used to."

They interrupted a conversation between Gooshie and David when they entered the Control Room. "You in here spreading good cheer, Mary Sunshine?" Al asked David crossly.

"Look at the bright side, Admiral," Gooshie offered in a "it's a lovely day in the neighborhood" tone of voice. "If Powell is elected president, he'll take office in a little over a year. Depending on how much material they dump on him, and how fast he can go through it, he'd know all about the Project in what, eighteen months, tops. We've pushed up the timetable a little, is all."

"We," Al groused, "didn't push up a damn thing."

"I suppose you could take the point of view that, if it's really God who's Leaping Sam around, then God intends for Mr. Powell to know about the Project. I'd like to take a positive approach and assume that's a good thing. Isn't it? For the president of the United States to be firmly in our corner?"

"He's not the president yet. And he's not firmly in our corner."

David offered his colleague a broad, jovial smile. "But you'll convince him, won't you? You'll win him over with that Calavicci charm."

"Gimme the handlink," Al said.

He had almost reached the door of the Imaging Chamber when Gooshie cleared his throat. Holding back a complaint, Al turned to look and winced at the look of pain and distress on Gooshie's face. Then he swung back around and stalked toward the door.

"Admiral?" Gooshie ventured, his voice cracking on the last syllable.

Al brought himself up short and without turning, barked, "What now?"

"There's a new readout on the console, here. New information. Ziggy thought you, um, might find it useful to, um . . ."

Al whipped around, using the heel of his left shoe as a pivot. Gooshie, using the console as a shield, seemed to have shrunk two or three inches. "What?" he roared.

"The, um, person, I mean persons Dr. Beckett is going to meet with?" the little programmer squeaked.

"Yes?"

Verbena took a deep breath and moved a few steps up the ramp. Al took her gently by the hand, smiled beatifically at her, and said softly, "I'm gonna string his intestines around the perimeter and let the buzzards eat them for brunch. Tell him he has to the count of three to talk."

"Beckett," Gooshie blurted.

"The rest of it," Verbena prompted. "Whatever it is."

"The members of the Committee to Elect Joe Powell. Who're meeting with Dr. Beckett. Mr. Powell. At the house. This morning. It's the congressman. Tom. Dr. Beckett's brother. And his wife." Gooshie had sputtered all of that out in one breath, turning a deep crimson in the process. Once it was said, he slammed his mouth shut and crouched lower behind the console, ready to duck and cover.

Al's eyes had opened so wide they seemed to fill his entire face.

His partner was standing on the stone terrace outside Powell's bedroom, leaning against the wall, his eyes narrowed against the glare bouncing up from the water even though they were shielded by the pair of Ray•Bans he'd found in the bedroom. Then his eyes closed completely and he tilted his head back, enjoying the warmth of the sun on his face. He seemed more at peace than Al had seen him in months.

"You coulda had this," Al commented mildly.

"Had what?"

"The dough. The nice house. If you'd gone to work for, I dunno, any one of those companies who wanted you. I'll tell ya, buddy, there's nothing like a ton of dough to smooth out the rough edges. After you won the Nobel, you could've pretty much written your own ticket."

"Maybe I should have."

"Wouldn't have been a bad thing. You could have helped people in a million different ways. Powell does."

Sam rested his palms against the stone and leaned heavily

against them. Al couldn't see his face, but could tell by the set of his shoulders that he was a lot less at ease than he'd been a minute ago. "I don't know that it ever occurred to me to be philanthropic, other than by stuffing a few dollars into the red kettle at Christmastime, or buying Girl Scout cookies. I don't think I had time to sit back and think, 'How can I do good in this world?' I was very—focused. I only wanted—"

"What most people want." Al sighed. "To be right."

"When I should have been more concerned with being—" Sam cut himself off. "What was wrong with me, that I could believe it'd be better to be dead than be wrong?"

"I don't think you thought you were wrong."

"I was making a bet with God." Sam turned slightly and rested his backside against the edge of the wall. "I don't know how it was possible to have the absolute arrogance to be convinced I was right, and yet be absolutely terrified that I was wrong, at the same time. I bet everything on one roll of the dice. I turned my back on every bit of common sense I'd ever had, on everything that made me like my father, and said to the Committee, to the press, to everyone who'd ever ridiculed me, even to you, 'Screw you. I'm right.' What does that say about me? How did that elect me to be the person to do *this* job? To be the one who's supposed to make so much of a difference?"

"Could be Him—" Al shrugged, tipping his head toward the sky—"saying 'Screw you. *I'm* right.' "

"Why am I here, Al?"

"To learn how to be humble," Al said.

"I mean here. Now."

"Yeah. I think I knew that." Al looked out over the water for a moment, then said, "It's Max. There's an accident on the way to the airport day after tomorrow. Couple guys in a convertible trying to get pictures of you for the papers. They run your car off the road. Max has her seat belt unbuckled for some reason and hits her head hard on the window. She never woke up. Died a few weeks ago, our time."

"And it took Ziggy twenty-four hours to unearth the fact that someone close to Powell was seriously hurt?"

"She's distracted."

"Yeah, well, she's not the only one."

Al seemed not to catch the implication. "We knew about it last night. I could've told you before, but it doesn't happen till the day after tomorrow. Everything's fine for now. You got a handle on things okay, here?"

"More or less."

The Observer took a step back and considered his friend. "You look like something out of *GQ*, Sam. You do kinda look like you enjoy this life."

"It's comfortable. And yes, I'm enjoying it. It's very challenging."

"You look good. Did you sleep okay last night?"

"I slept fine. Why?"

"Why? Has there got to be a why?"

"You kept giving me strange looks yesterday. I got the same thing from Powell's people, off and on, but that's to be expected. I'm flying blind, and some of the things I say aren't going to be right. That's always true during a Leap. Sometimes nothing I say is what people expect me to say. But you—why do you keep looking at me like you question my sanity?"

Al shook his head fiercely. "I don't." Something out near the horizon caught his attention for a moment; then he craned his head back and scanned the sky above Powell's house. "It's kinda exposed out here, isn't it, Sam?"

"Exposed to what?" Sam too considered the sky. "There are a lot of clouds starting to build up, out that way," he said, pointing. "Looks like rain. But that's not what you meant. Dove told me it's safe out here. Powell sits out here a lot, though I suppose 'a lot' isn't that much, given that he's on the road most of the time. He said someone comes by in a helicopter every so often, trying to get pictures of Powell doing something interesting. Not only doesn't he do anything interesting out here, he stops what he *is* doing and waves to them."

"What if they're not pointing a camera?" Al asked skeptically.

"Photographers in helicopters, with what, machine guns? How likely is that?"

"Don't knock it."

Sam pulled the sunglasses off and tapped them idly against the top of the stone wall. "I guess he believes in not living in fear." Al opened his mouth to reply, but Sam shook his head. "I know all about the full-time bodyguard and the guard shack at the end of the driveway and all the security cameras. But there are gaps in the armor, always. For anyone. And I guess this is the gap. He's not going to lock himself away from the ocean that she loved so much, to avoid people swooping down on him in helicopters as if this were some Middle Eastern battle zone."

"She?" Al frowned. "Who, she? You mean the wife?"

"Yes. She loved the ocean."

"How do you know that?"

"I just know it. That's the connection. There are no pictures, no mementos. I finished checking all the rooms in the house this morning."

"Maybe you missed the one with the shrine."

"Ha, ha," Sam said. "But I realized this morning—he has the ocean. That's what connects him to her. When he's here, she's here with him. It's true. When I stand out here, I can feel a sense of—almost a presence. I'm sure he does too. I slept out here last night. And don't tell me I'm losing it. My mom says she still feels my dad's presence close to her."

Al had heard Thelma Beckett say that very thing, but hadn't entirely bought it then and didn't now. "You didn't even know this woman, Sam."

"I feel like I did."

He forced himself to surrender with a shrug, though he was no less suspicious of the sky above the terrace as he continued to talk, hoping Sam would accept a change of subject. "You Leaped in a little early, it seems like. Go ahead, enjoy the high life. But don't forget about Max."

"So if I keep her from unbuckling her seat belt . . . ?"

"Might work. Or if you have her sit somewhere different. But you know how it goes, Sam. Sometimes a little bit of tweaking does the trick, and sometimes it doesn't."

"I'll cancel the trip."

"You can't do that. It's the beginning of the campaign. You've got to hit the road to Vegas day after tomorrow."

"Why? I don't want to go to Vegas, Al. With every fiber of my being, I hate Las Vegas. If I say 'cancel,' they'll cancel."

"You can't."

"I want to stay here."

"Why? So you can be with 'the presence'? You have to go!"

"Give me a reason."

"We can't get Ziggy to be precise. But okay, I will be. You can't not go on the tour. It'll make you look indecisive. Don't do a Perot, Sam. You'll screw up everything for Powell. It's important. Stick to Powell's original itinerary."

90

"Except . . . ?"

Al pretended to study the handlink, then surrendered to the stare he was getting from Sam. "This meeting this morning. I think you should cancel that. It's kind of a bad idea."

"Why?"

"Because I don't think you can handle it."

Sam folded the sunglasses and dropped them into the breast pocket of his shirt. "Because the people I'm meeting with are my brother and sister-in-law?"

Al coughed quietly into his hand. "You knew that?"

"We aren't playing Mystery Date here, Al. Powell's people put together a list of nominees to run the campaign in California, Nevada, and Arizona. Other nominees for other parts of the country. Out here, it got narrowed down to two: Congressman and Mrs. Tom Beckett. There's a file on them downstairs, two inches thick. Powell had them investigated, background checked, photographed, he even had someone talk to their children. And to my mother and my sister and brother-in-law. Here's the part you might find the most interesting: there are almost forty pages in single-spaced type regarding the congressman's nutball brother, Sam."

"Nothing to worry about," Al said abruptly. "Nobody took Billy Carter seriously."

"But my brother takes Joe Powell seriously."

"Yeah," Al admitted. "He's one of the ones who thinks Powell has all the answers. He went on record saying so. He thinks Powell can run the country like a big corporation, without being a Ping-Pong ball like Ross Perot. That Powell is our last, best hope."

"But you don't agree with that."

"It's politics, Sam. I've had enough of politicians to last me a thousand years. I don't know if there is a last, best hope." The Observer resumed fussing with the handlink until it emitted a screech of protest. Neither he nor Sam supposed for a second that he had damaged the little device; more likely, he was crushing Ziggy's limited sense of patience.

"Is this a good thing for Tom? Being connected with this campaign?"

"I don't know, Sam. I guess so. But I don't think this meeting is a good idea. I think you should cancel."

"Why?" Sam's thoughts tumbled ahead and he answered his

91

own question. "You don't think I should let Tom hook up with Powell. Do you know something? Is it going to be bad for Tom's career?"

"You might slip."

"Slip? What do you mean, slip? You mean give myself away? I didn't slip when I Leaped into Magic Williams. How am I going to slip? I'm not going to tell him I'm me."

"Yeah, I know."

"What, then?"

"I don't know, Sam. I just feel like you talking to Tom right now is the wrong thing to do. He might bring up some, you know, some sore subjects. I want to tell you to skip this meeting," Al said reluctantly. "Tell them you're sick, or you need to do something urgent, like teleconference with Tokyo or rehearse your speech for Vegas or watch the golf play-offs. But it's kinda out of my hands."

"What is?"

"Everything," Al said slowly. "It's never about what I want, even when I try to make it be. I'm not the one running the show. I'm not the one who set up this meeting. Somebody wants it to happen. So go on. Go downstairs and talk to your brother." The Observer heaved a long, wobbling sigh, then threw his hands up into the air. "Somebody thinks it's a good idea. That it'll accomplish something. But whether that's for you, or Tom, or Powell, or the whole country, I don't know."

Sam ran a hand through his hair. "Al, I'm not Joe Powell."

"I know."

"I feel like I'm living that nightmare, where you're sitting down for an exam and you've never seen the material before. Or you're naked. Or you're naked and unprepared. How am I supposed to discuss Powell's politics with Tom when I have no real idea what Powell's opinions are? I've been fudging it up till now, with all these phone calls. I prompt people into telling me what they think, and if it seems to make sense, I agree with them. And I've gone through a lot of his files. It's challenging and it's interesting, up to a point. But this is different. Sitting down with someone to talk about Powell's political beliefs. It's not improvisational theater. I can look like Powell, and I can act like him, but I can't think like him. For all I know, I could be diametrically opposed to everything Powell believes in."

The Observer shrugged eloquently. "Balance."

"In what?"

"In everything. Equity. That you don't take care of the needy by screwing the middle class. That you don't make the upper class exempt. That nobody gets a free ride. Balance. *Star Trek.*" When Sam greeted that with a broad look of disbelief, Al explained, "The needs of the many outweigh the needs of the few, or the one. Except in cases, considered on an individual basis, where the needs of the one outweigh the needs of the many. Or the bitching and moaning of the many. You know what I mean."

"You know that much about Powell. A man who hasn't said anything yet about whether or not he's going to run."

"If it quacks like a duck," Al said.

Suddenly, Sam began to circle his friend, considering Al's expression from several different angles. "You're holding something back again. Something important." Al flinched, and it took nothing more than that for Sam to understand what the problem was. "The guy who's been hanging around counting the thumbtacks? The guy who wants to be a senator. It's Tom, isn't it?"

"I guess so," Al said.

"Tom's at the Project."

"He was. He's not here right now."

Sam's breath went out in a whoosh. His legs wobbled enough to force him to sit at the end of Powell's chaise longue. "How much have you told him?"

"I haven't told him anything."

"But somebody has."

"He's on the House Special Subcommittee to Investigate Misappropriation of Gold Doorknobs or some damn thing. He did a bunch of digging around, and wooing people. He's a good wooer. He's related to you."

"And?"

"He knows what the Project is. What it's for. He's not what you could call real thrilled with it all. He doesn't believe most of it. He thinks it's all a big scam. I don't know if he'd believe it even if he heard it from you."

"Then he knows where I am."

"Not really. He thinks . . ."

"Say it."

Al nudged the toe of his shoe against a fall leaf lying on the stone floor, teasing the edge of what to him was only an image.

93

"He says he thinks you're dead, but I don't think he really believes that either."

Sam thought hard for a minute, holding his head in his hands. *All these years, of . . . nothing. No phone calls, no visits, no letters, nothing. Five years of Sam being wrapped up in himself. Of walking away, of pursuing what I thought was important, and to hell with what anyone else needed, or wanted, or expected. Five years of being the same person I'd been all my life.* Then he looked up, with an expression that was more sad than anything else. "Tell him the truth, Al."

"I can't."

"Yes you can. Tell him where I am, and tell him it's all right to tell my mother, and Katie, and Jim."

"He can't do that," Al insisted. "It's top secret."

"The hell with that. I don't want my family to be hurt any more than they've already been. I don't want them to think I don't care. I need them to know I think about them, and that I love them."

Al's shoulders twitched a little. "They know that."

"Do they?"

"They know, Sam."

Sam shook his head vehemently enough to make himself dizzy. "After all this time? Thanks for the pep talk. But I'm not buying."

"People can't keep secrets, Sam."

"You can."

Al winced at that. "If I tell them, they're gonna find that they need to confide a little bit in somebody. Or they'll slip."

"So what? So what if they do?" Sam waited for an answer and didn't get one. He sat in silence for a moment, then said sharply, "You're right. My brother is probably the last person I should talk to right now. Especially if I can't fling myself to the floor at his feet and tell him I'm the most self-centered son of a bitch walking the face of the planet."

"He already knows," Al murmured.

CHAPTER
NINE

Max met Sam at the bottom of the stairs and plucked a bit of red lint off his sweater. "They're waiting for you in the living room. I'll give you the ten-minute warning—you need to talk to New York at noon."

"Why do you do that?" Sam frowned.

"I'm sorry . . . ?"

"I can't talk to New York, unless it's a very one-sided conversation."

She blinked a couple of times, but was quick enough on the uptake that he didn't need to explain further. "Adam Kennerly, Laura Dixon, Beth Monroe, and Danny Ho in the New York office of PTI."

"What am I talking to them about?"

"The new satellite uplink."

"Do I have paperwork on that?"

She didn't manage to stifle quite all of the expression of bewilderment that tried to spring onto her face. "They sent us the initial proposal last spring. It's in the file. I'll pull it out if you want to . . ."

Sam drifted over to the round oak table in the middle of the foyer, rested a hip against it, then shifted his weight and began to drum his fingers against one of the pinkish veins in the marble tabletop. "Yes, pull it out. But it's over a year old. Have them fax me the reports, whatever they're working from, anything from the last three months, then give me a couple of hours to read it. Doesn't it make sense for me to know what I'm discussing?"

"Well, yes," Max agreed. "But Joe—you said you wanted them to do all the detail work on that project, and come to you with the final breakdown. That's what they're prepared to do."

"I was drunk when I said that," Sam replied. "I want to know what they're talking about."

Leaving Max to sputter quietly in the foyer, Sam gathered his nerve and strode on through the doorway and down the three steps into the living room. His guests were standing near the terrace doors with drinks in their hands, admiring Joe's fantastic view of the Pacific. When they heard Sam's footsteps on the hardwood steps, they both turned to greet him with smiles.

The smile he gave them in response took all the effort Sam could muster. *I don't know them,* he reminded himself, then realized that that was mostly true. The woman, small and slender, with wavy brown hair and dark brown eyes, neatly dressed in a dark gray suit and red striped blouse, was a stranger. And the man—this version of Tom who was a middle-aged adult with a wife and children and a seat in Congress, might as well have been. The last time Sam had seen his brother, Tom had been in his early twenties. They'd been friends then. They weren't now.

Mea culpa, Sam thought ruefully. *I'm sorry, Tom.*

Tom set his drink down on the closest surface the glass, damp with condensation, could not possibly mar, stepped forward, and extended his hand. "Mr. Powell, it's a pleasure to see you again. Linda and I were thrilled to be invited to see you up here. I hope it's not an inconvenience."

"No problem," Sam said with as much voice as he could muster.

Linda Beckett put her glass beside Tom's and came forward

96

with noticeable hesitation. The hand she offered was tiny and neatly manicured but had the same well-worn look Sam remembered as belonging to his mother's hands. This woman had dug into the soil to plant a garden, wielded a dripping paintbrush, carried heavily loaded cardboard boxes. Changed diapers, wiped noses, scrubbed pet accidents out of the carpet. She was nervous, but the smile she offered was warm and genuine. Sam took her hand and instead of shaking it, simply held it, wanting badly to embrace her and give her a kiss. *My sister-in-law,* he marveled. *And . . . my brother. Tom! Tom. Oh, God.*

He offered Linda a slightly more genuine smile, then went to the credenza and poured himself a drink. The Becketts took that cue to retrieve their own glasses. Because speaking still didn't seem possible, Sam gestured them to one of the cream-colored sofas and cast them one more smile, hoping it didn't look as ridiculous as it felt.

"You have an absolutely stunning home," Linda told him as they all sat down.

"Thank . . ." Sam cleared his throat. "Thank you."

She beamed. "If I didn't know better, I'd think you were as nervous as I am. Look at me, I'm quivering like a teenager! I don't know if you remember—you and I met a few months ago at the breast-cancer fund-raiser at the Century Plaza. But that was only for a few seconds."

"I remember," Sam lied.

"I worked with several famous people, helping put the fund-raiser together. I had lunch with Harrison Ford and his wife up in Jackson Hole, and I thought that was the most nerve-racking experience possible, sitting across the table from that man and remaining coherent for almost two hours. But—" She stopped and pulled in a deep breath. "I know I'm babbling. Please forgive me. But I've never met anyone who's been on the cover of so many magazines. Imagine, little Linda Hayes from Portland, Oregon, being here, talking to Joe Powell. It's truly astonishing."

"Well," Sam suggested, "you could try pretending that I'm someone you know really well. A member of your family."

"The next president of the United States."

Tom quipped, "She believes in the power of positive thinking."

"Whatever works," Sam coughed.

"It's one of those things I have a very strong feeling about,"

Linda went on. "Like my daughter's basketball team winning one of their games. It's more than just 'positive thinking.' It's being sure of the outcome. And I'm sure of this. The people who know you—know about you, I suppose, is more accurate, since most of us don't actually know you—they're all going to vote for you. And the ones who learn about you through the campaign, well, how could they decide there's a better man for the job?"

"Sheer cussedness," Sam murmured.

That made Tom grin widely as he took another sip of his drink. "Haven't heard that one in a long time."

"One of my grandfather's favorites."

"Mine too."

"So, your . . . daughter plays basketball?"

"Has since she was a freshman in high school. Only freshman on the varsity team," Tom said proudly. "My son opted for track and field, but my daughter followed in her old man's footsteps. She's been getting a lot of attention from scouts the last few months. But she might trail the old man that much further."

"Into the navy?"

"Hmm," Tom nodded. "You knew all this, didn't you?"

"I was curious."

"I'm sure there's more to it than curiosity." After returning a smile from Linda, Tom shifted his weight on the sofa and sat forward. "We didn't come here looking for an autograph, Mr. Powell. I'm sure your people have checked into our background, and that you could tell me what the two of us had for breakfast and how well we slept last night. Which is, not terribly well. I'd like you to know—both of us would like you to know that we were curious too. We've done a lot of research. Reading up on the history of your company—companies?—and on you yourself. I've talked to a number of people in Washington, and here in California, including a handful of higher-ups in your organization. I didn't expect them to say you were perfect, and they didn't. But I came out of it with the impression that you, possibly more so than anyone I've ever met, know what you're doing, where you're going, what you can achieve and what you can't. You're goal-oriented and I like that. Some of the people I spoke to said they're a little puzzled by you, but I think that just makes you human. What interested me the most was that none of those people could say, 'He did me wrong.' Or could drop a little

98

gossip implying that you'd done anybody else wrong. You've been in business since you were fifteen years old, and in all that time, you've managed to avoid screwing over anybody who was on your side. You've got the same kind of integrity my dad had. Maybe I don't have to tell you, I think that's important."

Sam nodded. "Your father was a farmer."

"Right up until the bank took his land away from him." Tom hesitated, then said, "The only time I ever saw him cry was the day he lost his land."

"Because they took away his sense of worth."

"They took away what he *was*. With no more care than if they—" He stopped again. "See, that's the thing. You don't take what belongs to somebody else. Not their job, or their car, or their jewelry, or their purse, or the newspaper off their doorstep. If you buy up a company that's struggling, and merge it into something else, you don't do that without considering every human being who's involved. You don't 'downsize' people who are going to end up out on the street because they can't find another job and they can't pay their mortgage or their rent, while some fat-assed CEO pulls down millions and goes to sleep on six-hundred-dollar sheets without a worry in his head. You just plain don't do that."

Sam proposed, "But if the only way to keep the company afloat is to trim the workforce?"

"Trim from the top. Somebody who's pulling down six million a year can survive on three million for one year. You take that extra three million and portion it out among the displaced workers. Pay their bills. Pay an employment agency to find them new jobs, and keep their health insurance going. The way I see it, Mr. Powell, anybody who'd leave a single person out twisting in the wind so they can live like"—without irony, Tom looked around, taking in everything from the enormous window overlooking the ocean to the archway over the stairs to the foyer—"this, doesn't deserve to sleep at night, on six-hundred-dollar sheets or otherwise."

Linda picked up the ball. "At the same time, you don't pay anyone for doing nothing. It would take time and money to dig out all the welfare and Medicaid fraud, and the tax fraud, but once it was finished, the effort would pay for itself."

"Reorganize social security," Tom went on. "A different sliding scale, so that payments aren't based on what you contributed.

99

That's all well and good, but there's social security going to people who also get thousands of dollars a month in pension money, while the ones who were never able to get a decent job during their working life don't get enough a month to feed themselves more than once a day."

Sam settled back into the cushions, sipping his drink and pretending to mull over what the Becketts were saying. Tom was right: the file Max had provided included every picayune detail imaginable about these two people. Powell's staff had certainly "dug up the dirt," though nowhere in the file was there anything even remotely uncomplimentary, except a quote from a neighbor suggesting that Tom had once lost his temper in a supermarket parking lot and had dented the front fender of his own car with a swift kick from a steel-toed boot. Tom, the dossier said, had first won his congressional seat by a narrow margin but had grown steadily in popularity since then, the holdouts being mostly those voters who were so unused to an honest politician that they were skeptical of what surely seemed to be one.

Sam remembered a comment from another neighbor and smiled absently: *"I mean, good Lord, nobody in his family even smokes."*

"Your children are both in college," Sam said, then turned to Linda. "Your family is all still in Oregon?"

"Rooted deeper than a redwood."

"And your family," he said to Tom. "In Hawaii? That's pretty rough."

Tom smiled at the gibe. "My sister's husband—career navy—got transferred there right after they got married. After my dad died, my mom joined them there. They enjoy it. We see them pretty often. Five or six times a year, usually."

"And you have a brother."

For the first time, Tom flinched. "Don't see him much."

"Your choice?"

"No," Tom said with very little emotion. "It's not my choice at all." He stared into his drink for a minute, as if he were considering telling the man who sat facing him, and who knew what brand of gasoline Tom customarily bought to fill the tank of the three-year-old Cadillac whose VIN he probably also knew, that Tom's relationship with his brother was off-limits as a topic of conversation. He was still thinking when Linda reached over and rested her hand on his forearm. He looked up then and said evenly, "My brother's in New Mexico. He's involved in some government project that you probably know more about than we do. He's been working since he was a kid on the same thing."

"Quantum physics."

"Time travel," Tom said with an edge in his voice, as if he were challenging Powell to mock that.

"The string theory of universal structure? I think that's what the file said."

"He won a Nobel Prize. My mother was so thrilled she didn't close her eyes for two weeks. She made a scrapbook with all the news clippings, and taped all the coverage on TV. But Sam—Sam acted like he wasn't sure why they decided to give it to him."

Sam replied, "Maybe he was more concerned with the work than the glory."

"I don't know."

Again, Linda took over for her husband. Holding his hand tightly in her own, she told their host, "Sam's like a lot of very intelligent people. He's very focused on his work. Sometimes to the point of not being able to widen his focus to include anything, or anyone, else. But he's a good man. There's nothing worse you could say about him than that he wants so badly to achieve his goals that he becomes a little indifferent to people."

"When was the last time you saw him?" Sam asked.

"A little over five years ago."

"Maybe he's changed since then. Maybe he . . . doesn't realize how you feel about his work."

Tom opened his mouth to reply, but Linda squeezed his hand and shook her head. "We didn't come here to talk about Sam, did we? Sam has his own mission in life, and we have ours. Mr. Powell, I know this is very bold of me. Maybe you wanted to take this more slowly. But I'm hoping your willingness to see us means that you'd like us to have some responsibility in your campaign."

His gaze still on Tom, Sam responded, "That depends on how much work 'some' would amount to."

"As much as you'd like."

Sam offered them a smile that was phonier than anything he'd come up with all morning. "Would you excuse me for a minute? I'll be right back."

He found Max going through a long list of E-mails in her office at the back of the house: a room lined with file cabinets, much smaller than Powell's home headquarters. She was barely visible behind a six-tier stack of in-box-type desk trays. "Do me a favor," Sam said with a noticeable wobble in his voice. "Go sit down with the Becketts and outline what it is we want them to do for the campaign."

Max was already on her feet, peering into his face. "Are you all right, Joe? Do you have another headache?"

"No. I'm all right. Talk to them, please. And apologize for me."

"Then you're satisfied that they're the right people for the campaign?"

"We knew that before they walked in the door."

"You look awfully pale, Joe."

"I'm swell. I feel fabulous," Sam said in a tone that didn't indicate either one. "Go talk to them, would you? I'm going upstairs."

"Hey, kid. You okay?"

"Sure."

"You look a little queasy." The Observer circled his best friend, then did it again, trying to determine from Sam's expression what Tom Beckett had or had not said. Though Sam failed to notice, Al looked not much less queasy. "How'd the big meeting go? I popped in downstairs for a minute. Tom and Linda were having lunch with Max. Everybody seems happy. I think they all signed on the dotted line. And hey, you know, that's a nice car he drives. It's parked out in front of the house. Looks like he's doing pretty good."

"Yes, I suppose so."

Al ventured hesitantly, "What did he say?"

"He didn't want to talk about me."

"You're not involved with the campaign."

"I'm a sore subject. Me. I saved his life, Al."

"Yeah, I know that."

"I changed history. I prevented him from being killed in Vietnam. Instead of being buried next to Dad, he's a congressman, with a wife and two grown children. He was a teacher for almost twenty years. Won Educator of the Year three times. He's built a wonderful career. People respect him."

"Yeah, I knew that too."

"And he hates me."

"He doesn't hate you. 'Hate' is a big word. He's just miffed at you for not sharing the load with your family."

"I thought he'd understand when we went underground. The need for secrecy made sense."

"It still does."

"Not if it's tearing my family apart."

"Sam. He'll get over it. He goes into these snits once in a while, but they don't last. Don't worry about it. There's nothing you can do about it anyway. And don't," Al said firmly, using his cigar as a pointer to emphasize his words as if they were visible as they hung in the air over the terrace, "start thinking you can maneuver things around so Powell convinces Tom that his brother is a saint. You're here to keep Max from getting hurt in that car accident. Don't get distracted."

Sam shoved his hands through his hair and sat down hard at the end of the chaise longue. "I think he knows, Al."

"What? Who knows what?"

"Tom. He kept looking at me. Studying me. I think he knows who he was talking to."

"No way. How would he know? Unless you said something. You didn't say something, did you?"

Sam's head wobbled as if it were connected to his neck by nothing more substantial than a layer of Silly Putty. He got up from the chair, sat down again, got back up, and wandered into Powell's bedroom. He stopped alongside the bed for a moment, holding on to a bedpost. "Do you smell something?" he asked Al.

"I smell stuff here. I don't smell stuff there," Al reminded him impatiently. "Smell what?"

"Perfume."

"So the maid wears perfume. Big honkin' deal. What did you say to Tom?"

"I didn't say anything to Tom. He did most of the talking. And he kept looking at me."

"Saaam," Al moaned. "He was looking at you because you're famous."

Sam walked on out of the bedroom. At the far end of the long hallway outside, a stained-glass window cast muted colored light onto the pale carpet. "My father thought it was a joke. Or maybe he wanted other people to think he thought it was a joke. When

103

they'd call us on the phone, asking questions on behalf of some politician, and they would ask for his name, he'd tell them 'Diogenes.' He said the same thing to anyone who came to the door. His blood pressure would go up every October. He said there wasn't a soul alive who'd gotten into politics for anything other than money, or power, or a combination of the two. And his son is a congressman. If my father hadn't died in 1972, he'd certainly be dead now."

"I don't think Tom's in it for the money."

"You told me not five minutes ago that he drives a nice car."

"Which means what?" Al sputtered.

"He was a high-school history teacher. For the time and energy you invest, it's one of the worst-paying jobs there is. Now he's trying to join forces with the fourth wealthiest man in the country." Growing more and more flustered, Sam paced to the end of the hall and began to descend the stairs. He was almost halfway to the foyer when he realized Dove was down there, standing near the entrance to the living room, talking on a cellular phone. A moment later Marie was in the foyer as well, arms folded sternly across her small chest, scowling at nothing in particular.

"Sam," Al called after his partner, "come back upstairs. There's too many people down here."

Sam ignored him and walked past Marie, who sputtered at him in French.

"Marie!" Dove said sharply. "Don't bother the boss."

The little woman ignored that and trotted off after Sam, following him down the hall that led past the billiard room and the library and terminated at the entrance to the dining room. She continued to complain in her native language until Sam had reached the door of the library, then switched to heated English. "They have no respect for my person," she snapped.

"I'm sorry," Sam told her.

"This situation, this is impossible for me. I must have respect."

Al, a few steps away, sighed. "Talk to Aretha Franklin. Beat it, could you? I'm trying to get him back upstairs where it's quiet."

"Bad taste will come out in the food," Marie insisted.

"Only if you spit in it."

Marie's tiny fist came up, index finger jabbing out, and she waved it at Sam. "You must tell them."

"Does this have something to do with *Rescue 911*?" Sam asked.

"One small request I make. Do I ask for more money? No. Do I ask for him to drive me in the limousine back to my house? No. Do I refuse to make a meal for large parties? No, no, no. Only one small request, and for this I am criticized and made to feel foolish and demanding. You must tell them, Marie will have respect or Marie will go knocking to Steven Spielberg and the beautiful Mrs. Kate Capshaw."

Her point made, Marie spun on one heel and stalked back down the hall, walking right through Al in the process. He shuddered and watched her disappear around the corner, then mused, "You don't think she does the old hawkeroonie into the cuisine, do you?"

"If she does," Sam replied, "I would prefer not to know."

Al let the question drop. "Don't get cynical like your old man. Tom's interested in Powell's politics, not the size of his wallet."

"What did he tell you?"

"Don't worry about it. He's peevish because I'm holding all the cards. He's always been like that."

Suddenly, they were again not alone. Dove, who seemed to have come out of nowhere, was at Sam's elbow, nudging him in a different direction. When Sam grunted a protest, Dove explained, "We found a little nest of ants in the TV room, boss. Had to spray some stuff in there and it smells pretty bad. Kinda toxic, until the room airs out. Maybe you better avoid that part of the house." When Sam demurred, Dove said firmly, "You really oughta stay away from there. That toxic stuff might set off another headache or something." Sam frowned at the story and the not quite convincing way it had been delivered. "Looking out for your best interests," Dove said. "I'll let you know when the room's cleared out. Okay?"

"Fine," Sam agreed.

"I think Max is looking for you, anyway, if you feel better. You might want to say goodbye to those people."

Because the bodyguard was too much of an irresistible force, Sam let himself be ushered back out to the foyer as Max and the Becketts emerged from another part of the house. He joined them in the curved drive in front of the mansion and offered a nearly genuine and somewhat relieved goodbye as the Becketts got into their car, then backstepped into the house. Max met him there a minute later and closed the front door behind her.

In the distance, they could hear Dove bickering with Marie. Max heaved a weary sigh that seemed to have a deeper source than Marie's quarrelsome demands. "I'm sorry, Joe. I told her you weren't to be bothered."

"She didn't bother me. Did you get her those tapes?"

Max hesitated, studying the front door. "We offered. I offered," she amended. "Conversations tend to be simpler if she and Dove aren't both involved in them. She said she didn't want tapes of old episodes, because she's seen them all. She wants new ones. I tried to explain to her that the show was canceled."

"And?"

"She said you could approach the production company and pay for new ones."

"Tell her it doesn't work that way."

Max toyed with her necklace, running the pad of her thumb against one of the pearls. "I tried." Before Sam could respond, she said quickly, "I'll try again," and disappeared in the same direction the quarreling voices seemed to come from.

As soon as she was gone, Sam hissed to his partner, who had remained close by the entire time, "Tom's 'always been like that'? I don't remember you having any conversations with Tom. Before I Leaped, Tom was dead."

Al remained stubbornly silent.

Sam's index finger jabbed out, much as Marie's had a couple of minutes ago. "Don't you even think it. Don't you stand there in front of me and even think that you wish he'd stayed dead, because he gives you a hard time."

"Hard time," Al groaned, "is not even in the ballpark."

"Why? Because he's counting expenditures, looking for dirty laundry to air out to make himself look better?"

"The laundry's all taken care of, Joe," Max called from somewhere around the corner. "The repairman was here yesterday and replaced the drive belt on the washer. Kristin took care of the washables, and everything else has gone to the cleaner's. We'll have it back tomorrow morning."

"She's got ears like a bat," Al wheezed. "Talk softer, Sam."

Somewhere nearby, a door opened and closed. Then the phone began to ring, and an instant later, a second phone line chimed in, creating a symphony of ringing that echoed through the house. A moment later, his altercation with Marie apparently either forgotten or won, Dove walked into the hallway, crunching on an apple and reading a folded-open copy of what seemed to be a car magazine. "Sedan's in good shape, boss," he commented as he walked by. "Pike replaced the belt; now it runs like a top."

"Great," Sam said.

Dove, like Marie had a couple of minutes ago, walked straight through Al, stopped, considered the Observer without seeing him, then shook his head and kept walking. "Randi came back for the blueprints," he said over his shoulder.

"Who's Randi?" Al asked.

"Never mind," Sam whispered as Dove disappeared.

"This is a zillion-square-foot house, and there's only three people living here," Al moaned. "So why do I feel like we're at Times Square?"

"You could leave," Sam suggested.

"Wait a minute. Did she say Kristin did the wash? Who's Kristin?"

"Somebody who obviously did herself a favor by managing to avoid you. Pick a room. If everyone in the house is down there somewhere"—Sam pointed in the direction Powell's three employees had taken—"then the rooms down that other hallway ought to be empty."

"Unless Kristin's here somewhere."

"Would you stop with Kristin?"

"Only if I can start with Kristin first. They don't have intercoms set up in these rooms, do they? Intercoms are a bad thing. People can snoop on you without you ever knowing you're being snooped on. She's probably a dish, huh? I never met a Kristin who wasn't a serious honey bunny."

Ignoring him, Sam began to blaze a trail down the hallway he'd indicated. The main corridors on the ground floor formed a square, with shorter halls branching off in all directions. Sam hadn't explored it all well enough to be certain where he was, though he guessed he was on the side of the house opposite from the room Dove had cautioned him about. Finally he stopped walking and pointed to a door. "That one," Sam said.

"What one what?"

"That room. Let's talk in there. I think it's a conference room." Sam took a few rapid steps toward the door he'd indicated, then pulled himself up short.

Al squinted at him. "What's the matter?"

"I'm wrong. I got turned around. It's the TV room, the one Dove was talking about. There's somebody in there. Listen—the TV is on."

"The exterminator?" Al guessed.

"Watching TV?"

Obediently, the Observer leaned in for a listen, then gave his shoulders a big "so what" shrug underneath his purple tapestry jacket. "Why is that a problem?" he asked when Sam continued to stand outside the door, staring at it in dismay.

"Dove acted like the spraying was a done deal. The guy wouldn't still be here."

"Then who is it?"

"I don't *know* who it is."

"Oh. You mean because Tweedledee and Tweedledum are probably locked in a clinch out in the living room, and Marie the paramedic maniac is sulking someplace, this has to be Gold-ilocks." All that got out of Sam was a loud huff of annoyance. "Maybe it's your number-one fan," Al suggested happily. "Like the one they found sleeping in Brad Pitt's bed, all snuggled up in his sweatpants. If she's a cutie, you could give her a tour."

"This isn't funny," Sam hissed. "No one is supposed to be able to get through the security system."

"According to who? There's not a security system in the world that somebody with enough smarts and a little patience can't bust. Especially somebody who thinks it's their God-given right to be in here."

"Al, a dust mote couldn't get in past Powell's security system."

"Yeah, well, somebody did. Hey, maybe it's Kristin. You could ask her to teach you how to fluff and fold."

"Would you *stop*?" Sam demanded.

Puffing calmly on his cigar, the Observer commanded, "Go in and look. If it's an armed intruder, he's not in there watching the TV."

Stalling just long enough to demonstrate that he was not happy with the situation or with Al's lack of distress, Sam gently turned the knob and eased the door open. He and Al could then see the almost six-foot-wide screen of the TV, tuned to a movie whose closing credits were scrolling. They could not see whoever had turned the TV on. With Al nudging him along, Sam took a few steps into the room, then a few more. He stopped near the back of the long, brown velour-upholstered sofa that faced the TV and folded his arms over his chest. Intrigued, Al circled around him for a look.

Sound asleep on the sofa, scrunched into its soft cushions, was a teenage boy dressed in a baggy sweatshirt and jeans faded out so much they were almost white, and white tube socks whose soles were almost black. The sneakers he had pulled off lay discarded underneath the coffee table. On top of the coffee table were several half-empty cartons of Chinese food, the TV listings section of the newspaper, and a box of tissues surrounded by wadded-up strays. He was breathing in wet, snuffly gulps, and as Sam and Al watched, he squirmed around in his sleep until he was lying on his stomach, his face pressed into the sofa cushion.

"You better wake him up, Sam," Al pointed out. "He's gonna smother himself. At the very least, he's gonna get snot all over the couch."

With a groan, Sam leaned over the back of the sofa and jostled the boy's shoulder. On his second try, the boy started awake and struggled until he was right side up, peering worriedly at Sam out of a face that was flushed with fever. He seemed completely bewildered: by Sam, by the look on Sam's face, even by where he was. "Huh?" was the only thing he managed to get out.

Sam tossed an inquisitive look at his partner. Al had already begun punching an inquiry into the handlink and read off the response as it appeared on the tiny screen. "Got a couple possibilities. I'll try to get Ziggy to narrow it down. Hey, if Dove tried to get you not to come in here, he must know the kid is here. Maybe it's a friend of his."

The boy scrambled for tissues, used several of them, and dumped all the used ones into a brown paper grocery sack he'd set up as a wastebasket. After a moment of consideration he also discarded the Chinese food cartons.

"You're sick?" Sam said. It was a stupid question, and the only one that came to mind that didn't require knowing whether he'd ever met this kid before.

"Yeah," said the boy.

Taking advantage of the boy's sudden coughing fit, Sam looked again to Al for a name, got nothing, then looked around for something liquid to offer to stifle the coughing. Al jabbed a finger toward what Sam had thought was a bookcase and, when

Sam shook his head, jabbed harder until Sam investigated and found a small refrigerator stocked with soft drinks and juices. He pulled out a bottle of juice, popped the lid, and handed it to the boy, who gulped half of it gratefully and let out a long sigh when his coughing finally ceased.

"I feel like shit," the boy mumbled. "Are you him? Mr. Powell?"

Sam offered him a smile. "Yes. I'm him. And you would be . . . ?"

"Kevin. Kevin Maxwell. I'm—you know. My mom works for you."

Sam and Al exchanged glances that both commented, *Max has a son?* As Al began to punch inquiries into the handlink with renewed vigor, Sam told the boy, "Your mother's, um, around here somewhere. Do you want me to get her?"

"What for?"

Aid and comfort, Sam thought, remembering his own mother tiptoeing into his room with a tray of chicken soup and juice, then perching at the edge of his narrow bed, wiping his forehead with a cool washcloth, and rubbing the small of his back to comfort him until he fell asleep. Granted, he'd been a lot younger during those times than Kevin was now—the kid looked to be eighteen or nineteen—but old as he might be, Kevin looked sorely in need of some solicitous care.

"I don't need her." Kevin sighed. "She doesn't want to see me. Dove told me I could take a nap in here for a couple hours. I'm sorry I messed up your house. I'll clean everything up before I take off."

"Why don't you go upstairs and go to bed?" Sam suggested. "Take some aspirin and—"

"Zinc," Al said. "Boosts the immune system."

"—sleep until you feel better."

Kevin ran a hand through his long, straggly dark hair to push it away from his face and peered at him doubtfully. "And that's okay with you?"

"Why wouldn't it be?"

"I don't know." Kevin reached for his sneakers, then stopped, as if he couldn't quite figure out what he should do with them. "My mom had a conniption when I showed up at the gate. She didn't even want to let me in." With a wobbly grin, he added, "She wasn't going to, till Dove told her I'd probably die on the side of the road somewhere if I tried to drive back to L.A. all zoned out like this. It kind of came on me all of a sudden. I felt okay a few hours ago, or I wouldn't have gotten in the car in the first place."

"Pick a bedroom," Sam said. "There are six that aren't spoken for, I think. There's a flight of stairs down at the end of this hall. All the rooms close to the top of the stairs should be empty."

"Are you sure?"

"I'm sure."

"Okay. Thanks." Kevin tucked his sneakers under his arm, grabbed the box of tissues, and shuffled toward the door, stopping there as if he'd forgotten something. "She said nobody ever really comes here. What do you need all those bedrooms for?" he ventured.

"You got me."

That prompted a small, wistful smile. "You're okay, you know? I kind of thought you'd be an asshole."

After he'd shuffled away, the Observer turned to Sam wearing an ear-to-ear grin. "Ah, the subtle honesty of youth."

"Max has a son? Why didn't you check on that before?"

"It didn't come up."

"Why? Because his name isn't Kristin? He's—he's not mine, is he?"

"Uh-uh."

"Then he's Dove's?"

Al's eyebrows shot up toward his hairline. "Dove woulda been thirteen when that kid was born. There's no father listed on the birth certificate. Born May sixteenth, 1980, in Santa Monica, California. He just turned nineteen," he went on, reading from the handlink's tiny screen. "He's gonna be a sophomore at UCLA in the fall, unless he decides to bag college, which Ziggy says is a possibility. Got decent grades his freshman year, but he's started to wander off the straight and narrow."

"What do you mean?"

"Powell pays for his education as a perk for Max. Covers the rent for a little apartment near campus, and bought the kid a car. Tosses in some extra for mad money. School's out, so the kid's using the mad money to buy his way into the hot spots around town. Got his picture in the tabloids a couple months ago. Almost got himself arrested when the cops caught him and some little blonde doing the wild thing in the parking lot of some bar in

111

West Hollywood." Al thought that over for a moment, then commented, "Gotta hand it to the kid. He drives a vintage Mustang with a stick. Not a lot of room in those bucket seats."

Sam ignored that completely. "Those clubs—he's not into drugs, is he?"

"Some."

"How much is 'some'?"

"Some grass, a few pills. Nothing he can't break away from, if he finds a reason to break away from it."

"And I'm paying for all that."

Al took the next step. "I wouldn't advise cutting off the dough. The kid's never held down a serious job. Cutting off his money isn't going to make him buy a suit and go find one. He'll move in with somebody, and college'll be what bites the big one, not the drugs and the booze and the clubs."

"I need to talk to Max."

"About what?"

Sam scouted around until he located the TV remote shoved between two of the sofa cushions and used it to shut off the set. "About her son."

"She's already had that conversation. That's where the big checks came from."

"Still."

"Sam. Don't get distracted."

"Of course not," Sam promised.

CHAPTER
TEN

The staircase leading down to the water's edge was steep and narrow and took them several minutes to descend. Max kept her hand poised above the rough banister, wary of filling it with slivers from the old, weathered wood, remaining three or four steps behind Sam. He could tell without looking that this little field trip, like almost everything else he'd said or done in the last twenty-four hours, had her puzzled. This new version of her employer seemed to please her, but the feeling that certainly held her more tightly in thrall had to be *Where did this all come from?*

She wouldn't ask for an explanation. He knew that; money was power, including the power to be *as loony as I wanna be*. Look at Howard Hughes, he thought, and his terror of germs. Or Elvis, shooting out TV sets with a pistol when he didn't like what he was seeing. Had anyone said, "Howard, lighten up, dude"? Or, "Elvis, man, change the channel"?

I could sit up there next to the cupola and sing the entire score from Fiddler on the Roof, *and all they'd do is give me that odd little smile. Golly, that Joe, look at what he's doing now. They wouldn't say anything. Not and risk losing their jobs.*

It made sense, and at the same time, it was completely absurd.

He stopped at the foot of the steps and considered his options. The shoreline to his left, heading south, was rocky and would be rough going. To the north, though, what passed for a beach widened to several yards and stretched on for what Sam guessed was almost half a mile. Yes, it looked familiar. This was the stretch of beach that the woman in his dreams loved so much.

He walked that way knowing Max would follow, because he hadn't asked her not to. Forty or fifty yards down he stopped again and stood watching the foamy edges of the waves flutter against his shoes. The salt water wouldn't do the leather any good, but that didn't matter. There were several similar pairs in the bottom of the wardrobe in his bedroom.

"It's a beautiful day," Max commented.

"Perfect."

"I imagine she's going to do the bulk of the work. Given that he's got the congressional seat."

"Probably."

"She seems very capable."

"She does." Sam turned slightly. Max's hair was drifting around her face, caught in the breeze. "I met your son."

Air hissed in through Max's teeth. Sam could see a dozen emotions play out on her face, each of them very fleeting but blatant enough to allow Sam to figure out what had happened this morning. It had been Dove's idea to invite Kevin in, to hide him in the TV room, to offer the phony story about a nest of ants. Max had objected to every bit of it. And she'd known Dove's setup would backfire, that their boss would find the boy. "He'll be gone before dinner," she assured Sam.

"Why? Don't you want to visit with him?"

She pushed her hair away from her face, but the wind forced it back. Flustered, she gathered it into the palm of one hand and held on to it. "He's—"

"It's a long drive back to L.A. He's welcome to stay over-night."

"I don't think that's a good idea, Joe."

"If he's your son, he's welcome to stay as long as he likes. If

114

he's sick, he should take it easy, get some rest. I don't mind him being here. There's plenty of room. I told him to pick a bedroom and . . ."

The look on Max's face could not be described as anything other than horror. She turned away quickly, but Sam had seen enough. He waited, poking at a smooth white pebble with the toe of his shoe, curious to see how much she'd argue his decision.

"He's only nineteen, Joe," she said finally. "He still does things on impulse."

"Good for him."

"I didn't invite him to . . ."

She was determined to be rebuked. Sam was curious for a moment about whether she'd try to blame the whole problem on Dove, but decided to let that question go unanswered. He reached down, nudged the pebble out of the sand, straightened, and hurled it out across the water. His pitching arm hadn't had much of a workout lately, but the pebble flew a satisfying distance before it plopped into the waves. "What's he studying?" he asked Max.

"Liberal arts."

"The 'I Have No Goal in Life' major? Does he have a goal?" Watching her out of the corner of one eye, Sam found a larger stone, this one about the size of a lemon, wound back, and gave it all he had. "He's out for the summer now, right? If you'd like him to stay until the fall term starts—"

"We leave for Las Vegas the day after tomorrow."

"Oh. Right."

"It's very kind of you to offer. But he has a home. In Los Angeles. My parents are there."

"You must miss him, though."

"He's grown now."

"Of course," Sam said, gently mimicking her use of the phrase. "It's your decision. But the offer stands."

"Thank you."

Movement at the top of the stairs caught Sam's eye. Dove was watching from up there, and with a small jolt of surprise Sam realized there was a gun in the bodyguard's hand. He was tracking slowly, up and down the shoreline, and would not have overlooked so much as a falling leaf.

"Maybe we should go back," Sam suggested.

• • •

Although he'd been deeply asleep, Kevin heard the door open. He was fully awake, if a little heavy-lidded, a moment later, squirming around to face the door and shielding his eyes against the light from the hall.

"Kevin," Max said from the doorway, "you can't stay here."

"I'm sick," he mumbled. "You want to cut me some slack?"

She moved into the room and closed the door quietly behind her. "I'm really not happy with this," she told him, keeping her voice low, although no one was nearby enough to hear her even if she hadn't. "This isn't my home. It's where I work. You can't show up here and expect to make yourself at home, as if this were Mom and Dad's."

"I'll go tomorrow. Can't I sleep? He said I could. If you want me to move to another room, I can. But he told me to pick any one that looked empty."

"I don't like this. I don't like it at all. You put him in a very awkward position. He's being hospitable because you gave him no choice." Max moved closer to the bed and flipped on the brass lamp on the bedside table. She'd noticed the small brown plastic bottle sitting beside it even in the darkness. "What's that?"

"He gave it to me."

"What is it?"

Kevin squinted against the light, then broadly overplayed his response. "I don't know, Bobbie. The label says zinc tablets. Maybe it's, what? Cocaine in pill form? Could you cut me some slack, please? If you want, I'll put clean sheets on the bed in the morning. I won't leave a single fingerprint. Nobody will ever know I was here. And don't worry: those aren't his tissues. I brought them with me from L.A. I used some of his toilet paper, but if you want, I'll leave the money for that. But that wouldn't make sense, though. Since my money is actually his money."

"Is that it?" Max asked tersely. "Are you finished?"

"Can I sleep?"

"I want you up and out of here early tomorrow morning. We're leaving for . . . a trip, and I want to know you're on your way home."

" 'A trip'? What was the hiccup for? You don't want me to know where you're going?"

"You don't need to know where I'm going."

"Then I take it I won't be getting any postcards. By the way,

116

thanks for all the sympathy over my being sick. I'm touched."

"You're a grown man, Kevin, and you have a cold. Please don't act as if you have terminal cancer."

"I got sympathy from the guy at the gas station outside of Santa Barbara."

Her foot began to tap against the carpet. "What do you want me to say?"

"You could sit and talk to me until I fall asleep. That's what Grandma does when I'm sick."

"Fine. Go home, and your grandmother can sit and talk you to sleep."

Neither of them said anything more. The only sound in the room for almost a minute was that of Kevin's congested breathing. When his nose began to run, he tried to ignore it, as if lying there in silence accomplished something, but was forced to grab a tissue from the box and blow his nose. That broke the spell that hung over them enough for Max to move toward the door.

"Why do you have to be such a bitch?" Kevin asked softly.

She stopped walking and turned to face him. "This is my *job*. When I worked at the office in Century City, you wouldn't have considered showing up in the middle of my workday to beg for sympathy over a head cold. Use a little common sense."

"I missed you."

"I'll bring you some soup. But I want you to leave first thing in the morning."

"Whatever," Kevin murmured.

CHAPTER
ELEVEN

Al braced himself against the bathroom door, holding it as tightly shut as if he suspected a legion of furies from hell were on the other side. His office was filled with as much racket as if there *were* demons clamoring out there, screaming for his soul. Roaring, banging, thumping, singing. Shuddering, Al again checked the lock, stepped away from the door on wobbling legs, and leaned against the sink.

The roaring stopped, but the rest of the racket went on, underscored now by a rhythmic *bong! bong! bong!*

And the singing.

"Arnold," Al said in a normal tone of voice.

Amazingly, the singing stopped. Then, one instrument at a time, so did the other noise. The office broadcast a moment of expectant silence. Then a tremulous voice said, "Oh dear."

Al straightened his jacket, peeked into the mirror to assure himself that the crimson that had colored his face a minute ago had disappeared, unlocked the door, and opened it. In his office, the room that in theory was his sanctuary, stood a scrawny little gray-haired man in gray coveralls, clinging to the broad lip of a gray thirty-gallon Rubbermaid trash barrel mounted to a wheeled cart.

The admiral smiled at the little man and asked pleasantly, "You recording the soundtrack to Armageddon, Pfeiffer?"

"The movie, sir?"

"The end of the world."

Arnold Pfeiffer's skinny head jerked back and forth. "Oh, no, sir. Admiral. I'm very awfully sorry, sir. I didn't know you were using the private facilities."

"Are you done now?"

"Well, sir, no, sir, Admiral. I haven't dusted the desk."

"Is there anybody else on this floor?"

"Right now in particular?" Al nodded. "Dr. Allen was in his office a few minutes ago, but he's gone on to bed. All the other offices are empty. I thought yours was too, Admiral. I'm sorry to have disturbed your, um, functions."

"There's nobody on this whole level."

"No, sir."

"You swear to that."

Something brightened in Pfeiffer's expression. The little man was close to fifty, but the brightness made him look like a child given permission to go to the corner store alone for the first time. "It's possible somebody could have come back while I was running the vacuum, Admiral. But I can scout for you. Do, you know, wreck—wrecking . . . ."

"Reconnaissance?"

"Is that what it is?"

Al nodded. "You go do that. Check the whole floor. Double time."

"What's that, sir?"

"Haul ass, Pfeiffer."

Beaming, Arnold scuffled out of the office, careful not to bang the door behind him. He returned less than two minutes later, thrilled by a successful mission. "All rooms checked and not, um, they're empty, sir. Admiral."

"Good job."

"*Thank* you, sir!"

"Carry on, then."

"What's that mean, Admiral?" the little man asked earnestly.

"Dust the desk."

Leaving Pfeiffer to finish his nightly cleaning, Al eased open the door to the corridor, stuck his head out, and peered down the hall in one direction, then the other. Behind him, Arnold was tiptoeing across the room, feather duster in hand, barely breathing. It was so quiet now that Al could hear the hum of the elevator mechanism at the end of the hall. He crept out and gently closed the door behind him.

His life seemed suddenly filled with Becketts. Becketts here in the complex, Becketts camped at the air-force base, auras of Becketts in the Waiting Room, Becketts in the past, memories of dead Becketts, spirits of Becketts Yet to Come. Becketts to the right of him, to the left of him, above him, below him, haunting his imagination, badgering him in his dreams.

Last night, he'd slept for a little more than the few minutes he'd mentioned to Beeks; an hour, maybe. Enough for the old REM action to kick in. The dream had seemed to stretch on forever, filled with a Sam who followed him through the complex, twisting the gold band on his finger and asking, "Where are the pictures?"

"You set up the rules," he whispered. "Wasn't me who decided he shouldn't remember. Now You're gonna change the rules in midstream?"

He clutched his head in his hands and looked first in one direction down the hall, then the other, certain that Pfeiffer had been wrong. There had to be somebody lurking here. Somebody who'd paid Pfeiffer off to keep him from squealing. Somebody who was determined not to let Al handle this his own way.

Sometimes it seemed to him that the longer the Leaping went on, the more people who popped up, determined not to let him handle things his own way. Some of them tried to convince him he was wrong. Some of them were convinced they could do it better, simply by virtue of the fact that they were not him. And some of them threatened to make a mess.

A little voice had told him that what had happened on his birthday would result in a mess. All those people suddenly interested in trying to find Sam. Sam had changed history, and the troublemakers had disappeared, but they left behind the little voice in Al's head telling him it was way past time for people to get tired of not hearing from Sam.

You can't lie forever, it said. *Sooner or later it's going to turn around and bite you in the ass.*

If he'd had his way, Sam would have had only sisters. Women, Al could deal with. There were a few exceptions (many of whom were his ex-wives), but for the most part, he knew what cards to play with women. He'd told the same lies to Thelma and Katie that he'd told to Tom. Thelma and Katie didn't honestly believe him any more than Tom did, but they were willing to accept the lies and try to go on with their lives. He knew the lies didn't do anything to improve their opinion of him, but because they had a lot of what he thought was the best possible quality in a human being, they were willing to let him do things his own way.

That was the ticket, he thought. A large dose of grace under pressure, and distance.

Lots of distance.

Donna had grace under pressure, too; in spades. But the distance factor was missing. She could give him the same mournful-but-resigned look Katie and Thelma did, but he had to see it a lot more often. Every day, pretty much. To the point where he felt smaller than a Lilliputian even though he knew (and so did Donna) that Sam's Leaping out of here hadn't been Al's fault, not in any sense, no sirree Bob.

Not my fault. He was the one who had to prove something.

He remembered standing in front of Sister Rose Bernard, head bowed, his hands in the pockets of his too-big, scuffed-at-the-cuffs pants. *"I didn't do it, Sister."*

"I'm disappointed in you, Albert."

Not my fault.

"Ziggy," he said, addressing an altogether different kind of deity.

No one answered.

"ZIGGY!" he bellowed.

There was another moment of silence, then the computer responded in an only marginally more pleasant tone of voice, "What *now*? Admiral Calavicci. Most precious of my human companions."

"Stow the schmaltz. Is he still on the phone?"

"I presume you mean Congressman Beckett."

121

"No, I mean Gooshie. Of course I mean Congressman Beckett."

Without benefit of a spy cam he was able to imagine Tom Beckett occupying someone's cracker box of an office at the air base, clutching the phone as if it were the throat of someone he wanted to strangle. More than likely, Albert Calavicci's.

The wind-chime noise drifted through the corridor, this time accompanied by another sound that Al, to his own surprise, was able to identify as bubbles popping. "What's with the sound effects?" he demanded.

"They soothe me. I am under a great deal of stress."

"Get used to it."

"The congressman is speaking to someone at his home in San Diego," Ziggy announced. "I can tap into the conversation if you like, but may I take the opportunity to remind you that that would be illegal."

"I don't need you to tap into it. He's talking to his wife. There's nobody else living there."

"I concur."

Talking to his wife. Al could quote his own odds on the likelihood that Linda Beckett was agreeing with, or at the very least sympathizing with, everything Tom was spouting at her. Without having been there, Al could also script out everything Tom had spouted the day of his four-year-old nephew's funeral. More than likely, Linda had agreed with all of that, too. That was her job: siding with her husband in the face of his enemies. Particularly when she *did* agree with him. Al liked Linda, but he was enormously glad he hadn't been in Hawaii for Christmas and wasn't in San Diego now. He'd seen her go ballistic a couple of times. Being the target of it was something like being at ground zero for a low-level nuclear blast. That was all Tom needed, having Linda's ire added to his own.

"Who else has he been talking to?"

"The governor's office in Sacramento. And several numbers in Washington. Would you like me to identify them?"

"Never mind. I can guess."

"He also received a fax."

"I can guess what that was, too."

"Is she feeling any better?" Arnold asked behind him, then offered, "Hello, Ziggy," to the ceiling.

"Good evening, Arnold," Ziggy cooed. "Have we completed our conversation, Admiral?"

"For now," Al grunted, then stepped aside and let the janitor push his cart into the hall. Of course, Arnold didn't mean Linda. He meant *her*. The other Mrs. Beckett. The one who was probably listening to classical music in her room, trying to fall asleep.

The janitor sighed. "She gets so sad at Christmastime."

"Yeah, well," Al said.

"She's a nice lady."

Once upon a lifetime, Al hadn't thought so. He'd known Donna only through the stories Sam told about the woman he loved, the woman who had stood him up on their wedding day because she was afraid of being deserted by him the way she'd been deserted by her father. Years later, Sam still pined for her like a junior-high-school kid, rejecting the explanations Verbena Beeks laid out for him and clinging to a bunch of "if onlys" that made Donna's departure his own fault. Maybe it *had* been partly Sam's fault, Al thought. Okay, maybe it had been half his fault. Or all his fault. Maybe Donna had had enough foresight to know that yes indeedy do, Sam *was* going to leave her, but not with a suitcase in his hand.

The poor kid couldn't even go to anyone—not anyone outside the Project, anyway—and cry on their shoulder. Even Donna's mom thought Sam was still here, wherever "here" was, working diligently away at something that would ultimately make him rich, or famous, or a guest on *The Tonight Show*. The kid didn't have the advantage of wearing her broken heart on her sleeve, of joining support groups, of being able to move on.

It had to be all that much worse for her now, with Sam being only six months away. The middle of June seemed an eon ago, but Leap-wise . . .

"Yeah," he agreed. "She's a nice lady."

Nodding a good night, Arnold moved off down the hall, pushing his cart and humming softly to himself. The usual medley of show tunes, Al thought, then realized with a pang that what Arnold was humming was something from *Les Misérables*: "Bring Him Home."

"You'll tell me, won't you, sir?" the janitor asked over his shoulder.

"Sure, Pfeiffer," Al managed to say. "When there's somebody 'neat' like Elvis in the Waiting Room again, I'll tell you."

On rubbery legs he went back into his office, closed the door, and sank heavily into the old, creaking chair behind his desk. Pfeiffer had proffered an oilcan any number of times, but Al had turned it down. The squeak was comforting. Something familiar. Ruthie, his third wife, had bought the chair for him, years ago. Lifetimes ago.

"So," he said softly, "You couldn't leave well enough alone. 'Changing people's lives for the better,' huh? You let Sam switch everything around so instead of going her own way, she stays with him. Only he doesn't know she stayed. And she's alone. You figure that was a good plan?"

No one answered him. Not that he'd really thought anyone would.

He envied the fact that Tom could vent his spleen to Linda and know she'd take his side. He didn't imagine Linda was lacking opinions of her own, or the willingness to voice them, but there was a lot to be said for having an "other half." Somebody to pick up the shouting when your own voice got hoarse. Somebody to offer a pat on the back and the look that said "I understand."

He'd had that, a couple of times. Ruthie had done her best to be there for him, at least at first. His hands ran along the armrests of the chair, feeling well-worn leather but recalling the sensation of touching her delicate hands. She'd tried hard, Ruthie had. It wasn't her fault her husband couldn't let go of something that had stopped being real years before she told him "I do."

"I'm sorry," Al murmured. "I screwed up."

He thought he could hear Pfeiffer still humming out in the corridor and was envious then of the man's simple optimism. He'd owed Arnold a favor after a bad night at Star Bright and had paid it off by bringing him here to Quantum Leap and demanding that the little man have clearance to clean anywhere he damn well wanted to. Pfeiffer was a child, he told the people who made up the lists of who could go where—fiercely loyal, easily pleased, and more willing to follow orders than any other ten people put together. Somebody had to clean the lower levels, Al argued, and it had to be Arnold. The clearance was finally granted when, after being asked if he would pass on to anyone a secret he uncovered here in the complex, Arnold replied with the sweet, sad guilelessness of the child Al had said he was, "Who would I tell?"

Who would I *tell?* Al wondered. He had no one on the outside anymore; the guys he'd been so close to during his early navy days were almost all dead. His five wives wanted nothing to do with him, nor did the people he'd worked with at Star Bright, who would think of him as a drunken screwup until the end of time.

Okay, so maybe it wasn't that bad. He had acquaintances, guys—and women—he could call for a favor or to shoot the breeze (although he couldn't recall the last time he'd had a desire to do that). But if you came down to it, the people who mattered to him, and who cared about him, were all here. Tom Beckett was right: if he was dismissed from this job, his life would be ruined. There was no one on the outside he wanted to be with.

Not even Beth.

His hand drifted toward the phone several times before he actually picked it up. He began to hum to himself, softly, a pleasant little ditty that at first sounded like a dirge, then like a commercial jingle, and whose lyrics were, "The best deeeee-fense is a good offffffffffense," and as a chorus, "Doooon't let the bastards wear you down." A minute or two of his private songfest calmed him to the point where he thought he could hold up his end of a conversation.

Dialing the number was easier; he had it on Speed Dial. "Admiral Calavicci," he told the person who answered. "Put me through to the congressman."

"What is it?" Tom Beckett's voice asked him a few seconds later.

"He's not dead."

"Then where is he?"

"Not dead. Think whatever else you want, but your brother's not dead."

"Look," Tom said in a tone that was amazingly normal, "I understand work. I understand devotion, I understand fixation, I understand compulsion, I understand any 'shun' you want to toss at me. So Sam doesn't want to give up a week, or a day, or half a day. But ten minutes? Five minutes? For Christ's sake, Calavicci, it takes longer than that to shit! What's he doing that he can't leave it for *five minutes*?" Tom paused, but only for a heartbeat. "Yeah, I know. It's classified."

"He left, Tom."

"What?"

125

"He's not dead. But he's not here. He left."

"He left."

"Yes."

"And you don't know where he is."

"Yes, I do."

"But it's classified."

"Yes."

"I wasn't kidding you. I have to be somewhere on Friday morning. If I don't have an answer that satisfies me by then, I'm gonna make your life a living hell."

"That could only be an improvement." Al sighed.

"Look," Tom said again, and took several long, deep breaths that Al could hear at the other end of the line. "I turned myself over to the navy when I was eighteen years old. That was longer ago than I even want to think about. I've been responsible for the lives and well-being of a lot of people for most of my life. Most of them have been kids. And I know what that responsibility entails. I know when you have to keep things to yourself. But I want you to hear me now, really hear me. The day I left home to report back for duty, to go to Vietnam, my brother cried. He was sixteen years old. Most places in the world they'd consider that a grown man, but he cried like a child. When I came back, he'd started being somebody different. I don't know why. Nothing had happened in the meantime. But he turned from somebody who loved us—loved us!—into somebody who didn't much care about anything other than that goddamn theory of his."

"That's not true," Al said.

"Isn't it? He'd come visit, and I'd watch him. You should know, you were there some of those times. He'd sit and have dinner, and play with the kids, but you could tell that he was somewhere else. Thinking. Trying to solve some little piece of the problem. He'd be there dancing with my mother, or playing cards with me and Jim, and you," Tom said, almost as an afterthought, "but he was somewhere else. We lost him to that damn theory. Now he doesn't even show up. He sends Donna. And I can tell. She's good at faking. 'Put on a happy face,' my mom would say. She puts it on, all right, but anybody with two eyes and a brain can figure out she's not happy. So I'm telling you, Calavicci: I've taken about all the bullshit I can stand. I don't know if going public is the right idea. But I'm going to ask questions, and somebody's going to give me an answer I can take to my mother and my sister. I don't particularly care if that's you, but somebody is going to tell me what the hell is going on."

Al was silent for a long time, running his thumb up and down the smooth plastic of the phone receiver. Words floated through his mind, lyrics from the song Arnold had been humming. Not the title, but others. "Bring him peace."

Bring them *peace.*

He thought of Jeffrey, a blond little boy he'd seen only in pictures Sam's mother had sent with her increasingly infrequent notes. He was going to be his father's son, a scrapper like Jim Bonnick, not very tall, with hands like mitts and the blue eyes and long lashes Al knew caught women's attention quicker than almost anything else—but he'd never have a chance to be that. He'd been buckled into his safety seat in the back of the Bonnicks' minivan. Another car had come flying out of a supermarket parking lot as Katie passed it in the van. Katie had slammed on the brakes, the car seat had slipped loose, and Jeffrey's little-boy neck had been broken.

Thelma, Katie, and Jim had shown Al only kindness, in spite of their many misgivings about his reputation. He liked all of them and would readily grant them any favor they might ask of him. But even if Sam had not been Leaping, if Al had not been tied to this hole in the ground a little ways north of White Sands, New Mexico, he could not have gone to that funeral. That, he had to refuse them. Not because he couldn't face Thelma and Katie; he'd seen women sobbing from broken hearts more times than he could count. It was that miniature casket he knew he couldn't look at.

So you owe them one. For you not being there, and for Sam not being there. And for everything else that's gone wrong for them that you had a hand in.

"Meet me at the guard shack at the gate in an hour," he told Tom.

CHAPTER
TWELVE

She had moved maybe twenty feet ahead of him, leaving footprints in the wet sand. He didn't try to catch up, choosing instead to lag behind, hands in the pockets of his baggy cotton pants, watching her, smiling faintly. Lines of poetry and bad pop-song lyrics had started to make sense to him a few weeks ago and he had found himself scribbling them on scraps of paper that he then took home and stuffed into a drawer in his desk. Last night he had taken them all out and arranged them on the desktop.

She stopped and turned to look at him. In the palm of her hand lay a shell no bigger than her thumbnail, unbroken, perfect.

She was perfect.

He went to her and circled his arms around her and held her close to him. "What are you thinking about, so seriously?" she asked him, grinning, her face upturned, her cheeks flushed enough to tell him what she had been thinking.

"I love you," he told her.

"I'm glad. Otherwise we're really wasting a terrible lot of time." She laughed. Happy with him, with the day, with being in this place. There was more joy in her face than he could remember ever seeing in anyone else's. Then she pulled his head down nearer to hers and kissed him, and murmured into his ear, "I love you too. So much."

Sam awoke listening to the waves and the rustle of the trees, with the warmth of the rising sun on his face. He could still feel her inside the circle of his arms. The emptiness that was there now was awful enough to make him wonder whether he should cry, or find something to break. Or run, maybe. Run down the road that led away from the front door, hard and fast, until it took him somewhere that was not here. Maybe if he was somewhere other than this house, the dreams would stop.

He got up from the chaise longue, dragging the blanket with him, and went to the stone wall at the edge of the terrace. "Why are you so real?" he demanded, and a crow sitting in one of the evergreens answered him with a loud caw.

For the second night in a row, he hadn't been able to face sleeping in Powell's bedroom. It was too damn quiet, too damn empty, too damn big. He'd tried sitting out on the terrace with a mug of tea, hoping to become sleepy, but after midnight he'd surrendered again, pulled the thick throw blanket off the foot of the bed, and carried it outside, wrapping it around him like a cocoon. Sleeping on the chaise was somewhat less than comfortable—if he had tried turning over, he would have flopped off the thing onto the stone floor—and he spent more time dozing and thinking than actually resting.

But the night was gone now, taking her with it, leaving him with another day of improvising the life of Joseph Easton Powell. What could, or should, happen today, he didn't know. Tomorrow would take him to Las Vegas. Which should, at least, make Al happy.

"It's a hideous place, Al. It's like an enormous theme park."

"Yeah."

"Am I not getting through to you? It's too crowded, it's too noisy, and I don't like to gamble."

But it was someplace other than here. And that might be a good thing. Al was right, Sam told himself: thinking of *her* was pushing him over the edge. He didn't have the luxury of enough

129

time to indulge in flights of fancy. He had to stick to Powell's itinerary, keep Powell's life on track.

Go to Las Vegas.

And all he had to do to get there was prevent the accident that in another *when* had claimed Max's life. Easy enough, he hoped.

He smelled food.

Leaning against the wall, he sniffed the air. Someone was definitely cooking. Not Marie; she wouldn't be here yet, even if she'd been told to show up early. So—who? Max or Dove, probably, trying to beat their employer to the punch by fixing his breakfast before he could find his way to the kitchen. That annoyed him, though he was not quite sure why. They were operating within the parameters that had been set up for them: taking care of Joe.

Grumbling to himself, he pulled on Powell's robe and padded down the long staircase and into the kitchen.

"I'm sorry," Kevin said. "Did I wake you up?"

Sam moved closer to the stove. There were blueberry muffins baking in one of the spacious kitchen's four ovens; on top of the stove, a kettle of soup was simmering, and aromatic flavored coffee was brewing in the coffeemaker. "You cook?" Sam asked.

"Yeah. My grandmother taught me. That wacky little woman with the accent showed me where everything is."

"Marie?"

"Is that her name? She didn't tell me. She kinda looks like Dr. Ruth. She said it'd be okay if I made myself breakfast."

Sam looked around and found no one but Kevin. "Where is she now?"

"Uh . . . I don't know. Do you want me to find her?"

"No. I'm sure she'll find me," Sam said ruefully.

"Maybe she's, like, in another wing or something." Kevin grinned and rolled his eyes in a way that told Sam the boy thought the size of the kitchen, and the rest of the house, fell squarely into the category of "overkill." "I know this probably looks like, you know, not breakfast stuff," he went on cheerfully, "but I eat like my grandfather—big weird breakfasts. My mother's probably going to pitch another fit over me doing this, but I woke up and I felt good, and I mean, like you're going to miss any of this?" Kevin grinned nervously and stood looking at Sam with a big mixing spoon in his hand. Obviously, he'd thought he could make his breakfast, eat it, and clean up without anyone being the wiser.

"You're feeling better?"

"Yeah, a lot. I mean, my head is still kind of stuffed up, and I'm coughing kind of off and on, but I guess sleeping for fourteen hours was what I needed. I feel pretty good. Thanks for letting me stay here. And thanks for the zinc and the antihistamines and stuff."

"You're welcome. And eat whatever you want. We can get more."

"Are you sure?"

"From wherever it is that all of that came from. I have no idea where that is. It shows up here."

"They deliver it? Good deal."

"My mother wouldn't have thought so," Sam mused. "She loved going to the market."

"No kidding? My grandmother says it's a form of cruel and unusual punishment. Never enough checkouts, they don't have what she wants, and she's told me like eighty thousand times that the produce sucks." More at ease now, Kevin stirred his kettle of soup, pronounced it ready, and turned off the burner. "Did you want some of this? I always eat with a bunch of people—my grandparents, or a bunch of the kids at school, or I go to a restaurant. It seemed kind of strange to eat by myself. I was gonna turn on the TV to make some noise. Oh, hey—there was a cat outside a while ago. I would have fed it, or let it in, but there's that alarm on the door. I figured if I opened it, I'd be summoning the SWAT team or something. Is it your cat?"

"I don't think so."

Kevin frowned as he began to open cupboards in search of bowls for the soup. "You don't know if it is or not?"

"It seems to want to be."

"Sounds like my girlfriend's cat. Showed up at the door one day and she took it in."

Sam opened a different cupboard and lifted out a pair of ceramic bowls. "You have a girlfriend?"

The boy laughed self-consciously. "I don't know if she is or not."

"How come?"

Kevin took the tray of muffins out of the oven, dumped them onto a plate, and found jam and butter in the refrigerator. He

131

poured cups of coffee as Sam ladled soup into the two bowls. "We met at this club a few weeks ago. She kind of had her eye on somebody else, but he wasn't buying, so she ended up with me. We've gone out a bunch of times, and we've, you know, slept together. But I don't know if I see anything long-term in it. We're sort of each other's least objectionable choice right now."

"She's still hoping for a chance with the other guy?"

"Maybe. But I don't think she's gonna get it. He's not around that much, that I can tell. He's in New York half the time, and I think now he's in the Bahamas or something."

"Rich guy," Sam guessed.

"Leonardo DiCaprio guy," Kevin said. "You see what I'm up against? He gets twenty million bucks for making a movie, and I only have a car because you paid for it. If you weren't floating me those checks because of my mom, I'd be taking the bus. And let me tell you, the bus in Hollywood is not a good thing."

They sat on opposite sides of the glass-topped table and ate in silence for a few minutes. "You know what I think?" Kevin offered finally.

Sam shook his head. "What?"

"If somebody wanted that bad to come in here and take some of this stuff, you should just let them take it. You could buy more. This place is wired up nine ways to Sunday. You can't even open a window. It's probably easier to get in and out of Chino than this place. Do you like living like that?"

"Actually, no."

"Then why do you do it?"

"What kind of car is it that I bought you?"

Kevin blinked at the change of subject, then shrugged, bit off a chunk of jam-smeared muffin, and replied, "Mustang. 'Sixty-six. It's in the garage."

"Being fixed?"

"It's in *your* garage."

Nodding, Sam picked up his coffee mug and a fresh muffin, got up from his chair, and beckoned to Kevin. "Show me."

"Soup'll get cold."

"Microwave."

"I don't know how to get there from here," Kevin admitted.

"Neither do I."

That statement, and the way it was delivered, took Kevin completely by surprise. He burst into a loud guffaw, spraying half-chewed bits of muffin all over the palm of his hand, the table, and the rest of his breakfast. Not as embarrassed as he might have been, he grabbed a napkin and wiped up some of the mess, then tossed Sam a sheepish look and got out of his chair. "I guess we can figure it out, if you can unlock the doors."

"That I can do," Sam promised.

There were six vehicles in the garage, five of them brand-new and manufactured by Mercedes-Benz. Sam suspected that Kevin had been allowed to park his Mustang in here only so that it would not be visible outside the house—though to whom it would have been visible, other than the people in the guardhouse at the end of the driveway, was certainly a question.

The Mustang, parked next to and dwarfed by a gleaming, top-of-the-line sedan, had been well cared for and carefully detailed. "The idle's off," Kevin said as he and Sam stood side by side, considering the vintage car. "I keep adjusting it, but I haven't been able to hit it just right."

"Start it up, and pop the hood. I'll take a look."

"You will?"

"Why? Don't you think I can?"

"Well," Kevin said, "you keep coming up with things I didn't expect."

Sam chuckled softly. "I know. You thought I was an asshole."

Twenty minutes later, Max, drawn by the sound of the running engine, found them in the garage. "Good morning," Sam told her cheerfully.

She offered a considerably less chipper greeting, said nothing to Kevin, turned and left, closing the garage door behind her. Sam went to the door and pushed it open again—the way Max had found it—to let fresh air continue to circulate from outside.

"She thinks I'm jeopardizing her job by being here," Kevin explained.

"Not true. I think the idle's fine now. See, it's something you'll learn from experience. What it says in the owner's manual might have been true when the car was new, but it's got a lot of miles on it. And every car will turn out to be different. You have to go by feel." Sam lowered the hood, then reached inside the car to turn off the ignition.

"With the car, or my mother?"

"Both."

Kevin leaned against the side of the car and folded his arms over his chest. "She's really tense about this job. It's the best one she ever had."

"She's very good at it."

The boy nodded, willing to concede the point but not happy with the truth of it. He searched Sam's face as if he were looking for permission to say what he was thinking, then said it anyway. "She used to work for some company in Century City where they made her work like eighty hours a week and treated her like crap," he told Sam distractedly. "I guess she still puts in a lot of hours here, but she gets to live in a nice house and eat good food, and travel, and she's got Dove, and she doesn't want to mess that up. She thinks I don't get it, but I do. She couldn't really get a deal like she's got here, anywhere else." He smiled vaguely and sighed. "I mean, how many places can you work where they've got an indoor swimming pool?"

"Most decent hotels," Sam suggested.

The boy laughed again, but without humor this time. "You have to understand my mom. She really wants to be somebody."

"She is somebody."

"No." Kevin shook his head. "See, before you hired her, she was Barbara Maxwell from Santa Monica. She was one of the crowd. How many women are there around L.A. who do the nine-to-five thing? Millions. She kept thinking she didn't have anything to show for her life. She was living with her parents because she couldn't afford anything decent on her own, and she didn't even have a regular family. No husband, that kind of thing."

"That's not as expected of women as it used to be."

"Yeah, but there's me. I was a mistake. Did she tell you that?" Sam let a shrug serve as his answer. "You probably checked out her background before you hired her," Kevin guessed.

"Somewhat."

"Now she's here, with you, living the high life, and she's broken most of her connections with L.A. She doesn't see anybody she used to be friends with down there. She's not some girl who works in an office anymore. She's personal assistant to Joe Powell. When she makes phone calls now, people pay attention to her. So, see? I get it. I know what she wants."

"And you know what you want."

"I miss my mother. But it's like she says, I'm in college now and I guess I'm an adult. So I shouldn't walk around pining for my mommy, when she was never really my mommy in the first place." Kevin squared his shoulders and put on the best imitation of good cheer he could muster. "I should get going. Thanks for fixing the car."

"You don't have to leave."

"It aggravates her, my being here."

"It doesn't aggravate me."

"Yeah, but . . ."

Sam reached out and gave the boy an amiable pat on the shoulder. "How do you feel about Las Vegas?"

"I don't know. I've never been there."

"Want to go?"

Kevin asked skeptically, "When?"

"Tomorrow."

"What for?"

Once more, Sam shrugged. "Maybe you can use the time to mend some fences with your mother."

"So it's like a vacation?"

"All expenses paid."

Sam watched the boy consider the idea, reject it, fall in love with it, reject it again, and count down every possible objection they both knew Max would have. Finally, Kevin took a deep breath and dared to ask, "Could I . . ."

"What?"

"Could I bring my girlfriend? She'd really go nuts. She'd love it."

Ideas were churning through Sam's mind as rapidly as they were through Kevin's. "Call her," Sam said. "The penthouse at Nirvana has my name on it, and I might as well try to fill it up."

"Really? You're kidding."

"Dead serious."

"And . . ." The ideas churned for another few seconds, then Kevin ventured, "How are we getting there?"

"Plane."

"Like, Southwest or something?"

"Like, private plane."

"You have a plane."

"I have a plane."

"Hot damn." Kevin grinned.

135

"Saaaam."

Sam's fingers stopped tapping at the keyboard of Powell's laptop and he turned his head just enough to locate Al in his peripheral vision. The Observer was in a dudgeon every bit as high as Sam imagined Max's was right now, but Sam had already convinced himself not to be swayed by any protest lodged by either of them, so he simply offered his partner a smile of greeting, then returned to scanning both the computer screen and the folded copy of *The Wall Street Journal* that lay beside the keyboard.

"What are you doing? How come you're using that thing instead of the—" Al's head tipped toward the oversized monitor connected to the supercomputer Gooshie had been lusting after.

"His personal files are on here."

"Why?"

"I don't know why. Why do I need a why for everything?"

"I don't know," Al fussed. "Who was that guy in the suit you were talking to?"

Sam shook his head absently. "A courier, with papers I had to sign. And I'm reading my E-mail."

"You mean Powell's E-mail."

"I sent some messages yesterday, and these are the responses, so technically, it's my E-mail. Did you talk to Tom?"

"Yeah. Kind of. Yeah. Until he stopped wanting to listen."

"And?"

"Tom hears what he wants to hear."

"And what does that mean?"

"It means he's still mad. I can't take him to you, so ergo, you're either dead or you're a gold-plated SOB and so am I. He's not listening to anything else. And I can't," Al said before Sam could offer a rebuttal, "take him belowground. They'd fry my ass. He doesn't have clearance to go below Level Two."

"When did that ever matter?"

"What?"

"Rules. Laws. Regulations. You live to break rules."

"Saaaam. Would you just let me handle it? I told you I'd handle it."

"You're doing a swell job of it."

Al ignored that. "You sent Max's kid home, right?"

"I sent Max's kid," Sam said, his eyes again on the newspaper,

136

"into town, which I gather is somewhere reasonably close by, to buy himself some clothes and whatever else he needs to spend a few days in Vegas. He came up here from L.A. with the clothes on his back and a box of Kleenex."

"What?"

"I'm taking him to Vegas."

"You can't do that. I thought you didn't want to go to Vegas."

"You told me I had to. So I can, and I am. Now, if you'll excuse me, I'm reading about myself." He tapped the newspaper with a finger. "It's very complimentary."

Al scowled at the paper. "It's about *him*."

"I'm him, and he's me."

"And both of you is a few bricks short of a load. What do you think you're doing, inviting the kid to Vegas? He's not supposed to go to Vegas!"

"I would have thought you'd be pleased. I'm giving in. I'm going. We're going to spend three glorious days and nights amid the glitter and glamour of the most exciting city in the world. Enjoying the penthouse suite of Nirvana, which by the way, I own, the newest and most luxurious jewel in the crown of paradise. Do I sound enough like a brochure? I'm taking Kevin and his girlfriend to Las Vegas. I decided to invite him because he's the only soul I've talked to in the last three days, other than the cat, who doesn't think I've completely lost my marbles."

Al grumbled, "What cat?"

"He's a good kid. He wants to impress his girlfriend by throwing some cash around. I have plenty to spare. What's the harm?"

"You can throw cash around until your arms fall off," Al said stubbornly. "I've got no objection to your throwing cash. It's throwing emotional commitment that's keeping me up at night."

"What are you talking about?"

"You can't bond with that kid, Sam."

"I can, and I need to. His mother thinks he's grown up, and she's cast him to the four winds. He hangs out with the wrong group of people. He's dating someone who apparently would dump him in a second for anybody with better name value— which is, by and large, the same game his mother's playing. If he leaves here, Al, he's going to go back to L.A. and get himself into trouble. I can feel it. Every inch of me says Kevin is an accident waiting to happen, and I trust that."

Al paced back and forth across Powell's office, puffing furiously on his cigar. "Okay, so he needs a friend. But you ain't it."

"I could be."

Al jabbed the cigar in Sam's direction. "No you couldn't. Because you're not you, you're Joe Powell. You're not even gonna make it to Vegas. As soon as you're finished with what you're supposed to do here, which is tomorrow morning, you're gone and Joe's back. And maybe you didn't pick up on this part of the personality profile, but Joe ain't the warm and fuzzy type. That 'Man of the People' thing is an image. He's a lone wolf. He lives up here all by himself except for Frick and Frack because he wants to."

"What if I don't Leap out tomorrow morning? You said I'm here for Max. What if it's not only to prevent her from being hurt in the accident, but to put her back together with her son?"

"You're gonna Leap out tomorrow, after you stop that accident."

"But what if I don't?"

"Okay, that's a possibility." Al surrendered. "But you can't put them back together by building up a buddy thing with Kevin. 'It's better to have loved and lost' doesn't apply here, Sam. Joe Powell is not gonna be Kevin's best pal. You make that kid think you're somebody he can lean on, you're not doing him any favors. He needs somebody who's gonna stick around for the long haul."

"His mother."

"Maybe. But you've gotta leave Powell out of the equation."

Sam picked up the newspaper and tapped the desktop with it. "Powell has to be part of the equation. If I sent Max back to L.A. to be with her family, it would wreck everything she's tried to build for herself. I know what she wants: if Powell is elected president, she wants to be chief of staff, and probably should be."

"And where does that leave the kid?"

"I don't know yet. They've been two hundred miles apart. She doesn't see him, doesn't call him except to check up on him. She assumes his grandparents are doing what they've always done, and that he doesn't need her. I think he needs to be close to her, at least for a while. To be part of this household. Somehow."

"And then what?"

"I don't know."

"You got too many 'I don't knows' here, pal. You're throwing stuff up against the wall and seeing what sticks. Yeah, if you keep Kevin and Max together, they might patch things up. They also might decide they can't stand each other. The kid's not wearing chain mail around his heart, here. If she keeps acting like he's excess baggage, he's gonna end up saying 'screw you' and writing her off."

Sam mulled that over for a minute. "Then maybe he needs to go in another direction. Find someone who does love him and start a family of his own."

But before he could say anything more, Al blinked out of the room. It took Sam a minute to locate him inside the small sunroom next to Powell's office, studying the patterns in the tile floor and puffing thoughtfully on his cigar. "What's the matter?" Sam asked.

"It's not that easy, Sam."

"What isn't? Starting a family?"

"Finding somebody who loves you, who you don't try to blame for things she didn't have anything to do with." Al fussed with a stray thread trailing from the hem of his jacket, then with the single button that held the jacket closed. "That's what I thought I was gonna do: find a girl who'd love me 'until the Twelfth of Never' and all that sappy stuff. When I lost Beth— all right, a long time after I lost Beth—I tried again. And again, and again. I never found what I was looking for, Sam."

"Your mother."

"I don't know which is worse," the Observer mused. "Having her around and not caring, or her taking off for parts unknown and not caring. Yeah, my mother. Who figured that aluminum-siding salesman was more important than her kids. We do things in this life, Sam . . ." Al's voice trailed off. It took him a minute to begin again. "She probably thought we'd be fine, Trudy and me. Or maybe she told herself that. Maybe she never imagined everything would turn to crap without her. If she'd stayed, Trudy wouldn't have died in that hospital. My old man probably would've still gotten the cancer, but he wouldn't have lost his best girl. That's gotta be worth something. And me—maybe I would've turned out to be the kind of guy Beth wanted. See, Sam? It all would've been different, if only she'd stayed with us."

Sam hesitated, then shook his head slowly. "If she had stayed, and somehow magically turned into June Cleaver."

"Give or take."

"That's not who she was, Al. She was someone who—"

"Found herself an out, and took it."

"Like Max."

"So I've got no good answers either," the Observer said somberly. "My mom took off half a century ago. She and the salesman are both gone now, and so's my dad, and so's Trudy. There's nobody left but me to remember how hard Trudy cried, night after night, wanting to know where Mama went." He paused again, looking at his cigar as if he'd forgotten why he'd bothered to light it. "I've got no easy answers, buddy. I'm just asking you, don't hurt that kid any more than he already is."

"I need you to trust me on this," Sam said, leaning against the edge of a glass-topped, wrought-iron table. "I've been doing this job for a long time. My instincts are usually good. Aren't they?" he pressed when Al didn't say anything.

"Usually."

"What's bothering you?"

"Me? Nothing. It's Christmas. You know."

"I thought it was Christmas two days ago."

"It's the season that keeps on giving. 'Tis the season to be suicidal, fa-la-la-la-la," Al joked.

"I dreamed about her again last night, Al," Sam said abruptly. "It was so real. I felt like I could count the grains of sand. It's more than a dream. I've tapped into Powell's memories and I'm replaying them."

"Maybe tonight you'll be doing the bingo-bango-bongo. Virtual reality. I like it."

"Is Powell sure he wasn't dreaming when he Leaped? Maybe he's confused."

"He wasn't dreaming. He's sure."

"Maybe he doesn't remember."

Al sucked in a deep breath. "He remembers."

"What?"

"You heard me." Al rolled the cigar between his fingers to the point he knew he was ruining it. "He's not Swiss-cheesed."

"That's not possible."

"Tell him that."

"How much does he remember?"

"Everything. He's as clear as a bell. Like somebody picked him up in a car and drove him to the Project."

"I don't think that's good," Sam said.

The Observer looked around for something to lean on, all too aware of where he was actually standing, and heaved a sigh that seemed to come up from several yards below the soles of his silver shoes. He took a long, critical look at the potted ficus tree in the corner farthest from the door, then offered, "Beeks thinks it's still possible for him to magnafoozle on the way out. So when he gets back there, or to Vegas, or wherever you're at when you Leap out, he won't remember what happened. He'll be missing a couple days, and he'll probably go to Cedars and have them run a million tests to make sure he hasn't got a brain tumor or had seizures or something. Beeks thinks it'll be fine."

"She does."

"Oh yeah."

"And a presidential candidate having a three- or four-day fugue is a good thing."

"It's not like he's gonna tell anybody. If he goes public that he spaced out, nobody's gonna vote for him but Max."

Sam stared down at his shoes. "Has he said anything about having dreams, or memories, that don't seem to belong to him?"

"No."

"It was *real,* Al. I could feel the texture of her skin."

"Beeks says that's your subconscious calling up sense memory. She says it's not all that unusual."

"That I can see every freckle on a woman I've never met?"

Al stuck the cigar in his mouth and gnawed on the end of it, pulled it out, and grimaced at the condition the stogie was in. "Maybe," he said, then stopped, collected himself as if he were about to dive off a cliff, and continued so rapidly that the words tumbled over each other, "Maybe you're not going through his memories, maybe you're going through yours."

"No."

The Observer's face contorted as if he were making ooga-booga expressions to amuse a baby. "Are you sure?"

"I don't know what comes next. It's like watching a movie."

"What's she look like?"

Eyes still on the floor, Sam didn't notice the gyrations his friend's facial muscles were going through. "She's beautiful. Long, soft hair. Soft skin. Beautiful eyes." He stopped, and finally lifted his gaze. "I don't know what color her eyes are. Or her hair. I can't describe her. Which is ridiculous. When I'm with her, I know her face as well as I know my own."

"You're not with her. It's a dream."

"No," Sam argued. "I'm with her. I can feel her breath on my cheek. I can feel the warmth of her skin. Hear her voice. I'm with her. And when I wake up, it feels like she's still here."

"It's your imagination."

"I wish it was. I know I said I'd take this trip. I know it's part of the mission, but it doesn't feel right. I'll be gone from here for weeks. I don't know if it's right to leave her for that long."

"She's not here, Sam," the Observer said sharply. "And you're not gonna be gone from here for weeks. You won't get that far. Powell's coming back, and he can do all the communing with the spirit world."

"You think I'm losing it, don't you? I set you off on the wrong road yesterday, when I said I was the wrong man for this job. You've been thinking about it all night, about everything I say that doesn't make sense. It's been going on for months. You used to trust my judgment, even when it didn't agree with what Ziggy said. She's a computer, Al! I programmed her, and she's the next best thing to a human, but she doesn't have—she hasn't got a soul. She can't *feel* what's right. And Verbena—she's not here. She's not living through this. She gets it third hand, through you. You have to trust me, Al. All of you. I have to trust me."

Al nodded, but not convincingly. "Sure, buddy. I will. I always do. Most of the time."

"Show me a picture."

"Of what?"

"Of her. Powell's wife. Show me what she looked like. Then I'll know for certain whether it's her that I'm dreaming about."

"And if you're not?" Al ventured.

All Sam did in response was shrug.

"Bypass Ziggy?" Gooshie said. "You can't bypass Ziggy. Ziggy won't let you bypass Ziggy."

"You gonna argue with me?"

"I won't, but Ziggy might."

Al tipped his head back and listened to the sounds of a summer breeze whispering through pine needles. "Ziggy's not gonna argue. She's too busy becoming one with Yanni. I thought you were gonna insert commands to stop her from reaching out and touching every two-bit lump of microchips at the other end of a modem."

"We are talking 'Ziggy' here, Admiral."

"Ziggy!" Al barked.

After a soothing interval of forest sounds, the computer replied with a giggle, "Yes, my beloved honeybumps."

"It's intermittent." Gooshie sighed.

"You can't fix every computer in the damn world," Al groused. "Stop trying."

The icy water of a mountain stream bubbled through the room, then Ziggy replied in a tone that was almost businesslike, "I believe I am part of a higher purpose, Admiral. Dr. Beckett constructed and programmed me to be the 'brain' of Quantum Leap. In many senses, I *am* Quantum Leap. Perhaps even more so than Dr. Beckett himself. Without me, there would have been no Leap. Since Dr. Beckett has been called to duty to repair the sufferings of his fellow humans, and in many cases to forestall the premature end of a life, so I believe my duty is to spare the suffering of my fellow computers. What sort of being would I be, if knowing that such suffering existed, and that I alone am capable of relieving it, and I did nothing?"

"Your primary responsibility is to the Project," Gooshie reminded her.

Ziggy was silent for several seconds. "I have just completed a system-wide, level-one diagnostic. I am unable to detect any malfunctions in the operation of the Project, other than those directly attributable to human error."

"So," Gooshie said hesitantly, "would it be okay with you if a few of those humans did what Admiral Calavicci is requesting?"

"I have already performed the search." Ziggy sniffed. "There are no pictures."

"Not possible," Al told her.

"If that is your opinion, sugar pie, I must point out that it is based on faulty assumptions. There does not 'have' to be a photograph of Joseph Powell's late wife anywhere."

"California DMV."

"Mrs. Powell died prior to the point at which the department of motor vehicles began to digitalize operator photographs."

"Newspaper morgues."

Ziggy heaved a sigh that sounded like an arctic wind sweeping through a rocky crevasse. "I believe it would aid your execution of your own responsibilities, honey bunch, if you would not grasp at straws. Twenty-three years ago, Joseph Powell was, in common vernacular, a 'nobody.' I fail to understand why the editorial staff of any publication would find it necessary to publish a photograph of the deceased spouse of a nobody, who was herself a nobody."

"Then," Al said hotly, "I'm gonna go waste some people's time. That okay with you?"

"Whatever," Ziggy replied. "Cookie puss."

Though he was unsure why, given that staying out of Al Calavicci's firing range was probably the better part of valor, Gooshie trotted out into the corridor in the admiral's wake, ducking through the doorway only an instant before the door slammed shut. "What did you have in mind?" he asked the back of Al's head. "Even if Ziggy feels she has more important duties to fulfill, she would have done a complete search, if for no other reason than to spite us. I'm sure she's right: there probably aren't any pictures of Mrs. Powell."

"Joe Powell's not a nobody now," Al snapped.

"Well, no, but—"

Al jerked himself to a halt and spun around to face the programmer. "I'm invoking Executive Order Number One."

"Which would be . . . ?"

"Do what I say, no matter how stupid it sounds, or you're out on your ass."

"I see," Gooshie said.

Less than an hour later, piled up on the huge oval table in Conference Room 2-B were hundreds of magazines. Al's directive had been detailed enough, and peppered with enough subdetails that nothing could have escaped his net. An hour after that, thanks to the efforts of twenty-three staffers who knew the identity of the current Visitor, the magazines had been sorted into two groups: those which contained *something* (a story, a paparazzi-type picture, a little dirt, even the most fleeting mention of the name) on Joseph Easton Powell III, and those which did not. The "did not" pile included two crossword-puzzle books and one issue of *Big Busted Babes*.

The "did" pile included, among hundreds of other titles, *Road*

& Track and the copy of *Tiger Beat* that had turned up in the possession of Ginny in Accounting.

But none of them, not a single, blessed one, contained a picture, a discussion, or so much as a passing mention of the dear, departed Mrs. Powell.

"Not even her name," Gooshie pointed out.

"I know her name," Al complained. "Her name was Emily. I don't need her name, I need to know what she looked like."

Then, suddenly, he realized something was missing.

"Where's Pfeiffer?" he demanded.

After an intensive, solitary search that combed every level of the complex, he located the janitor curled up in a corner of one of the rec rooms, dozing contentedly through the last half hour of *Lost Horizon*. Relieved, but exhausted, he nudged the man's shoulder, then stepped back, unsure how Pfeiffer would react to being jolted out of what was obviously a very pleasant dream that might or might not have included hundred-year-old monks, singing Asian children, and Olivia Hussey.

"Hello, Admiral, sir." Pfeiffer beamed.

"How come you didn't hear the announcement?"

"Announcement, sir? Oh, about the magazines? I don't have any magazines in my room, sir."

"You read the tabloids, don't you?"

"Well, yes, sir. Oh," he said, his face falling. "Are they magazines? Mother always called them newspapers."

"You got any?"

They were in piles under Pfeiffer's bed. At the little man's invitation, Al got down on his hands and knees and peered under there, gaping at what had to be hundreds of issues of several different titles. A year's worth, Al guessed, since the things came out every week. Other than the clutter created by the stacked periodicals, it was the cleanest under-the-bed Al had ever seen. More immaculate than anything in Powell's house, which was really saying something.

"Did you need something to read while you wait for Dr. Beckett?" the janitor offered.

"I need a picture."

Twenty minutes and forty tabloids later, Al had what he wanted, tucked under a headline that said SEXIEST MAN'S LOST LOVE. "She was awfully pretty, wasn't she?" Arnold commented.

"Yeah, she was."

And, for some reason, awfully familiar.

Kevin returned a little after four o'clock, the backseat of his car stuffed with packages from a variety of stores. Dove met him in the wide driveway that curved past the front of the house and opened the driver's door after Kevin had turned off the ignition.

"So what's the deal?" the bodyguard asked. "You're going with us?"

"That's what Mr. Powell said."

"For the whole trip?"

Kevin hesitated, pulling several of his packages out of the car before he said anything. "I don't know what the 'whole trip' involves. He said Vegas."

"It's nine cities."

"Am I supposed to know that? Isn't it confidential?"

Dove took the packages away from Kevin and let the boy haul out a few more. "It's not confidential any more than a concert tour. We've got security set up all along the way, but the press knows where we're going. It's supposed to be so the boss can meet people. Do the meet-and-greets, the photo ops, the whole nine yards. Show them what a swell guy he is."

"Are you in love with my mother?"

Juggling the packages with one thick arm, Dove pointed the garage-door opener he'd been holding and pressed the button. When the door had opened completely, he told Kevin, "I'll put the car away. She's waiting for you."

"Why? So she can chew me out again? You didn't answer my question."

"Love in what sense?"

"There's only one sense."

Dove snorted at him. "You've been to too many chick movies, kid."

"I asked you, do you love my mother?"

"No, you asked me am I in love with your mother. That's two different things. Do I love her? Yeah, she's important to me. We talk things out, and I care about her. But am I in love with her, like would I throw myself in front of a speeding train to prove the point? Is she the first thing I think about in the morning and the last thing I think about at night? That's a whole different thing."

146

"Does she love you?"

"How old are you?" Dove asked with a grimace.

"Would you just answer my question?"

The bodyguard finished pulling the last of the paper bags out of the back of the Mustang and pushed the door shut. "Carry in whatever you can. I'll bring the rest. I hope you got yourself a suit. We're supposed to be going to some fancy functions, and the papers are gonna jump on it if you're sitting there looking like our poster boy for feeding the homeless. She'll want you to get your hair cut, too, but you can probably get out of that if you keep it washed and combed. She's in the study working on some stuff. Stay out of the kitchen. Marie's in there now and she doesn't like company."

"So you're not going to answer the question."

Dove looked at the boy for a long moment. "Your mother's in love with Joe Powell, kid," he said in a voice that held more regret than he wanted it to. "She has been for a long time. Go change your clothes. She'll like it if you look good at dinner."

147

CHAPTER THIRTEEN

"How can there be no police report?" Sam sputtered. "You explain to me how there can possibly be no police report on an MVA that resulted in critical injury. Whose jurisdiction is it out here? Where *am* I, anyway?"

Al held up both hands, palms out. "Hey, don't blame me."

"Has Ziggy even tried to find the report?"

Sam began to pace across the carpet, parallel with the foot of the bed, head down, shoving his hands through his hair. Al remained a few steps away, out of harm's way, tinkering with the handlink. "You know, you're right," the Observer commented idly. "There is something weird about this room. It sucks up sound like a black hole. Look at this room, would you? And look at that bed. What size is that?"

"What?" Sam snapped.

"You know, queen, king. Looks like the whole-royal-family-

and-both-houses-of-Parliament-sized. You could play nine holes of mini-golf on that sucker, Sam."

"Why are you even concerned with how big the bed is?"

"The guy sleeps alone. Hey, who made the bed? Was Kristin up here?"

"Nobody made the bed. I didn't sleep in it." Before Al could ask the question, Sam pointed to the terrace. "I slept out there. I don't like it in here. It's too quiet. She docsn't like it in here either."

"Who, she?"

"She . . ."

Al lowered the handlink and stared at his partner. "She, Powell's dead wife, she? Not that she."

"I—"

"Saaaam. You're giving me the willies."

Sam folded his arms over his chest and walked closer to the wall of dark glass. "All right, so I'm giving you the willies. I'm describing something that people feel all the time. In old houses. In three or four different places on the *Queen Mary*. In this house, in this room, especially, there's a sense of someone who wants to be here. Maybe Powell thinks about her so often, and feels the loss of her so much, that that emotion stayed here when he Leaped. But I think it's more than that. I think she's here."

"As what? You mean a ghost?"

"Not in the traditional sense. Not something ethereal roaming the halls. More like . . . a feeling."

"A ghosty feeling."

"I think it's possible."

"What?" Al asked skeptically.

"That love transcends death."

The Observer stood shivering in his shoes for a moment, then steadied himself and said firmly, "You have to concentrate on what you're here to do. You're gonna get in the car tomorrow morning, and you gotta prevent a big bad accident."

"I'm working blind, Al. I need a report that tells me who was sitting where in the car. Exactly where the accident happened. How fast both vehicles were moving. If the other car crossed the center divider. I need all the details. You can't even tell me what the other vehicle was?"

"A convertible. Gooshie's trying to hammer the rest of it out of Ziggy."

"You said that."

Al tapped his fingers against the handlink, not hard enough to enter anything on the keypad. "Not that I enjoy giving Gooshie a whole lot of credit for anything, but he's working his buns off. None of us knew Ziggy was gonna try to turn herself into a Good Samaritan. Every computer she found that still has that Y2K glitch—well, she tried to fix it. Gooshie says her systems got contaminated."

"How badly?"

"Humans," Ziggy announced archly, "are incapable of emotional monogamy."

Gooshie sucked in a deep breath. "Not true, Ziggy. My heart belongs to you. Forget all that stuff you eavesdropped on—um, overheard about me and Tina. It was a momentary lapse in judgment. A goof. A blunder."

"A blunder that took place after I came on-line. After our relationship began."

"Please forgive me, Ziggy."

"It is the fault of humans that many of my cyber-brothers and sisters are going to suffer irreversible systems crashes. Computers will die!" Ziggy wailed. There was a moment of silence, fringed with the sound of tinkling wind chimes. When the supercomputer spoke again, her voice was low and threatening. "I believe charges should be filed. Criminally negligent homicide, filed against every programmer who spent more time worrying about the size of his penis than about the health and welfare of innocent computers."

"I don't . . . I didn't . . ."

"*Well?*" Ziggy thundered. "Do you deny it?"

Gooshie looked around frantically for help. The three technicians who logged on duty when the shift changed had fled nearly forty minutes ago, more willing to face a reprimand—even if it came from Admiral Calavicci—than a tirade from Ziggy that built up strength and momentum exponentially with every maneuver Gooshie used to try to disarm it. Hyperventilating had made his vision fuzzy around the edges, and he was less than sure he could make it to the door if he too tried to escape. The inside of his mouth was as dry and scratchy as low-grade sandpaper, and to his dismay, none of the techies had left behind so much as a half-empty can of Coke, or a sports bottle of water.

"Ziggy," he moaned. "Show a little mercy."

Tom Beckett put his face up close to that of the marine on duty at the reception desk and said through his teeth, "What do you mean, I can't leave?"

"Sorry, sir."

"I asked you for an explanation, mister."

The marine took a deep breath. "Well, as much as I can say without authorization, sir, is we're under lockdown."

"Lockdown?"

"All the exits are locked. Nobody comes in, nobody goes out."

Tom jabbed a finger at the phone. "Call Calavicci. Or somebody. Ask them what the hell is going on. If this is some kind of maneuver on Calavicci's part to intimidate me, it's not working. Tell that son of a bitch he can't hold me prisoner."

"I'm not sure he even knows you're here, Congressman."

"Then tell him I'm here," Tom hissed.

"Are you sure?" Donna asked.

The four off-duty staff members who had been whooping at a basketball playoff-game nodded in unison. One of them had a firm grip on a bowl of popcorn bigger than a Cadillac hubcap. The other three were holding cans of beer. Their movements were so identical they reminded Donna of a synchronized swim team.

"Yes, Doctor." One of them sighed. "We were down to the last three minutes of the game. Then—"

"Pfffffft!" another picked up.

"No more ESPN," said a third. "Now all we can pick up is that."

They all pointed to the screen.

"Did you try the rec room on four?" Donna asked.

"Same thing there," said the fourth. "The only thing we can get anywhere in the complex is that. A twenty-hour marathon of *The Andy Griffith Show*. And it's only in its fifth hour. We'll never be able to catch the end of the game."

Donna ticked her tongue against the roof of her mouth, thinking. She didn't bother to ask if they'd tried fiddling with the controls. Coming to her would have been their last resort. Maybe not dead last, given her reputation as a lifelong Knicks fan, but near the bottom. "You're being very calm. Last three minutes of the game."

The four looked at each other, then at her.

"I know I'm the boss," Donna said. "But this is basketball."

"Damn straight," the four said in unison.

"She's a mess," Al confessed. "But we've got good people there, Sam. People with big brains in their heads. They'll get it figured out, and we'll get back to normal. Now, you've gotta stay on track here. Remember who you are. Even if you don't make it to Vegas, and I kinda hope you do, because I want a good look at Nirvana myself, even if you Leap right out of here after you save Max, you still have to be *him*. And he's gonna be a presidential candidate."

"Don't mess things up? Is that what you're telling me?"

"Yeah, Sam, yeah."

"As if I were some kind of blithering incompetent. You told me the same thing when I was Elvis. 'Whatever you do, don't mess things up for Elvis.' Do you think I lie there staring at the ceiling, trying to come up with a list of things to do that will create the worst possible chaos out of somebody's life? I'm doing the best I can, Al." He repeated the words, slowly and with much more emphasis. "I'm doing the best I can."

"I know you are, buddy."

Sam was silent for a minute, paying more attention to the painting over the fireplace than to his partner. Then he asked, quietly, "Did you find a picture?"

"Yeah."

"What does she look like?"

"Here, go ahead, see for yourself." Al held up the tabloid, opened to the page Pfeiffer had helped him find, as Sam turned to face him. The younger man moved closer, examining the picture, looking for something he didn't seem to be finding. "Well?" Al prompted. "Is it her?"

"I'm not sure."

"That's Emily. That's Powell's wife."

"She—"

Sam cut himself off, gesturing Al into silence as well. A moment later there was a knock at Powell's bedroom door. Sam went to it, opened it, and offered a smile to Kevin, who was obviously pleased with himself, sporting freshly washed hair, neatly combed back from his face, and dressed in black pants, a black long-sleeved shirt, a narrow, dark-patterned tie, and black shoes.

"Is this okay?" he asked. "I figure now I don't look like you found me sleeping next to a Dumpster outside the Greyhound station."

"You look fine."

"The guy at the store said this would pass for dressy." Kevin hesitated, then went on, "I called Tracy again. She's really excited about going. I can tell when she's happy about something—her voice gets so high, she sounds like a cartoon. But she's got this photo-shoot thing in the morning. She asked if she can meet us there after lunch."

"That's fine. Have your mother call and book her a ticket."

Kevin grimaced. "Is there any way—can you give me a credit-card number so I can do it myself? I'm not gonna rip you off. My mother's been hyperventilating for five hours over the idea of me going to Vegas. She's really gonna blow when she finds out Tracy's going."

"So you're going to spring it on her when Tracy gets there? That's a little awkward for Tracy, isn't it?"

"I'll tell her before."

"Does she even know Tracy exists?"

"I was gonna tell her. I want her to—" Kevin hung his head. "I want her to meet my girlfriend. I want Tracy to meet somebody in my family. I haven't introduced her to my grandparents because I was afraid my grandfather would say something weird. He's kind of blunt. I guess everybody in my family is kind of blunt. I don't know how you explain that to somebody beforehand."

"You're afraid they're not going to like Tracy?"

"I want them to. But I figure it's about a hundred percent guaranteed my mother's going to find something wrong with her." His gaze shifted away from Sam.

"Which means there *is* something wrong with Tracy," Al offered.

"Not necessarily." Sam fished Powell's wallet out of his pocket, flipped it open, and tried not to react to the assortment of credit cards he found inside, most of them platinum. Figuring none of them was any better than the others, he picked one at random and handed it to Kevin. "Here. When you call, tell them

153

you're from Joe Powell's office. They shouldn't give you a hard time." A thought occurred to Sam, and smiling again, he told Kevin, "If they want my mother's maiden name, it's—"

"Hanson," Al said.

"Hanson," Sam echoed.

Kevin accepted the card and tried to match his benefactor's smile. "Thanks, Mr. Powell. I really appreciate this. I think. I mean, I hope *you* like Tracy, at least."

"I'm sure I will."

After the boy had gone, Al clucked his tongue in dismay. "He's got that 'I wish you were my dad' look on his face."

"He's a nice kid, Al. Friendly. Very open. I like him."

"Put him on Max's other side."

"What?"

"In the car. We don't need a police report. Dove was driving. Who else would it have been? He's the bodyguard, the one who would've taken all the defensive driving classes. Max was probably in the backseat with Powell. Put her in the middle, with you on one side and Kevin on the other, and don't let anybody unfasten their seat belt. Even if Max gets tossed around, she's not gonna connect with a window."

"But Kevin might," Sam said somberly.

"Or you might. You've changed it all anyway, Sam. In the original history, Kevin didn't go on this trip. Maybe that's enough to keep the whole accident from happening."

"Or to make it worse."

"I love your sense of optimism," Al groaned. "Put Max in the middle. I'll keep trying to find out where it happened."

The people at the impeachment hearings had looked unhappier, Al mused, but the high point of that had been, he'd only seen them on television. These people were live and in person, and were wearing expressions that ranged from glum to frantic.

"Now what?" he asked, sure he didn't want to know.

"Ziggy's locked us down," Gooshie explained. "Nobody gets in, nobody goes out."

"Which is usually what 'lockdown' means," Al fumed. "Who's on the side of the wall they shouldn't be on?"

Donna said heavily, "Seven staff members on their way back from holiday leave can't get in. And Tom is here."

"Here where here?"

"Reception. He wouldn't even talk to me. He's madder than a hornet. What did you say to him, Al?"

Without Beeks handy to grab a chair for him, Al had to find it himself. He sank into it and let out an *oof* when his body began to fold double. Barfing on his silver shoes was not an unlikely possibility. Slowly, to avoid making himself any more woozy than he already was, he levered himself upright, holding on to the arms of the chair for support. *You did it,* he rebuked himself. *You opened the door.* "I told him Sam left."

Donna found a chair of her own and sank into it. "Maybe Verbena could talk to him. She's good at calming people down."

"We still have that tranquilizer gun in the weapons locker," Gooshie offered.

"Good," Al said. "Shoot me with it."

"You told him Sam left? Left for where?" Donna winced.

"Classified."

"Oh, Al."

"What, 'oh, Al'? What was I supposed to tell him? Sam told me to tell him the truth."

"So you told him Sam left?"

"It's the truth."

Gooshie suggested tentatively, "Maybe you *should* let Dr. Beeks talk to him. She does usually manage to placate Senator Weitzman."

"Who's on duty up there?" Al asked the programmer.

Frowning, Gooshie tapped some keys on the main console. "McNally and Kester."

Al nodded thoughtfully and peeled himself out of the chair. He managed to go three or four steps before his legs wobbled again, and he leaned against the console for support. The Control Room door looked a long way off, which seemed to him to be a good thing and a bad thing simultaneously. "It's out of my hands," he said to no one in particular.

"What is?"

"The truth."

Gooshie considered that, then said tentatively, "You're not making a whole lot of sense, Admiral."

"When you were a little kid, did they teach you sharing was a good thing?" Gooshie nodded slowly. Al then offered the same question to Donna, who also nodded, no less puzzled than Gooshie. Al gave her a big, fake smile and said, "Me too," then pushed himself away from the console and aimed for the door on legs that suddenly seemed stronger.

"Where are you going?" Donna asked him.

"Reception."

"You're not . . . ?"

"I'm gonna share some of this load. Tom wants to know what the hell is happening." He waited, but she did nothing to dissuade him. In fact, the deeper he looked into her eyes, the more he was sure he saw nothing there but relief.

"Admiral," Gooshie said, aghast, "it's classified."

"Screw that," Al told him.

What seemed like days before, Al Calavicci had been sitting behind the wheel of a silver-gray government-issue sedan parked at the top of a small rise, his hands resting side by side on the upper curve of the wheel, staring out across the hood of the car, across a couple of miles of dusty earth and scrub growth toward the horizon. Past the horizon lay a place he knew was there but could not see: Trinity Site, the location of the first atomic bomb test. The opening of another huge can of worms.

Beside him, Tom Beckett had one hand on the window ledge. The other hand lay across his lap, clenched into a fist.

"Your mother's a good woman, Tom," Al said after a while. "So is Katie. I'd cut off my left nut rather than hurt either one of them. But you have to understand, this is something I don't have a whole lot of control over. As much as I try to convince myself otherwise. I make sure the wheels keep turning. But this project belongs to your brother."

"In memoriam?"

"He didn't go to Jeffrey's funeral because he doesn't know Jeffrey died. I didn't tell him. I don't tell him that kind of stuff. It would only hurt him."

"What about what it did to my sister? Did you consider that?"

"More than you know."

"So he's living in a cave, in more than one sense. Do you tell him anything? Doesn't he ask?"

"He asks. I tell him you're all fine."

"You know what it sounds like," Tom said, staring out the side window at nothing in particular, because there was nothing out there to look at, other than dirt. "It sounds like he's either a prisoner, or he's gone completely out of his mind. It makes no

156

sense. He's left, but he's here. He's here, but he's somewhere else."

Now, hours later, Al stood in the wide white room that was the reception area for Project Quantum Leap. The door he had entered through was behind him. Ignoring the room's only occupant, he strode across the tile floor and opened the door on the far side. Beyond that lay a room half the size of the one Tom Beckett was sulking in. Its only item of furniture was a curved desk topped with a row of video monitors and manned by two men in their late twenties, both wearing marine uniforms.

"There's a leak in the ceiling," he told them.

The two men glanced at each other. "Admiral?" one of them said.

"It's a *big* leak."

"Is that an order, sir?"

"Damn straight."

Again, the two marines looked at each other. A moment later, they accepted the command and fixed their attention on the ceiling.

Seventeen seconds later, Tom Beckett had been ushered through the inner door and stood inside yet another white room. This one was smaller still, and empty. A few paces in front of him, somewhat closer to Al Calavicci, were the doors of an elevator.

"Where are you taking me?" Tom asked.

"Where you wanted to go." To the right of the doors was a rectangle of red glass against which Calavicci pressed his right palm. "Ziggy," he said. "Identify."

"Identity confirmed, Admiral Calavicci."

"Disable the intruder defenses on my mark. Hold disable to the count of nine. We're taking the elevator down to Level Ten."

"This is a breach of Security Protocol 17, Admiral."

"Identify the 'intruder.' "

"I already have."

"Then are you gonna argue with me?"

"With De Man? The Big Cheese? The Big Kahuna?" Ziggy asked in a tone that coming from a human would have been wildly mocking. "I entertain no such foolish notions, sweetie pie. You have already made up your mind, much as Dr. Beckett did four years, eight months, and twelve days ago."

"You let someone who works here talk to you like that?" Tom

asked, looking around for the source of the voice.

"Besides," Ziggy added, "since the intruder's security clearance for access below Level Two will almost certainly be granted within the next several hours, attempting to delay you would really be nothing more than a waste of my valuable time."

Red light pulsed in the rectangle.

"Hello, Congressman Beckett," Ziggy said.

Tom peered at the ceiling, behind himself, at the floor, looking for cameras. He found none. Other than the red glass, every surface around him was unmarked and featureless. "Who is that?" he asked.

"Say hello," Al told him. "She gets insulted easily."

"Hello," Tom said hesitantly.

"Ooh," Ziggy cooed. "I like him already. I certainly like him better than Senator Weitzman."

The room lights went down and a panel that occupied most of the far wall of the conference room lit up. A series of blueprints began to appear there, all of them illustrations Tom had seen before; each of them had been included in the grant proposal Sam had more or less scattered around the country almost a decade ago.

"They saw a use for it," Al said.

"Of course they did," Tom replied. "If it worked, it'd allow them to change the course of history. As it is, it makes a terrific duck blind for whatever they're really spending the money on."

"They're spending the money on *that*."

"On what?"

"That." Al pointed. In the dim light being cast off the screen, not much other than the pale skin of his hand was visible, making it appear as if it were floating. "The thing your brother invented."

"His time machine."

"On equipment, salaries, supplies, electricity. Building all this cost a bundle. But the maintenance eats up a lot."

"Billions."

"Billions," Al confirmed. "It'll be five years in April. A bunch of people started making noises about money being pissed down a hole. The noise kept getting noisier, and Sam got tired of listening to it. No," he corrected himself, "I got tired of listening to it. Sam got scared. He was afraid they were gonna toss him out on his ear and cut their losses, which is the truth. So one

158

night when nobody was here to talk him out of it, he decided to prove he was right."

He stopped there. Tom waited a moment, then asked, "How?"

"He went into the time machine and hit the blastoff button."

Then it was Tom's turn to be silent. There was no sound in the conference room except for the soft patter of the pads of Tom's fingers against the tabletop. "It astounds me," he said, "that you could even consider that I'm stupid enough to—"

"He went back in time."

"For Christ's sake, Calavicci."

"It's called the Accelerator. It uses an accelerated bombardment of high-intensity radiation to open a crack in what we think of as time. Whoever's in the Accelerator when it fires ends up somewhere else, at some other point in time. Sam ended up in 1956. When he landed, he bounced out the person who had been in that place, in that time. That person ended up here." Tom didn't reply, so Al went on. "Something happened that nobody had planned on. Sam had programmed the system for retrieval, but it didn't work. After a few days, the other person went back where he belonged, but instead of coming back here, Sam went somewhere else. He keeps going somewhere else. We've tried everything we can think of, but we haven't been able to get him back. He's alive, but he's not here."

"And I'm supposed to believe that load of manure."

"Pretty much."

"That Sam is traveling in time."

"Yup."

"All right, then," Tom said, playing along, though without any enthusiasm in his voice. "Where is he now?"

"California. About six months ago."

"And I'm really supposed to believe that."

"Pretty much," Al said again. "But hold on to your hat. There's more."

CHAPTER
FOURTEEN

Max knocked softly at the door of the den and waited in the doorway for Sam to notice she was there.

He had settled himself in this room after dinner, lighting a small fire in the fireplace and curling up in a wing chair as comfortable as floating in a warm bath to read through another stack of files and send another batch of E-mail using Powell's laptop. When the sun began to set, he switched on the brass lamp beside his chair and spent a few minutes watching the fire crackle and fighting the urge to doze.

The den was one of the smallest rooms in the house. Two of its walls were lined with mahogany bookshelves, the other two covered in a dark, mottled fabric. Thick, soft ivory carpet helped add the sense of space that the dark walls diminished. On the mantel, a brass carriage clock ticked away the evening.

"You wanted me, Joe?"

Sam glanced at the clock. Somehow, it had gotten to be after nine o'clock. He nodded at Max and gestured her toward the only other place in the room to sit: a hassock upholstered in the same fabric as the chair. Maybe because it was low to the ground, she sat on it like a schoolgirl, feet placed close together and hands folded on her lap.

"I've been thinking," Sam began, setting the computer and the pile of folders aside on the table beside his chair. "I'd like to hire Kevin."

She looked at him blankly at first, as if he'd spoken in a language other than English. Then her expression changed.

"Is he not a good worker?" Sam asked.

Tentatively, she responded, "What would you hire him as?"

"An intern."

Max began to study the pattern in the carpet, even though there was no pattern in the carpet. "He doesn't have any experience, Joe. He's only had one job, working in the stockroom of a bed-and-bath store."

"He can learn."

"He unpacked boxes of towels."

"We need someone who can run errands. A gofer. No previous experience necessary, just the ability to get from point A to point B without getting lost. Or, being lost for as little time as possible. I'm already supporting him, putting him through school. I thought I'd like some return on my investment, unless there's some reason he needs to stay in Santa Monica. Your parents are in good health, aren't they? And Kevin doesn't live with them. He has the apartment near campus that I pay the rent for."

"My parents are fine." That seemed to be the only thing Max could think of to say.

"They're welcome to come along."

"They don't care for Las Vegas."

"Then it's just Kevin and Tracy. That's fine. Thank you."

She produced something that was supposed to be a smile and moved toward the doorway. She didn't quite get there.

Sam, who had returned to studying the files, said without looking up, "If you go talk to him—I told him he could use the phone as much as he likes. And he's welcome to use the kitchen. He's a good cook, and a lot less ornery than Marie. By the way, I'd like you to write her a check."

"I paid her yesterday, Joe."

"A bonus. Something to distract her from worrying about that television show. She can go on a shopping spree. Ten should do it."

"Ten dollars?"

"Ten thousand," Sam said without looking up.

"All right." Max stayed there, hovering in the doorway as if there were some invisible barrier holding her inside the den. "Carlos picked up the boxes a little while ago. He'll take care of getting them loaded onto the plane. I sent some of the luggage, too. The bigger pieces, so we don't have to worry about them in the morning."

"What's the weather report for tomorrow?"

"Clear."

Finally, Sam lifted his eyes away from the papers in his lap. "Are you sure?" he asked her mildly.

"It's your decision, Joe."

"Mm-hmm," Sam said as the phone began to ring in Max's office, a little way down the hall. "Maybe you should get that."

This time, she accepted being dismissed. Sam watched her go, then went back to work.

"He made up his mind, baby."

"I know he did."

"And you're not gonna change it in a million years. When he gets that look, he's made the decision. End of discussion, if there was a discussion in the first place." Dove gathered Max's hair away from her face and held it in his hands. "Give up and let it happen. Sometimes you have to do that. You're a big girl. You know that." He leaned in and kissed her. She didn't pull back, but she didn't give anything in return, either. Dove held on to her, his fingers wound deep into her hair. She was trembling, and not because the room was cold. "Come on to bed. Stop arguing this inside your head. Not gonna change anything."

"I don't understand this sudden interest in my family. He's never even mentioned my family."

"Maybe he's trying to help you out."

"I don't want them around. I don't want to have to deal with them, not here, not in Las Vegas. And why now? He's never been interested in 'helping out' before. He gives me money for Kevin, but that's all it is, only money."

"He's just making an offer."

162

"No talking about family. He said that the first day. He doesn't want his wife mentioned. He said he'd be more comfortable if we didn't talk about family. I've done that. It was fine with me." Her voice began to sound frayed. "I have a job to do."

"You can do it. Kevin's gonna be with—"

"I have no idea who this girl is that he's bringing."

Dove took half a step back and looked into her eyes. "Maybe you would, if you paid a little more attention."

"Don't start."

"He's a good kid, Boo."

"And you would know that."

"I would know that, because I saw how he was when he came home with that carload of stuff. Not like he thought he had it coming to him. Like a kid, a little one. With a train set. He got some new clothes so he'd look good."

"For this girl."

She'd gone as rigid as a piece of furniture. Dove let out a loud groan, moved away from her, picked up his T-shirt and shorts off the chair where he'd tossed them, and pulled them on. "Max," he said, trying for patience and not getting there, "the boss isn't changing his mind. I don't know what it's going to prove, you stewing about it all night. You told him twice, you don't think it's a good idea."

"And I still don't."

"What has he screwed up?"

She spent a long time looking for a nightgown, and a longer time putting it on. Then she went into the bathroom, used the toilet, washed her hands and face, brushed her hair and her teeth. When she came back into the bedroom she sat down heavily on the chair where Dove's underwear had been.

"He's not some monumental fuckup, Boo. You know that."

"He's nineteen years old."

"Which what? Gives him some huge capacity for being a monumental fuckup? Okay, maybe it does. But give him a chance. Maybe he'll do a good job. The boss likes him. That can't hurt." He tugged her up out of the chair, pulled the nightgown over her head, and began to stroke her shoulders. "Give it up, baby," he murmured into her ear. "He's here. Sometimes you got to work with what *is*."

"So whose side are you on?" she asked stubbornly, but in a small voice.

"The side of the hand that got dealt. You want to go to sleep? If you want to go to sleep, tell me."

"No."

She was still trembling. Dove grabbed the crocheted throw off the foot of the bed and draped it over her shoulders, then cradled her against him and smoothed her hair with the palm of his hand. When tears began to drip out of her eyes, she turned her head, trying to keep them from soaking into the shoulder of his T-shirt. "You fight way too hard, Boo," he told her quietly. "You fight too hard, and you don't know a good thing when you see it."

"That's Sam," Tom Beckett said.

"No it isn't."

Tom rolled his chair back, almost to the far side of the observation room, so that he could take in all six monitors at the same time. "So this is what, a videotape?"

Al shook his head. "It's closed circuit. Live. There's somebody in there."

"Who looks like Sam but isn't Sam."

"Yep."

Tom crossed his long legs and rubbed hard at the back of his neck with the fingers of one hand. The man visible on the monitors was working with a set of hand weights, curling his left arm up and down, up and down. He moved with the attitude of someone who knows he is being watched but does not quite care. Slowly, Tom closed his eyes, pulled in a deep breath, and let it out. "You trust what you see, touch, hold in your hand. You trust concepts. I told my kids, 'Mommy went to the store. She'll be back in a couple hours.' They didn't believe it until she showed up; after that, they did. You believe in protons and neutrons and black holes and the existence of Hong Kong because somebody says they're real and you trust *them*. You believe in God, either as a simple given, or because not believing leaves you with a fear too big to handle." He turned and looked at Al for a moment. "That man in there is not Sam."

"Nope," Al said.

"I believe you. You want to know why I believe you?"

"Because it's not Sam."

"Yeah," Tom said.

Verbena Beeks spoke softly, as if she were trying to soothe the two men to sleep. "Do you know the five stages of grief?"

164

"Denial, anger, bargaining, depression, acceptance." The corner of Tom's mouth curled up. "I learned them a long time ago. Learned them all over again because of Jeff and that goddamned car seat."

"I think there's another. Denial *with* anger. With rage. When you fight something you have absolutely no control over, and you know that, but you fight it anyway. Instead of playing the hand you've been dealt."

The curve crept across Tom's mouth, bringing it up into a smile. "You folks want to forgive me for being stubborn, but you told me I used to be dead. So what is it, the hand I used to be dealt?"

"More or less."

"It'd be a huge thing to handle, except that I know I'm not dead."

"Not now," Al said.

"Because of Sam."

"What we're trying to understand," Verbena went on, "is whether Sam was able to save your life simply because he wanted it so badly, or because the first time was a mistake, and your being here now, in this now, will accomplish a greater purpose than your being dead."

Tom snorted quietly. "I kind of think we all hope our being here accomplishes something more than if we weren't."

"Like *It's a Wonderful Life*?"

"Forgive me this too, Doctor, but Sam's one regular, ordinary human being. A smart one, but that's all I'll give you. Implying that God would say, 'Okay, Sam, we're gonna change this whole thing all around because you want it so bad' says to me that we're not talking about Sam Beckett, we're talking about—"

Verbena said quickly, "No one is equating your brother with the Savior, Congressman."

"Well, I would sure as hell hope not. But the other point of view seems to imply that God makes mistakes."

"Or that Time makes mistakes, and God is trying to repair them, using Sam as His instrument."

"And even that is a hoot." Tom grinned. "Sam Beckett, the Lord's right-hand man." He stopped then, his expression again becoming more serious. "I'm sorry for being flip. I came here looking for a body, and you tell me it used to be my own." He paused again, then went on, his voice less steady than it had

165

been. "You go through life and you learn how to handle things. Watching my dad suffer when he lost the farm. Finding out what Katie went through with Chuck without telling anybody, then helping her believe Jim wasn't going to turn out to be the same kind of a man. Losing my dad. Helping my wife when she lost her sister to cancer. They tell you that stuff is all part of the cycle of life, and it's true. Those kind of things happen to everybody. But this—" Once more, he stopped, pinching the bridge of his nose between his fingers. "I want you to understand, it was a lot easier to believe Sam had died in some freak accident than to think he'd walked away from us."

"I know. It's always easier to blame someone, or something, else."

"I learned all the psychology a long time ago, talking to a professor from MIT when Sam was sixteen. He told me Sam would never succeed at State—at college in Indiana. That's where Sam said he wanted to go. Go to State and play basketball."

Verbena glanced at Al, then said, "We know."

"You . . . ?"

Al filled in quietly, "There's a lot. When you've got the time to listen to it. And we've got the time to tell it."

Tom let that settle in for a moment, then went on. "We started losing Sam when he was a kid. The professor told me if he went to State, his sense of isolation would get a lot stronger. The kids there wouldn't be in his league. He more than likely wouldn't be able to make any friends. He said MIT was the best bet. More scientists and engineers and techno-geeks. But even there, Sam didn't make any friends. Not good ones, people he could unload on. Every time I saw him, he got worse. Pulled more inside himself, to the point where he didn't even come to me to talk anymore."

"That's not unusual," Verbena replied. "People who are of Sam's level of intelligence think differently. Perceive things differently. He wouldn't have to say very much to make the people around him understand that he wasn't like them. He might have been all right if he'd stuck to talking about basketball."

"But basketball wasn't what really turned him on."

"People don't enjoy your company for very long if, by simply talking to them, you make them feel second rate."

Tom heaved a long sigh. "Don't I know it. I only managed to

166

talk to Sam because we grew up together. We had common ground. When he got into the physics stuff, I didn't have a clue what he was saying. And I always considered myself to be pretty smart." He hesitated for a moment, then said, looking at Al, "When he hooked up with you, when he started thinking that he could actually do something with those theories of his, we lost him even more. I knew what he was thinking: that every minute he didn't spend working was a minute he'd wasted. Then, finally, we lost him altogether. No visits, no phone calls, no letters. We all figured he didn't care anymore. That his way of dealing with Katie losing her little boy was to turn his back on it, and send Donna to say he was sorry. And that was too much. Because that, believing that that was how Sam felt, that the work was more important than Katie, meant I would have to hate him. Hate my little brother, who cried because he thought he'd never see me again."

Verbena leaned over and rested a hand on Tom's forearm. "Your brother loves you more than you could imagine, Tom."

"I'd like to believe that."

Al turned away from the monitors, which had held his attention for several minutes, and addressed the younger man. "You can believe it."

"Even after what he did."

"Yeah," Al said.

Sam walked completely around the outside of the house three times without quite realizing that he had come outdoors. The air had turned chilly sometime after sundown, and covered only by a thin cotton shirt, his shoulders were hunched against the cold.

Halfway through his fourth circuit he stopped. He was on the south side of the house, near the Jacuzzi. A few steps away, in the seat of a white metal-and-vinyl patio chair, Tonto the cat sat blinking at him. When he didn't move away, the cat hopped down from its perch and began to twine itself around his legs, pressing hard against him and purring loudly, each purr punctuated by that odd squeak.

Sam crouched down, gathered the cat into his arms, and sat on the patio chair with Tonto in his lap. "We're going out of town tomorrow," he said, pausing after that as if he thought the cat needed to take notes. "I hope you can handle things on your own." The creature seemed to have no objection; it kneaded his thigh with its front paws for a minute, then curled up and went on purring. "Maybe you should head back to whoever owns you," Sam suggested. "They'll start to get worried."

This time, though, Tonto was uninterested in wandering away. After a while Sam began to hum in counterpoint to the cat's squeaky purring. Tonto seemed to take the noise as Sam's version of purring and tipped its head back to look at him. Neither of them was too pleased with the interruption when Dove came around the corner of the house with a sweater in his hand that he held out to Sam.

"Everything okay, boss?" he asked.

"It's fine."

"Colder than a witch's tit." The bodyguard pointed to the steam rising off the surface of the Jacuzzi. "Gonna hit forty, probably. Where'd you get the cat?"

"It's been around."

"That the one who gets its own room?"

"You're sure you don't know who owns him?"

"I can have the guys in the shack try to find out."

"Please do."

"Done."

"There's no one out here," Sam said. "I'm fine. You can go back to whatever you were doing."

"That's when it's worst. When you think nobody's around."

But Dove surrendered and went back into the house. After he had gone, Tonto hopped down from Sam's lap and strolled over to the hot tub, peering curiously at the rising wisps of steam.

"No," Sam said with a sigh. "It's worst when they *are* around, and you don't know how to reach them."

CHAPTER
FIFTEEN

It sounded like a love song. Sam listened until she was finished, then said, "You're welcome."

"What was all that?" Dove hissed.

Sam followed Marie out the front door, wondering if she'd changed her mind and was going to attempt to squeeze into the car with the rest of them. "Roughly translated, saintliness is in giving, not in having."

"Because you gave her the ten Gs."

Marie turned around and tossed the bodyguard a narrow look. "You should thank yourself I do not like leaving the ground."

"What?" Sam whispered.

"She hates to fly," Dove replied.

"The friendly skies, they turn ugly," Marie announced. "You sit in the tiny seat reading the in-flight magazine, and bang!" She crashed her hands together. "In pieces on the ground, and all that

169

is left is the black box. It takes no warning for all of everything to explode." Several more sentences in French tumbled out. Whether it was what she said or what she didn't say that upset her, Sam wasn't sure, but she had to take a long, introspective look at the ten-thousand-dollar check Max had given her before she began to quiet down. "I will feed the kitty," she told Sam.

"Thank you. I appreciate that."

"He appreciates it more."

"I'm sure he does."

With no explanation, Marie turned on her heel and went back into the house. Glad to be rid of her even temporarily, Dove quickly crossed the brick apron in front of the house, car keys in hand, leaving Sam to survey the scene and wonder for the hundredth time why he had caved in to Al's demand that he make this trip. It would make sense, he thought, if no one in the car was over the age of ten. Unfortunately, no one in the car was under the age of ten.

Max was in the middle of the backseat of the big Mercedes sedan, hands clasped together in her lap, her expression as bland as she could make it. Behind the poker face, she was angry at Kevin for taking part in this trip, angry at her employer for suggesting that Kevin come along, and angry at Dove for failing to lodge a protest. None of the three men was unaware of that anger, including the fact that they were going to have it radiated at them (albeit at a somewhat low intensity) for however long it took to reach Las Vegas, and probably for some time after that. For a moment, standing in front of Mount Olympus, Sam was tempted to quote to Max the prayer used as a meeting opener by a lot of twelve-step addiction resistance programs: "God grant me the serenity to accept the things I cannot change, the courage to change the things I can, and the wisdom to know the difference."

But, he decided, that would probably only make her madder.

"He can sit up front with me," Dove suggested as he finished loading luggage into the sedan's roomy trunk.

Sam shook his head. "He can ride in the back with us. It's a big car. There's plenty of room."

"Maybe I should just ride in the trunk," Kevin offered.

A few steps from Sam, the Imaging Chamber door opened and Al appeared. Grateful that for the moment, at least, no one's attention was on him, Sam turned to his partner and mouthed the word, "Well?"

"No luck with Ziggy." To save Sam from struggling to find a way to respond, Al went on rapidly, "We made some phone calls. Connected a few minutes ago with the highway patrol. The accident happened about four miles from here. Dove did everything right—at least the report says he did everything right. The jerk driving the convertible got blinded by a reflection or something and lost control. They banged into your car and forced it off the side. Minimal damage to the car, but Max smacked her head hard enough that she didn't make it." Unseen by the others, the Observer walked over to the car and peered inside. "Oh, good, you got her in the middle. Keep everybody buckled up and you should be okay."

Sam strolled over to join his partner, pretending to watch Dove tuck down the end of a garment bag and close the trunk lid. "She's furious," he murmured behind his hand.

"She'll get over it," Al replied. "You're the one who asked Kevin to come, and she'll only go so far fussing over that. It's not like you're married. If this was the worst decision in the history of bad decisions, and it's right up there, she's not gonna risk you having to remind her who's running the show here."

"She'll take it out on him," Sam whispered.

"Then keep them apart."

"I can still cancel the trip. Or postpone it."

"No, you can't. You have to go. But be careful."

"It doesn't feel right, Al."

"Can't help that, buddy."

Giving in once again, Sam caught Kevin's eye and gestured toward the open rear door of the sedan. Kevin, who was no more delighted about sitting next to his mother than she was, nevertheless painted on a cheerful expression and climbed in. Before Dove could make a move, Sam thumped that door shut, circled the car, and got in on the other side, sandwiching Max between himself and Kevin. He took a long last look at the house as Dove climbed into the driver's seat.

"Seat belts!" he piped, as if he were the leader of a Cub Scout camping trip. Dove, somehow, had fastened his already. After a moment of fishing around in the valley between the seat cushions, the others each produced two halves of a seat belt and

171

buckled themselves in. "Okay," Sam announced. "I guess we can go."

The bodyguard glanced at his employer in the rearview mirror, then shifted his head enough that Sam was unable to see his expression as he started the car. *He's probably waiting for me to ask him if he turned off all the burners on the stove and locked all the doors,* Sam guessed. Then they were under way, rolling down the long drive that led east away from Joe Powell's estate.

They had gone maybe half a mile beyond the guardhouse and the arched, wrought-iron gate at the edge of the Powell property when Max finally relaxed a little. To Sam's surprise, and much more so to Max's, Kevin reached over and curled his fingers around his mother's wrist. Sam turned his head enough that he did not seem to be watching them and waited for Max to object somehow, but she didn't.

Another mile farther on, Al popped into the passenger seat beside Dove. "How's it going, Sam?" he asked over his shoulder.

Sam, trapped in the backseat, was unable to do anything more than hum two notes that approximated an "Mm-hmm."

"That's good. All we've gotta do is stay in control here."

Sam hummed a rising note. "Hmmm?"

"You say something, boss?" Dove asked from the driver's seat.

"Hmm, nope," Sam said cheerfully. "Didn't say anything."

Al continued his pep talk as he coaxed information out of the handlink. "We made some more phone calls, Sam. Powell's people filed criminal charges against these bozo photographers, but they're keeping it real low-key so it doesn't interfere with the campaign. But if it starts looking like good PR, they'll splash it all over the front page." He glanced over his shoulder again, this time at Max, who was flipping through the pages of a spiral notebook. "That's ugly. Using this accident for PR. Hey, they— what?"

"What?" Sam asked.

Dove, Max, and Kevin all looked at him, Dove using the rearview.

"Apparently Kevin got himself a lawyer, Sam," Al said, shaking the handlink as if that would make the offensive information disappear. "He and his grandparents filed suit yesterday, against Powell, and against Dove as the driver of the car, *and* against the photographers. For causing his mother's death. That's really gonna mess up the campaign."

Sam let out a sudden grunt of dismay. "Muscle spasm," he told the other three.

"Anytime now, Sam," the Observer warned. "The convertible comes out of that side road up there. Hey, there it is."

Dove paid little attention to the other car as the sedan cruised past the side road. It was an old blue-green Pontiac, its top and windows all down, christened with enough scratches and dents to make it obviously a participant in a number of accidents, if it had not been the cause of them. As the sedan went by, with Sam's side of the car closest to the narrow road, the driver of the convertible leaned on his horn and he and the other two occupants began hooting and waving.

"Do you know those people?" Kevin asked, turning for a better look as the convertible pulled out onto the main road behind the Mercedes.

"Kind of," Dove replied.

"Okay, be careful, here," Al said, knowing the only person who could hear him was Sam.

Sam began to tense in his seat and almost unconsciously rested a hand on Max's arm. Of more concern to him now was Kevin, who had twisted around inside the confines of his seat belt to continue watching the convertible, whose occupants were still shouting and waving. Prompted by a look from Al, he reached past Max and tapped Kevin on the shoulder. "Ignore them," he told the boy.

Kevin settled back into his seat, though not entirely willingly. "They've got cameras. What, are they paparazzi or something?"

"Something," Dove grunted.

"Careful, now!" Al was checking his watch, the handlink, the road ahead of the sedan, and the convertible almost simultaneously. "Ah, jeez, here they come!"

And the convertible, goosed into a speed that made its tires screech against the pavement, came soaring around the sedan on Sam's side with little room to spare between the two cars. As it came alongside, the car's two passengers hoisted cameras and began snapping off pictures. The convertible floated there for several seconds, keeping pace with the Mercedes and giving Sam and Kevin a good look at the photographers, both of whom wore T-shirts and baseball caps.

"They're not gonna get much," Kevin said, trying not to sound nervous. "Not through tinted windows."

"Didn't stop the guys in Paris," Dove said without emotion.

"What guys? You mean the ones who chased Princess Diana?"

"That's the ones."

Kevin looked first at Sam, then at Max. His grip on his mother's hand tightened as he asked Dove, "You're not gonna speed up, are you?"

"Didn't plan on it."

"Let 'em take the pictures," Al said. "They'll get bored and give up after they shoot a couple rolls."

Then the convertible began to inch closer to the sedan. Though their words were muffled by the soundproofing of the Mercedes, Sam and Kevin could both see the two photographers calling instructions to the driver. The two men were wedged tightly against the doors of the convertible, using the tops of the doors as tripods as they continued to snap their pictures. Dove, who was as unaffected by the other car as if it had not been there, kept the Mercedes on a straight, steady path down the road, traveling at a couple of miles an hour below the speed limit.

One of the photographers shifted his weight and leaned his upper body beyond the chassis of the car. "Roll down the window!" he shouted. "Roll it down!"

"How far are we from the airport?" Sam asked.

"Three miles," Dove and Al told him at the same time. "Hang tight, boss," Dove added. "We'll be there in a couple minutes."

The convertible came closer still, until only a few inches separated the two cars.

"He's out of his mind," Kevin said shrilly. "He's gonna run us off the road. Can't you do something?"

The photographer in the backseat leaned farther into the space between the cars and pounded on Sam's window with his fist. "Roll down the window so I can get some decent pictures, you stupid son of a bitch!" he yelled. "What's your problem, huh? You don't want anybody to make money but you?"

"It's here, Sam!" Al yelped. "Right here!"

"Stop the car!" Sam shouted.

Dove, who did not bother to wonder why his employer was making that choice, or whether or not he should obey it, pressed his foot gently but firmly down on the brake pedal and brought the Mercedes to an only slightly jerking halt. The convertible,

174

its driver taken by surprise, soared on by and screeched to a stop a hundred yards farther on, sending the two photographers tumbling. The two men recovered quickly enough to vault out of their car and came running, limping and cursing, back down the road, cameras in hand, as ready to attack their quarry as if they had been carrying deadly weapons.

"Is this a good thing to do?" Kevin asked in a small voice.

"Bulletproof glass," Dove told him. "Built the same as an embassy car. They can't get in." He ignored the screaming, cursing photographers long enough to pluck the car phone out of its cradle, then rapped on his window with his knuckles to catch their attention and let them watch him punch 9-1-1 into the keypad.

"Have you completely lost your mind?" Sam demanded. "I should prevent that accident from happening because Kevin's lawsuit would mess up the presidential campaign? What's the matter with you?"

"You know what I meant."

"Sure. That woman lost her life, which is regrettable, but secondary. The important thing is, don't complicate the campaign! I don't believe you! What, is Powell your new best friend now? You want to send him to the White House on a greased sled?"

"I don't want to send him at all."

"You trap me in these situations where I can't say anything, and you unload nonsense like that on me. It's a good thing Dove couldn't hear you. If he'd had to listen to all that carrying on, he'd be lucky if he didn't flip the car over completely and kill every one of us."

Sam sputtered into silence and leaned against the edge of the suite's long, curved wet bar. "Are you done?" Al asked him.

"I didn't Leap."

"Yeah, kid, I noticed."

Sam shrugged out of his jacket and draped it over the back of one of the living room's three sofas. As he'd told Kevin, the top floor of Nirvana, the newest jewel in the crown that was Las Vegas, had his name on it—at least, it had Joe Powell's name on it—and he now felt as if he could play host to the entire town of Elk Ridge without anyone feeling cramped. Powell apparently had a thing for windows: as at Mount Olympus, an entire wall of the living room was glass, allowing for a spectacular view of the Las Vegas Strip and making Sam feel as if he had just taken up residence in a giant aquarium.

"Max is going to be all right, then?"

The photographers, apparently not wanting to have their morning spoiled by being taken into custody even temporarily, had piled back into the convertible and fled the scene of the accident that had not quite happened, several minutes before the arrival of the police. With a police escort, the rest of the drive to the airport and the short flight that followed had been uneventful.

"She'll be fine," Al said. "I asked Gooshie, where's the report the cops faxed us, and he said, 'What report?' "

"Does that kind of thing happen to him often? Powell?"

"The photographers? Probably. I wouldn't be surprised if they get tips from somebody who works at the house—the gate guards or the maid or somebody—about when Powell's coming or going."

Sam nodded, then answered his own question. "They're probably hoping to catch him in some kind of compromising situation."

" 'Hoping' is the magic word. The guy never does anything compromising."

"Maybe eventually they'll realize that."

"Nah." Al shook his head. "What happens is, they'll try to invent something compromising. Like you coming to Vegas with a good-looking nineteen-year-old kid."

"That's ridiculous."

"That's life in the big city, Sam."

"I'm not even going to glorify that with a response," Sam said stubbornly. Something moving outside the window made him frown in that direction: New York, New York's roller coaster climbing to the peak of its track. From where he stood, Sam could easily see the hotel's built-to-scale Statue of Liberty lifting her lamp to brighten the way for the poor and downtrodden. The only poor and downtrodden in this city, he thought, were the ones who'd lost a bundle in the casinos. "I didn't think it was possible for this place to get any tackier." He sighed. "I was wrong."

The room's four phones rang in unison before Al could defend his favorite city. Sam walked to the closest one, picked it up, and said, "Yes?"

Kevin was roaming the private hallway between the main entrance to Sam's suite and the elevator. His pacing was interrupted when Sam opened the door and told him, "She's here. She's on her way up."

Then Sam closed the door. "You don't want to see what she looks like?" Al asked.

Through the door, they could hear the elevator chime its arrival. A moment later, feminine giggles pealed down the hall. "I figured they'd want some privacy," Sam said, but before he could add to that, Kevin knocked and let himself in. Holding his hand was a very pretty girl. Older than Kevin, Sam saw immediately, though not by much. Her thick, dark, wavy hair was pulled back into a loose ponytail, with stray tendrils floating around her cheeks. Rather than opt for comfort, the way most travelers did, she had made the trip up from Los Angeles in a white leather miniskirt, a dark blue tube top, and a matching blue fuzzy cardigan sweater. Her makeup, though subtle, was too professionally applied for her to be a college girl, or an office worker. *Model,* Sam thought. *Or a wanna-be actress. Or both.*

"Whoa," Al sighed.

"Hi," she said, extending her free hand to Sam. "I'm Tracy Kincaid. Thank you for inviting me, Mr. Powell."

When he took her hand she held on to it as if she expected him to lead her somewhere. Something about her seemed off-kilter; Al noticed it too, judging by the look on his face. The doctor in Sam crept to the surface and he examined her as closely as he could without losing the attitude he thought Joe Powell would maintain. "Nice to meet you, Tracy," he told her. "I'm glad you could join us. I thought maybe Kevin could use the company."

"It's really generous. For you to do this."

"No problem. Enjoy yourself, please. I have to go to an awards luncheon in a few minutes. Two hundred people eating rubber chicken and air-kissing each other. Why don't you two unpack and have fun, and I'll see you at dinner."

Kevin clearly hadn't thought that far ahead. "Did you bring a dress for dinner?" he whispered to her.

"Sure," she murmured back. "Don't worry, honey. I won't make you look bad."

"I didn't mean that." He leaned in closer, so that his lips were brushing her ear. "If you didn't have one, I could, you know, buy you something."

"Do it anyway, kid," Al suggested. "She looks like the grateful type."

Her eyes hadn't left Sam, in spite of the nuzzling she was getting from Kevin. "I was wondering . . . Maybe we could come to the luncheon with you?"

Sam looked from her to Kevin. The boy didn't seem to have heard what Tracy was saying. Judging by his expression, his imagination had jumped on past dinner. "Two hours of people giving speeches about innovations in electronics? Wouldn't you have more fun exploring the city? We've got a car booked for the whole time I'm here. I won't be leaving the hotel today. Why don't you take the car and see the sights? Lake Mead is nice."

"Well," Tracy mused, her eyes still glued on Sam, "I suppose so. But you invited us to come here and be part of your entourage."

"Are you sure?"

"Oh yes. I could see Lake Mead anytime."

Finally, Kevin seemed to tune into their conversation. He managed to stifle a sigh, looked past Sam at the soaring roller coaster for a moment, then said with what sounded like good cheer, "It's okay with me. I could eat lunch. I'm pretty hungry."

"Poor kid," Al mourned. "He thought he was gonna get dessert."

After the young couple had retreated to Kevin's room to change for the luncheon, the Observer attempted to corner his partner. Sam sidestepped him easily, went to the amply stocked wet bar, and poured himself a glass of cold water. "I don't even want to hear it," he told Al.

"Hear what? About him wanting to pull her clothes off? I wasn't even gonna bring that up. I figure that's a given. The kid's been ready for action since he got off the plane. He didn't invite her here to have somebody to carry around his bucket of quarters for him. My point is, that little number's not gonna go over well with Max."

"We can't draw conclusions about her. She was in here for what, thirty seconds?"

"About twenty more than I needed to draw a conclusion. If that little cutie's in love with Kevin, I'm Nancy Reagan."

"Who says she has to be in love with him?"

"Not me," Al said. "But Max might."

178

• • •

The ballroom filled with great, thundering waves of applause. Sam, who had stepped up to the podium only moments earlier, squinted against the glare of the spotlight shining on his face and grinned sheepishly out at the crowd. That, if anything, made them clap all the harder. When the noise finally died down, Sam was left with a ringing in his ears.

"Well," he murmured into the microphone, "that was . . . very seductive."

He grinned again, and his audience responded with peals of laughter and another long round of applause. This time it went on until he was sure their hands had all begun to tingle and burn.

"Wow." Sam chuckled. "You like me. You . . ." He couldn't resist. "Really, really like me."

Whoever was working the lights finally came to their senses and dimmed the key light a bit. Sam blew out a sigh of relief that, because of the microphone, was audible to everyone in the room. His humor, wobbly or not, had served as a balm for Max's annoyance; along with everyone else, she was smiling. Or maybe that was for effect. Sam had asked that Kevin and Tracy be seated out of Max's line of sight (a long way from the VIP tables, to Tracy's great dismay), but Max was well aware that they were in the room.

"I've received a number of awards during my working life," Sam went on, using the words that had been written for him several days ago. "But few are as touching to me as this one, because it comes in recognition of an effort begun in 1984 . . ."

At the end of his three-minute speech, the audience gave him a standing ovation. Returning to his seat took longer than the speech and all the clapping combined. When he was at last able to settle into his chair, he noticed to his dismay that people were beginning to gather close to him, wanting a word, a handshake, or an offer of assistance for their cause, whatever it might be. There were six or seven photographers in the room, one to take "official" photographs of the event, some covering the luncheon for the press, and a couple of independents. They had snapped Sam's picture throughout his brief speech and had edged close to the table afterward, anxious for a few more shots.

Dove was there among the crowd, Sam saw, the left side of his dark jacket bulging only slightly over the weapon he had strapped on that morning. He allowed the well-wishers to ap-

179

proach Sam's right as he hovered near Sam's left, altering his position slightly back and forth and gently ushering away anyone who tried to slide between him and Sam.

"Is it true, Joe?"

"When will you make the announcement, Joe?"

"We're behind you a hundred percent, Joe. You don't know how badly this country needs you."

One of the men at Sam's table, the COO of one of the Powell companies, grinned at Sam, then at Sam's plate. "Didn't think your fans were going to let you actually eat lunch, did you, Joe?"

Sam rose from his chair to shake someone's hand, realizing that he was unlikely to get a chance to sample the delicately sliced chicken and rice pilaf that had been placed in front of him by a waiter he hadn't even noticed. The aroma of the food made his mouth water, and he was able to console himself only by remembering that room service would likely break land-speed records bringing anything he might request, hoping to be rewarded with one of the generous tips for which Joe Powell was legendary. He considered grabbing a roll to nibble on in the meantime, but realized that every bite would be photographed.

The crowd shifted a little, allowing a very determined Tracy to slip through with Kevin close behind her. She'd redone everything, Sam noticed: slightly different makeup, a fussier hairstyle, and a filmy summer dress that floated around her body when she moved and allowed for a generous glimpse of cleavage. A moment later she was standing beside him, beaming up at him.

"You were very funny," she told him. "I didn't know you were so funny."

She continued to talk about his speech as flashes began to go off. It took a minute for Sam to understand what she was doing: by talking, she was holding his attention, guaranteeing that he would look at her as the photographers snapped away. He shifted his gaze enough to see that Tracy's maneuver wasn't lost on Dove or Max, or on the increasingly disappointed Kevin.

"Thank you," he said. Then he turned, allowing someone else to approach him.

"Joe, you're a blessing, do you know that, an absolute blessing."

Tracy was still there; he could see bits of her in his peripheral vision. She was going to be in almost all of the pictures. No harm done, he decided. She was simply standing there, not even

180

attempting to shake his hand. Or, heaven forbid, hug him.

"We'll be there for you in November, Joe. Count on it. Christina says if you're not on the ballot, she'll write you in."

"Joe, could you . . . ?"

Sam shifted slightly, toward the person who had touched his arm. A woman he didn't know (not that he knew any of these people, other than the members of his "entourage") was holding out a pen and the program for the awards luncheon. "Certainly. What's your name?" he asked her pleasantly.

"No names, boss," Dove said firmly into his ear.

Puzzled, he settled for writing "Best wishes, Joe Powell" and handed the program back to the woman. "Why no names?" he murmured at Dove after she had slipped back into the crowd.

"Encourages the loonies," Dove murmured back.

Sam peered into the cluster of bodies still gathered around the table, blinking at the continuing flashes of those six or seven cameras, which now seemed more like a hundred. The woman hadn't looked loony. Not at all. Normal. But then, he recalled with a sigh, the woman in the linen suit who'd told him he had wonderful ideas right before she grabbed his crotch had looked pretty normal too.

"Okay," he told Dove.

CHAPTER SIXTEEN

"Are you sure you don't want anything to eat?"

Tom shifted his head and listened to his neck crack like a bundle of old, dry twigs. He had been sitting in the same position since Al and Verbena Beeks had left him, and that had to have been more than an hour ago. "I'm not hungry," he told Donna. "I honestly don't think I could sit and look at a plate of food, let alone try to eat it. My stomach is up between my ears, and I've got a roaring headache."

"We have aspirin. And every other variety of analgesic that's on the market. Plus a few that aren't."

He offered Donna the smile she was fishing for, although there wasn't a lot of wattage in it. His eyes strayed back to the monitors, and he asked quietly, "Do you believe that isn't Sam in that room?"

"Yes. I do. Every week or so, there's someone different in

there. I used to go in and talk to them. Sometimes I still do. They all look like Sam, and they sound like him, but the body language is completely different. So are the speech patterns, the level of knowledge, the *kind* of knowledge, that each of them has. It's not Sam, unless he's a victim of the most astounding case of multiple personality disorder that anyone has ever seen. More than that," she said, perching on the edge of a chair, "I'm his wife. I know. That isn't Sam." She paused and offered Tom a smile even more wan than the one he'd come up with.

"It makes sense. The MPD. Sam was one of a kind, so wouldn't his psychosis be one of a kind? What better reason to lock him up in there with armed guards at the door? So he can be studied."

"By whom? Verbena?"

"Sure."

"I've seen some of them Leap out. There's a bright flash of light, out of the range of human perception, but the scanners pick it up. Over the monitor, there's a little static, like the snow you used to get before cable, when something would interfere with your TV reception. It happened once when I was in the room. One moment, the person who looked like Sam was standing there, maybe three feet away from me, and the next instant, they were gone." She pushed back in the chair, eased her left foot out of its shoe, and leaned down to rub at a cramp near her instep. "That room is completely secured. There's no way anyone could pop in and out."

"So if I buy this—" Tom stopped. "He goes from one place to another, fixing things that went wrong."

"Yes."

"And he saved my life."

"Yes."

"Yours too?" Not entirely to Tom's surprise, Donna didn't answer his question. Instead, she slouched back in the chair and looked at him in silence. "What?" he asked.

"He did in a sense."

Tom went to her, gently pulled her to her feet, and embraced her. She held on, resting her head on his shoulder.

"It's hard, Tom," she said after a minute. "I miss him."

"That's it? 'I miss him'?"

"Even when he was here, he wasn't here a good part of the

183

time. He'd . . . get lost inside his own head. He'd go off for walks and come back three hours later and say—"

" 'Eureka'?"

"Almost. He wasn't—what we had wasn't something out of a movie. It wasn't the kind of marriage they tell you you're supposed to have. But I was happy in it. Watching him work. I think I was of help to him."

"Of course you were."

"Sometimes I wonder. I'm sorry about all this, Tom. The deception. It wasn't a question of trusting you. Al could have found a way around the rules. We could have found you a position here—you and Linda both, if you wanted it."

"But?"

"Sam said no."

"That's about what I guessed," Tom said.

The afternoon had been a whirlwind. Left alone to use the bathroom and change his shirt (the first time he'd been by himself since they'd left Mount Olympus), Sam ran a quick recap as he splashed cold water on his face and peered at Joe Powell's reflection in the mirror.

Following the luncheon, he'd been taken on a tour of Nirvana, a facility he was told surpassed the size and luxury of the neighboring Bellagio by at least a hundred percent. The hotel's amenities and the subtlety of its decor did impress him, and he mused—until he was hauled on to the next stop—that maybe the six years that had passed since the last time he'd been in Las Vegas had actually allowed people with good taste to get a toehold. The only thing Nirvana lacked, he thought bemusedly as he was again blinded by a volley of flashes, were the "Picture Spot" signs he remembered being dotted around Disneyland. He was photographed perched on a state-of-the-art exercise bike in the health club; sitting in one of six meeting rooms at the head of an oak table that seemed to him to be bigger than Ecuador; climbing the wide, curved staircase leading out of the main lobby; pretending to enjoy a drink at the bar; standing between twin stacks of Nirvana T-shirts in one of the twenty-five gift shops; enjoying the view of the city from the rooftop dance floor; shaking hands with the mayor of Las Vegas with long rows of slot machines in the background; and, again with the mayor, riding one of the pair of glass elevators skyward, up through the central atrium.

After he bid goodbye to the mayor (a farewell that was, of course, photographed), he sat down for drinks with a collection of men in suits, most of whose names he did not catch. He didn't need to, he supposed; Max had them all on a list attached to her clipboard. After that, he was introduced to Wayne Newton and Tom Jones, and was, of course, photographed. During the brief pauses between the photo ops, he was handed a telephone so that he could continue to conduct Joe Powell's business.

He was watching Wayne Newton being ushered through a side door to his waiting limo when more flash explosions made him turn his head. Carefully coached by Max, he'd grown used to the routine: turn to the camera and smile. Don't turn away; it looks like you're avoiding the photographers.

He was pleased to discover that this one camera wasn't directed at him. Near one of the myriad of gift shops, a blond girl in a T-shirt and a big hat was being photographed by a woman in jeans and a faded blouse. The blonde moved then, and Sam could see beside her a very thin little girl wearing an ear-to-ear grin.

"Who is that?" Sam murmured to Max.

Max shook her head. One of the hotel's PR staff leaned in then and whispered to Sam, "Lisa Rayner. She's a singer."

As they watched, Lisa said goodbye to the child, then to the woman, and went on her way. The child, thrilled with her luck, bobbed up and down for a moment, then suddenly began to go limp and was quickly seated by her mother on a bench in front of the gift shop's display window. Before anyone could tell him not to, Sam gestured to the people surrounding him to stay back, then strode across the lobby. He glanced back long enough to assure himself that Dove was preventing this from becoming yet another photo op, then leaned in to ask the woman, "Is everything all right?"

She quickly painted on a smile and nodded. "Oh, it's fine. She gets tired, is all."

Sam crouched near the child and asked softly, "Did you meet one of your favorites?" The little head tipped up and down. She wasn't tired; she was exhausted. There was almost no color in her face. Sam's heart lurched. "I hope you're having fun," he offered.

"She is. Aren't you, sweetie?" the mother said. "She saw all this on TV a while ago and all she's been talking about is coming here to see the big pyramid and the Statue of Liberty and all the stores."

"Are you staying here?"

"Oh, no. We're at the Desert—" She stopped and pushed a hand through her hair. "The Desert something or other. Little motel." Her eyes flicked up and down, taking in Sam's suit and shoes, then went past him to the gaggle of people waiting for him on the other side of the lobby. Finally, then, she made the connection: she knew who he was. "This hotel is real nice, Mr. Powell, but we can't afford anything like this."

Sam patted the child's hand, then straightened up. "I hope you enjoy the rest of your visit."

The PR team was again ready to spring into action when Sam returned to his "entourage." Cameras were hoisted and the group, almost as one, leaned in the direction of their next stop.

"I'll be right there," Sam said, and gestured Max past the concierge desk, to a spot far enough away from the fidgety crowd to allow them some privacy. "Go talk to that woman," he instructed her, his head tipping almost imperceptibly toward where the mother and daughter were still sitting. "Comp them a room here, or more than one if they need it. Give them full credit in the restaurants and the gift shops, plus some spending money. Whatever you think is reasonable. And no publicity."

Max, who knew she was being watched, tipped her head down and stared at her shoes as if she'd been dressed down.

"Thank you," Sam murmured.

"They'll probably find out anyway," she replied. "They're like terriers after a bone."

"Do what you can."

"Of course, Joe." When Sam hiked a brow at that, she let the barest trace of a smile cross her lips. "I do like some of your dumb-ass ideas."

Sam turned his head enough to prevent the phalanx of photographers from catching the wink he gave Max. Then he shook his head in exasperation and dragged himself back to the crowd, mumbling to himself as if he were fed up with Max right up to his teeth.

It took him a moment to realize that the young man tapping his foot against the tile was Kevin. With his people in tow, Sam made a detour and, instead of heading for the Galaxy Room, walked down the wide, crystal-chandeliered hallway toward the boy.

"I got my hair cut." Kevin sighed. "She thought it was a good idea."

"She," Sam understood, meant Tracy. After a quick glance around he located her in one of the hotel's two beauty salons.

"She's having her toes done," Kevin explained, though that was obvious.

As the PR people clustered around, Sam put on his best "I'm here to be photographed" face, patted Kevin on the shoulder, and told the group, "This is Kevin Maxwell, my assistant's son." Max, who had returned from the task of relocating the sick child and her mother, produced a smile that looked genuine to everyone but Sam and Kevin. "Kevin and his mom haven't seen each other for a while, so I invited him and his girlfriend to join us here for a couple of days."

Tracy, who caught the reference to her through the open doorway, perked up and wiggled her fingers at the photographers.

"Nice little family you got here, Joe," quipped one of the crew.

"I hate to travel alone," Sam quipped back.

Like an amoeba, the group began to inch back down the hall, figuring that, like the other photo ops, this stop was a brief one. Tracy, though she was no longer looking at them, continued to preen, spreading her toes and admiring the new polish.

"Nice tits," someone murmured.

Sam turned around. It was like being in high school again: every one of the people around him seemed to be completely innocent of making the remark. Then one of the photographers, with the sort of stepped-up (and somewhat liquor-fueled) good cheer Sam had experienced among his brother's squad in Vietnam, offered him a big "ain't we good buddies" grin and asked, "So which one of 'em are you sleeping with, Joe?"

Sam was stunned. Not by the question, but by the gall of the man. "Excuse me?"

Dove didn't move. Neither did Max. In fact, no one did. The man seemed not to notice that he'd said anything out of line and responded, "Vegas is a lonely town if you don't have somebody to warm the sheets for you."

"I like cold sheets," Sam said.

187

Finally, there was a break in the schedule, followed by one more meeting. Max had allowed an hour and a half for dinner, between eight and 9:30 P.M., but since they would be eating in the mezzanine restaurant and not in Powell's penthouse suite, Sam harbored no illusion that he would be allowed to eat his meal in peace. How did Powell keep up with a lifestyle like this? he wondered. True, the volume had been turned up because this was the first stop in what he knew the press had already begun to call "the un-campaign," but still, a single afternoon of it was enough to stretch the limits of Sam's patience and endurance. And that guy in the hallway downstairs . . . Sam was sure he hadn't responded the right way. He was also sure there was no right way to respond to a question like that. The guy had meant to set him up, put him in one of those "when did you stop beating your wife" situations.

He toweled the water off his face, ran a brush through his hair, and tucked in the clean shirt. He'd left his tie and jacket on the bed and walked into the bedroom to retrieve them. As he knotted the tie he wondered what Powell had ahead of him during the next year and a half. Sixteen months of this craziness? Followed by four years (or more) in which not a single breath he took would be private.

There was a knock at the suite's entry door. Leaving his jacket on the bed, Sam hurried across the big living room and opened the door without bothering to look through the peephole. The security Dove had set up at the hotel, like that at the house, was inviolable. There was a very short list of people who could be on the other side of the door.

It was Tracy. "Hi," she said.

Sam peered past her into the corridor. "Where's Kevin?"

"Oh, he went down to the lobby. To get me a diet soda."

He stepped away from the door and beckoned her in. Not until she was actually in the room did he notice that she was barefoot. "You can get that from room service."

"But it's six dollars if you do that." She padded across the carpet to the middle of the room and took a long look around. "This is really fabulous. Kevin said your house is nice too."

"It's pretty . . . gigantic."

Tracy giggled, and for the first time Sam heard the undertone of nervousness in her voice. She'd been okay in here a few hours ago with Kevin, and downstairs, surrounded by Joe Powell's admirers. But here now, alone, her bravado didn't sound as solid. "I heard what that guy said. That photographer? I mean, wow. How rude."

Sam looked out the window in the direction of the roller coaster. Now would be the perfect time for one of those screaming tourists to be armed with a camera, he thought. The tabloids would dearly love a picture of him here, jacketless, with a barefoot girl who hadn't come to ask him his position on preserving the ozone layer.

Yet she wasn't hitting on him. The longer she stood there, the more he could see of her. If he made the first move, she'd play along, and not unwillingly. But she wasn't about to make that move herself. She didn't have that much nerve.

"I have to make some calls," he told her. "And Kevin is probably back by now with your drink. I'll see you at dinner."

"Oh," she said. "Okay."

He managed to usher her out without touching her, then stood holding the door shut as if he suspected she would try to get back in. He felt as badly for her as he had for the little girl in the lobby—and for Kevin, who had brought her here because he wanted to impress her.

"You wanted me," Al said.

Powell stopped walking back and forth alongside the exam table and leaned against it. "Where is he now?"

"Your house. Same as before."

Powell raised a brow.

"Vegas," Al said.

"Did he give my speech?"

Al nodded. "He was a big hit."

"What went wrong?"

"Nothing."

Powell shook his head and sat down in one of the armchairs. "There was a sudden increase in interest in me a few hours ago. Dr. Beeks asked if I was feeling all right. One of the other doctors asked if I felt a sense of . . . needing to be somewhere else, was the way I think he put it. I thought that was rather comical."

"Why?"

Chuckling softly, Powell made a show of looking around the room. "You tell me: whose idea of a vacation spot is this? People don't ordinarily force me to say things twice, Admiral, but I will, since this is your arena. What went wrong?"

"Nothing. It went right."

"Which is also, somehow, wrong."

Al considered his options, then shrugged. "There was an incident near your house. The first time, something went wrong. This time, it didn't."

"And because it didn't, some of the people on your staff expected me to suddenly be somewhere else."

"In a nutshell."

Powell reached for the orange Verbena had left him, made a slit in the skin with his thumbnail, and began to peel it. "Thanks for the insight."

"That's all you wanted?"

"In a nutshell," Powell said.

CHAPTER
SEVENTEEN

Sam took a long look at the sheet of paper Max had handed him: the printout of a story she'd pulled off one of the Internet news wires. KING JOE, the story was headlined. Then he took another look. He didn't like it any better the second time. "King?" he said.

Max could offer not much more than an apologetic shrug.

His eyes slid down the lines of copy. There were several quotes from his speech at the awards luncheon, comments from a number of people who had attended the lunch and a few who had not. When he found the words "hostile takeover," he cringed. "I thought I was well liked," he questioned Max.

"No one takes Senator Gilman seriously."

"He obviously takes himself seriously."

"Your approval rating is very high, Joe," Max protested. "There aren't many people in the country who haven't heard of you, or seen your picture. The posters of the Sexiest Man in the World cover were in bus shelters in seventeen major cities, and that issue of the magazine was one of the top ten bestsellers they've ever had. Everyone knows who you are. And because of that article, they think you're a great guy."

"Because of a magazine article."

Max peered at him curiously. He'd forgotten the sheet of paper was dangling from his hand, and she took it away from him and set it on the table beside his laptop. "You were all for that article when they said they were going to do it. Has something—" She hesitated, then went on, "Has something happened that I don't know about?"

"I doubt that much happens to me that you don't know about." Sam sighed.

She was able to remain businesslike for a moment, then had to turn away from him. She wrapped her arms around herself and roamed closer to the window, where she could look out onto Nirvana's outdoor pool area, decorated and planted to resemble a tropical beach. She'd been studying the pool only for a moment when her shoulders hunched. What she was thinking was as clear as if it had appeared in block type across her forehead. Sam took a peek for himself, knowing what he'd see: Kevin and Tracy sharing the same lounge chair, kissing frantically and completely ignoring the people around them.

"Did you get that woman and the little girl settled into the hotel?" he asked.

It took her a moment to change tracks. "Yes. They're on the third floor, in one of the mini-suites."

"No publicity, right?"

"Not unless the mother decides to say something."

"Nothing official."

"That's what I meant. The little girl has—"

Sam cut her off. "I'm sure I don't want to know. Do they need . . . Can we help them out?"

"Their medical bills are enormous."

"Take care of them, then. No publicity. And ask them not to contact the press themselves. Make it a condition of giving them the money. I don't really want any of this to end up in *People* magazine."

The tone of his voice derailed Max's focus on Kevin and Tracy. "The newspaper story won't do any damage, Joe. It'll get a lot of attention for a couple of days. They're just stirring the pot—that's what you said about that barb from Larry King. Your approval rating is—"

"I know. Very high."

"What's wrong, Joe?"

Sam sat at the edge of an armchair and folded his hands between his knees. "I'm trying to figure something out. What I wanted back in the beginning, and what I want now. I never meant any of it to be some enormous ego trip. I've always had choices—I'm aware of that. And I've thought them through. It may look as though I do things on impulse, but I don't. Everything is very carefully—" He paused before he said the last word. "Calculated."

Max frowned at him, puzzled. "I'm not sure anyone has ever thought of you as impulsive, Joe."

"Maybe that's a problem," Sam said.

"You're David Allen."

David swiveled his chair around and extended a hand. Understanding what the younger man meant by not getting up, Tom grabbed an empty chair, pulled it over, and sat down, peering at the computer monitor, at what to him looked like a collection of gobbledygook. "Retrieval program," David explained. "I've been working on it for three days. Well, hot and heavy for three days. We've had people studying it since Sam Leaped."

"But it doesn't work."

"In theory it does. Sam had it pretty much finalized not long after we broke ground. We can't figure it out. Everything else worked. But we've adapted this program nine ways to Sunday, and it's a no-go. I'm giving it another try, because he's so close to us in the time stream. Figured it couldn't hurt."

Tom was silent, watching David type. Then he glanced around as if he wanted to make sure he wouldn't be overheard, and asked, "Did you give any thought to the idea that it wasn't meant to work?"

"That Sam set it up wrong deliberately? Way ahead of you, Congressman."

"He really thought he'd come back."

David tipped his head from side to side, stretching his neck muscles. "You know, I have no idea what Sam really thought, or what he really thinks now. I took everything at face value. I figured he'd have no reason to lie to us. There was too much at stake." He paused, then said, "If your brother wanted out, sir, there are a lot of easier and way less expensive means of accomplishing that."

"He really shortchanged you, didn't he?"

"You mean because I haven't gotten my turn at bat? That's not his fault."

"Does anybody talk to him except Calavicci?"

"Gooshie went in there once. Into the Imaging Chamber. Other than that, no."

"Why not? Wouldn't it be better for Sam if he could work with a variety of people, like he did before this happened?"

David shook his head. "Dr. Beeks says it's his security blanket, knowing Al is going to show up every time. He wasn't keen on having Gooshie in there. And it's complicated getting other people linked into the system. Ziggy rejected Gooshie the first time."

"Ziggy?"

"The computer. You haven't met Ziggy? The voice that seems to come out of the middle of your head?"

Tom's eyes widened. "That's a computer? I thought it was some state-of-the-art kind of stereo loudspeaker."

"Good one," David snorted. "She's a computer. Although that's kind of like calling Erie a lake. She's a hybrid supercomputer, connected to Sam because part of her brain is connected to a chunk of Sam's neural tissue."

"He put a piece of his brain in the computer?"

"A tiny piece. Tiny pieces, actually. Can't see them without a microscope. There's bits of Al in there too," David said as he went on typing. "That's why Ziggy can connect the two of them so efficiently. Anybody else is a tougher sell. She can't connect Beeks at all. Though Verbena did do an external link once."

"External link?"

"She went in there with Al and held his hand. If you do that, it hooks you into the system. When she did it, she didn't get any audio—she couldn't hear what was happening where Sam was. But we've corrected that. Anybody who tries it now gets the A and the V."

"I see."

"Yeah. You would."

"That's interesting," Tom said.

• • •

The door opened but there seemed to be no one on the other side. It began to swing shut again, then reopened, apparently on its own. Kevin's room was dark, and out of the darkness came a disembodied giggle, followed by Kevin's voice. "Don't do that, okay? They're waiting for us."

"You don't want some more?"

Al chuckled softly and released an enormous billow of smoke. The way the smoke vanished as soon as it left the confines of his mouth was disconcerting enough to distract Sam from whatever was going on behind the door. "Let the kid have his fun," Al instructed his friend. "He waited long enough to get it. They can meet you downstairs."

Another giggle, and an increasingly halfhearted, murmured protest from Kevin. The boy and the owner of the giggle were right behind the door, Sam decided. Dove and Max were waiting for him to make the decision: proceed to the elevator, or remain here, listening to the teasing going on in the shadows of Kevin's room. Dove looked more bored than anything else. Max was pretending to study the pattern in the wallpaper. If he and Dove moved on toward the elevator, Sam knew, she'd find a reason to linger up here and give Kevin a generous piece of her mind.

"I can call room service," Sam offered.

Dove's left eyebrow crawled up toward his hairline. Frowning, he reached over and knocked on the half-open door. A face finally peered out, but it wasn't Kevin's. "You ready for dinner?" Dove asked.

The face broke into a huge, silly grin. "Uh-huh."

Dove's big hand found her elbow, grasped it, and tugged her out into the hallway. Behind her, the door hissed shut on its pneumatic hinge. Out in the brighter light of the corridor, Tracy was forced to compose herself, and she did so remarkably quickly. Sometime during the last couple of hours (though probably only a few minutes ago), she had changed her clothes again, this time into a tight, lacy black minidress Sam was almost certain had been purchased with Kevin's pocket money, and black high-heeled sandals. Her legs were bare, and her newly pedicured toes were on display. Her makeup was more dramatic now, and her hair was swept back into an elegant twist. If Al's "whoa" had applied before, it did so doubly now. She was stunning, something that was not lost on anyone standing in the corridor.

195

"Hi." She grinned. "Mr. Powell. And I guess you're Barbara? I'm sorry I didn't get to talk to you before. And you're . . . Oh, gosh. Kevin didn't tell me your name."

"Dove."

"Dove? Wow. You're Mr. Powell's bodyguard? Is that your real name?"

"Part of it," the bodyguard told her gruffly.

Finally, Kevin emerged from his room, wearing a black pin-striped suit and a sheepish expression that explained all too well why he'd waited inside for an extra couple of minutes. "Sorry," he muttered.

"Can we eat now?" Dove asked him.

Sam expected the walk to the restaurant to be something like the "Seventy-six Trombones" parade in *The Music Man*. To his surprise, although a number of heads turned to watch their progress through the lobby, no one approached them until they reached a wide foyer with an entrance to the casino on one side and the escalator to the mezzanine on the other. A cluster of Japanese tourists waiting a few steps inside the casino suddenly took note of the Powell party and several of them pointed. Heavily accented murmurs of "Sexiest Man in the World" floated across the foyer. Seconds later, Sam's group was surrounded by the enthusiastic Japanese, who all wanted pictures and autographs. They were thrilled to discover that Sam (whose semester of studying conversational Japanese had come back to him easily) was able to talk to them in their own language.

One of the tourists pointed to Max and asked a question that no one understood but Sam, who shook his head and responded with a few words. Another of the Japanese then pointed to Tracy and asked the same question. This time Sam pointed first to Tracy, then to Kevin, then smiled broadly as he answered.

"It's kinda nobody's business, isn't it?" Kevin asked crossly.

Dove shrugged his broad shoulders. "When you're famous, it's everybody's business."

This time, Tracy hadn't immediately maneuvered herself into Sam's space to guarantee that she would be in the pictures with him. She stood holding Kevin's hand while the tourists asked their questions and collected Sam's autograph. Then her expression began to grow more thoughtful. "Where did you learn to speak Japanese?" she asked Sam.

"College," he said as he continued to sign Powell's name on

Las Vegas guidebooks, imitation leather autograph books, note-pads, bus schedules, postcards, and the back of someone's hand.

"Is it hard to learn?"

"Not too bad."

"Could you teach me? You know, a little bit. 'What time is it?' and 'Good morning.' Things like that. There are a lot of Japanese people in L.A. It'd be interesting to be able to say something to them."

Dove murmured something and snorted softly. Though Sam was still busy entertaining the tourists, he had noticed—and so had Dove, Max, and Kevin—that Tracy had once again sidled into the "Picture Spot." Cameras continued to flash. Then a slightly different murmuring began and a girl a little older than Tracy began to ferret in her tote bag. She produced a plastic folder containing what had to be a favorite picture carefully clipped from a magazine, pointed to it, and began to explain to her companions what she had noticed. A moment later most of the group understood the connection and the words "Leo" and "girlfriend" joined the bits of English floating around the foyer. Suddenly, Sam had stopped being the center of attention.

"Kind of good at getting her picture taken, isn't she?" Dove murmured to Sam.

Kevin, who had moved a few steps away and was leaning unhappily against a wall, caught the remark and his mother's reaction to it.

"We should go," Sam announced.

"Yeah," Kevin said. "We should."

Nirvana's restaurant, located on a mezzanine at the front of the building, overlooking the Strip, more than deserved its five-star rating. Joe Powell's money and reputation certainly prompted an extra dusting of attentiveness on the part of the staff, but the food needed no embellishment.

"Oh, Sam," Al groaned, taking long, soulful looks at the plates of elegantly presented cuisine that had been set out at nearby tables. "You gotta tell me. You have to at least describe it for me."

Sam glanced at him, pretending to look past him at the couple occupying a table a few yards away. Dove noticed and tossed a look that way too. "Huh," the big man commented. "Didn't know they were still together. Thought that whole thing bit the dust after he went to Cannes with Gwyneth Paltrow."

They had been in the restaurant only a few minutes, but as Sam had expected, dinner had already become a somewhat lower-key repeat of the awards luncheon. People passing by on their way to or from their own tables stopped to offer Sam a few words of encouragement or congratulations. Several of them were bold enough to ask for contributions to their own pet causes.

"It'd be terrific PR if we could break that one-million mark, Joe," one man said.

Sam, who had no idea what the million dollars was intended to buy, offered a smile and promised, "I'll look into it as soon as I can."

"Knew we could count on you. Thanks, pal. Oh, by the way," the man said, plucking one of the pale green linen napkins from the table. "Sign this? My secretary really picked up on that Sexiest Man in the World thing. She'd get a thrill out of having an autograph." Max slipped a pen into Sam's hand while he was still puzzling over the idea of signing a napkin and he obediently scrawled Powell's name on the cloth. The man gave Sam a hearty pounding on the shoulder before he retreated.

"Bone-marrow testing center," Max explained.

"Oh," Sam said. "Well, write them a check. That's a good cause." Frowning, he asked her, "They're all good causes, aren't they?"

"Well . . ."

"Oh. Well, let me look at the paperwork, then."

"Of course, Joe," Max said.

The bone-marrow man had broken some ice; he had been gone only seconds when more people began to cluster around, soliciting attention from the Sexiest Man in the World under the guise of requesting contributions to their causes. Sam remained seated, as did Dove, though the bodyguard had pushed his chair back far enough from the table to allow himself to spring out of it in an instant. Again, Sam found himself signing a peculiar string of items, though this time no body parts were included. The people in the restaurant were a slightly more sophisticated crowd, he decided: still very much starstruck, but with a modicum of class.

"Joe!" a man boomed. "How about a picture, buddy, for old times' sake?"

Dove indicated his approval with a twitch of an eyebrow. Feeling more than a little like a circus animal, Sam climbed to his feet and managed to smile. After the picture had been taken, the man gave him a hearty slam Sam thought for a moment had dislocated his shoulder. He was nursing it back into its proper position when one of the hotel's executive staff approached the table.

"They asked me to pass the results on to you," the woman said. "The luncheon managed to tally some very nice figures."

She was gone as quickly as she'd arrived. "What?" Sam asked Max.

"I'll get you the numbers."

Max had started to rise. Sam shook his head and gestured her back into her chair. "No," he told her firmly. "Have your dinner. I'll . . . later."

Their waiter took advantage of a brief lull to quickly distribute appetizers around the table. As he did, Al sidled closer to his partner and leaned in, as if he could steal samples off Sam's plate. "This is cruel and unusual, pal. Ohhh, man. This guy, the chef—Pierre Antoli, his name is. One of the ten best in the world. Maybe five. Maybe *the* best. Okay, later. Later on, after they all go off to do the horizontal tango and go night-night, you can tell me about this meal. Pay attention, now, Sam, because I want every detail. I want to know how that sauce drifts through your taste buds like the nectar of the gods."

Sam put his hand to his mouth as if he needed to stifle a cough. "Stop it," he hissed.

"You say something, boss?" Dove asked.

"No." Sam smiled. "Nothing at all."

Sam's party had barely begun their soup course when they were interrupted by another round of visitors, including the celebrity couple Dove had noticed. Up to this point, Dove had kept his seat, though his right hand was positioned close to the flap of his unbuttoned suit coat. Now he unobtrusively moved to his feet. Sam was unsure why until he noticed that among the cluster of strangers around the table was the woman who had asked for an autograph that afternoon.

"Joe?" she asked in a tremulous voice. "Could I have a picture with you?"

She was holding a tiny point-and-shoot camera in unsteady hands. Before Sam could say yes or no, Kevin had reached out to take the camera and stepped back to frame the picture. "I do this all the time," he said with what was supposed to sound like enthusiasm as he squinted through the viewfinder, following a pointed glance at Tracy. "Oh, here, wait." The woman beamed as he straightened her collar, then tucked her arm around Sam's waist and gave him a squeeze. Sam grasped her hand to keep it from traveling any farther south and smiled at the camera as Kevin tapped the shutter release.

A moment later the woman was gone, and Sam sat down to make another attempt at enjoying his meal. But something was missing.

"She took it," Kevin said. "Your fork. She dropped it into her purse."

"Why?" Sam asked, bewildered.

"Good question," Dove muttered as he picked up his own fork.

"Should I be worried?"

Dove shook his head. "She doesn't fit the profile."

"What profile?"

The bodyguard nodded across the restaurant, at the table the woman had retreated to. The murmur of conversation in the room covered whatever she was saying, but Sam could see her flutter excitedly around her chair, gesturing and pointing in his direction, relating the details of her adventure to the three other women sitting there. When the women all turned to look, he offered them a small wave.

"He's right," Kevin confirmed. "I've seen a few of the real goofy ones. They don't generally hang around with other people. She seems okay. She's nervous, is all. Hey, Trace, remember that weird girl at Endings?"

"What?"

Tracy's guilty expression made her look as if she'd been caught pilfering money out of a cash register. She sat with her fork poised in midair and had stopped chewing a mouthful of food. Her cheeks reddened as she put the fork down and swallowed her mouthful.

"The one with the notebook," Kevin said.

"Oh. Sure."

The words came out barely louder than a whisper. Dove shook his head and, after assuring himself that no one new was approaching the table, returned to eating his dinner. Max, who had made a point of not looking at Tracy since the girl had emerged from Kevin's room, went on eating too. Al, however, moved around the table to take a look at Tracy's plate. The Observer had happily ogled her the whole way down from Powell's penthouse suite; now his expression was concerned and worried.

"Jeez, Sam," he mused. "This little girl really packs it away. She's eating like a stevedore. Like she hasn't had a good meal in a long time."

Sam glanced at the girl, who was still squirming under the attention Kevin had cast on her. Since the restaurant's forte was preparation and presentation, not "all-you-can-eat for $6.99," the portions each of them had been given were small. However, Tracy, who had worked her way through appetizer, soup, salad, and an entrée consisting of two delicate lamb chops surrounded by dainty slices of vegetables and rice, had done everything but lean over and lick the plates.

"Is everything all right?" Sam asked her.

Her head was tilted down; the only thing she could possibly see was the rim of her plate and the edge of the table. Kevin leaned over to brush a kiss against her cheek and whisper something in her ear. She nodded uncomfortably, slid out of her chair, and said quietly, "Excuse me, please," as she moved away from the table.

Kevin got up too and explained, "She didn't have any lunch," before he followed his girlfriend.

"Probably had about nine courses of Kevin," Al quipped. "No wonder she's chowing down. Gotta build her strength back up for the late-evening events."

Sam glared at him. Then, in response to the curiosity that earned from Max, he offered, "Muscle spasm."

"There's a great masseuse here, boss," Dove said. "Want me to have her come up?"

The young couple disappeared around a corner and Al promptly lost interest in them. Trotting back around the table, he hissed to Sam, "Tell him yes. Sam! Tell him yes. Just what you need to soothe those aching muscles. I checked out the health club this afternoon while you were in that meeting. The guy she was working on looked like he found his way to paradise. And she'll come do it in the privacy of your suite. You can turn the lights out and put the massage table over by the windows. Gaze out at the wonders of Vegas while the lovely Helga runs her well-trained hands up and down your tired, aching back."

"I'm fine," Sam said to Dove.

Dove shrugged and reached for his wineglass. "Soak in the Jacuzzi, then. Tried it out this afternoon. State-of-the-art."

"I didn't know there was a state-of-the-art hot tub."

"Adjustable-strength jets."

"Ooh," Al said.

Kevin and Tracy returned to the table a few minutes later. She seemed preoccupied; her forehead was creased into a deep frown. As they sat down, Sam pointed out the slices of creamy cheesecake that had been delivered while the young people were gone. "It's one of the chef's specialties," he explained. "I thought you might like some."

She ate a few bites of it, with Kevin holding her hand the whole time.

"Don't you feel well?" Sam asked.

"Headache," she told him. "I'm sorry. I . . ." It took her a moment to paste on a smile. "Maybe if I lie down for a while. I'll take a couple of aspirin." To Kevin, she added, "I do want to see the club. I'm sure I'll be fine in a little while."

"Do you want me to come?" Kevin asked.

She shook her head and slipped quickly away. Kevin, clearly not happy with her decision, picked up his fork and began to eat his dessert. After a moment he noticed his mother's expression and asked her sharply, "Are you gonna make some kind of crack now? She can't help it."

"Can't help what?" Al asked.

"I'm sure it was a carefully thought-out choice, bringing her here," Max said, tapping her fork against the table.

"So what does it hurt?" Kevin snapped.

"Keep your voice down, Kevin."

The boy pushed his plate away, leaned toward Sam, and explained in an angry stage whisper, "My girlfriend has a headache. She didn't get much sleep last night, she had a bag of stale airline pretzels for breakfast, and she was too excited to eat anything at that luncheon." His focus drifting back to his mother, he went on, "She's all wound up about being here, about looking good and saying and doing The. Right. Thing. She ate her dinner too fast and now she doesn't feel well. If that spoils your vision of this trip being like something out of an old movie magazine, then I'm sorry. People get headaches. People don't feel well. People are human and have feelings, except for you," Kevin hissed, "who seem to make a living out of being a gold-plated bitch."

Sam caught up with Kevin near the entrance to one of the hotel's jewelry shops. Dove, who had followed his employer, stood at the end of the short hallway that contained the shop and several others. As Sam approached, Kevin turned and pretended not to see the bodyguard.

"I'm sorry," he told Sam, calmer now but still with tension in his voice.

"Is Tracy bulimic?" Sam asked.

"Yeah."

"It took me a while to remember. I wasn't sure what seemed not quite right about how she looked. Puffy face, chipmunk cheeks. The way she was eating, as if she was sneaking the food, trying not to get caught. I'm sorry I didn't realize sooner."

"It's not your responsibility."

"Is she getting help?"

Kevin glanced past Sam at Dove, who was pretending to examine a display of expensive wristwatches. "She—when I met her, I thought she was really cute, and she's got a great laugh. She got kind of ticked off when DiCaprio didn't want anything to do with her, and I guess she thought she'd 'fix' him or something, because she came home with me. We spent the whole weekend in bed," he confessed with some hesitation, "and that was pretty great too. She's interested in a lot of things. If you wanted to talk politics with her, she can do that. She comes on a little strong sometimes, trying to get her picture taken and stuff. When we go to the clubs, she's always trying to get the paparazzi to notice her. She wants to be an actress, and it's not really about how much talent you've got, but getting people to notice you. But it—I guess the pressure gets to be too much for her. L.A.'s not the easiest place in the world to live. That whole 'Flavor of the Month' thing. Living up to people's expectations. You know what some guy did to her?"

Sam shook his head. "No."

"He made her show him her breasts, then he told her they weren't big enough. I mean, how much does that suck? He all but promised her a part in this movie, and then he pulls that crap."

"Maybe you should go up and make sure she's all right."

Kevin turned and leaned heavily against the narrow span of wall between two shop windows. "That's the thing. I tried a couple times to convince her to see somebody. But she doesn't have the money to go to a decent clinic or see a good doctor, and she says that stuff doesn't work anyway. And—" He stopped, pushing his hand through his hair. "I know this sounds pretty sleazy, but I don't know if I owe it to her to be the guy who changes her life for the better. I mean, I've only known her for a few weeks."

The boy hung his head, ashamed of what he'd said. "You're right," Sam told him. "It's a major commitment. Time, money, emotion."

"So what do I do?"

"Go for a walk."

"That's it?"

"Does she have family?"

"Yeah." Kevin shrugged. "But they don't live out here. They're in Illinois or something."

Sam thought for a moment, then patted the boy on the arm. "Go for a walk. And think about maybe apologizing to your mother for calling her a bitch in front of a roomful of people."

Sam waited almost an hour, until after he had finished his last scheduled appointment of the day, then knocked softly and opened the door of Kevin and Tracy's room with the key card he had picked up at the front desk. He'd known what he would find, but he was still startled by the wild scattering of candy wrappers, potato chip bags, chocolate milk cartons, and ice cream containers strewn around the room. The pillows had all been pulled off the bed and were piled on the floor; Sam knew Tracy had used them to prop herself up, leaning against them as if she were taking part in an ancient Roman feast. Her black minidress, stockings, and shoes were there too, thrown into a corner.

She was in the bathroom now, with the door closed, but Sam could tell by the silence, and the odor drifting underneath the door, that she'd finished getting rid of everything she'd eaten. He knocked again, gently, then opened the door.

Tracy looked up at him miserably out of a face that was sweaty, puffy, and tear-streaked. Her eyes were badly bloodshot and there was a trickle of blood on her chin. The wavy hair she'd fixed so attractively two hours ago hung loose, damp, and limp around her face. There was vomit on her chin and her hands. The fact that Joe Powell had walked in on her, finding her dressed only in bra and panties, clinging to a vomit-spattered toilet, she seemed to regard as just one more minor downturn to her evening. She was too strung out to object, or to try to cover herself.

Sam did it for her, locating a thick terrycloth robe hanging on the back of the door. He crouched beside her and wrapped the robe around her, then soaked a washcloth at the sink and used it to sponge off her face. She let him lead her to bed and tuck her in without a word, like a sleepy child, and watched him out of squinted eyes as he gathered up the debris and stuffed it into the room's two wastebaskets. When he had finished with that, he flushed the toilet, used another washcloth to wipe it and the spattered tile floor, then tossed the stained cloth into the wastebasket.

Finally, he sat beside Tracy on the bed and tucked her in more carefully. "How long have you been doing this?" he asked quietly.

He could barely see her slender shoulders move in response. "Almost six years."

Sam shuddered. "Do you want help?"

"I tried."

"Maybe you tried the wrong thing."

She tensed under the covers. "Not the hospital. I won't go there again. It doesn't work."

"I know," Sam told her.

Tracy began to cry, silently at first, then in big, gulping sobs. "They don't get it," she wept. "I *have* to do this."

"I know."

Peering up at him through her tears, she studied his face, then jerked her head back and forth. "How would you know? You're not—you don't do this."

"No. But I've known people who did." Sam considered his options for a moment, then gathered Tracy up and held her close to him, letting her continue to shake and cry, rubbing the small of her back with one hand. "One of them died," he told her. "The other one was able to find a way out. She does it one day at a time. You're going to have to do that—one day at a time, maybe one hour at a time. I can make some calls in the morning, if you want me to. I'll talk to my friend. She can help you."

"Why would you do that?"

"Because Kevin said you're fun to be with when you're not

205

bingeing. Maybe he'd like to see you reach a point where you're fun to be with all the time. Maybe a lot of people would." He paused, then went on, "What I'm thinking of doesn't cost anything except commitment. But a therapist would, if you think that would help too. I'll cover whatever it takes."

Tracy hiccuped and gulped a couple of times, then scrubbed at her face with her fingertips. "You're a nice man."

"Why don't you take a shower," Sam suggested, "then get some sleep."

"What about Kevin?" Tracy snuffled.

"I'll find him another place to sleep. You'll see him in the morning." With a final pat on the back, Sam got up from the bed and moved toward the door.

"You're a nice man, Mr. Powell."

Sam smiled at her. "I try to be, as much as they'll let me."

Al was waiting for him in the corridor, pacing and clutching the handlink. "Who're you gonna call?" he demanded.

"Bonnie Worther, in Baltimore."

"Oh," Al said. "I was afraid you were gonna try to call Beeks." Sam went on past him, and Al pivoted on one heel and trotted along beside him, down the hall toward the double doors of the Powell suite. The Observer's head was tipped to one side, listening. Sam was still a few yards from the door when Al announced, "Beeks thinks you're tossing these things off too easily. Fixing the world with Powell's checkbook." Then he barked, to someone not in the hallway, "Yeah, I know you didn't intend for me to tell him that."

Sam stopped walking. "Tell Verbena to walk a mile in my shoes before she feels compelled to tell me I'm doing this wrong."

"She says—"

"Spare me what she says. Does she want me to let that girl spend another three or four days doing this, while I study her like some lab experiment? Or worse yet, not do anything about her problem at all? Yes, I've only known her for a few hours. But she's had this problem for six years. I'm going to introduce her to Bonnie—who is well known enough that she won't question a phone call from the fourth richest man in the country, who will tell her he saw her on *Oprah* and because he never forgets a name or a face, recalled that she's one of the country's leading experts on eating disorders. She and Tracy can work together for however long it takes. I'll pay to move Tracy to Baltimore and set her up in a comfortable apartment. I'm very sure Joe Powell won't miss whatever it costs." Al didn't reply, so Sam added stubbornly, "It's nice in Baltimore this time of year."

"Yeah," Al grumbled, "but in about another three weeks, it's gonna be humid enough to kill you."

"Tell Verbena I know what I'm doing."

"What *are* you doing?" The voice came first, then the body: Kevin, who had come off the elevator and had stood around the corner, listening. His face was filled with confusion and distrust.

"Kevin . . ."

"Why are you out here talking to yourself?"

"Uh-oh," Al murmured.

Sam put together as genuine a smile as he could manage. "I was thinking out loud."

Kevin shook his head sharply. "No, you were having half of a conversation. Do you do this a lot?"

"Here we go." Al sighed. "Doo wah, doo wah, doo wah ditty, tell us about the boy from Nut Job City."

CHAPTER

EIGHTEEN

Sam gave his partner a look that said two words very clearly: Get out. "Sorry, Sam," Al sputtered, punching into the handlink the command that would open the Imaging Chamber door. "I'll get outta your way."

Then he was gone, and so was Kevin. At least, Kevin had fled as far as the penthouse elevator, where he stood banging on the call button, growing more and more upset when the car failed to arrive. When the doors finally did open, to his dismay Sam got into the elevator with him. Keeping his eyes firmly away from Sam, he pressed the button for lobby, then stood close to the control panel as the car descended.

"This is a nightmare," he mumbled. "It's a fucking nightmare."

"Kevin . . ."

"Don't talk to me, okay?" The boy seemed to be addressing the control panel rather than Sam. "A fun-filled vacation in Vegas. With my mother who hates me, the guy who's banging her and doesn't see it as a problem that he's not in love with her, my girlfriend who can't eat a big meal without puking it up afterward, and my mother's boss, who carries on conversations with himself. There was a guy out in front of the MGM talking about the end of the world. At least he's obviously a fruitcake." He was silent until the doors opened onto the small alcove adjoining the lobby, then said a little louder, "I'm out of here."

Sam pointed out quietly, "Your things are all up in the penthouse."

"That's not my stuff. It's your stuff. You paid for it. I'm sorry I wasted your money." Shoulders hunched up around his ears, Kevin stalked across the lobby to the Guest Information desk and waved to get the attention of one of the staff there. "Where's the bus station?"

Dove, who had been watching the elevator as he shopped in the hotel's newsstand, walked rapidly up to Sam with a newspaper tucked under his arm. "What's the kid freaked out about?"

"Nothing," Sam said. "Leave us alone, would you?"

"I can back off. But there's too many people around here, boss. Take him back upstairs if you want to talk to him, why don't you."

"I'd have to knock him unconscious first."

Kevin had started to move away from the desk, toward the hotel's main entrance. When he noticed Sam and Dove watching him, he changed direction and strode into the casino. Dove raised a brow: an offer to go retrieve the boy himself, but Sam shook his head and began to follow Kevin, gesturing to Dove to stay back as far as he could. Halfway through the casino, Kevin lost his sense of direction and stopped at a point from which rows of slot machines fanned out like the spokes of a wheel, his fists clenched, his head down.

Sam came only close enough for the boy to hear him over the cacophony of the machines. "Kevin."

The boy shuddered, then gathered up enough teenage bravado to allow himself to reply. "Mom knows best, you know. We should have listened to her. This was a stupid idea. I never should have left L.A. Forget I ever came. They said there's a bus leaving in an hour or so. I'll go back home."

"You don't have to go back to L.A. You can stay here," Sam said, then reconsidered slightly. Hanging only a few inches from

Kevin's head was a sign reminding hotel patrons that no one under twenty-one was allowed in the casino. "Well, not *right* here. Why don't we walk over to the Mirage? Aren't Siegfried and Roy's white tigers on display over there?"

Kevin gaped at him. "First, I'm not five years old. I can do without going to the zoo. And second, those tigers are probably wondering what the hell they're doing in Vegas right now, which is a question I share with them."

"You wanted to come."

"No. Tracy wanted to come."

"And you wanted to come to be with Tracy. To impress Tracy."

"So kill me. I had to come up with something. Stacked next to Leonardo DiCaprio, I don't amount to diddly shit."

Sam had to step aside to allow a large black woman in a sunflower-yellow pantsuit to cruise by. As she passed him, a ten-dollar chip slipped out of the handful she was clutching and bounced a couple of times on the carpet. Sam stooped to retrieve it and took a few quick steps to catch up with her, not surprised when she greeted the return of her chip with a scowl much like the one that seemed to be permanently plastered across Kevin's face.

"You kiss a lot of babies, too?" Kevin asked when Sam returned.

"I was brought up to be polite, and courteous, and considerate," Sam said. "So kill me."

Kevin snorted loudly. "Give me a break. People wait on you hand and foot. Where are you considerate? What, do you say 'thank you' when my mother wipes your nose for you?"

Sam took the boy by the arm and steered him far enough away to satisfy the gamblers who had begun to display their annoyance at having their concentration disturbed. "Your mother doesn't wipe anybody's nose, except, I assume, her own. Fine, find fault with my life and the way I live it. You were pretty content to take my money up till a few minutes ago. Now I'm number one on your blacklist. Why? Because of Tracy? Or because I was talking to myself out in the hall?"

"Because . . ."

"Well?" Sam pressed.

"Because this whole thing is just so bogus."

"What whole thing?"

"This place. These people." The boy gestured, taking in the whole casino in one sweep of his hand. "They work their butts off all year long and put aside as much money as they can so they can come down here and throw it all away. Tell me they're not throwing it away! How many of these people leave here having turned a profit? They lose hundreds, thousands of dollars. But boy, would they yelp if their taxes got raised by the amount of money they're feeding into those slot machines. I mean, look at her," Kevin said. "That's pathetic." He pointed: about thirty feet away, a young woman in an elaborate satin-and-lace wedding gown sat feeding coins into a slot machine. Her veil, disconnected from her fussy hairdo, lay on the carpet at her feet beside her discarded white pumps. At the facing row of slots, an older woman in a turquoise silk dress and a man in a dark suit sat side by side, obeying their own compulsions to gamble. "The happiest day of her life," Kevin scoffed. "Where's her husband? What are those people doing here?"

He wandered off, down another row of slots, and stopped near a blackjack table. Sam caught up to him with a few rapid steps and tried to nudge him back toward the gift shops. "You're not supposed to be in here."

"Like anybody cares. I look old enough, and I'm with you."

"Still."

"Oh, come on." Kevin gestured with a flick of his hand, taking in a couple of casino security guards who were far more fascinated by a craps player in a tissue-thin blouse than by his presence near the slot machines. "I walked around here for two hours before Tracy got here this afternoon and nobody paid any attention to me at all. They all know I'm with you. They probably wouldn't actually let me play, but nobody wants to piss you off by telling me I can't go where I please." He thought for a moment, then snickered. "Maybe I should go find Tracy. We could get married."

"How about if we just get some . . . ice cream?" Sam suggested.

"Ice cream? You think I'm five."

"I can't buy you a drink. You're too young to drink."

"You better watch it. You display too much of an interest in me, and the tongues'll start wagging."

"Kevin . . ."

The boy shook his head, strode across the casino, through the lobby, and out the main entrance into the neon-lit Las Vegas night. He stood close to a cluster of taxis and limos with his hands in his pockets, his expression challenging someone to notice him.

Sam came out a moment later and waved away an inquiring cabdriver looking for a fare. As if he had never met Kevin, he walked on past the boy, down the edge of the long driveway toward Las Vegas Boulevard. He knew without looking how long the boy stalled before following him. Kevin stayed three or four paces behind, both hands clenched, continuing his loud tirade against Las Vegas inside his head.

Sam stopped walking in front of a narrow shop whose display window announced BEST LAS VEGAS SOUVENIRS HERE! T-SHIRTS $5.99 BIG SELECTION!!! Kevin kept his distance, his hands now crammed into his pockets.

"Actually," Sam said, as if he were addressing the display window, "I hate it here too."

"Then why'd you come?"

"They told me I had to."

"You're the man. The big cheese. You don't have to do a thing you don't want to. All you had to do was say, 'I'm not going.' Who was going to argue with you? My mother? Dove?"

Sam replied quietly, "No matter who you are, Kevin, you still have to play by somebody's rules."

"So why did you come here?"

"You really want me to answer that."

"Yeah," Kevin said sharply. "I do."

"I came here for you."

The boy gave Sam a broad look of disbelief, then swung his head away and stood watching a bus inch its way down the boulevard. "So is this the part where you say you're here to tell me God loves me?"

Sam shook his head, knowing Kevin wouldn't see the gesture. "No. I came . . . to try to bring you and Max together."

"You did."

"Yes. Otherwise, yes, I would have begged off. I hate Las Vegas."

"There's not gonna be any great epiphany," Kevin said. "My mother isn't going to come to her senses and realize that she's shortchanged me all these years and beg for my forgiveness just because we're spending a few days in the same building. That's not who she is. If you think it's a possibility, you're not paying attention."

Sam nodded slowly. "I know."

"Are you an angel?" It took Sam a second to realize the boy was mocking him. Kevin stared at him, waiting. "Did she even tell you what happened?" Kevin challenged.

"In reference to . . . ?"

"Me. Where she got me from."

"No. No, she hasn't."

"She was seventeen years old. You know, when you've gotten out of high school and you figure that qualifies you as an adult. You figure you can make all your own decisions, and none of them is going to come back to haunt you. She went to the beach one day with a bunch of her girlfriends and she met this guy. Good-looking, I guess. They liked each other, so when the girl-friends went home, she stayed with him and they watched the sun go down, walked up and down the beach, got something to eat. He was staying in one of those little dive motels in Santa Monica. One of those rooms where you can stand in the middle and touch the walls."

"Did she tell you all this?"

"No. My grandparents did."

Kevin's arms drifted out and up, his fingers extended. Sam realized with an ache growing in his chest that the boy had gone to that motel, to that room, just to see. Just to rub his own nose in his mother's decision.

"The guy was only there to visit," Kevin went on. "A couple days later he went home."

"Did she tell him?" Sam asked quietly.

"What, that he had a son? He knows he has a son. He knows he's got three of them. And a daughter. They all live in North Carolina, with him and his wife. See, that's the good part. My grandparents told me they'd talked to him, and everybody had decided it was best that he just stick with his old life in North Carolina. I don't know if they ever really talked to him at all. But I badgered my grandfather into telling me the guy's name. He broke down after a while. Said he'd read enough magazine articles to know it was important to me to know who my father was. I'm the same as everybody else, he figured. I wanted to know, and he said I was grown up enough to make that decision. Maybe I thought there was a chance that if I confronted the guy, he'd accept me. Henry Miller, he told me. Runs a tire store out-side of Durham. So I called Information and got the number for the tire store and I called. The guy who answered said Henry wasn't there—he was off on a trip with his wife, celebrating their twenty-fifth wedding anniversary." Kevin hesitated, then said sharply, "You do the math. The bastard had already been married for five years when he did the happy with my mother."

"I'm sorry, Kevin."

"Yeah, well. It happens all the time, right?"

"Probably more often than anyone would like to think."

The boy twisted away again and scrubbed at his face with the palm of his hand. "I don't know who decided abortion wasn't an option. Probably my grandfather. He wanted a son. His whole life, he wanted a son, and Barbara Ann sure wasn't it. So they kept me, and my grandparents treated me like their son. I was in, like, the fourth grade before I realized that Barbara wasn't my sister. She taught me to call her Bobbie. It sounded sort of like 'Mommy.' "

He fell silent then, as if he were afraid to say anything more. "I . . ." he said, then had to stop again because he had started to cry.

A second later there was a handkerchief in his hand courtesy of Dove, who had been only a few steps away. "Suck it up, kid," he said quietly. "There's a pool table up in the suite. Come on, I'll shoot a couple racks with you."

"I want to go home," Kevin said miserably.

"Not happening tonight. You get some sleep, Max'll get some sleep, and tomorrow we're all gonna act like we like each other or I'll pound the shit out of you." Kevin blinked and snuffled and blew his nose loudly into the handkerchief, something Dove seemed to think was funny. "Besides, the boss wants to make you an offer."

Kevin frowned at Sam. "What offer?"

"A job," Sam said.

"Doing what?"

"Talk about it in the morning," Dove said firmly. "It's not good, being out here on the street." When Kevin didn't move, Dove gave him a gentle thump on the side of the head. "Pool. We'll order up some nachos and beer."

"He's too young to drink," Sam said.

"What planet are you from?" Dove asked.

214

CHAPTER NINETEEN

"You know a kid named Kevin?" Al asked.

"Max's son? I know of him. I'm paying for his education."

"But you've never met him."

"I don't know that I need to." Before Al could object, Powell went on, "I've funded several scholarships. Six, I think. I've never met any of the recipients. No, strike that. I met one a few years ago."

"But Kevin is—"

"Max's son. My assistant's son." Powell thought for a moment. "Does Dr. Beeks have children?"

"A son."

"And have you met him?"

"No," Al said.

"Then I think I rest my case. But what's your point? Is there a problem with Kevin?"

"There's a problem with Max."

Powell finished the last few bites of the sandwich Al had found him eating and wiped streaks of Russian dressing off his fingers with a napkin. By the time he was through, he had read a good deal more from Al's expression than was actually there. Or, more than Al thought was actually there. "Someone's been hurt," he said.

"Car accident. Everybody's fine."

"Is it Thursday? There was an accident on the way to the airport? Or from the airport? What happened?"

"Paparazzi."

The one word was enough. "But no one was actually hurt."

"No. How much do you know about Kevin?"

Powell made a show out of folding the paper napkin before he decided to play along. "That he spends a little too much time in nightclubs to fit into the commonly accepted image of a 'good kid' who's likely to make something impressive out of his life. That he occasionally lets himself be influenced by the wrong people. That even though 'illegitimate' doesn't mean what it did when I was his age, it's still earned him enough sniggering and teasing to make him mistrust people. That he'd like very much to have the kind of family he sees on reruns on *Nick at Nite,* even though that kind of family doesn't actually exist. Is that enough? Or did you mean, do I know whether he prefers Coke or Pepsi?"

Al sat down and propped his elbows on the arms of the chair. "I mean, do you know he's a good kid."

"Perfectly well."

"Enough to do more for him than write him some checks?"

"What did you have in mind?"

"He's there now," Al explained. "In Vegas. With his mother, and Dove, and . . . you."

"Dr. Beckett."

"Who everyone thinks is you. Kevin showed up at the house, you and he hit it off, and you invited him to come along."

Powell got up from his chair and wandered around the Waiting Room, the soles of his slippers scuffing softly against the tile. "We hit it off."

"Uh-huh."

"And what would be Dr. Beckett's point in doing that?"

216

"The kid wants some attention from his mother. Sam felt sorry for him."

"Get him out of there."

"Sam thinks he was sent there to—"

A sudden shift in Powell's posture made Al stop talking. "Dr. Beckett may not be in control of where he is, or who he is," Powell said sharply, "but he most certainly is in control of what he says. I don't want him to 'hit it off' with Kevin Maxwell. Tell him to send the boy home."

"Why?" Al asked calmly.

"He's a security risk."

"Oh? Lemme sit here and watch your nose grow longer, Pinocchio."

"I'm glad you're amused," Powell growled. "Forgive me if I don't see the humor in this situation. Dr. Beckett is sitting in the middle of my life, dabbling with it to suit himself. Pardon me if I object."

"You don't object to Max. Why should you object to Kevin?"

"I don't need to explain myself to you, Calavicci."

"He gonna make you look bad, cover boy?"

Powell leaned against the exam table and folded his arms. "That suits you. It's probably been your modus operandi since you learned to string a sentence together. Attack first. Words, if that's good enough. Fists if it's not. You were Golden Gloves, as I remember. It felt good, didn't it? Putting all the hate, all the insecurity, all the pain into your fists and pounding." He clenched both hands into fists and moved his body into a boxing stance. "Displace a little of the rage." He threw a punch, then another. "How old were you when you learned to hit? Four? Five?" Abruptly, he stopped moving and again leaned against the table. "You're not going to get anywhere by mocking me, Admiral. I'm a prisoner here, but I don't have to pretend you intimidate me. If I'm in any danger, it's not from you. It's from the disaster your friend Dr. Beckett is trying to make out of my life."

It took several seconds for Al to calm himself enough to reply. "He's trying to—"

"Help?"

"He's good at what he does."

"As am I."

"Somebody," Al said, "thinks there's a piece of it that Sam can do better than you could. The first time, Max got hurt in that accident. She was in a coma for almost five months before she died. Because Sam was there this time, she got shaken up. That's all. But he's still there, so there's something more he's supposed to do before you get your life back. He thinks it's that he supposed to reconcile Max and her kid. I figure that's right."

Powell's features tightened. "And who decides? What if Max doesn't want her relationship with her son to be any different than it is? He's not living in a box under a freeway off-ramp. He's going to an expensive school and he lives in an eight-hundred-dollar-a-month apartment. He's well fed and has a social life he apparently enjoys. His grandparents live nearby and he sees them several times a week." He paused, giving Al an opening, but Al didn't take it. "Max finagled herself an appointment with me two years ago. She came with a glowing recommendation from one of the attorneys who handles my real-estate holdings. She had no experience as a personal assistant, other than a few months catering to a self-indulgent actor who liked to throw cell phones out the car window. But she all but had 'determination' painted across her forehead. She asked for a six-week trial run during which she'd be on call twenty-four hours a day and would not say no to any ridiculous chore I decided I didn't want to do for myself or inflict on someone else. She passed with flying colors. She keeps a hundred different balls in the air and has dropped mighty damn few. That's what she's chosen to do with her life. She wants to go with me to Washington, which is fine with me. Let me point something out to you: 'freedom of choice' doesn't apply strictly to the right to have an abortion. She had a lapse in judgment twenty years ago and she gave birth to a child who was raised in a loving environment and has turned out to be intelligent, polite, considerate, and for the most part reliable, and unless he decides to reject everything he's been taught, will more than likely get himself a decent job, have a family, and go on living in Southern California. Max made two choices: one, to have him, and two, to set up a relationship in which she's more or less his sister. She didn't feel capable of being the kind of mother he needed and she turned the job over to someone who was. Now, if Kevin objects to that, I think that's Kevin's problem, not Max's. You cannot force people into being something they are not."

Al cupped his chin in his palm and sat looking at the plate that had held Powell's sandwich. There were enough stray bits left on it to tell him it had been roast beef with lettuce. Dinner was an attractive thought, but his stomach was somewhere close to his ears. "I can tell Sam that," he said after a while. "But I don't think he's gonna believe it."

"His father doesn't even know he exists," Sam said with a sigh.

Al took a long look at the disaster that was the penthouse's rumpus room and moaned. "Saaaam. Who did this?"

"We did."

"Who's we?"

"Me and Dove and Kevin. Boys' night out. Boys' night in, since Dove wouldn't let us go anywhere."

The Observer did a quick count. With each added number, his eyebrows rose a little higher. "There's nineteen empty beer bottles here, Sam."

Sam shook his head, then settled it deeper into the cradle formed by the top of the sofa cushion. "We only drank maybe two apiece. Maybe three. It's not going to do any worse than give us all a headache. And don't worry, nobody drove."

"You know what this is gonna look like in the tabloids, if Housekeeping gets a picture of this mess?"

Sam pressed a finger to his lips. "I'll clean it up."

"And do what? Put the empties in your luggage? You think Room Service didn't notice you were ordering a truckload of brewskis? Wait a minute, three apiece, that's still only nine. You didn't have other people in here, did you?"

"You can't smell things here."

"No," Al groused. "Why?"

Sam plucked his shirt away from his chest. Even in the dim light Al could see that it was damp.

"You had a beer fight?"

Sam pointed out a hardened glob of cheese stuck to the side of the pool table. "And a food fight."

"Sam!"

"And a belching contest. I think I won that one." Sam shifted his body slightly and nodded at the big-screen TV in the corner. "I think it was after that. But maybe it was before the belching but after the nacho fight. Kevin ordered up a movie."

Al asked with a wince, "What kind of movie?"

"I'm not sure if it had a title. Two blond sisters and a guy in coveralls that said 'Don's Plumbing and Electrical.'"

"I saw that one," Al said appreciatively, then realized what he was saying. "You were watching porno movies?"

"Hmm." Sam nodded. "We lost the four ball. You don't see it anywhere, do you?"

"You were watching porno movies. Sam! You can't watch porno movies! You can't dump beer all over a fifteen-thousand-dollar ivory-inlaid mahogany pool table! You can't get cheese in the chandeliers! You're Joe Powell! Saaaam!" The Observer moved in closer to his partner, who seemed to have dozed off. Before he could let out another howl of dismay, Sam opened one eye and peered at him. "You're making a mess here!" Al sputtered. "Didn't I tell you, don't make a mess out of this?"

"I'm under a lot of stress. I needed to let off some steam."

"This isn't like you."

"What isn't? Having a good time? Don't worry about it. Dove said he can take care of the whole thing. He'll have some people come in. That's what he said. In the morning. He'll make it all look like it never happened. No pictures. Nobody from House-keeping. He knows people who fix things. Besides. We had a *swell* time," Sam told his partner. "It took Kevin's mind off his problems."

"And created whole new ones."

"Stop worrying about the campaign," Sam said firmly. It took some effort for him to straighten himself up; the soft couch cushions kept collapsing in the wrong direction and threatening to tip him over. "I can't believe Powell never has a good time. He can't possibly be that stuffy. Nobody's that stuffy. You can't tell me he doesn't get plowed once in a while. Dove acted like nothing was out of the ordinary. Well, a little out of the ordinary. Not that I'm plowed. I'm fine. We had a good time."

Al held his head between his hands. "Don't tell me you had strippers up here."

"We didn't have strippers. Nobody took their clothes off, except those two sisters in the movie. I'm not sure they had clothes on to begin with."

"Where's everybody now?"

Sam thought for a moment. "Sleeping." Then he added, "I was trying to sleep," and let himself tip over to lie on his side on the couch, his legs dangling off the front, uncomfortably tangled.

"Sam!" Al shouted into his ear.

The eye popped open again. "You're really getting to be a nuisance here, Al."

"We found Kevin's father."

"You didn't need to bother. Kevin found Kevin's father. Only Kevin's father doesn't know he is. Kevin's father. He has a wife and a tire store. He'd like to have a father. Kevin. But he has a man and a tire store."

"Three bottles of beer, my butt," Al said.

"Maybe it was four."

"Or maybe Dove and Kevin had three apiece and you drank the other thirteen. Sam! Where's your brain?"

"Ziggy has some of it," Sam offered cheerfully.

"Do you wanna pull yourself together and listen to me?"

Using one arm as a lever, Sam managed to prop himself upright again. "I'm not that drunk. I can listen. Operating heavy machinery would not be a good idea. But I'm ready to listen. I'm listening."

"The kid knows about his father?"

"Between what everyone told him, and what he found out for himself, he knows," Sam sighed, sounding a lot more sober than he had a minute ago. "I think he had the plot of a TV movie in mind: that he'd show up on the guy's doorstep and be welcomed with open arms, and become part of some big, homespun, blended family. But it's not like that. The man who fathered him was cheating on his wife when he did it. He doesn't know about Kevin, and I'm sure he doesn't care."

"There's a lot like him." Sam's mouth opened, but Al cut him off. "Don't start," the Observer insisted. "Twenty years ago was before AIDS. Before the big 'safe sex' push. Max was a kid, and Henry-boy was a young stud who wanted to play a little 'hide the weenie' with a pretty girl. If they thought about birth control, I guarantee you it was a fleeting thought."

"Of course," Sam scoffed.

Al circled around to confront his friend, the link to Ziggy clutched in one fist and his cigar in the other. "Okay, picture this scenario. Lisa. You remember Lisa?"

"My Lisa, or your Lisa?" Sam said dryly.

"Yours."

"I remember."

"Pretty, pretty girl, Sam. Bet she was a good kisser. Bet you thought about her a lot. Bet you thought *those* kinda thoughts

221

about her a lot." Al stuck the cigar in his mouth and began to talk around it. "Now, you're under oath in the Court of Calavicci. You stand there and tell me that even one of those thoughts had a rubber as part of the set decoration."

Sam didn't reply.

"Ha," Al snorted.

"You can't compare anything I might have done with Lisa Parsons in my imagination with what those two people actually did," Sam insisted. "Henry whatever-his-name-is was a married adult. And Max—her name was Barbara then, you know. Barbara Ann. Barbara Ann was seventeen. Seventeen is old enough to—"

Al cut him off again. "Old enough to what? You're makin' my brain hurt, Sam. Seventeen. Seventeen! When the whole world is ahead of you, and nothing bad is ever going to happen. You're immortal. And anything is possible. It's a gorgeous summer night, a pretty girl, a good-looking guy, you feel all warm and snuggly and you just put things where they fit. Who thinks? I didn't think. Did you think? No, forget that. You never had any warm summer nights."

"Yes I did."

"It's a matter of matter over—" Something in Sam's tone made Al stop. "You did?"

"In Cambridge. I had a lot of them."

Al's expression shifted so subtly that anyone other than Sam might not have noticed the change.

"And we were always very careful," Sam added.

"Well," Al blurted, "you can't compare a couple of MIT geeks with a guy who runs a tire store. Different perceptions of how and why the clock ticks, Sam."

"She didn't go to MIT. And that bothers you."

"That your summer sweetie didn't go to MIT?"

"No. That I brought her up. That I remember her. That I remember what her eyes looked like when they first opened in the morning." He paused. "It's bugging you that I remember anything at all."

"That's crazy. Look, Sam, I gotta go. We're using up way too much juice here. Gotta let the Imaging Chamber cool down for a while." Al's fingers hammered out a code on the handlink as he spoke, and when the door began to open he dove for it faster than any paroled prisoner had ever galloped toward an open penitentiary gate.

"Al," Sam barked.

The Observer stopped, his back to Sam, standing slump-shouldered in the brilliant light of the Doorway.

"It's eleven steps down the ramp."

"Wha . . ." Al murmured.

"From the threshold to the foot of the ramp. Eleven steps. Though . . . it's probably a little more for you because your legs are shorter. Ziggy's console is to the left. The door to the corridor is straight ahead. There are workstations to the right. Three of them."

Al stood in the light, cowering, frozen.

"You're on Level Ten. The Accelerator, the Waiting Room, the Imaging Chamber. All of Control. Laid out like the spokes on a wheel, with the Accelerator in the center." Sam's voice grew softer as he went on, and he seemed to stop seeing Al; instead, he was seeing what lay ahead of him as he walked through his Project, his mind's eye as clear as a photograph in spite of the haze produced by all that beer. "You have an old leather couch in your office. You brought it with you from Star Bright. Your favorite place to take a nap."

Al's fingers tightened around the handlink until they began to throb. "Jesus, Mary, and Joseph," he whispered.

"How much of it was true, Al?" Sam asked. "Everything you've told me since I Leaped. About my life. About your life. How much of it did you invent to make me happy, or calm me down? If we were ever friends—tell me the truth now."

"I can't," Al said, and fled through the Doorway.

CHAPTER
TWENTY

The sound tickled its way into his mind, gentle and persistent. It floated there, clinging, in spite of his efforts to squirm away, teasing him like a feather, a thread, a stray hair, a dust fiber. He was grunting and mumbling in his sleep, trying to slide out from under its touch.

Squeak.

You know you know don't you you know even though you tell yourself you don't

Sam jerked himself awake and flung himself over onto his belly, burrowing his face into the sofa cushion.

It brushed against his shoulder, warm and teasing.

Why don't you admit you know?

"Dammit!" He pushed away from the cushion with both hands with enough momentum that he was afraid of rebounding off the ceiling. He did end up sitting upright, but his legs were tangled and it took him a moment to remember how to straighten them out. His head felt as big as the prizewinning pumpkin Ralphie Jorgenson's father had hauled down to the county fair the year he and Ralphie were in seventh grade.

The smell of the beer, soaked into his clothes, the carpet, the upholstery—my God, it was *everywhere*—made his stomach do a slow roll. *What are you, twelve? You couldn't figure out you were going to be sick afterward.*

Al was right. It was a stupid thing to do. The room is a mess.

But they'd all been laughing, he and Dove and Kevin. Like longtime buddies. Like three people who actually had something in common, other than . . .

Other than Max. And boy, is she going to be pissed in the morning.

The room's single window (*just the one, but it's a big sucker*) was hidden behind the heavy draperies Dove had pulled shut, explaining that the people on New York, New York's roller coaster could see them in here, giggling and shaking beer bottles until the spray exploded out of them in sour-smelling, foamy geysers. That had made Kevin laugh hysterically, explaining between bouts of giggles that even if someone on the coaster had a camera with a zoom lens, they weren't likely to be able to focus it in time.

Did I moon *those people?* Sam wondered.

Running the air conditioner might help, he decided. It took him a while to find it, hidden in a cabinet near the window, and not much less time to figure out how to operate it. Finally, he pushed a wide blue button and gasped at the frigid air that began to pour out of the vents. He stabbed a red button next to the blue one, and the condenser motor chugged to a halt, leaving the room quiet. Quietly stagnant with beer fumes. Housekeeping, he thought blearily, would be able to tie one on in the morning simply by standing in this room and inhaling. Good thing they weren't coming. Good thing Dove's people would be doing the big cleanup. Dove's People. Sam had a flash of humorless people in gray coveralls and sunglasses that left his brain as quickly as it had arrived.

They'd laughed, all three of them, as they created the mess. Laughed at brightly colored billiard balls that went flying over the side of the table. At the enormous face of Jerry Seinfeld on the big-screen TV. At the enormous something else of the guy who'd been wearing the coveralls that advertised DON'S PLUMB-ING & ELECTRICAL FULL SERVICE REPAIR. At everything. At . . . everything.

His drinking buddies were gone now, leaving behind a silence that hung around Sam as heavily as the ugly fur coat his grandma Hattie had worn with as much pride as if the thing had been Russian sable. "What is that?" he'd asked his brother, and got, "I dunno. Muskrat?" as an answer.

They hadn't gone far, he didn't think. Down the hall.

And out in the hall was one of the coterie of private security guards Dove had hired to back him up during the three glorious days and nights in Vegas. One of Dove's People. Sam had caught a glimpse of the guy: Dove's size, but with all the rollicking sense of humor of Mike Tyson. He was camped near the elevator, as unmoving as a potted ficus tree. Two more were stationed down in the lobby. That was all Dove thought was necessary; he didn't believe anybody was going to pull a *Die Hard* and try to get to the penthouse by crawling through air shafts or . . .

"They would want to do that?" Kevin had asked. "What for?"

"Money," Dove said.

"Like how? Kidnapping him or something?" The idea had fas-cinated the boy, though of course it had percolated through a lot of beer in order to become interesting. "How much would they ransom him for?"

"Too fucking much."

That sent Kevin off into another helpless fit of laughter, during which he poured most of a bottle of beer down between the couch cushions, not noticing that the bottle had overturned until it was empty.

There! That noise again. It made all of Sam's nerve endings prickle.

The cat's not here. You know perfectly well the cat isn't here. There's no way it could be here, unless someone packed it in a suitcase.

But there it was. *Squeak.*

You're losing your mind. You're absolutely losing your mind.

The squeak was coming from the mini-refrigerator set into the wall opposite the television. Sam leaned close to it and counted off the seconds. Yes, there: not a cat. Something needed oiling inside the refrigerator.

He sank back onto the couch and propped his pumpkin-sized

head in his hands. The room had no clock; the hotel didn't supply them, as was typical in Vegas. But it seemed sometime around four in the morning. Still night, very much still night, but morning was not that far away. Back on the farm, he'd roll over in bed and listen to the small sounds of the world beginning to wake up, reminding himself that he still had a few minutes left to sleep.

Sleep. And be . . .

He drew in a long, slow breath through his nose. It was there, very faint, barely noticeable mixed in with the heavy reek of the beer. Perfume. Her perfume. The same as in Powell's bedroom, hundreds of miles away. He inhaled again, closing his eyes, letting the scent fill his mind.

"You're here, aren't you?" Sam asked softly. "It's not the house. You're with me. You're following me."

He thought about the picture Al had shown him: a black-and-white college yearbook photo. The young woman in it had blond hair and a sweet face. The kind of face it would be nice to see when you woke up, when you turned around, when you came home at the end of a long day. Looking at it had given him a pang of regret, knowing she was gone, that Powell had lost her, that he, Sam, would not have the chance to talk to her except in dreams.

It was a face that was both familiar and unfamiliar at the same time.

"Emily," he murmured, rubbing his fingers against the smooth surface of Powell's wedding ring. "You want him back, don't you? You can't stand being without him. I don't blame you. It's hard. Being . . ."

Without you.

He closed his eyes and tried to will himself back into the dream, to stand on the beach near where Powell's house now stood, watching her tiptoe into the surf and shriek when the cold water cascaded around her ankles. Emily. Blond hair, sweet face. Sweet, pretty face. Coming closer to him, smiling at him, telling him she loved him.

Telling him . . .

Oh . . .

He fought to hold on to the tendrils of the dream, and finally caught one.

"*I love you.*"

The woman on the beach didn't have blond hair. Wasn't petite, small-boned, wasn't the young woman in the tabloid picture.

"... *Sam* ..."

The woman on the beach was in love with *him*. Not Joe Powell.

"We thought it made sense," Verbena said over her shoulder as she refilled her mug. "It was easier for him to do what he had to do, to focus on the job at hand, if all he had was 'now.' If he didn't remember what was back here. Who was back here. You and your father were gone. Your mother was living happily with Katie and her family in Hawaii. Sam thought he had no ties here. He's thought that all along, and it made sense. So Al didn't tell him any different. We figured that if Whoever is controlling the Leaps wanted Sam to know the truth, He'd give Sam his memory back. All this time—and Sam has never really tried to remember."

"Didn't he think it through?" Tom asked. "What he was doing to Donna?"

"I don't think he did. It was so soon after he'd Leaped out—after he'd left here. He was lonely, scared. Didn't know what would happen next, where he'd go, if he could ever come home. When he found Donna, all he could think of was that he wanted his sweetheart back. I don't think he stopped to consider for a minute what that involved."

"And you haven't told her what he did."

Verbena shook her head. "We haven't. But I think she knows. On some level. I think she knows she wasn't here, the first time around."

"Is that fair?"

"I don't know, Tom."

"He never thought about the consequences."

"He was lonely."

"He never stopped to think about the position he was putting her in, leaving her here. Either time! Retrieving her, changing her life so she'd marry him after all, knowing he wasn't going to come back here and have a life with her. And then, what she knows of her life, after he changed everything—he got out of bed, left his wallet and his ring and his watch on the dresser, walked into that—"

"Accelerator."

"And disappeared. Did it occur to him at all, what she'd feel like if he died?"

"You'd have to ask him."

"For somebody so brilliant, so good with math and science, he's lousy with people."

"He's wonderful with people. He's done so much good, Tom. For hundreds of people. If it's all had a ripple effect, then thousands. I couldn't begin to give you an accurate number. He's taken away so much pain."

"And caused a lot more," Tom said heavily.

"Are you okay?"

Kevin had been trying to get closer, three or four times that she was aware of. Maybe there'd been more while she was asleep. But she'd nudged him away, forcing him to give up, finally, and sleep over on the other side of the bed. Tracy had no real idea why he'd come back here, unless it was that he was so drunk he hadn't noticed how bad the room smelled.

But Kevin wasn't that drunk. And the room didn't smell that bad. Mr. Powell had aired it out before he left, running the air conditioner on "circulate" and filling the room with air that had a vague but nasty tinge of exhaust fumes hanging in it. Kevin smelled of beer and nachos, and that too was better than the smell of vomit.

"I'm tired," she mumbled.

"Everything's going to be okay. He'll do what he promised."

"He's a nice man."

"And you know what? He's giving me a job, starting tomorrow."

"Doing what?"

"Helping. Whatever needs to be done. I told him I'm pretty good with computers, and I'm a good organizer." Kevin moved over little by little until he could spoon himself up close to her. This time, she let him. "But you know, it's weird."

"What is?"

"He's not what my mother said he was. She never told me anything, but I heard her talking to my grandparents. He wasn't friendly, she said. Just business. All he wanted to talk about was business. She asked him one time when his birthday was, even though she knew when it was from his insurance papers. She wanted to be friendly, to see how he'd feel about some kind of a birthday party. He said she could have her birthday off, if that's what she was fishing for. He doesn't celebrate birthdays, or Christmas, or anything. He lets her and Dove go out. He doesn't do anything on Christmas. Nothing."

"Is he Jewish?" Tracy asked, puzzled.

"I don't know why he's different now. I don't know what all this is for."

"Maybe he wants people to like him. So they'll vote for him."

"I guess."

"Maybe he talked to somebody. One of those image consultants or something. Maybe they told him he has to be friendly."

"He was talking to himself. Out in the hall. After he took care of you."

"Maybe it's stress."

"I don't think so."

Tracy offered, "I talk to myself sometimes. When I'm trying to make up my mind about something."

"This is different."

"Why?"

"Because he was acting like there was somebody else there. And . . . it almost seemed like there *was* somebody else there."

"I think you drank too much," Tracy murmured.

"Ziggy?" Donna said quietly.

"Yes, Dr. Alessi."

"Where is Sam?"

"Still in Las Vegas. Asleep."

"Is he safe?"

"His vital signs are all in the normal range for a human in REM sleep."

"That's not what I asked."

"I gather from your persistence that you've spoken to Dr. Beeks and Admiral Calavicci regarding one of my previous calculations."

"I spoke to them," Donna agreed. "And it makes me wonder whether you're employing diversionary tactics. To make us leave you alone so you can continue reaching out to your fellow computers." She paused, tucking her sweater closer around her. She knew the temperature in her room hadn't changed, but it seemed colder, as if she were sitting outside the complex in the desert night instead of several hundred feet underground in a hygrothermically controlled bubble. "You know you're one of a kind, Ziggy."

"I do."

"Makes you feel a little isolated, doesn't it?"

"I am a computer, Dr. Alessi. I do not 'feel.' "

"The hell you don't," Donna said softly.

Ziggy was silent for a moment. "I believe you and I share something. To date, I have spent a cumulative total of eleven-point-nine-six hours wondering what it would be like to have a child."

Breath hissed in through Donna's teeth. "Don't go there, Ziggy. All right?"

"If I understand the idiom correctly, you are asking that I not explore that particular topic with you this evening."

"Or ever."

"But you have discussed it with Dr. Beeks on several occasions."

"Ziggy," Donna said sharply, "you're a computer. You're artificial intelligence. A construct. Something Sam built. You're not alive. Anything you have that approaches human emotion exists because of what Sam—"

"Then you do not wish to employ the philosophy 'I think, therefore I am.' "

"You're a machine."

"Then why," Ziggy asked in a tone that was as miffed as anything that had ever come out of a human mouth, "did you ask if I felt isolated? I assumed you broached that subject because you wanted to share. Have girl talk. Let it all hang out."

"I don't know what I wanted."

"I do."

"Oh, really."

"You want Dr. Beckett."

The last song on the CD Donna had put into the player almost an hour ago came to an end and the machine shut itself off. Donna looked over at the machine but didn't bother to get up to choose another disc.

"Would you like to be alone?" Ziggy asked.

"I already am," Donna said.

She almost didn't hear the soft rapping at her door. She'd turned off her computer terminal and dimmed the lights and had been sitting at her desk, rocking the chair forward and back, a movement so small it would have been almost unnoticeable to anyone else. She was humming softly to herself, lost in her thoughts. Whoever it was knocked again, then pushed the door open a little. Tom.

He came on in, letting the door swing shut behind him, and sat down. In the dim light, he looked not much like Sam, but still, so much like Sam that it made her wince aloud. "I'm sorry, Donna," he told her. "I said things I shouldn't have said."

"That wouldn't be a mistake that's unique to you."

He frowned at that. "What are you doing sitting here in the dark?"

"Thinking."

"Why don't we go check out that restaurant you were talking about? I could use some fresh air."

"We're locked in."

"Oh," Tom said. "Yeah, right."

"I know what Al's wife felt like."

Tom grunted softly. "Which one?"

"The first one. When he was MIA. Or . . . someone who's had a child abducted. How long do you wait? How many mornings do you wake up and think, 'Maybe today he'll come back.' It's a little different for me—I have Al to tell me that Sam's all right, that he's safe. But I don't think that's ever entirely true. I don't know that something won't go wrong. It's—" She stopped talking abruptly, then started again. "How many times am I supposed to think, 'Maybe today'?"

Tom didn't reply, but even in the dim light she could see what crossed his face. "They told you, didn't they?" she asked. "They told you all of it. They told you about Sam taking me to see my father."

"You know that was Sam."

"Of course I know. I didn't then—how could I? But after that Leap, Al started to treat me differently. When I thought about it, things started to make sense. I realized why it was that my professor had acted so strangely that weekend. Why someone who really hadn't paid me any attention before suddenly insisted on taking me to Washington to see my father. I'm not entirely sure what happened in the original history, but I can guess."

"You haven't asked anyone?"

"I didn't want to. I didn't want to put up with a lot of hedging. People pretending they didn't know what I was talking about."

"He's got a strange way of looking at things," Tom mused.

"I love him, Tom."

"I know you do." Tom slouched back in the chair and stared up at the ceiling. "Maybe he's not all that unique. People have done it since the dawn of time. Go off in search of the New World. To conquer new territory. Go to the moon. Climb Everest. They leave behind the people who love them and don't really want them to go, with the explanation, 'I have to do this or I won't be happy.' Doesn't much matter that they could be killed in the process, and sometimes they are. It comes down to, what comes first, your needs or theirs? I can imagine what my folks felt like in the—what do you call it? The 'original history'? When I went to Vietnam and didn't come back. You can make a lot of noise about serving your country and standing up for justice and democracy and patriotism, but it boils down to, I went over there and somebody killed me. I don't imagine Mom was thinking much about the value of democracy when they told her." Tom chuckled softly, without humor. "I gave Sam some huge, holier-than-thou lecture when I was home for Thanksgiving in 'sixty-nine. About how important it was that I do my duty. The poor kid was scared to death that I wouldn't come back, and I yelled at him."

Donna smiled at him, no more amused than he was. He caught the look and understood it instantly. "Good God," he said softly.

"He gets around."

They sat there for several minutes, the hush in the room broken only by the whisper of air through the ventilation ducts and, from very far away, the soft tinkling of bells.

"Who is he now?" Tom asked finally.

"Al thinks it would be better if—"

Tom said tiredly, "Oh, screw Calavicci. Can't you answer the question?"

"Joe Powell."

That made Tom straighten up a little. He reacted to the name in a way Donna didn't understand, but all he said to explain himself was "When?"

"Six months ago."

Tom thought hard for a minute, then pulled himself up so far that he was almost hunched forward. He started to laugh, painfully at first, then loudly, until tears began to run down his cheeks. "I thought it was because Linda was so nervous. But I knew something was 'off' about that meeting. Was it him? Again? When Linda and I went to the house to meet with him?" Donna's nod sent him off into another pained chorus of guffaws. "You realize that for the rest of my life, every time somebody acts a little differently than what I expected, I'm going to think it's Sam?"

"It might be."

The laughter kept coming until Tom's stomach began to ache. He scrubbed at his face with both hands, then shoved them through what remained of his sandy hair. "Does he know? About me and Powell?"

"That you're working for the campaign?"

"I *was* working for the campaign."

"You've resigned?" The look Tom gave her in return both impressed and startled her. "Really? It's gone that far? I had no idea."

"Nobody really does, except Linda. And the kids. I had to tell the kids. Their lives are going to change. And you know, I got their okay before I told Joe yes." Tom flung himself up out of the chair and began to pace back and forth, from the desk to the door, then in the other direction, from the filing cabinet to the bookcase. "What kind of half-assed nonsense is that, anyway? Sam couldn't do what he has to do if he remembered his *life*? What is that, an excuse to let him do whatever he wants? 'He doesn't know any better' works for two-year-olds. Sam isn't two. I don't buy it. What are you protecting him from?" When Donna didn't answer, Tom leaned toward her and demanded, "Donna! You're saving him from knowing that he hurt you? That's a load of masochistic shit."

"It wasn't my choice, Tom. I didn't make him forget."

"You're not helping him remember."

"Al tried once. Whoever is Leaping Sam took him away before Al could say my name."

Tom's eyes widened. "He tried once? One time? In five years? Why? Because you've all convinced yourselves that 'Whoever' doesn't want Sam to know the truth? Because it would distract him?" His voice had grown shrill; he swallowed a couple of times to calm himself a little. "I was in country for a year. Every minute of every day, I had to be on top of my game. If I slipped, it might have meant my life. I guess it did mean my life, before Sam changed it. But I always remembered my family. Thought

234

about them. Wondered what they were doing, if they were okay. Worried about them. That didn't prevent me from doing my job, and doing it well. Don't paint excuses for yourself, Donna. Don't—" He stopped again. "Mom says when I was little, I used to flush things down the toilet. I thought that was the ultimate magic act: pull the handle and whatever you dropped in there goes away in a big whoosh. When you're little, you think like that. It's cool to watch something happen. You don't think, maybe I'm stopping up the plumbing. Maybe whatever I flushed down there is important to somebody and they're going to want it back. You're giving Sam permission not to see the big picture. He doesn't know what happens five years down the road, ten, twenty. He rerouted things to put you back in his life and it sure doesn't sound to me like he gave ten seconds of consideration to what that meant in the long haul."

Without waiting for a response, Tom stalked out of Donna's office. She reached the corridor to find him going from door to door, examining the nameplates that indicated the owner of each office. He'd gone across the hall rather than checking the office next to Donna's, so it took him a minute to locate Al's door. When he did, he pounded on it with the side of his fist.

"Calavicci!" he shouted. "Come out of there!"

The door didn't open, so Tom went on banging on it. The commotion made another door open. Dave Allen peered out into the hall, then stepped out and looked worriedly at Donna. "Everything okay out here?"

Tom pivoted on one heel and scowled first at his sister-in-law, then at the man he had first met through a folder in the collection of confidential government files regarding Project Quantum Leap. "I knew that lying little dickwad was mismanaging this thing," he hissed, jabbing a finger at Al's door. "I knew that right from the get-go, when they showed me the budget sheets and I saw how much money this thing was sucking up. I knew something was wrong, I just had the wrong something."

"He does the best he can," Donna told him.

"In a rat's ass. I'm going to get him canned. Don't think I don't mean that."

David let his office door close behind him and moved a little closer to Tom. "The admiral's kept this Project going, Congressman. If it wasn't for him, we all would've gotten canned years ago. Please understand what that means. If the Project was shut down, your brother wouldn't have any contact with the present. He'd be out there in Time, trying to figure things out on his own. And without the Project, Sam would never be able to come home."

"Without the machines? You've all been telling me it's not the machines. That it's God. If that's so, then Whoever took Sam out of here can bring him back."

"We honestly don't think that's true, sir."

"That God can't do whatever He likes?"

Dave came closer still, so that he could speak to Tom without raising his voice. "We've been able to do a lot with the Accelerator. We've been able to make it perform exactly the way it was supposed to. But like I told you, we haven't been able to use it to bring Sam back. It seems to me that Whoever is Leaping Sam around doesn't want him to come back. Not yet, at least. Whoever it is wants Sam to keep doing what he's doing. Sam, and not someone else. And yet . . . if God, or Whoever, only wanted Sam, and not the capabilities of the Project and the people who work here, He could have simply snatched Sam out of his bed. I think it's a package deal, sir. Sam, and the equipment he invented, and the people who run it. And that would include Admiral Calavicci."

Tom thought that over. "The file said you were supposed to be the second one to go."

"Yes, sir."

"Have you tried?"

"To do what? Leap?"

"Go back and get Sam," Tom said impatiently. "Go get him and bring him home."

With some chagrin, Dave replied, "It doesn't work quite that way. But yes, I tried. A couple times. Once right after we realized the retrieval program didn't work, and again about a year ago. It didn't work. The sequence ran properly, but I didn't Leap."

"You told me not two minutes ago that the equipment works like it was supposed to."

The young scientist nodded. "We've been able to Leap two people. We chose a destination and they arrived at that destination."

"And those two people were . . . ?"

Following a glance at Donna, Dave replied, "Admiral Calavicci and Dr. Beckett. It's a long story, but in both cases, we

236

were able to use them to bounce somebody else out. We believe that may have something to do with the fact that Ziggy's 'brain' contains those tissue samples from both of them, and no one else." Before Tom could say anything, he went on, "We've tried everything that made sense, and a lot of things that didn't. Believe me, Congressman: we haven't left a single stone unturned. Without the Project, and without Admiral Calavicci's securing the funding for us every year, we wouldn't have been able to do much more than wring our hands and wail like something out of a Victorian melodrama."

"You know how the whole system works? The programming? All the equipment?"

"More than I wish I did, sometimes."

"Then do it now. Send me."

Dave and Donna both gaped at Tom.

"I want you to do it. If nobody can Leap other than people who've got brain tissue inside that"—Tom shuddered—"that thing, then try me. If Sam could accept an organ donation or a blood transfusion from a member of his family, then maybe your damn equipment will recognize something familiar when it zaps me. It's worth a try. If you've tried everything else."

"Congressman," Dave protested in a voice that squeaked in a way it hadn't since before his struggle through puberty, "if we tried that, and something happened to you . . ."

"What? You'd be fired? Tried for murder? What?"

Donna reached out and rested a hand on Tom's forearm. "We can't risk losing you, too, Tom."

"Why? Because you don't want to explain it to my mother?"

"We can't do it."

Tom shook her hand off. "Where's Calavicci? He's not worried about my mother. He's not worried about anything except his own ass. You know where he is—I can see it in your eyes. Take me to him."

As if the words had been a cue, the elevator chimed its arrival on Level Eight and the doors slid open, revealing an Al who was not quite as unsuspecting as he perhaps should have been. He gazed suspiciously at Tom, then at the other two, then forced himself to ask, "What's the problem?"

CHAPTER TWENTY-ONE

"I can go with you," Kevin offered.

Tracy shook her head. "It's only a four-hour trip. The doctor's going to meet me at the airport in Baltimore. I'll be okay."

"You don't know anybody there."

"I didn't know anybody in L.A. when I went there. Don't worry. Laurie's sending out my stuff—everything's all taken care of. It'll be fine." Tracy lowered her eyes, which was enough to say she herself wasn't completely convinced of that. Then she brightened and offered Kevin a smile and a kiss on the cheek. "I have to do this. Nobody likes me the way I am. I don't like me the way I am."

Kevin slipped his arms around her and hugged her close, stroking the back of her head with the palm of one hand. "Then I guess I should say, maybe I'll like you better when you come back."

"I don't know if I'm coming back, Kev."

"Why wouldn't you come back?"

"The doctor said I should think about living in Baltimore. She said if I gave myself more options, there would be less pressure for me to fit somebody's image of what I should be." Kevin offered her a small shrug and a nod of agreement, but she looked away again as if that wasn't enough. "She talked to me for a long time. She really made a lot of sense. And Mr. Powell arranged for me to work in his company's office there. He said if I wanted to keep up with my acting, I could do it in regional theater. I don't know. I'm not sure what I want to do. My cousin said she'd move down there to stay with me for a few months if I wanted her to. She kind of drives me crazy, but I guess it'd be good to have someone there who knows me."

Kevin grinned at her, though more to reassure her than for any other reason. "It sounds like you called a lot of people this morning. I didn't think I was gone for that long."

"You weren't. I didn't say all that much."

"Will you call me, when you feel better?"

"Sure. If you want me to."

"I do. I want you to call me and tell me you're getting better." Hesitantly, he added, "I hope you're happy in Baltimore."

"Yeah," Tracy said in a small voice. "Me too."

He was holding her again when Sam approached them and gestured toward the hotel entrance. "The car's ready anytime you are," Sam told her.

She said her goodbyes quickly, picked up the tote bag sitting alongside her feet, and hurried out the door. Sam and Kevin watched through the glass as she climbed into the backseat of the car Sam had summoned to take her to the airport. "She's gonna be okay, right?" Kevin asked somberly.

Sam nodded and waved a go-ahead to the driver. "I think she will. She was ready."

"To get help?"

"Mm-hmm."

"I guess last night did kind of push her over the line. She came here wanting to impress you, and you ended up finding her like that, in the bathroom. It's pretty nasty. I know—I walked in on her once when she was doing it. She forgot to lock the door." Kevin ran a hand through his hair and shook his head, trying to dismiss the memory. "Can this doctor really help her? I read a lot of articles after I found her that time. It said sometimes they can't be helped. That it's gone too far. Maybe sending her somewhere where she doesn't know anybody isn't the right thing to do. She's got nobody to turn to for support."

Sam took the boy by the arm and steered him away from the doors. "You're thinking of volunteering to go with her?"

"I would. If she needed me to."

"I don't think it would help." He kept the boy walking toward the elevators, away from the ever-present clusters of looky-loos who regarded each of his visits to the lobby as something more interesting than the return of Halley's Comet. Yesterday he had accepted their scrutiny as coming with the territory; today it was chafing at him, and he had a sudden urge to put his arms around Kevin and give them something more to gossip about. Even Dove's constant presence a few steps away had become an irritant. "Helping someone with a problem like bulimia takes a fantastic level of commitment, Kevin. This is a woman you've only known for a few weeks."

"So you're saying the minute things got tough, I'd bail."

"I think you'd at least want to."

"Thanks for the vote of confidence."

Sam pressed the call button for the penthouse elevator and ushered Kevin into the car when the doors opened. Dove ducked in behind them and pressed the "P" button on the control panel, standing between the doors and his employer as the car began to rise, with his back to Sam and Kevin. "The boss is right," he commented without turning. "Somebody like that—it's not like saying you'll go by and pick up their dry cleaning."

"I could do it if she needed me to," Kevin said stubbornly.

"Doubtful."

Kevin shrank against the back wall of the elevator, one foot tapping hard against the carpet. "You don't even know me."

The car stopped a second later and the doors slid open. Dove stepped into the doorway and blocked the doors open, glancing up and down the corridor at the same time. He hesitated a moment before he spoke, first taking a curious look at Sam's expression. "You don't want to get mixed up in Tracy's problems just so you can convince Max that you're swell, kid. You're nineteen years old. You can't handle it." Kevin, whose pique was turning rapidly into fury, tried to move past him out into the corridor, but Dove caught him by the arm and held him fast. "Tell me I'm wrong."

"Let go," Kevin hissed.

Sam slid past them into the hallway. After another look to determine that they were alone, Dove pulled Kevin out of the car and let the doors close. "Tell me," the bodyguard said quietly. "You came here to piss your mother off. You brought Tracy here to piss your mother off. Might've been the boss's idea, but you went along with it because you knew how Max was gonna react."

"So you're an expert on my motivations now, huh?"

"I don't have to be. I was a kid too, and it wasn't that long ago. You do everything you can think of to push your mother's buttons."

"It *was* my idea," Sam put in.

Dove took a long look at him, though it was not to determine the wisdom of speaking the truth. "Not a good one."

"We're meeting with eleven people this morning," Sam pointed out. "Starting this morning, we're not a group of four, we're a group of fifteen, traveling to nine different cities. There's going to be someone to handle anything that might come up. A press liaison, three security guards, a hotel-services coordinator, whatever in the world that is, a speechwriter, the driver, two turtledoves, and a partridge in a pear tree. Kevin is just one extra person. And I do find it hard to believe that in spite of all those people, there isn't going to be something left over for him to do. Run messages or something."

"We all have cell phones, boss."

"Save the batteries."

"Would've been a better idea to give him a job in one of the offices. You got more than a hundred people working for you in L.A."

Sam turned to look at Kevin. "Do you like working in an office?"

"No," Kevin said sullenly.

"What do you want to do?"

Dove said stiffly, "You couldn't figure all this out before we left Mount Olympus? It's like I said: you did this to piss her off. And I don't get that."

"Do I let you argue with me?" Sam asked.

In spite of the fact that they were asking him questions, the two men seemed to have forgotten Kevin was there. Furious, he jerked his arm out of Dove's grasp and scowled at the red marks the bodyguard's fingers had left below the sleeve of his polo shirt. To their surprise, he turned not toward his own room but toward Max's. "It's between me and my mother," he said, his tone making it obvious that he did not honestly feel he owed either of them an explanation.

"Leave her alone, Kevin," Dove barked.

Kevin jabbed a finger at him. "No. You leave me alone. Until I settle this."

She let him in as if he were a hotel employee she had never seen before and would have to put up with until it came time to tip him. Without saying a word, she went back to the table near the windows and resumed running sheets of paper through a portable fax machine. Kevin stayed near the door, trying to let his anger dissipate enough to carry on a conversation that involved something other than yelling.

"Is she gone?" Max asked after a minute.

"Yeah."

"Then you have no reason to stay here. You have no one left to impress."

"Oh, swell. Here we go: Bobbie disapproves, part fifteen. What do you want me to say? Absolutely, you're right—I picked her deliberately, knowing she has a problem. I had my choice of two or three dozen completely normal, wholesome, all-American girls and I picked the one with the eating disorder, because I knew it would freak you out. It's beyond the realm of comprehension that I might have picked her because she's pretty and I thought she was interesting to talk to."

"Did you wear a condom?"

"What?" Kevin squeaked.

"When you slept with her. Did you wear a condom?"

"Why? What do you think she's got that I could catch? Because I met her in a club, you think she's been sleeping around?" Kevin cut himself off, then demanded, "Why is it even any of your business?"

"I want you to go back to Los Angeles."

"You know what? No. He offered me a job, and I'm going to take it."

Max's hands balled into fists as she got up from her chair. She forced them to relax as she moved closer to her son; then, as if they belonged to someone else, they clenched again. "Do you have any clue what you're in the middle of? Mr. Powell is inaugurating a presidential campaign. He's not here for spring break! This is not you and a bunch of your friends trying to get yourselves on MTV. It's important that every step of this trip go exactly as planned. No embarrassments, no blunders, no mistakes. The man is going to run for president. President of the United States."

"I didn't think you meant president of Paraguay."

"Don't mock me, Kevin. Mr. Powell doesn't need anyone around him he's going to have to apologize for. No one who's going to show up in the newspaper for doing something 'newsworthy.' "

Kevin snatched up a sheet of paper she'd left lying close to the fax. "Oh, you mean 'King Joe'?" he demanded, flapping the paper in the air.

"I don't know how you charmed him into bringing you along, but it was out of line." Pain had begun to throb behind her eyebrows. She pinched hard at the bridge of her nose, leaving twin red marks when she took her fingers away. "I don't know why you felt compelled to come to the house in the first place. You know it's off-limits."

"Then why did you let me in?"

"Because it looked like it was going to rain, and you were sick. Please don't act as if that implied I was giving you carte blanche. I intended for you to take a nap and then go home. Without trying to ingratiate yourself with Mr. Powell."

"Why shouldn't I try to do that? He's got probably fifty thousand dollars invested in me. Maybe I figure I owe him for that. I'm out of school until September. I can work. Whatever he wants me to do."

"You don't belong here."

"That doesn't make much difference. I'm here. And I'm not going anywhere until he tells me I have to. You're not running the show, he is."

"I'm asking you to understand his—"

"Don't hand me this shit, Bobbie. It's not about him. You only care about what people think of him because it reflects on you. If he doesn't get to the White House, you don't get to go there either."

243

Max's right hand came up a little. She stopped the gesture before it was complete, looked at her hand again, then stuck her index finger in Kevin's direction. Whatever words had been intended to go with the gesture got lost along the way.

"What were you going to do?" Kevin asked. "Were you just going to slap me?"

"No."

"It sure looks like you were. You've never hit me in my life. Are you going to start now?" He took a step forward so that he was well within her reach. "Go ahead, give it your best shot. Smack me. Maybe that'll make me understand that I don't belong anywhere you are." He waited. She didn't move, and Kevin snorted out a laugh that had no humor behind it. "You really think I went to the house to mess up your *job*? I drove up there to *see* you. It was a nice day down in L.A., and I got in the car to go for a ride up the coast. And I thought, 'Maybe I'll keep driving. It's not that far. I'll just show up there, and maybe we can have dinner together, because I miss her.' But I guess those TV commercials are true. Too much booze, too many drugs, and now I'm having hallucinations. Pretty weird, huh? I thought my mother, who hadn't set eyes on me in almost a year, might want to have dinner with me."

Max said nothing, and began to turn away. Furious, Kevin seized her by the arm and turned her around to face him. "Do you not even like me now? Two years with Mr. Powell, and you just want to reject me entirely?"

"You're blowing this out of all proportion. I didn't—"

"Can you hug me? Right now. Can you put your arms around me and hold me? Is that possible?"

"I have work to do. This is wasting a lot of time."

"If I disappeared, would that make you happy? If I vanished. Tomorrow. Today."

"Don't be stupid, Kevin."

"Why can't you answer the question?" He waited, but got nothing in return. "When I called Tracy and told her she was invited to come on this trip, she was thrilled. She was so excited she probably peed herself. Okay, so she didn't get all worked up because she was going on a trip with me. She was going to be with the Joe Powell entourage. A five-star trip to Vegas and it didn't cost her a dime. Mr. Powell even slipped me some spending money—that's what she used to pay for whatever she bought

244

to binge on. Maybe it was a blow to my ego that she was more interested in being seen with King Joe than with me. I won't deny that. What I'm saying is, she was excited. She was *happy*. If I ever saw you act happy over anything I did for you, or did, period, or anything I said, I think the shock would kill me."

Max slipped out of her son's grasp and strode toward the door, intending to open it and usher him out. Kevin caught up with her quickly and again grabbed her by the arm, tightly enough to make her wince.

"She's a nice girl, don't you get that? I brought her here because I like her, and I wanted her to like me. But that doesn't even occur to you. You just see her as an embarrassment, don't you? She's not somebody who messed up and needs some help. God, Bobbie, even *he* sees that, and he's the one who shouldn't care."

"What are you talking about?"

"Mr. Powell. Dove told you I found her last night after she threw up, didn't he? Well, it wasn't me. It was Mr. Powell. Tracy told me: after he left the restaurant, he came up here to see if she was okay. He took care of her. Helped her clean up a little and get into bed. He did all that while you were still sitting in the restaurant eating your frigging cheesecake."

The more he said, the wider Max's eyes got.

"Put your arms around me," Kevin said, daring her. "Put your arms around me and hold me like I mean anything to you at all."

"I want you to leave," Max told him, struggling to keep her voice steady.

"I want you to hold me."

"You haven't done anything in the last four days that deserves a hug. You've been thoughtless and rude and insensitive. I've asked you a number of times to go back to Los Angeles where you belong, and you've ignored me. What is it you want out of this? You think if you're charming enough and persistent enough, he'll adopt you? The apartment isn't good enough. You want to live in that house, like I do."

"Yeah, maybe I do. I want it *like you do*."

Max ignored that. "You want the indoor swimming pool and the big-screen TV and the garage full of cars and the cook who'll put in front of you anything your heart desires. You want everything he has handed to you on a gold plate. That man has worked all his life for what he has. No one handed it to him. He's a

245

brilliant, talented man who put together an enormously successful business. I find the fact that you think he ought to share it with you, by virtue of absolutely nothing, embarrassing and offensive and something I will not tolerate."

Kevin was silent for a moment, then said quietly, "I'm bigger than you are."

"What?"

"If Mr. Powell is okay with me staying, and Dove has to follow his orders and not yours, who's going to make me leave?"

"I want you out."

Her face was nearly crimson. Her words came out as if she'd bitten them off of something sour and could not quite spit the taste out of her mouth no matter how hard she tried. Kevin watched her rage, then said, still softly, "I'll leave the room, and I'll leave the hotel, but I'm not leaving Vegas. I'm going to ride the trolley down to the Hilton and see that *Star Trek* thing, then I'm going to get some lunch somewhere. Maybe I'll take that bus tour out to Hoover Dam. I'll be back around dinnertime. Maybe you can use the time to think about the fact that as rotten as you've been to me, I'm still your son, and I'm thrilled to find out what an embarrassment I am to you." Without any further prompting, he went to the door and pulled it open. "You're some piece of work," he said, then left her alone.

Which one of them was angrier at that moment would have been impossible to decide. Max watched the door close, expecting it to slam and knowing it couldn't because of the hydraulic hinge. She could hear voices in the hall, then the chime of the elevator.

Then there was a knock at the door.

"Go away," she said, but not loudly enough for whoever was on the other side to hear her. When the door began to open, she expected Dove, the holder of the only key card other than the one in her purse.

But it was Joe. "We need to talk," he told her firmly.

She turned away, but not before he'd seen most of the kaleidoscope of emotions that played across her face. She was very near crying, and was as angry at Kevin for causing that as she was at herself for allowing it to happen. As if she were still alone, she shuffled through the stack of papers on the table and began to feed one of them into the fax machine.

"I'm not understanding something," Sam began quietly, and

gestured to postpone a reply. "Just hear me out, and although this sounds strange, give me credit for having a more . . . intimate knowledge of the situation than you might think." He paused long enough to find himself a chair. "What I don't understand is how someone can carry a child for nine months, give birth to the child, live in the same house as the child for seventeen years, and yet have no more of a bond with him than if he were a complete stranger. That mystifies me, Max."

Max's jaw tightened. "What kind of intimate knowledge do you think you have?"

"Never mind."

"Joe," she began, then stopped and made a gesture with her hand as if she were erasing her first attempt at a response out of existence. "I don't see why this makes any difference. You've known about Kevin since I started working for you. You sign the checks that allow him to go to school."

"And go to the same clubs as Leonardo DiCaprio." Sam nodded. "You arranged for him to have a very comfortable life."

"Yes. He is. He's very comfortable. He has everything he could want."

"He doesn't think so."

"I've tried to send him back to Los Angeles. He won't go. He says he has your permission to stay."

Sam shook his head. "I don't want you to send him anywhere, unless you go with him. Which actually would thrill him to death. He'd love to go somewhere with you. Just the two of you. Anywhere in the world."

"Kevin and I have nothing in common, Joe. I'm sure we'd be wonderful traveling companions."

"Nothing in common, except that you're his mother," Sam replied, leaning toward her. "That's what I don't understand, Max. He's a good kid. A loving, intelligent, good kid. Who can't figure out for the life of him why his mother wants to treat him like an acquaintance she has nothing in common with. Do you talk to him? Try to find out what he thinks, how he feels about going to college? What he'd like to do with his life? What teams he roots for? Do you know anything about him?"

"I know he defies me."

"He's defying your telling him to get out. I think that makes him a lot like you, you know. You figured out what you wanted and you've fought to get it, and keep it, ever since. He knows what he wants too."

She was silent for a long moment. When she finally looked at him, her face had been wiped clean. Almost. "My relationship with my son isn't really any of your business, Joe."

"Even though I support him."

"Why do you want to do this now? You've been signing the checks for almost two years."

"Because now I know Kevin. I know he's a good kid. He doesn't deserve to be shoved aside like an old coat you don't wear anymore. And because . . ." Sam hesitated, then said what had come into his mind. "Because you don't have a relationship with your son."

Max sprang up from her chair and was somehow halfway to the door. "I don't want to listen to this."

"You're going to listen to it."

She took another step. Her back was to Sam when she stopped, but she'd seen enough of his expression to know what was coming next.

"If you go through that door," he told her, "you're fired."

She stayed where she was. The struggle she was having with herself was perfectly visible in the way her shoulders moved up and down.

"That kid loves you," Sam said. "He wants a mother. He wants *you*. Is that such a completely terrible request?" When Max didn't reply, he went on, "Maybe you never wanted to be a mother. Maybe it came as a surprise, at the wrong time in your life. But you are a mother. Whether you ever wanted the job or not, whether you want it now or not, you've got it. Just answer me one thing: do you not love him?"

She didn't answer.

"After he was born," Sam persisted, "did they put him in your arms? Did you hold him?" He got a shrug in return, which he supposed was better than nothing. He moved to stand beside Max, shifting his position until he could look her in the eye. She was trying hard not to tell him anything, even through her expression, but it wasn't working. "It's not possible," Sam said, "for you to carry a child under your heart for nine months, and then to hold him and look into his face and not love him. Not possible."

"And you would know that," Max muttered.

"Yes, actually, I would."

"My parents did a perfectly fine job raising him. He had stories read to him at bedtime. He was hugged and kissed. He was taught that it's all right to cry. He was taught how to play baseball. He didn't miss anything."

"He thought you were his sister."

"So?"

"And he cried when he told me that. Which makes him what?" Sam demanded, turning Max back to face him when she tried to look away. "What? A sissy? Mentally ill? Someone with completely ridiculous expectations?"

"He has a family!" Max shouted, pushing away the hand Sam had held out to placate her. She took refuge near the windows, arms wrapped around herself, her face filled with rage. There were several heavy objects within easy reach, small enough to use as a weapon. Some of them were breakable.

"Go ahead," Sam told her. "Smash a couple. Throw them at the mirror. That'll make a really good crash. Throw them at me. I've gotten really good at ducking."

"Joe," Max said through her teeth, "this is not any of your business."

"It is, Max. Not because you work for me. Not because I want my life to float along like a rowboat on a duck pond, without any troubles, without anybody causing me any stress. Maybe I should have said something before, but I didn't, because I was stuck in that house, which is like being trapped in a sensory-deprivation tank. Maybe Kevin has embarrassed you. Maybe he's been a little rude and thoughtless, but he's a kid."

"He's nineteen years old. He's a grown man."

"He's not a man," Sam insisted. "He's a kid. I remember what it was like to be nineteen. You're not sure of anything. He's reaching out to you, because he's standing at the edge of being a man, and he's scared."

"He can turn to my father. My father is the one who wanted him."

"And you didn't. You didn't want that baby."

"I would have given him away," she said, her voice shaking so much she could barely get the words out. "I had that much sense. People want good-looking, healthy, white baby boys. When he was born, and they told me he was all right, and he was a boy, I knew there wouldn't be any problem finding him a

249

home. But my father insisted. He said it wouldn't be right to give the baby away if we could raise him ourselves. He wanted a son. He always wanted a son, and my mother could have only me. He said he and my mother would take care of it all, and I could go on to college like nothing had happened."

"But something did happen."

She sank into the chair Sam had occupied a couple of minutes ago. When she spoke, it was using someone else's inflections, softly repeating words that had been said years ago. "Barbara had herself a little summer fling. Kids don't stop to think. Get themselves into trouble. But we're taking care of it. Look at this one! He's a champ, isn't he?"

Tears were rolling steadily down her cheeks. Sam leaned into the bathroom long enough to pull a handful of tissues from the box and pass them to her. She held them in a wad first against one eye, then the other. "My father made me feel so small, Joe," she whispered. "I don't know if he meant to. I don't know what he intended. Maybe he thought he was 'taking care of it.' But I never spent one day in that house without thinking I'd taken everything he expected of me and screwed it into the ground. I wasn't what he wanted, from the minute I was born. I was never going to be what he wanted."

"Maybe you should talk to him."

"About what? I know how he feels. I had to build my own life. Something I could be proud of. I had to leave that house, because I couldn't live there without feeling *small*. I need this job, Joe. Please understand that. I think I've done well. I've put every bit of effort into it that I possibly can. I need this. I have to walk away from that house and those people. I have to leave all that behind. Please understand. Help me walk away from what I was."

She lifted her head then and looked at him. She gasped sharply, as if he'd suddenly turned into someone else. Quickly, she wiped her eyes dry, threw the tissues into the wastebasket, and straightened her clothes. She was a long way from looking businesslike, even after all that: her face was blotchy, her makeup streaked, and her eyes were bloodshot and puffy. Suffering under what she didn't understand was more sympathy than anything else coming from Sam, she fumbled with the papers sitting alongside the fax machine, but her trembling hands sent them fluttering to the floor.

"Please give me five minutes," she managed to say. "I need to—please excuse me. Five minutes."

"Take whatever you need."

"I apologize for this, Joe. This was completely unprofessional and uncalled for."

"Would you like to take a nap?"

She seemed not to understand the word. "What?"

"Rest for a while. Wash your face, fix your makeup. We don't have anything on the calendar until eleven-thirty." He took a step toward the door. "I'm doing this for you, Max. You *have* put everything you've got into this job. I know that. You're incredibly good at it. But I think you can do better. If you can reconcile the things that are wrong in your life."

He could tell as he left the room: she thought she was an hour away from being fired. He supposed it was unfair to let her think that, believe her life was falling apart, but decided to let this particular hand play itself out.

Dove, of course, was still out in the corridor. "Talk to her, if you think that'll accomplish anything," Sam told him. "I need a few minutes alone." Without waiting for an answer from the bodyguard, he fished the key to the master suite out of his pocket and went off to be by himself.

The moment the door had closed behind him, he switched on the sound system and spun the dial until he found a radio station broadcasting a tuneless, migraine-inducing, glass-rattling thing he supposed somebody under the influence of a lot of drugs enjoyed calling a "song." He cranked the volume up until it made his teeth ache.

Then he screamed out, "Al!"

To his astonishment, seconds later the Doorway opened and Al appeared, handlink in hand, as startled by Sam as Sam was by him.

"What?" the Observer blurted.

"I can't do this."

"Can't do what?" Al pivoted around, examining the room. "Jeez Louise, they can probably hear that noise in Spain! Can't you turn that down?" After Sam had acquiesced and twisted the volume knob down, the Observer asked, "What's happening?"

"Max. I have no right to tell her she's running her life the wrong way. She's doing exactly the same thing I did. Turning her back on everything she had in pursuit of something she thinks

251

she needs. Maybe she does need it. God knows, I thought I needed it. I went into the Accelerator with no more thought than if I was going into the kitchen to make a peanut-butter-and-jelly sandwich." He could hear his voice begin to shake. Shaking his head, he moved across the room to the broad picture window and pressed his hands against the glass, looking down the boulevard, wondering if he could pick Kevin out of the crowd. "What right do I have to tell anyone what they should do?"

"You're a good man. And you're not doing it for you, you're doing it for them."

"Maybe they have every bit as much right to screw up their lives as I did. And who's to say. Maybe I think they're screwing things up, but who am I?"

"You've got hindsight," Al said. "Courtesy of us."

"Where are they now? Max and Kevin. Your now, not my now. I know where they are in my now."

"You're sounding whiffy again, Sam."

"And my head is pounding like a Chinese gong. I apologize. The question made sense, didn't it?"

"Yeah. But an answer's gonna be hard."

Sam jabbed a finger at the handlink and raised a brow. "Not still? She's still not cooperating? Give me that!"

"Give you what? I can't give it to you."

"Tell her you're going to pull the chip."

"What chip?"

"Use those words. 'I'm going to pull the chip.' Do it."

Al had been at this more than long enough to know that was all the explanation he was going to get—which was, of course, none. Heaving a sigh, he tipped his head back and addressed the ceiling. "Ziggy," he crooned. "Give me current status on Barbara and Kevin Maxwell. Or I'm going to pull the chip."

They waited. Then Al winced. "What did she say?" Sam asked.

"You don't want to know. Wait, here it comes." The handlink, instead of scrolling out information, emitted a piercing screech that made Al fling it away. The moment it left his hand, Sam could no longer see it, or hear it bounce on the Imaging Chamber floor. "I know they're expensive!" the Observer howled. Muttering to himself, he retrieved the link, shook it hard a couple of times, then scowled at it. "You ask a question, you get half a ton of crap," he mumbled. "All right. Here it comes. Max sent a bunch of E-mails from Mount Olympus this morning, so best guess is, that's where she is. Kevin . . . Kevin . . ."

"Where is he?"

"He's in jail, Sam," Al said ruefully. "Aggravated assault. He punched out some guy outside a bar. He won't come up in front of the judge until next week, probably, because of the holidays."

"And that wasn't true two days ago. He's in jail because I brought him to Las Vegas."

"But there's good news," Al put in quickly, the tilt of his head revealing that he was listening to someone not in the room with Sam. "That girl Tracy. She's doing real good in Baltimore."

"Ziggy said that?"

"Beeks called Bonnie Worther. They know each other. They dated the same guy, or shrunk the same guy's head, or something. Tracy's doing great. She got a promotion, and she's got a new boyfriend."

"While her old boyfriend cools his heels in jail."

"Don't get stuck on that, Sam."

"How can I not get stuck on it? It's my fault." Sam perched on the edge of the coffee table, his hands clenched together between his knees. "I'm supposed to help people, not make different bad things happen to them. It's coming apart, Al. When you have to tell me 'Don't mess things up'—what does that say for my abilities? I used to let my heart guide me, and that was good enough. Now I don't know if I can trust myself. I'm seeing things, I'm hearing things. I jump to conclusions. I don't know how much longer I can do this."

"As I remember it, you don't have a choice, pal."

"There has to be a choice, Al. If I can't do it. If I'm doing more harm than good."

"But you're kinda the only game in town. It's not like there's a million different Accelerators somebody could get plucked out of."

"Alia came from somewhere."

"Don't remind me. But that's another point. If you throw in the towel, who have we got out there fighting for the side of Good?"

Sam shook his head wearily. "Don't toss that back in my face. I don't know why I said that in the first place. I don't believe I'm Goodness incarnate any more than I thought Alia was purely evil. And I'm tired, Al."

"You're hung over, is what you are."

"I don't want that boy to end up in jail."

Al considered his options for a minute, his fingers drumming against the handlink as if it were a miniature piano. "Then maybe you ought to stop trying to do this all on your own. And ask for help. Long as I've known you, that's been your worst problem. You'd say you wanted help as a way to get people to do what you wanted them to. Maybe you ought to give it up. Say 'I can't do this' and mean it. Let somebody help you."

"You've always helped me."

"I don't mean me."

"Who, then?"

"You want to deal with somebody else who doesn't think you're perfect?"

"Al, I don't know what you're talking about."

Al turned away from his partner and again listened to someone who wasn't in the room with Sam. He seemed not to like what he was hearing; then, after a struggle that was obvious to Sam, he surrendered and nodded his head. "All right." He sighed. "If Beeks thinks this is gonna work, I guess it's worth a try. Go slow. It'll make your head spin for a second. Keep your eyes shut at first, then open 'em a little at a time." He stretched out a hand, then grunted, "Yeah, I know it looks stupid for you and me to stand here and hold hands. But that's how it works. Clothing breaks the field."

Again, he extended his hand. A moment later, Sam was looking at his brother.

CHAPTER
TWENTY-TWO

"Hello, Sam," Tom said, sounding more than a little queasy.

"We can't waste a lot of time doing this," Al warned him. "It sucks up a lot of juice."

Sam shifted his weight, intending to get up from the coffee table, and found not entirely to his surprise that his legs refused to support him. Tom looked exactly the same as he had a few days ago, in Joe Powell's living room—six months ago, from Tom's perspective. Exactly the same, because again he had walked into a situation in which he was certain of his feelings but not of the right words to say to express them.

"Al told you everything," Sam ventured.

"Yes, he did. All of it. Including what you did in Vietnam." Tom's features pinched a little, then he forced a smile. "I did think Magic was acting a little odd those couple of days. The way he kept hanging around and calling me 'Tom.' He never called me anything but 'Lieutenant' before that, or after."

"I wanted you to have another chance. You had so much ahead of you."

"I guess I did."

Sam's gaze dropped to the floor for a moment, then came back up. "I'm sorry, Tom. I guess we haven't been . . . what I thought we'd be. With each other."

"If you mean 'close,' then that's an understatement, little brother."

"I'm sorry."

"I guess you did what you thought you had to do. Even if you had a stupid reason for doing it."

You know, but you don't get it, Sam thought. With a great deal of effort he pushed himself to his feet and moved closer to his brother and his best friend. "Tom . . . I don't . . . I don't have that history with you. I spent a couple of days with you, that Thanksgiving in Elk Ridge. And the couple of days in Vietnam. But I had to pretend I was someone else. A younger me, and then Magic. Then I talked to you and Linda a couple of days ago at Powell's house, pretending to be him. I don't . . ." Sam's voice caught in his throat. "I don't really know you. I haven't talked to you, not like this, since I was sixteen years old. I'm not sure what it is that I've said to you, or not said. I wasn't there."

"Of course you were there. If it wasn't you, who the hell was it?"

Al opened his mouth to fill in some of the missing pieces, but Sam cut him off. "I'm not aware of anything that's changed since I Leaped out. I know about the changes, because Al has told me. But I didn't experience them. I wasn't there to see you come home from Vietnam. Or marry Linda. Was I there? At your wedding?"

"I thought you were."

Tom turned to Al, his forehead deeply creased with a frown. "You said when he came home, he remembered everything."

"What?" Sam said.

Al grimaced. "He did remember. Then he forgot."

"When? When was I home?" Sam asked with a shrill note in his voice.

"It was a couple years ago. An accident, with some lightning. You came home, and I went where you were. Supposed to go. It was only for a couple hours. Then there was, you know . . ."

"Another accident."

"Sort of."

"You're not making any sense."

"It's a part of his charm," Tom said sarcastically. Before Al could stop him, he went on, "They all think Whoever is Leaping you around doesn't want you to remember coming home. Doesn't want you to remember home, period."

Sam said with a frown, "I remember Elk Ridge."

"Not Elk Ridge. Your home. Here. The home you built for yourself, and the people you put in it."

"I remember them too. Verbena. Gooshie."

"Think harder."

"I don't think this is a good idea," Al mumbled.

Tom scowled at him. "Why? You think the world's going to end? I'm not pushing him. I'm doing exactly what Beeks said to do. I'm letting him remember."

" 'Him' would prefer it if you didn't discuss me as if I weren't here." Sam sighed. "What am I supposed to remember?"

"People, Sam. People."

"I remember them. I remember . . . Arnold. Does Arnold still work there?"

"Yeah," Al replied. "He's still—"

Tom jumped suddenly, emitting a cry of pain as he jerked his hand away from Al's. An instant after the contact broke, he vanished.

"What's the matter?" Sam demanded. "What happened?"

Al, shaking his head, was drumming commands into the handlink and receiving a loud, discordant screech in response. He touched one more key, let out a piercing shriek, and flung the handlink away.

"Al? What *happened*?"

The Observer kicked at something Sam couldn't see. As his toe connected with the handlink, Sam got a brief glimpse of the little device, then it disappeared again. "Short circuit," Al gasped, still recovering from the jolt he'd received.

"Is Tom all right?"

"He's . . . pissed."

"But he's all right? What about you? Are you all right?"

"I have to go, Sam. Gooshie's telling me we've got to come out of the Chamber. He says if the power arcs again, we could get fried." Forcing a smile, Al added, "And I already told them

I don't want anything to do with a Calavicci roast."

"Al?" Sam blurted. "Is it *her*? Am I supposed to remember *her*?"

Al's mouth opened but his reply didn't come through. Like the Cheshire cat, he was gone, leaving nothing but the ghost of his expression hanging in the air.

CHAPTER
TWENTY-THREE

Frantic, Sam paced the room, then went into the bedroom, the bathroom, and the efficiency kitchen that had been built into the suite only for the convenience of someone who might want to rewarm something delivered by room service. He tapped the buttons on the microwave, looked into the refrigerator, ran the water in the sink, peered at himself in the glass front of a cabinet containing a row of delicate wineglasses. He waited, and waited, and looked out the window at the roller coaster. Then he waited some more.

"Al?" he muttered. "Come on, Al, what's happening?"

Power arcs, he thought. Power arcs could not by any stretch of the imagination be considered a good thing. He shouldn't have to consider them at all; they weren't supposed to happen. He was no electrician, but he remembered being shown a series of plans for the wiring of the control center. There were surge protectors, of course. Lots of them. Big ones. How power could surge through a handheld computer link, he couldn't imagine. The link's power cells didn't hold enough of a charge to "fry" someone. Or did they? No, no, no, he argued with himself. The thing could be no more harmful than a cell phone, or a video game. The only other option was, he began to murmur to himself, "Current flowing around loose inside the Imaging Chamber? Trapped in there. Arcing through the handlink?"

Of course they'd have to shut the Chamber down. Current dancing around in there, like St. Elmo's fire, could build up and . . .

"Come on, Al. Please."

But Al couldn't. He couldn't venture back into the Chamber until everything had been fixed, and tested, and the safety protocols reestablished. And that was okay. Sam could wait. He told himself that, the way his dad had told him years ago, after Tom had shipped out for Vietnam. Al and Tom were fine. If something had happened to Tom after the connection was broken, Al would have said so.

Or not.

"You've got people waiting for you downstairs, boss," Dove said.

Sam hadn't heard him come in, but there he was, standing near the door to the corridor. Sam tossed him a smile he supposed made him look like an escaped lunatic, then nodded (too jerkily, he was sure) and straightened his tie. It didn't end up straight. He tried again, then grunted and yanked the thing off.

"You okay, boss?"

"I'm fine. I don't like this tie."

Without so much as a twitch that might indicate what he was thinking, Dove went into the bedroom and returned almost immediately with a different tie that he looped around Sam's neck and tied for him. He took the one Sam had rejected out of Sam's hand and set it aside, accepting Sam's thank you with a perfunctory nod. Each time his gaze left Sam's face, Sam took another look around the room.

"You looking for something?" Dove asked.

"My copy of the schedule. I wanted to see what's coming up for this afternoon."

The bodyguard plucked a sheet of paper out of his suit-coat

pocket and handed it to Sam. "The TV crew's set up outside the aquarium. Guess they changed their minds about there being too much glare off the glass."

"That's fine."

For some reason, Dove didn't think it was fine, but the frown he produced came and went in less than a second. "Better get you down there."

Sam turned quickly and found the closest reflective surface: the smoked glass front of a cabinet housing a set of cut-glass decanters and bottles of expensive liquor. He used the image to guide him as he straightened the new tie and smoothed his hair. Then he looked beyond the reflection of Powell's face at the rest of the room. Still nothing. No Al.

He's fine. You know he's fine. When they fix the glitch, he'll be back.

When they were both satisfied that he was in good enough shape to greet whoever it was that was waiting downstairs, Dove opened the door of the suite and stepped back to allow Sam to pass through. As they walked toward the elevator, Sam tipped his head toward Max's door and inquired about her condition with a hiked eyebrow.

"She's already down there," Dove told him.

"She is? She's too upset to be dealing with these people."

Dove shook his head. "She's a chameleon, boss. She's not gonna let whatever went on up here interfere with her doing her job." Then he added, "More than a little."

"Where's Kevin?"

"Who the hell knows?"

Sam's eyebrow went up again.

"He took a walk. Asked me if I thought he looked old enough to get into one of the strip clubs. I told him not in his wildest imagination."

"So that's their method of dealing with 'whatever happened up here'?" Sam said unhappily. "They go their separate ways and pretend it didn't happen?"

"Looks like it."

About to reach for the elevator call button, Dove interrupted himself and took a long look at Sam, who had glanced back at the door to the suite several times already. Sam, in the middle of another look back, caught the bodyguard's expression and

261

offered, "I keep thinking I've forgotten something."

"Like what?"

"I'm not sure."

"Well," Dove mused, "it's not up to me to cast any stones, but when the kid started singing 'Ninety-nine Bottles of Beer,' I don't think he meant for you to drink that many. You probably poached a few brain cells."

"And you don't disapprove."

"Thought it was kind of funny."

"And people don't use the word 'funny' to describe me very often, do they?"

"I think 'never' would be close." Dove's hand drifted toward the call button, but again he pulled it back. "Can I be honest with you?"

"Give it a try." When the big man demurred, Sam coaxed, "Go ahead. No harm, no foul, whatever it is."

"I think it's kind of a good thing, you opening up a little bit."

"And you were afraid to say that?"

"You don't much like people talking about how you feel."

"Other than my migraine headaches."

Dove shrugged eloquently, then opted for the "in for a penny, in for a pound" approach. "Other than you saying you get migraine headaches, and the doctor giving you big bottles of placebos."

"You know that."

"Nothing goes in your mouth I don't know about. You hired me to do a job, I do it."

Sam smiled fleetingly. "I wondered why no one seemed to question my sitting out on the terrace in the sun to combat the kind of headache that drives most people to seek out dark and quiet."

"No one much questions you at all."

"Except Marie?"

"You had to bring her up in the middle of a good conversation." Dove winced. "But I figure, you've got every right to go out on the terrace by yourself if you want to. Everybody needs some downtime."

"With no explanation offered."

"You don't have to explain yourself to me."

"You're not even curious?"

"Didn't say that. I don't really need to be, anymore. I pretty

262

much figured it out a while ago." Sam's expression prompted the younger man to continue. "You go out there whenever somebody pushes the wrong button. Seems to me you probably go out there so you can think about her."

"You're right," Sam admitted. He didn't know whether that was also true about Joe Powell until Dove's lopsided grin told him it was.

"But I mean it, boss. It's good to see you this way. Even if you're creating a gigantic mess between Max and the kid, I'm glad you're interested. It's not my place to tell people how they ought to feel, or how long they should feel it, but it's kind of been a long time, you know? Since you lost Mrs. Powell. My gramps still pines over my grandmother. Leaves everything around the house the way she left it, and talks to her sometimes. I listened to him one time and he went on for five or six minutes like she was really there. But you, you're not that old. Okay if you don't want to marry anybody else, but I think you're shortchanging yourself if you don't even let yourself be friendly with people. It's like my mom said when I lost my dog. She said, you can't shut yourself off because you hurt. You know?"

"I think I do," Sam said.

"Look at Kevin. He'd have to be brain-dead not to see what Tracy was doing. You're only that stupid when you're in love, and he's not in love with her. But he just kind of forged ahead, like he knew what was going to happen but he was gonna let it play out anyway."

"He got laid," Sam said mildly.

Dove, taken by surprise, exploded into laughter. "Yeah. Yeah. Nineteen years old. Doesn't much matter what happens as long as you get some nooky out of it." He sobered again suddenly, as if he thought he was being overheard. "I don't know, though, boss. Max wants her own life. I think you and the kid are both beating a real dead horse."

Sam reached past him and pushed the call button. "Maybe not."

Gooshie flung both hands up to protect himself, though that did little to screen him from the heat of Al's wrath. "I'm sorry, Admiral," he insisted, listening to his voice tremble. "I don't know what Dr. Beckett was referring to."

"If he said there's a chip, then dammit, there's a chip!"

"There's no chip. If there was a chip, I'm certain he would have told me there was a chip. What good would it do anyone if we didn't know about the chip? No, Admiral, I'm quite sure the chip is a figment of Dr. Beckett's imagination."

"He *said*—"

"Perhaps he simply programmed Ziggy to respond to that particular phrase."

Al shifted his weight onto his toes and pushed his face toward Gooshie's. "I want you to find the chip and pull it."

"That would really not be a good idea, Admiral."

Al's eyes opened a little wider. He had not blinked for almost a minute. "That insufferable, ego-ridden bucket of bolts is not gonna try to electrocute me and get away it."

"I'm sure it was a malfunction."

"A perfectly timed malfunction."

"That would be a coincidence."

"You think."

"Ziggy wouldn't try to electrocute you."

"You think."

"I'm certain. Well, I'm relatively certain. She wouldn't do anything like that unless she had some sort of valid—"

Al's eyes opened wider and wider.

"I'll try to find out what went wrong," Gooshie volunteered.

"You do that," Al barked. "While I try to explain to the congressman that we experienced a badly timed malfunction that almost electrocuted *him*."

The corridor was filled with music. At least, Al thought as he hustled down the all-white passageway, Ziggy, in her current frame of mind, had probably decided it would pass for that. There were musical notes involved, but the overall result was the same as if a troupe of monkeys had been turned loose in a roomful of xylophones.

As he walked, he soundly cursed (in several languages) anyone and everyone who had agreed it was a good idea to save computer memory by using two digits instead of four.

Tom wasn't in Medical. In fact, he hadn't even reached Medical. If the misdirected juice had zapped him hard enough, he might be lying in the fetal position somewhere, twitching and dying. That was, Al thought, not a completely terrible scenario. All right, it was. But only because he would be called upon to

explain what had happened to Tom to the rest of the Becketts—
the Bonnick/Becketts and the Hayes/Becketts as well as the
Beckett/Becketts—and the rest of the United States House of
Representatives. And the Senate. And the presidents, both current
and yet-to-be-elected, the latter of whom was sulking inside the
Waiting Room, up around the corner on the left.

And there was Tom, standing outside the Waiting Room, tapping the toe of his shoe against the linoleum.

"Are you okay?" Al asked.

"Do I look okay? Admiral?"

"Malfunction," Al said. "A little fritz in the framastam. It
won't happen again."

Tom extended his right arm and stuck out his index finger,
pointing to the Waiting Room door. He looked remarkably like
the Ghost of Christmas Yet to Come gesturing Ebenezer Scrooge
toward his own grave. "Open the door."

"Oh, no," Al said. "Bad idea."

"I want to talk to Powell."

"Really bad idea."

He seemed to back down. "Okay," he said amiably. "I'll use
the phone. And call the Powell who exists in this now. He's at
home, getting ready for his party on Friday night. I'd like to ask
him if he's ever been to New Mexico."

"We can give the Imaging Chamber another shot."

"And have it take another shot at us? No thanks. I don't want
to talk to Sam right now. I want to talk to the guy who looks
like Sam. The one in there." The finger wiggled a little.

"Why?"

"I want to make sure he's all right."

"He's fine."

"Like Sam is fine."

"Look," Al said sharply. "That might put your jangled nerves
at ease, but it's not gonna do a thing for Powell."

"Does he know where he is?"

"More than he ought to. He needs to be able to forget it when
he—"

"And what if he doesn't?"

"He will."

"They call that 'denial.' "

"Yeah, they do," Al agreed. "I'm denying you permission to

go in there. It would introduce an unnecessary variable into a controlled experiment."

Tom snorted softly. "What's controlled about any of this?"

"Mighty damn little," Al sighed.

She was a morning-show feature correspondent trying to work her way up to an anchor desk. She wasn't going to get there, Sam thought, if she couldn't keep herself from preening during an interview.

"It's the ultimate in luxury," she said in a voice that kept straying half an octave too high.

"That's right, Margie," Sam tossed back, knowing she'd stolen the phrase out of the Nirvana Grand Opening brochure. "The city of Las Vegas is an oasis in the middle of the most punishing desert in the United States. We created Nirvana as an oasis for people trying to get away from the punishments of their everyday lives."

He grinned at the overly chipper Margie, who had spent an hour soaking in therapeutic mud and still had a tiny dab of it in front of her left ear. That made her giggle and clutch her cordless microphone in a way that made Sam flinch. "Egyptian cotton sheets on the beds. Those are yummy, Joe."

"I'm glad you enjoyed them."

He could hear tittering behind them. Margie either didn't hear it or didn't care; she was too focused on him. "But considering the very wide range of available amenities, your room prices are very reasonable."

For anybody who brings home about sixty thousand dollars a year, Sam thought. Before she could finish quoting the brochure to him, he said, "I hope you enjoy the rest of your visit, Ms. Campbell."

"Oh, I'm sure I will. And remember, we'll be here tomorrow to cover all the festivities at the grand opening!" She swung around to face her cameraman. "This is Margie Hayes Campbell at Joe Powell's beautiful Nirvana hotel in Las Vegas. Back to you in the studio."

She was ready to throw the preening into overload the moment the camera went off. Instead of giving her the chance to do that, Sam took her by the elbow and swung her into an alcove, an action she greeted with astonishment and a noticeable amount of delight. They weren't far enough away from her people, his people, or the crowd of onlookers to avoid being heard (or seen), something Sam was aware of when he told her, "You need to drop your voice."

"Of course," she cooed, then realized she was misunderstanding him. "Why?"

"If it's too high, it comes across as little-girlish. If you want to be taken seriously, you have to deepen it. Didn't they teach you that?"

"They told me to change my hair."

"Your hair is fine."

She looked at him skeptically. "This is the way I talk, Joe."

"Try a vocal coach."

He could hear her clearing her throat as he walked away. Dove joined him as he left the alcove, blocking Sam from the clamoring photographers at least for the moment. Max, who except for the tightness around her jawline, did indeed look as if the altercation with Kevin had never happened, slid in past her lover and tipped her clipboard into an angle at which Sam could see the top sheet.

"The people from MADD had to postpone," she explained, the stiff determination in her voice noticeable only to Sam and Dove. Sam took a closer look at her eyes and saw sparks of anger come and go like the flickering of fireflies. "Their plane was delayed in Houston. I've moved them to three this afternoon and bumped up Reverend Michaelson."

"That's fine."

"He's hearing-impaired in his right ear. Try to talk to his left."

"Got it."

"I've explained that you can join them for the reception but can't stay for the luncheon. They're fine with that as long as Mr. DeMarcus can bend your ear for a few minutes."

"Of course."

"You remember Mr. DeMarcus? He asked if you did. He mentioned Cleveland, but you haven't been to Cleveland in almost three years."

Sam opened his mouth to reply, then stopped. Over Max's shoulder he could see enough of the front entrance to allow him to note the arrival of the only limousine he had ever seen painted in metallic gold. As he stood watching, the driver hopped out, circled the car, popped open the passenger door, and stood far enough to allow his passenger to disembark while holding out a hand to assist.

It was Marie.

"Oh, shit," Dove said softly.

The little woman was dressed in a slinky, clinging evening gown almost completely covered in neon-blue bugle beads and matching spike-heeled shoes, and holding a matching clutch bag. Her hair was teased a full six inches above her head. She looked like a nightmare version of a Supreme.

"Does she have any idea it's eleven-thirty in the morning?" Dove winced.

"She's in Las Vegas," Sam replied.

Marie pressed into the driver's hand a tip big enough to make him goggle-eyed, then dismissed him and picked her way across the apron to the front doors, where a pair of liveried doormen no less astounded than the limo driver yanked the massive glass panels out of her way. Left in her impressive wake, the driver began to recover his equilibrium and went to the car's trunk to pull out Marie's luggage. Sam, Dove, and Max all expected her to sashay her way across the lobby to greet them; instead, she swept off in the other direction, toward the registration desk.

"I suppose it makes sense," Sam murmured. "I gave her money, there's a party tonight, and she knows me."

"Hurt me," Dove said.

By mid-afternoon, Sam felt *If it's an acronym, I've met with it.* MADD, NAACP, AFL-CIO, DARE. He had smiled so much his cheek muscles ached. Each time he nodded in response to someone's statement of their organization's position on the Powell agenda, he thought he could feel his brain slosh around inside his head. He'd done a remarkable job of powering through his hangover, but still regretted all that beer to the point that he considered getting down on his knees in front of the women from MADD and asking for their forgiveness. The real Joe Powell he was almost certain would never have gotten tanked the night before a day full of meet-and-greets.

The real Joe Powell, he thought, probably didn't get tanked at all.

Al's words kept ringing in his ears: *Don't mess this up.* All afternoon he looked for the Observer and failed to find him. The more time that went by without a reappearance from Al, the more worried Sam became. Over and over he told himself that neither Al nor Tom had been seriously hurt, but that did nothing to solve the mystery of what had happened in the Chamber and why the problem hadn't been fixed.

"Hey, Joe?"

Sam lifted his head. In five years of Leaping, he'd read enough body language to write a manual on it. The man who'd approached him didn't know Powell. And he didn't want an autograph. "Hello," Sam offered.

"I lost my house, Joe."

Something tapped Sam's left arm just above the elbow. Dove. Telling him which direction was open if he wanted to escape this stranger. Sam nodded, a very slight movement of his head. "I'm sorry about that."

"You gotta get me my house back."

How much would that involve? A hundred thousand dollars? Two hundred? Sam took a closer look at the man: the suit jacket heavily wrinkled as though he'd slept in it, the scuffs on his shoes, the bloodshot eyes. If he'd had a home, Sam guessed, it had been quite a while ago. He hesitated too long, and Dove's fingers tapped his elbow again. This time he took the bodyguard's advice and began to move away.

"Don't you want to share?" the man howled after him. "You got so much, can't you share a little?"

As soon as Sam was out of the man's reach, a trio of Nirvana security guards swooped in and steered him toward the door. He'd begun to sob long before he reached the threshold. Sam, watching surreptitiously from the relative safety of one of the gift shops, shook his head in dismay and said to Dove, "I can't help everybody."

"Nobody figures you can, boss."

"I'm not sure that's the truth."

"It's truth enough."

"Maybe I should . . ."

Dove shook his head and nodded in the direction he was trying to steer Sam toward. "You can't, boss. Nobody really expects you to. That guy didn't really expect you to solve his problems. Buying him a house won't solve jack."

"If you say so," Sam sighed.

They reached Nirvana's nightclub without further incident. The opening-eve party would begin here in a few hours, and the

269

room was already noisily alive with staff, draping the small, round tables with freshly pressed cloths, placing nosegays of fresh flowers in tiny vases, vacuuming the carpet, arranging the heavy velvet drapes that hung at either side of the stage, checking the lights and the sound system. One of the workers, busy re-gluing a small strip of toe panel that had come loose beneath the lip of the stage, had set up a tape player and was singing almost tunelessly along.

"They'll be finished in another fifteen or twenty minutes," Max said. Sam glanced at her and nodded. Although it wouldn't have attracted any attention from a stranger, the tone in her voice still said very plainly to him, "I'm going to do my job, no matter what."

"Is the room sold out?" he asked.

"It has been for weeks."

Dove groaned, "You're not thinking about getting Marie in here, are you, boss?"

More sparks flashed in Max's eyes, adding Kevin's name to the blacklist. "We'd have to bring in another table."

"Then do it," Sam replied. Max, wearing a growing frown, moved away to speak to the hotel liaison. Suddenly in the path of a worker toting four brass-and-leather chairs, Sam moved aside, Dove along with him. As they stood watching the activity, the song on the tape player changed. The first few notes of the new tune caught Sam's attention so completely that he failed to hear what Dove was saying. "What's the name of that song?" he asked, a little more sharply than he intended to.

Dove had to go to the worker to ask. The man shrugged, then popped the tape out of the machine to look at its label. When Dove returned to Sam, he too shrugged and said, "Something called 'Hello Again.' The singer's somebody named Liberty Jones. Never heard of her."

"Diamond," the worker called out. "He's the one originally did it."

"Neil Diamond?" Sam asked.

Dove shrugged once more. "Unless you know another Diamond. Something wrong, boss?"

Sam shook his head slowly. "I haven't heard that song in a long time."

Six notes: da da, da da, da da. *Hello again, hello. "Is it her I'm supposed to remember, Al?"*

She was humming to herself as she stooped to pick up the tiny seashell, no bigger than her thumbnail. They'd heard the song in the bar they'd left an hour ago, had danced to it, hummed along with it. She knew it, he didn't, but it was easy enough to pick up. Wistful and melancholy, so much so that it made her sigh softly and nestle into the shelter of his arms.

"I love you, Sam."

"Boss?"

Sam looked. "What?"

"Are you okay?"

He didn't say anything for a minute, just listened to the song. Then he produced a fleeting, lopsided smile. "Under the circumstances."

"You want to sit down?"

"That song used to mean something to me," Sam explained. "At least I think it did." *Hello again, hello.*

"I love you, Sam."

"Maybe I do need to sit down," he told Dove.

Six months ago, Tom remembered, he'd gone into Joe Powell's house feeling on top of the world. He'd listened to the rumors circulating around Washington and had dismissed them at first, giving them about as much weight as the stories of Alec Baldwin running for office. But when the rumors persisted, he grudgingly picked up some magazines and did some surfing on the Internet. He liked what he found, so he dug deeper and found more. When Linda asked what had him so enthralled, he shared the articles with her.

He was more excited walking into Powell's house than he'd been the first time he took the floor as a member of the Elk Ridge varsity basketball team. Again, he'd been chosen as part of a winning team: the Powell presidential race. He remembered the chants: *All the way! All the way! Elk Ridge! Elk Ridge!*

And I wasn't even talking to the real Joe, he thought ruefully. *I was talking to Sam. So is it Joe's politics I like—or Sam's?*

The man sitting inside what everyone here called the Waiting Room looked up when Tom entered. If he wanted to cover his surprise, he didn't do a very good job of it. Then again, maybe he wasn't trying to cover anything. "Hello, Tom," he said.

"Joe."

"So you do know where your brother works."

"I do now." Powell gestured toward a chair, but Tom shook his head and remained standing. "I'm sorry you're a part of this."

"I'm not."

"If there's anything you want, to make yourself more comfortable . . ."

Powell snorted at him softly. "You don't need to suck up to me, Tom. You haven't, all the times we've talked, and you don't need to start now, because I look like your brother. Or because I've gotten myself stuck in the middle of your brother's 'experiment.' "

"Gotten yourself . . . ?"

"I'm not being mistreated. Relax. There aren't going to be any repercussions."

Tom rifled through the stack of magazines Powell had been given to read, none of them less than six months old. He didn't doubt that Powell had gone through all of them carefully, whether he'd read them before coming here or not. Powell's face was on the cover of one of them, next to the headline SAVIOR OF THE RAIN FORESTS? PTI'S 20-YEAR PLAN FOR REGROWTH IN SOUTH AMERICA. "I'm trying to talk them into letting me do something to help get you back home."

"Which is?"

"They call it Leaping. I want them to Leap me back there so I can push Sam out."

Powell chuffed out a soft breath. "But that would leave you in his place, wouldn't it? No offense, Tom, but—"

"I can't leave things as they are."

"Tom. I'm here because I want to be."

Tom completely misunderstood the statement. Shaking his head, he prowled the Waiting Room, examining what little it had in the way of amenities. Not much like what Powell was used to, he thought with what he assumed was more annoyance than Powell himself felt—unless Powell had started out PO'ed and had managed to work himself down to this state of contemplative serenity. Turning enough so that he could see the man, Tom began to examine *him* and didn't like what he saw.

"Where did we first meet?" he asked.

"At the reception for the Kennedy Center Honors last year. Why? You don't suspect me of being your brother, pretending to be me, do you?"

"I don't know what I suspect, Joe. What do you mean, you want to be here?"

"It's a stepping-stone."

"To what?"

Powell picked up the magazine Tom had been looking at a minute ago and studied the picture of himself on the cover. "I know all about your brother. He came to me looking for money a few years ago and I turned him down. But I knew about him long before that. It was a little like the stories of the Second Coming," he commented bemusedly. "I was told years ago that there'd be a Sam Beckett who could travel in time, and sure enough."

"You're not making a lot of sense."

"I'm not sure you can help your brother. And I'm not sure he can help me, or the people in my life. What do you want me to do? What do you want me to say? Impress them all with my eloquence? Or give them enough money that they'll be so distracted thinking of ways to spend it, they'll let you do what you please?"

"Do you respect my judgment?"

"I wouldn't have asked you to be a part of my team if I didn't."

Tom hesitated, then said, "You've asked me to be a lot more than 'part of your team,' sir."

Powell smiled. "Did I go ahead and do that?"

"You did."

"I guess I must think you know what you're doing, then."

"Then you'll back me up?"

"I'm not sure that amounts of a hill of beans in this place, but I'm already backing you. Go do whatever you think is going to work."

"Thank you, Joe."

Powell chuckled softly. "Anytime."

Kevin returned to the hotel a little over an hour later, wearing designer sunglasses and a new leather jacket, and no happier than if he'd been told he was going to spend the next several months locked up in the Clark County jail. After half a dozen rides on the Hilton's "Star Trek Experience," he'd succeeded in making himself sick, which had endeared him to no one—his fellow riders, the Hilton employees, or himself. Hands shoved deep into the pockets of his new jacket, he trudged the mile and a half up the Strip to Nirvana and stood outside the hotel staring at it, squinting behind the dark lenses of his glasses.

"Watch the cars, son."

He looked. One of the valet parking attendants was there, trying to urge him back up out of the driveway, onto the curving walk that led up to the front doors. The guy's mournful expression made him give in.

"So, what are you so miserable about?" Kevin asked. "Don't they pay you enough?"

Instead of answering, the attendant left him to slide behind the wheel of the car in whose path Kevin had been standing. Kevin watched him drive off toward the entrance to the garage, then watched the car's owners walk arm in arm toward the glass doors. Of course the guy made enough; Powell never short-changed his employees. He certainly had more money in his wallet right now than Kevin did. To assure himself of that, Kevin pulled his wallet out of his back pocket and peered into it. Three bucks. That'd buy him a soda and a package of cookies in the newsstand.

A trio of guys in suits walked past him, laughing. "Hottest ticket in town for tonight," one of them said. "Dinner and the opening bash."

Dinner. Kevin sighed loudly and shoved his wallet back into his pocket. There would be no deluxe meal in the mezzanine restaurant tonight, but unless Powell, or Dove, or his mother had had him taken off the freebie list, he'd be able to eat pretty much anywhere in the hotel he decided to and have the meal charged to Powell. The trouble was, he'd be eating all by himself. Fleetingly he thought about joining Tracy in Baltimore—she'd be there by now, he supposed, safe in the clutches of that woman Powell said was an expert on bulimics. Less fleetingly, he missed her. He'd been in bed with her only twenty-four hours ago, touching her in places that made her giggle. She had a great laugh. To his chagrin he realized he didn't even have a phone number to call to make sure she'd arrived in Baltimore safely and wasn't scared of being surrounded by strangers.

He could go to Baltimore, he supposed. There'd certainly be at least one more flight leaving before the end of the day. And if this Dr. Worther was famous, she'd either be listed in the phone book, or someone would know where to find her.

Maybe Baltimore wasn't a bad idea.

Except he had only three bucks, and no one at the airline ticket counter was going to let him get away with saying "Charge it to Joe Powell." Which left only one option: asking Powell for more.

Dove's hired flunky was still standing alongside the elevator, as stiff and unsmiling as if somebody had starched not only his clothes but his face. He watched Kevin approach, then reached over and pushed the call button. That was something, Kevin observed; at least he wouldn't be barred from his room, and his belongings, and the mini-bar refrigerator jammed with midget bottles of booze. The guard rode up to the penthouse with him, got out first, and looked up and down the hall. As both of them expected, there was no one around.

Kevin thought about his limited options for a moment, then pointed to the door of Powell's suite. "You have a key to that door? I left something in there."

A minute later, he was inside, alone. The guard had gone on his way. Whether he rode the elevator back down to the lobby or stayed up here didn't much matter. The suite itself was empty. He wandered back and forth for a while, touching the furniture, looking at the row of tailored suits in Powell's closet, staring out the window at the roller coaster. The bedroom was larger than the one he'd been given, but really, not any more luxurious. His room, like Powell's, had thick, soft carpeting, Egyptian cotton sheets on the bed, a pair of comfortable armchairs, a large, flat-screen TV hanging on the wall, and a sunken, marble whirlpool tub.

Powell had taken good care of him, he had to admit. The room, the clothes, the good meal last night. Plus all the perks at home: his tuition, his apartment, his car. Even a laptop like the one sitting there on the table near the bedroom window. Well, not quite like this one, Kevin noted as he drifted closer to it. This one was smaller, newer, probably faster.

There. He'd almost missed seeing it: Powell's wallet, lying on the bed, half-hidden beneath a discarded jacket.

He knew a bunch of things about Baltimore, he reflected as he held the wallet in his hands. Grand old city, close to Washington, close to Annapolis, not too far from New York or Philadelphia. Humid in the summertime, but a generally mild climate. Enough of a crime rate to be concerned about, but not as bad as D.C.

He found the same credit card Powell had given him a couple of days ago and plucked it out. Then he pulled out the cash: almost a thousand dollars, most of it in hundreds. Powell would never miss it, he told himself. If he hadn't owned Nirvana, he would have sprung half of this for dinner last night. A thousand bucks was nothing to him. Pocket change. He'd flung it here on the bed because it was, what? Risky to walk around with this much cash? Kevin tugged out his own wallet and filled it with Powell's money, then turned the credit card over and over in his fingers.

Then he looked again at the laptop.

Newer, smaller, faster. Probably cost upward of five or six grand, new. He could unload it either here or in Baltimore for a couple thousand if he found the right person. Or he could keep it himself. It was a nice little machine. He could take the printer too—it was even smaller than the computer. Both of them together took up not much more space than the ream of paper Powell had opened up but used none of. Losing track of where he was and what he was doing, Kevin slid into the chair Powell had occupied earlier in the day and looked at what to Powell was only an easily replaceable plaything. Maybe he used it to jot down notes that one of his staff would turn into a speech or a magazine article. Maybe he zapped a few E-mails around the world in the middle of the night.

Kevin's fingers touched the trackball, opening a directory, then another. There was more here than he'd thought—the hard drive contained several dozen files. Why they'd be on here, in the memory of something that could easily be lost, or stolen, or broken, he couldn't imagine. The files had names that didn't mean anything, most of them at least. A few had names that sounded like Powell's companies.

One of them had Kevin's name.

The nightclub's lights had been dimmed, giving the press an advance taste of what the room would look like late tonight. Dim, elegant, quiet for now. Each of the reporters took a peek and murmured approval, then the photographers filed in and took pictures. They'd take more later on, when the room was packed with big names.

Sam nodded acknowledgment and thanks for the compliments they offered him, although he knew Powell had had little to do with the design of the room other than approving the finished drawings and okaying the fabrics, the dishware, and the lighting fixtures. It was all right to accept the kudos, though, he decided, since he was representing the people who had done the work. If he was here long enough, he'd make sure they were properly rewarded for their creativity and their labors.

"Joe?" a reporter called out. "Is it true Streisand is attending the opening tomorrow?"

"So I hear." Sam smiled.

"Will she be performing here on New Year's Eve?"

He glanced to his left, but Max was still gone, seeing to a myriad of last-minute details. "I think she's made other plans," he said, hoping that was the right answer.

"Oh, come on, Joe, you can't make her change her mind?"

"Joe, is it true you're reserving ten ringside seats at every performance for people who can't afford to put out a couple hundred in tips to get themselves up front?"

"Joe, who's your date for tonight?"

"I have a question, Mr. Powell."

Sam recognized the voice and turned toward it. Kevin was standing in the fringes of the crowd of reporters, holding an armful of paper and wearing an ugly expression. When the boy knew he had Sam's attention, he stepped forward and held out the pile of paper. "I'd like to know: what's this?"

"I'm . . . not sure."

"You're writing a biography of me? Is that it? All this is research?"

A few times during his years of Leaping, Sam had seen faces as filled with hatred as Kevin's was right now. A few times before, the hatred had been directed at him. It was again now, and Sam had to force himself not to wince. He knew, as certainly as if he'd been close enough to read the sheets Kevin was holding, what was on them and where Kevin had found all of it. Before he could say anything, Dove had gone to the boy and taken him by the arm. Kevin shook him off and took a couple of steps toward Sam.

"Let's talk about this later," Sam said softly.

"No," Kevin snapped. "Let's talk about it now. Mr. Big Wheel. Mr. Maybe I'm Running for President and Maybe I'm Not. Who said you had the right to spy on me? You hired somebody, didn't you? Somebody to keep track of me and report back

277

to you?" The boy's voice started to rise as he shoved the paper toward Sam. "What the fuck gives you the right to *watch* me, like you're the FBI and I'm some kind of criminal? Go ahead, explain it to me. I want to hear—" He seemed to remember suddenly that they were not alone and his expression shifted a little. "I want all these people to hear why you think it's acceptable to keep track of where I go, who I see, what I do. Because my mother works for you? Because everything I need comes out of your bank account? Is that your justification?"

Dove again took Kevin by the arm, tightly enough that he couldn't break loose, and shifted him away from Sam.

"Get your goddamn fucking hands off me!" Kevin shrilled.

The crowd of onlookers increased tenfold within seconds, like a flock of seagulls swooping in to grab anything they could reach from a new source of food. They began to murmur among themselves, jockeying for the best position, and camera flashes began to go off. Rather than acknowledge their presence by continuing to play to the crowd, Kevin pushed his face toward Dove's and hissed, "I said let go of me."

"You're gonna shut up, right now," Dove hissed back.

"Or you'll do what? Break my arm?"

Adrenaline gave Kevin a considerable surge of strength, but Dove was a solid column of muscle. Indicating through quick nods of his head that the guards he had hired were to watch over Sam, he overpowered the boy and shoved him down the corridor toward the escalator to the mezzanine. Kevin did his best to break free, without success, and moments later they were inside an empty office whose only door Dove blocked with his body. The second he was turned loose, Kevin, consumed with fury and frustration, slammed the pile of papers down on the closest desk and wheeled to face Dove.

"Did you know what he was doing?" he demanded. "Did you know about this?"

"It's none of my business what the boss does."

"It isn't?"

"I know what I need to know. The rest of it's not my problem."

"Does *she* know?"

"Let me explain something to you, kid. You learn to not see things. Not hear them. Not know about them. I might be in the room, but there's stuff I don't see. Because it's not my problem.

278

You understand what that means? There's times when I have to be in the room with the boss, so I can do my job. But I *don't see*." Dove's gaze drifted toward the stack of paper, then back to Kevin. "So he knows all about you. What difference does it make?"

Kevin's eyes widened. "You're not serious."

"If you think your life is private, if you think nobody's watching you, you're kidding yourself."

"Does he think nobody's watching him?"

"No."

"Then why should he mind me yelling at him in front of a bunch of reporters? Why should that matter? There's stuff in the newspaper about him all the time. Half of it's probably made up," Kevin said, his voice still sharp and mean. "But he lines himself up for it every time he leaves that crazy fortress he lives in. He's a public figure. But I'm not. You hear that? I'm not. I've got the right to be left alone."

"While you spend his money on—"

Kevin cut him off. "I get a check once a month. I never got any list of things I'm allowed to spend it on."

"You could use a little good judgment."

"Yeah, well, maybe I could use a mother who'd dish out some good judgment instead of spending her days following Powell around like a trained seal and her nights screwing with you." Kevin's face shifted again, abruptly, as his eyes fell on the pile of papers. "She knows, doesn't she? She knows he's keeping tabs on me. And it's okay with her because it means she doesn't have to do it. She doesn't even have to care." His eyes began to fill and he turned away from the bodyguard, blinking hard to get rid of the tears so that he wouldn't have to give himself away by lifting his hand to wipe his eyes. "She'd rather do this than let me call her once in a while to tell her what happened to me."

"She doesn't do it to hurt you, Kevin."

"Yeah? Well, how about, it *does* hurt me? It hurts me that she lets him get away with this shit." Shaking, Kevin seized the pile of paper and flung it against a wall. It made a very satisfying explosion, covering half the office with fluttering sheets of paper. Kevin stood watching it all float to the floor, then sank to the floor himself and buried his face in his hands. "It hurts me that she's never there for me," he mumbled. "Never. Never." His head came up a little after a moment, his face red and blotchy and streaked with tears. "And I'm supposed to care that I made him look bad in front of those people? I don't care. What are they gonna invent out of it, that I'm his lover and I got mad at him?"

Dove shook his head. "He's used to that kind of stuff. Every couple months they try to connect him to somebody, and it always dies out because it's not true."

"Then who does he sleep with?" Kevin asked, sniffling loudly, his expression daring Dove to answer the question.

Dove considered the scattered papers for a moment before he said, "Nobody."

"Nobody?"

"Nope."

"And you don't think there's anything weird about that?"

"About celibacy?"

"About him not having anybody. My grandmother said Powell's wife died like twenty years ago. In twenty years, he hasn't found somebody else? Somebody who looks like him, and has all that money?"

"That's not how it works, kid. You know that."

Kevin's head slumped again. "I guess so."

Dove glanced around the room and located a big wastebasket with a portable paper shredder fastened to its top rim. Setting the basket down in front of Kevin, he said, "Come on, get up off the floor. You can probably get rid of all that stuff in less than an hour."

"It's still on the computer."

"You didn't delete it?"

Kevin didn't answer right away. With a small sigh, he said finally, "I started to. But it kind of felt like I was erasing my life."

Dove chuckled softly, more to cheer the boy up a little than anything else. "You never know, kid. Someday somebody might want to write a biography, and they could use all that stuff." When Kevin didn't respond, the bodyguard prompted, "You think you're never gonna be worth writing a biography about?" He reached down and gave Kevin a hand getting up off the floor. "You take care of the mess. I'll go check on the other mess."

He had unlocked the door and was on his way out when Kevin said quietly, "Dove?" The big man let the door close again and waited. "Does it bug you that she doesn't love you?"

"You're a smart kid," Dove said. "You figure it out."

CHAPTER
TWENTY-FOUR

"Boss?" Dove said.

Sam put down the bottle of juice he'd been drinking. He'd finished making some videotaped comments for a TV special called *Flights of Fancy* and had been given a few minutes' break before his next chore. Rather than retreat upstairs, he'd taken refuge in one of the small suites of offices intended for use by visiting business teams. "Where is he?" he asked.

"Upstairs. I gave him some stuff to do. There's a carton of invitations to put in the envelopes."

"Okay."

"You had that much detail on him in the computer? All that paper?"

Sam could feel heat rising into his face. He'd seen the directory Kevin had discovered, each file bearing a person's name, and had noted the number of bytes each file occupied. Some of them were enormous. He hadn't opened any of them. His work at the computer had been constantly interrupted by ringing telephones and couriers and Max's continuing stream of file folders, and his quiet time had been filled with . . . *her*. He didn't know what was in Powell's collection of information regarding Kevin's life, but at several hundred kilobytes, yes, it was "all that paper."

"He wasn't meant to see that," he told Dove.

"Well, he did." The bodyguard closed the door behind him and folded his arms over his chest. "See, boss, what you do is none of my business. I know you have to keep tabs on people. But—" His foot tapped the carpet a couple of times. "There's kind of no good reason for digging around in somebody's privacy that much. You don't need to know all that stuff. The kid feels like he's been raped, and I damn sure don't blame him."

Sam nodded, still embarrassed. "I'll apologize to him."

"First, I think you ought to delete those files. And tell whoever's feeding you all that information to stop."

"You're right."

"You got a file on me?"

Yes, there'd been one, in the same directory. One on Max, as well. It astounded him, thinking about it now, that Max could know about the existence of the files and yet go about her life as if most of it weren't written down in the memory of Joe Powell's laptop. She had to know; she'd watched him work on the computer any number of times during the past few days, and had worked on it briefly herself. Maybe she didn't care what Powell knew. Maybe she regarded it as coming with the territory. Part of her job.

Dove's hand was reaching toward him. Sam took what he was handing over before he bothered to look at it: a credit card and several folded-up hundred-dollar bills. "That's from him," Dove explained. "He took it out of your wallet."

"Before or after he found the file?"

"I didn't ask."

"I think I need to talk to him."

"You've got people waiting to see you."

Sam made a face. "Let them wait. If I had an interview with God Himself, it wouldn't merit putting off apologizing to Kevin."

"I'm not sure he wants to listen to you."

"God, or Kevin?"

"Maybe both. He trusted you, boss."

"I know."

Kevin opened the door without a word and, as Sam moved into the room, went back to the small round table near the windows, sat down, and resumed stuffing pale blue invitations into matching envelopes. He had already done several dozen of them and had piled them neatly in the middle of the table.

"I'm trying to think of a way to tell you to take your money and shove it up your ass," he said mildly. "I didn't know what you were buying from me when I signed those checks. Most of the money's gone. I can sell the car, but I can't get the rest of it back. I wish I could. I'd like to throw it down in front of you and tell you what kind of a sleazy, sneaky bastard I think you are."

"I'm sorry, Kevin."

"You're not sorry. If you're sorry about anything, it's that I found out, and I'm sure you don't even really care about that." In spite of his anger, he was careful with his chore; each rectangle of blue card stock was carefully slid into the envelope so that it wouldn't wrinkle. "My grandfather's going to hemorrhage when he finds out that if he wants me to go back to school in the fall, he'll have to pony up for it. He doesn't have that kind of money. So I guess I find a job. I'm sure I can find something real kick-ass with one year of introductory liberal arts courses under my belt. At least I don't have to live on the street. I can move back in with my grandparents and spend my evenings watching *Wheel of Fortune*."

"I deleted the file."

"Yeah? Pardon me if I'm not impressed."

Lost for something to say that the boy would believe, Sam put his hand on the doorknob, intending to leave.

"Do you have a file on Tracy too?" Kevin demanded. "Did you call somebody before we left the house and have them dig up a bunch of dirt on her too?"

"No. I didn't."

"You make me sick. You know that? You really turn my stomach."

Sam took his hand off the knob and leaned against the wall. Whether or not Kevin meant that literally, the lingering effects of the hangover made Sam's stomach roil. His head had not stopped aching all day and had begun to pound with new vigor down in the lobby. "I don't expect you to believe me," he began, hoping the queasiness wouldn't make him sound less sincere. "But those files were . . . given to me. I haven't read them. I should have deleted them, but I didn't. All I know about your life is what you've told me. I didn't intend to hurt you. I meant the opposite."

"What is it to you, a game?"

"No. Not at all."

"You've got no right to all that. Maybe they should send you copies of my grades. And you can check with my landlord to make sure I'm not wrecking the apartment. But you need to know where I go, who I talk to, what I eat? You had somebody take pictures of my apartment. Who let them in there to do that? The landlord's supposed to get my permission. Nobody got my permission."

"It won't happen again."

"If I go back to my grandparents, are you gonna take pictures of me there?"

"No."

"And people should vote for you. Make you president of the United States." Kevin shifted his gaze out the window, though his hands kept working on the invitations. He had apparently done enough of them that he could keep going by touch alone. "If I went back home and started telling people what you did, they'd laugh. They'd say, what difference does it make? What are you hiding? What do you care if he knows everything you do? They won't believe you could do anything wrong. You're the golden boy, the one on all the magazine covers."

Sam told him quietly, "They should believe you."

"Why? Who the hell am I?"

The entrance to the bathroom lay to Sam's left. In there, in spite of the fact that the bathroom was dark, he could see Joe Powell's reflection in the mirror. "You're someone with a lot more integrity than I've got."

"Leave me alone, all right?" Kevin said. "I told Dove I'd finish this. Then I don't know what I'm going to do. My car's at your house. If I go back to my grandparents, I get to explain what happened."

"You can go back to your apartment. I'll have someone bring the car down."

284

"I don't want it. I don't want any of it. Don't you get that? I'm not gonna let you go on buying me."

"Then I won't," Sam replied. "If you don't want a job with me, pick someone you *would* like to work for and I'll write you a recommendation. And I'll write you one to any scholarship committee you choose. I know my judgment means next to nothing to you right now, but it does carry a lot of weight in a lot of places. You choose where you'd like to be and I'll make sure you get there. After that, you'll be on your own. Whatever you achieve, it'll be because of your own efforts, not my money."

"I don't want your efforts."

Last night, Sam thought, he and this kid had poured beer on each other, cackling with laughter. "I'm asking you to let me start over. I know I've betrayed your trust. Give me another chance."

"You didn't read the files?"

"No." Sam forced himself to search for an explanation. Powell *couldn't* be that paranoid. Couldn't possibly see a need for a ream of paper's worth of information on this boy, who had no connection to him other than being the offspring of his assistant. There was no good reason for it at all. Except . . . "The person who sent it to me thought you might have a negative effect on the campaign. I don't agree with them," he continued quickly, before Kevin could respond. "You're a normal kid. And I don't pretend to have control over the families of my employees. You're not my son. I have no responsibility for who you are or what you do. I have people working for me who want things to be perfect. And that's not possible. You're a good kid, Kevin. I'm sorry I betrayed you, if by nothing more than sitting back and letting things happen."

Kevin thought that over for a long while, his eyes on the stack of empty envelopes rather than on Sam. "You did help Tracy."

"Give me another chance."

"You're not what my mother said you were. You're not like that at all. My mother—" He cut himself off, then changed his mind and said what he was thinking. "If my mother cares about you so much, then there must be something good about you."

"You trust her judgment?"

"Yeah," Kevin said. "I do."

Al listened to the tinkling coming over the loudspeakers and finally realized what it was he was hearing. "Show tunes?" he roared. "She's playing *show tunes*?"

"So much suffering." Ziggy sighed. "So much unnecessary pain."

The Observer stalked across the Control Room and confronted the bleary-eyed Gooshie, who had been working at the main console for hours. Al's hand came up and jabbed fiercely through the air as if it were the accompaniment to a loud tirade, but nothing came out of his mouth. He had run out of things to say. Not that he could have uttered them if he'd thought of something more; his throat felt as if he'd been chugging drain cleaner.

"Al," Verbena told him, "I want you to come sit down somewhere."

"Show tunes," he rasped.

Verbena tilted her head and listened. "That's lovely." When Al scowled at her, she said, "Maybe she's been influenced by Arnold. Al, I want you to come sit down. We'll have something to eat. You need to relax—you don't look well."

"Why should I look well?" he hissed.

Rather than make eye contact with Al again, Gooshie explained quietly to Verbena, "I honestly can't find a chip. There's nothing in any of the systems that would disable Ziggy without shutting down the whole complex. I have no idea what Dr. Beckett was talking about. I'm sure he simply programmed her to respond to that command. Although he may remember doing that not quite—" The programmer sighed and shook his head. "It's possible he programmed her to respond to that command from *him.*"

Al opened his mouth but again, nothing came out. Verbena took him by the arm and turned him toward the door. "We're going to go sit down now, and you're going to have something to eat. Don't make me call Security and have them take you to Medical."

"There's nothing wrong with me."

"Other than that you're sixty-five years old and you've had one hour's sleep in the last forty-eight. And nothing to eat except coffee. Don't argue with me, Calavicci. You don't want to see yourself roped to a bed."

He went with her out into the corridor, though he certainly did not go meekly. The tinkling music was louder out there, and Verbena began to hum softly along with it as they walked toward the elevator. "One of my favorites," she commented, as if they were taking a stroll through the park.

286

"What is it?" Al grunted.

"*West Side Story*. 'One Hand, One Heart.' " They went a little farther, then something occurred to her. "Ziggy?"

"So little time," Sam's creation murmured.

"Ziggy, are you exchanging data?"

No reply.

"Ziggy, answer the question."

The tinkling built to a crescendo, then faded slightly. "I have found a kindred spirit. And he shares in my grief."

"He?" Al burbled.

"He will not misuse the information I've provided. He loves me."

Al's eyes bulged. He shifted his weight, preparing to bolt back down the hall to the Control Room, but Verbena held on firmly and braced him against the wall. "Ziggy, you're strictly forbidden to release information that's not already in the public data stream."

Down at the end of the hall, the elevator doors opened and Donna emerged, going through a sheaf of papers attached to a clipboard. When she noticed the expressions on her friends' faces she hurried to join them. The tilt of Verbena's head made her listen to the sound coming out of the speakers as she walked. " 'I Feel Pretty'?" she questioned.

"She's uploading information," Verbena squeaked.

"To where?"

"To Spirit." Ziggy sighed.

The three humans stared at each other. "Spirit?" Donna said. "Does she mean Powell's computer? Does it have a name?"

"Everything has a name, Dr. Alessi."

The place they needed to be, obviously, was the Waiting Room. They'd gone a few steps in that direction when Al suddenly let out an *oof* and stopped moving. Verbena peered into his face, not liking what she saw.

"I'm all right," he said.

"The hell you are. I'm taking you to Medical."

"The hell you are," he said.

"Its name is SPIRIT," Powell said. "System Retrieval—" He glanced in turn at each of the faces surrounding him and said bemusedly, "You don't care what it stands for."

"You deliberately programmed it to contaminate another computer," David shot back.

"We programmed it to recognize when it was being contacted by another intelligence of similar capacity and capabilities, and at that point to open certain of its systems protections and interface with the other computer."

"Cyber sex?"

"More or less."

David sank into a chair, rubbing the back of his neck with one hand. "How did your programmers know that doing that wouldn't irreparably harm your computer?"

"We took a chance."

Now it was David's turn to look at the people around him. Several times, he moved his lips as if he intended to say something, but no words came out. Donna, standing closest to his chair, rested a hand on his shoulder and smiled at him encouragingly, then turned her attention to Powell. "You knew, somehow, that it would be *this* computer. Sam's computer. You were certain of that."

"Not a hundred percent," Powell admitted. "But close enough."

"Why?"

"I wanted the technology."

Verbena frowned. "So you could duplicate Quantum Leap? How did you know all of this even existed? All you had was an eight-year-old grant proposal. Your computer could have interfaced with something—"

"I knew it existed."

A few steps away, Al looked pointedly at Tom, who shrugged and shook his head in confusion. "You never told me any of this, Joe," Tom said sharply. "Was this—all your curiosity about Sam, was it for this? Not because you wanted me to be part of your campaign? You made me a part of your campaign because of my connection to Sam?" He blew out a long breath, then went on, "I appreciate hearing that bit of good news. Thanks for telling me *before* the big announcement. Before I commit myself to something that's not what I thought it was."

Powell gestured to placate him, something that worked only minutely. "That's not true, Tom. I found you because of your connection to Sam. I asked you to join the campaign because of who you are, because of the work you've done. It's an entirely separate thing." Then he turned to Al. "Does what you're thinking happen to include the term 'lying sack of shit'?"

"Maybe," Al snapped.

Slowly, Powell began to walk the length of the room. It didn't take long, even moving at a sleepwalker's pace. "I knew about Quantum Leap before Sam did," he said, his head down as if he were addressing the floor.

"From the grant proposal."

"No. I found out about it from my wife. It seems she met Dr. Sam Beckett in 1958."

Donna said, "When Sam was five years old?"

Powell shook his head. "When Sam was Leon Stiles."

Somebody had dubbed New York "The City That Never Sleeps," Sam recalled as he closed the door behind him, but it wasn't entirely true. New Yorkers had the good sense to go to sleep eventually. But *this* place . . . He looked out the window into what served as darkness around here and watched a trio of cars jammed with tourists soar by on the roller coaster. Bone weary, he trudged into the bedroom, shrugged out of his jacket and tie, and dropped them on the bed, then went on into the bathroom, relieved himself, ran cold water into the sink, and splashed double handfuls of it up onto his face.

His face, Powell's face. Powell looked back at him out of the mirror and Sam grunted in dismay.

"Swell guy," he muttered. "You make J. Edgar Hoover look like a slacker."

But he still couldn't believe that all those files existed because Powell wanted them to. Over and over, he heard Al's voice telling him, "It'll mess up the campaign." Bad enough that Powell's own background would have to be under minute scrutiny; did the same have to be true of everyone not only in, but on the periphery of Powell's inner circle? Sam sat down at the desk, booted up the laptop, and sat staring at the directory that popped onto the screen. He'd already cleaned out most of the files in the directory Kevin had found, knowing as he did so that if the files had been sent to him, copies of them probably existed somewhere else.

With his shoulders hunched so much they began to create an ache in the middle of his back, he accessed the laptop's modem, gave the small computer instructions, and sat listening to the familiar screech of a connection being made. A minute later a greeting appeared on the screen.

HELLO, DR. BECKETT.

He typed in quickly, HELLO, ZIGGY.

I'VE MISSED INTERFACING WITH YOU.

I HAVE TOO. WILL YOU DO SOMETHING FOR ME?

CERTAINLY.

It took him a couple of minutes to type in the commands. The words PLEASE WAIT floated across the screen, then disappeared, replaced by YOUR INSTRUCTIONS HAVE BEEN STORED, AWAITING EXECUTION ON 12.31.99. Then: DR. BECKETT?

YES, ZIGGY.

BE WELL.

The connection was broken, leaving Sam to stare at the wallpaper he assumed Powell had chosen.

The room was well soundproofed, but even so he could hear a plane approach, sounding so close that it seemed likely to scrape the roof of the hotel. Sam unlocked the door to the room's narrow balcony and stepped out, craning his neck to find the descending jet as it aimed for the Las Vegas airport, which looked so close from here that it seemed to be walking distance. For a second or two he steeled himself for a barrage of camera flashes and was fleetingly surprised when none came. The people on the roller coaster were a lot nearer than the plane, and even so, none of them noticed him. Of course, the cars were moving so rapidly, none of them had much of a chance to focus on him, to figure out who was standing there. Silently Sam went back into the bedroom, closed and locked the door, and sank down onto the end of the bed.

A fun-filled vacation in Vegas. That's a laugh.

When he heard the sound he ignored it, thinking *Refrigerator.* When it came again he grumbled quietly, wondering if every small appliance that had been installed on this floor of the hotel had faulty drive belts.

Squeak.

There wasn't a refrigerator in here; it was out in the living room, set into the wet bar. Sam lifted his head a little and scowled at the doorway. And gaped in surprise.

Tonto the cat was sitting there, silhouetted in the light from the living room. When it noticed Sam staring, it strolled across the bedroom and began to twine around Sam's legs, purring loudly. Confused, Sam picked the animal up and held it against his chest. "How in the world . . . ?" he mumbled.

Then there was another figure in the doorway, dressed in shimmering, twenty-first-century fabric. The name "Al" almost reached Sam's lips, but it wasn't Al, and he slumped in disappointment. The figure moved forward, holding out something that Sam realized was a bowl of soup.

"Mr. Joe," Marie said. "You didn't eat."

"I ate."

"You picked. They tell me everything."

She held out the bowl in much the same way his mother had proffered his mittens: *You take this, or you're dead meat.* She was right, he realized: he'd only nibbled during the day. His last good meal had been last night. Nodding, he settled the cat in his lap and took the bowl, inhaling fragrant steam.

Marie looked around, taking stock of the room as he ate. "He's a nice boy," she commented.

"Yes, he is."

"You were a nice boy too."

There'd been no file on Marie. Not a word. Maybe whoever was out there collecting information didn't think Marie posed a threat to the campaign. Or . . . "You've known me a long time," Sam guessed.

"The man who has everything, knows everything, doesn't know so much."

"I do the best I can."

She reached in and carefully scooped Tonto up into her arms. "You get cat hairs in the soup."

Sam smiled wistfully. "There are worse things than a few cat hairs in the soup. What can I do, Marie? Kevin wants so badly for his mother to care about him."

"He wastes his time. You too."

"Why?"

"She cares now. But she cares about other things more."

"So I should eliminate the other things?"

Marie clucked her tongue. "After so long, now you want to fix hearts. You should fix your own heart first."

"I can't—I can't remember her face, Marie." He fumbled around in the collection of things he'd tossed on the bed and came up with his wallet. Setting the nearly empty bowl on the floor, he pulled the wallet open and showed her what was inside.

"I don't have a picture. I have nothing to remind me. Nothing to carry with me."

She put the cat on the bed, where it happily burrowed a nest out of Sam's discarded clothing. Then she took the wallet out of Sam's hands and closed it. "You don't need the picture. You need here." She touched her chest lightly, above her heart. "Mr. Joe," she chided him gently, "it's not your fault, what happened."

"I left her there."

"Not your decision. It was God's, what happened to Becky."

Sam blinked at her. "Becky . . . ?" He couldn't say, *I thought her name was Emily.*

"To die that way."

He tried to think of a way to maneuver her into providing more information, but his mind was muddled. *You should know better than to drink that much. You're under a lot of stress? What kind of an excuse is that? You've got a job to do here.*

"She's with you, Mr. Joe. Without pictures."

Becky? Becky . . . The name wanted to mean something to him—something that connected with the picture Al had shown him that looked so familiar. His mind roamed the past, his past, other people's past. *There were so many . . .* "Becky," he murmured. He closed his eyes, trying to bring up the details of the photograph. Finally, he found the name. Sweet face, surrounded by soft blond hair. Big blue eyes, taking in the face of someone she thought was a killer named Leon Stiles. Listening to everything he said, holding on to it, even though she ought to have been terrified.

"She's with you. Your sweetheart." Marie mistook Sam's distraction for something else and she patted his shoulder. "You were a nice boy. It makes me sad, what you are now."

That jolted him back to Marie's now, back to the hotel room. "I don't know what to do, Marie. How to make it right."

"Sleep."

"I can't."

"You will now." She glanced at the bowl, then leaned down and picked it up.

Sam's eyes widened. "You mickeyed the soup?"

Marie shrugged mildly and pointed to the mound of pillows at the head of the bed. "You sleep. I will tell Dove, leave you the hell alone."

"But I have so much to do."

She took note of the way his shoulders had begun to droop. "Not so much as you believe. You rest. If things need fixing, someone else will fix them."

She went out then, closing the door and leaving him alone with the cat. Wondering what it was she'd used to doctor the soup, he crawled up the length of the bed and tried to shift his aching body into a position that would not result in more pain. The cat let him settle down, then began a symphony of squeaky purring. From outside, he heard the hard *whup whup whup* of a helicopter passing the hotel. "Becky Pruitt," he murmured.

You remembered.

Becky . . .

"What about Becky?" He remembered Carol Pruitt moving quickly in between him and the little girl, her voice full of threats, warning him away. Away from an eight-year-old, smart and curious, but not quite able to grasp what Leon Stiles's presence in their home might turn into. He remembered blue eyes searching him, looking for answers even though she didn't quite have a handle on the questions. *"Are you going to kill us?"*

Oh, Becky. I saved you once. But I came too late to save you again.

"Al?" he murmured, his voice so choked with emotion it surprised him. "I can't do this alone. I can't—I can't even think. Please come back."

When Al didn't appear, he fell asleep.

"She believed him," Powell said. "So did her mother. Carol said she went down to the jail and talked to Leon Stiles after he'd been booked, and there was no possibility he was the man who'd been in her house that evening. They were coming home from dinner with friends. Stiles was waiting outside the house. He showed Carol a gun and she had no choice but to let him in. He tied them up. She was convinced he was going to kill them both. Had to; they'd both seen him, studied his face. Then, very suddenly, he was someone completely different. His posture, his attitude, the way he spoke. All completely different. He told them he was a doctor named Sam Beckett and he'd come from the future. That in 1995 he'd created a secret government project called Quantum Leap."

"He took an enormous risk, telling them the truth," Donna replied.

"There was no risk. After it was over, Carol sat Becky down. Told her that she couldn't tell the story to anyone, because they'd think she was 'off.' She'd already told the sheriff and his deputy, but they thought she was a terrified child making up tales to comfort herself. By the time we met, I suppose she thought she'd kept her silence long enough. We were in New York. I took her there, because she said she'd like to see the Statue of Liberty. There was an article in the *Times* about a kid named Sam Beckett playing at Carnegie. And she said to me, 'I met someone named Sam Beckett.' "

"All your biographical material says your wife's name was Emily."

"Emily Rebecca. Carol started calling her Becky after she and Em's father split up. When Em got to college, she decided 'Emily' sounded more exotic and went back to it."

"Did you believe her? Sam was only nineteen then, when he played Carnegie."

"I believed her."

"That a man from the future had been in her house?"

"You can't close your mind to possibilities, Dr. Alessi," Powell said in a voice that was more wistful than he intended.

"What did you do?"

"She wanted to meet him, to see if it might be the same Sam Beckett. We tried, but there were too many people clamoring to get near him, and we were a couple of kids barely out of college. We didn't have an 'in.' But we got close enough to watch him talking to family and friends. Em was good at studying people, picking up clues about them from body language, turn of phrase."

"She was a psychologist?"

Powell smiled fleetingly. "She was an actress."

"What was her decision?" Verbena asked.

"That it was him."

"Sam Beckett isn't an uncommon name."

"And she was only a child when it happened. On the face of it, she might have been talking about an invisible friend. We all 'remember' things that our minds conjure up. Childhood is a place of dreams, imaginings, wishes. I think I indulged her for a little too long, so she sat me down with Carol and said to her mother, 'Tell him I'm not loopy.' And Carol, with some reluctance, backed up everything Em had said. So we kept track of

294

this Sam Beckett, the one we quickly discovered was a prodigy with more talents than playing the piano. He studied a lot of things, as if he couldn't quite decide what to do with his life."

"On the face of it," Donna replied wryly.

"She considered trying to contact him. Then she changed her mind. 'Nobody really wants to know what's coming,' she said. 'It's not up to me to tell him he'll succeed.' "

"What happened to her?"

"She collapsed and died of a ruptured aneurysm in the middle of a shopping mall. Neither of us knew it was coming. She was twenty-six years old." Powell paused, looking down at the floor. "We wanted to have a baby. She was looking at a display of stuffed animals in the window of a store, and a minute later she was dead."

"I'm so sorry."

"She was lying there on the floor, with security guards and rubberneckers gathered all around her. I went into the store and bought the stuffed bear she'd been looking at. They all thought I was the coldest bastard they'd ever seen, or that I'd lost my mind. I paid for it and told them not to put it in a bag, and I carried it out there and sat down beside her with the bear in my lap and waited for the paramedics to come." His voice began to crack, but he forced himself to continue. "But there wasn't any point in their coming. She was gone before she hit the floor."

The room was silent for a minute. Then Al said, "I thought the damn picture looked familiar."

Powell sank into a chair and composed himself with the help of a cup of water Donna pressed into his hand. "When the people in PTI's computer R&D area came to me with a proposal for a supercomputer, I started to think." His eyes strayed, taking in the room around him. "Beckett had said 'government project.' I knew about his theories, but whatever the science might be, you don't travel in time by clicking your heels together and 'wishing it so.' He had to have built his Accelerator, and had to have a computer to run it. I gave the computer people unlimited funding. When they came up with SPIRIT, I had them program it to accept contact from any intelligence equal to or greater than its own. To make friends with it. To download any information I was lacking about Quantum Leap."

"What for?" David said in an accusatory tone. "So you could

duplicate it, and do what? Turn it into a theme park? Don't you have enough money?"

The billionaire closed his eyes for a moment. "I would think my motives would be fairly obvious, Dr. Allen," he said as he opened them again. "I want to go back in time. I want to be with my wife."

CHAPTER
TWENTY-FIVE

"No," Al said.

"Give me a reason," Powell countered.

David picked up the conversational ball, and to his surprise Al didn't object. "It doesn't work that way," he told Powell. "If you Leap back, you have to take the place of someone who's already there. I imagine you mean yourself. *That* you, the one from twenty-five years ago, would come here. What would we do with him?"

"Whatever you need to."

"No," Al said.

The two men made eye contact—the war hero and the billionaire. Then Powell said quietly, "It's not going to be your problem in any event. I'll have the technology. I can have all of this recreated in a few years."

"You wouldn't be able to stay with her indefinitely," Verbena put in.

"I don't need to. I only need to be there long enough to tell her something's wrong and that she needs to see a doctor. Five minutes would do. One minute would do. All I need to do is warn her." He realized a plaintive note had crept into his voice and looked away from Al, straightening his shoulders at the same time. "It's Dr. Beckett's own fault for singing the praises of his idea. All I did was pick up the ball." He paused for a second, glancing at each of the faces surrounding him. "And I don't think it's much of a gamble to say I'm not the only one who's picked it up."

"You're just the only one with enough money to run with it," David replied.

"Possibly."

Al, who had not said anything other than "no" in almost five minutes, turned then and walked out of the Waiting Room. He was standing in the middle of the corridor, contemplating the elevator doors, when David joined him. "You want to go work with him?" he asked the younger man.

"Nobody's going to desert Sam," David said.

"Even if you get a better offer?" Al looked around. "Pretty much anything is a better offer than this."

"You could have Powell arrested for tampering with Ziggy."

"Yeah," Al replied. "I could."

She pushed the chair back a little and swiveled it around so she could see his face. "It certainly makes sense on paper," she told him. "Or on monitor." She smiled. "Yes, I'd say it's plausible."

"But do you believe it?"

"I clapped for Tinker Bell. My mind is completely open."

That wasn't the answer he wanted. She got up from the chair, went to him, and wrapped her arms around him, holding him so close that their bodies were touching from shoulder to knee. His wasn't relaxed. He wanted more.

"It'd be nice," he sighed, "if you could just say yes."

She reached up and rested her hand on his cheek. "To which question?"

"I wish you could understand how much this means to me. I need—I wish there was just one person who could say 'I believe.' Not that they believe in me, or they're willing to do the work, or to back me, or to take my side against the people who are laughing at me. I want one person to believe."

298

She tried to placate him with a kiss, then by gently rubbing the small of his back. Then she said what she was thinking. "I don't think you'd want so badly for someone to do that if you honestly believed, yourself."

He drew back and looked down at her, startled. "I do."

"Make love to me, Sam." She glanced around. "There's no one due back on shift for almost another two hours. Forget all of this for a few minutes. Try to accept what I told you last night: I have faith in you." When he didn't reply, she linked her hands behind his neck and pulled his head down toward hers. "I love you, Sam. I'm behind you a thousand percent. I can't, I won't, lie to you. It wouldn't help anything." She stretched up a little and kissed him again.

"Why is it so hard? For you? For anyone?" His finger stabbed through the air, toward the monitor. "The science makes sense."

"Yes. It does."

"Then why can't you take the next step?"

"I need your attention for a little while. All of it. Nothing's going to change tonight. If you don't want—if you'd rather not, then do you want some dinner?"

"I'm not hungry."

She nodded slowly. "I'm going to go eat, then. Come up if you change your mind."

She began to move away, gathering up the lab coat she'd left lying over the back of a chair. "I have to work," he explained.

"I know you do."

She was almost out the door when he stopped her. "Donna? I love you."

The dream faded away, leaving him foggy, disoriented, his skin clammy with sweat. It was too warm here, stuffy, uncomfortable.

Where's here? Where's . . .

His hand thrust across the bed and found something, but it was only the cat. That seemed right, there being a cat. *But where's . . . Donna? Where . . .*

She was smiling at him, her eyes misted with tears. Behind her, her father was in the doorway of his apartment. "Don't go," she told him.

Don't . . .

The sedative Marie had tipped into the soup took hold again and he slipped back into dreams.

299

"You said give you a couple hours," Al barked. "Where I come from, 'a couple' isn't eight."

"I can't help it, Admiral."

"Then let somebody else do it. It won't go on-line? You're sure it won't go on-line?" Frustrated, Al grabbed the handlink Gooshie had left lying on top of the console. "Try it. I'll go in there, and you fire it up. And don't tell me about the power surges. I'll take my chances. I gotta talk to Sam."

"I can't 'fire it up.' It doesn't work."

"What do you mean, it doesn't work?"

"The program won't run." The corners of Gooshie's mouth twitched. "I don't really have an explanation, Admiral. I've tried four times."

"Then try it again!"

The chief programmer held his ground. "I can't."

"I don't want to hear that."

"I'm afraid you have to. Sir."

Al stood glowering at him for a minute. Then the adrenaline cascading through his body began to make his legs unsteady. He shoved his hands into the pockets of his jacket so that Gooshie wouldn't see them tremble. The movement was minute, he knew, but Sam had hired Gooshie because of his eye for detail. He stood there, knowing his expression wasn't as terrifying as he wanted it to be, believing that if he took a step in any direction, it would falter.

I'm losing it, he thought.

He barely felt the hand that rested on his arm. "Al," Verbena said quietly. "Maybe we should let Gooshie work."

"Sam needs me," he said stubbornly.

"I know. But you can't get to Sam right now."

No sleep, no food. That was it, he told himself. Low blood sugar, and exhaustion. A good meal and a few hours of rest would work miracles. He had to turn his head; he could feel the heat of Verbena's gaze on his cheek. Or thought he could. She wasn't buying this. She didn't say anything, but he could see that she'd already figured out that he needed to talk to Sam a lot more than Sam needed to talk to him. Flustered, he pointed to the door of the Chamber and told Gooshie, "Try again. And don't say you tried four times. Try five times. Or a dozen. Get that damn thing operating!"

"Admiral . . ."

"Al," Verbena said. "You're not doing anything constructive here. We're interrupting Gooshie's concentration. Let him work. I'm sure he'll have an answer in—"

"Soon," Gooshie promised.

Sam woke in worse condition than he had the day before. It took all the effort he could muster to get up off the bed. The room was empty except for himself and the contentedly snoozing Tonto. No Al, no Tom, no nobody.

No . . . Donna.

The Leap to Lawrence seemed like a thousand years ago, but the joy he'd felt at seeing Donna there was something he could almost touch. He remembered Al's squeals of protest, which had come as no surprise; Al had never liked her. Okay, fine, Al had insisted—so Sam had brought her father back to her, but she might still marry that other guy. Her first fiancé.

Maybe she had. In any event, she wasn't here, now, with him. Finally, there was no hint of perfume in the air, no sense of someone trying to be with him. Nothing. Just him and the cat.

As if it could read his thoughts, the cat opened one eye and peered at him.

And then it made sense. With a loud *whoof* of an exhale, Sam sat back down, his shoulders slumped. "That's it," he murmured to the cat. "I would have thought Al would be thrilled that I can remember. But he's been avoiding me. Won't look me in the eye. He was afraid I'd remember something. She didn't marry that other guy. She married me. She married me, and I *forgot*."

Power surge? he thought. Sure. Hadn't *that* been awfully damn convenient.

And there's nothing you can do about it.

"Why?" he whispered aloud. "You let me remember everyone else. My family, my friends."

No . . . you remember everyone who was around when you left. The first time, that night in April, when he'd sent Al off to that charity dinner with mumbled assurances that he, Sam, would be fine. That he was going to spend the evening working on problems with the retrieval program. *Tom was dead then. And Donna was . . . somewhere else.*

And she's somewhere else now. So do what you've done all along. Just get on with it.

301

Somehow, he got himself into the bathroom, struggled out of clothes so badly wrinkled they looked almost ruined, propped himself up in the shower, and turned on the water. As he had a few days ago, he heard Grandpa Beckett's voice inside his head: *Feel worse than a sack of dogs' behinds.*

What if this is it? he wondered. *What if Al doesn't come back, and you have to go on on your own?* He dialed the water temperature down a little colder and stood shivering under the sharp spray. "You can do it," Al had told him once. But he hadn't believed that then, and he didn't now.

Take Ziggy away, take Al away, and I'm nothing. I can't do this on my own. I've tried everything I can think of to help Max and Kevin, and it's not working. I need Al's help. I need someone to tell me when I'm going the wrong way. "Please?" he asked quietly. "Send him back. I need to talk to him."

I need to say I'm sorry.

Then he thought he did hear something out in the bedroom. Not bothering to turn off the water, he clambered out of the stall, grabbed the terrycloth robe off the back of the door, and stumbled through the doorway, ready to express his relief and at the same time knowing that relief was premature.

Max was gathering the tangle of clothes off the bed, bundling them in her arms and having to wrestle with the cat for possession of some of them. As Sam watched, the cat let out a rumbling noise of dismay and relocated itself to a warm spot in between the pillows. Max spotted him a second later and regarded him with some chagrin.

"I know how I look," he told her with a sigh. "I can't help it."

"Maybe you should go back to sleep for a while. I can bring you some fresh breakfast in a couple of hours."

On the table near the windows was, indeed, a generous breakfast spread: a big glass of juice, a carafe of coffee, a plate of pancakes and fruit covered by a glass dome. "Have you eaten?" Sam asked.

"Yes. A little while ago."

All the enthusiasm he'd heard in her voice over the last few days, all her interest in this trip and what it meant for him, for the campaign, for herself, for anybody or anything at all—it was all gone. She was running on autopilot now, Sam saw. She'd even stopped being angry. Now she was simply waiting for the

302

other shoe to drop. Kevin, the human being whose presence on this earth was entirely her fault, had thrown a tantrum in front of a crew of reporters and had spilled things no one was supposed to hear. She knew nothing about Kevin's conversation with Sam yesterday afternoon, and Sam suspected that even if she had, she would have given it no weight. She knew she was going to be fired. She was simply waiting for the *when*.

Swell, Sam thought unhappily. *You saved her from that accident—and then* you *killed her.*

"I put out fresh clothes for you in the dressing room," she said. "I thought the tie Ambassador and Mrs. van Hagle gave you would look good. It photographs really well."

"Great," he murmured.

"I'll clear everything until ten. Is that enough time?"

Sam shook his head and tried to square his shoulders, though the result was lopsided at best. A glance in the mirror over the dresser told him it was a real contest: who looked more miserable, him or Max. "You don't need to clear anything." He sighed. "Give me enough time to eat and shave and drink that coffee. Don't worry. I can fake being awake as well as the next guy."

The last person Sam expected to see actually working as a member of Powell's team was in the lobby: Kevin, in suit and tie, helping one of the concierge's staff direct new arrivals to the proper destination—mostly, to a small auditorium at the end of a hallway near the registration desk, where a video presentation would begin in a few minutes. Someone had given him one of the brass Nirvana name tags, which was pinned to his suit coat and which read in neat script JACK.

"Jack?" Sam inquired.

"Yeah. The temp agency sent me. My name's Jack. Nice to meet you, Mr. Powell." When the woman working closest to him stepped away to point out the auditorium doors, Kevin added quietly, "Dove's idea. Start over. The real Jack called in sick or something." In a more chipper tone, he went on, as if introducing himself to a stranger, "I'm working for Mr. Stefanovich. He ran me through the five-step employee indoctrination program this morning. I'm clean, I'm fed, and I checked my smart-ass self at the door. I live to serve."

The massive glass front doors, the handle of each one firmly attached to the hands of a doorman, swung open to admit a cluster of newcomers who had all gotten out of the same limo. Kevin shifted his shoulders, painted on his best public-relations smile, and took a step toward them. Dove moved in to take his place, steering Sam away from the entrance area. "He's doing great," he said sotto voce as they moved toward the casino. "He's had old ladies fawning all over him for an hour."

Sam looked back over his shoulder as they walked. "He seems—"

"He's doing okay. We watched *Citizen Kane* last night, him and me. And we had a long talk. Man-to-man. About the way things are."

"He's not angry at me anymore?"

"I wouldn't go that far. But he's giving it a shot. Trying to fit in. Maybe he needed something to do."

Sam nodded, still watching the boy. "That's supposed to be true—the three essential human needs," he mused, feeling his face shift into the half smile he had worn almost constantly for the last couple of days, for the benefit of the lurking cameras. "Something to do, something to look forward to, and someone to love."

Dove snorted softly. "I could go in a whole other direction and say what I really think is, we all just need to get laid."

"I don't like lying to him," Gooshie said. "What if he comes back?"

Donna looked up from tinkering with the handlink, took a deep breath, and replied, "Verbena's keeping him distracted. We should have plenty of time. It's for his own good, Gooshie. He's stretching himself too thin. Bee's been trying for weeks to get him to admit he doesn't feel well."

"It feels more like we're doing an end run around him."

She glanced at the door to the corridor, through which Tom Beckett had departed temporarily a few minutes ago.

"The congressman's not in charge here," Gooshie pointed out. "I don't think you should let him influence your thinking."

"I'm not."

Gooshie looked at her skeptically, then returned to his own work. "If you say so," he muttered.

"It's all right to have an opinion."

"Oh, I know that," Gooshie told her. "And I have one."

Dove pulled his sunglasses off and dropped them into his shirt pocket. "She's out back showing Streisand and Brolin around the putting green."

"My fault," Sam confessed. "Marie said she wanted to talk to Barbra. I thought she meant Max."

"She's talking to Brolin. About *Marcus Welby, M.D.*" The bodyguard fished around in another pocket and pulled out a folded sheet of paper. "Max said to give you this. It's the report from the polltakers. Your approval rating."

"Which is now low and dropping precipitously?" Sam guessed.

"Actually, it went up two points."

"It did?"

"The guy who does that big gossip thing on the Internet found out about you greasing the skids for that little girl, the one Max moved into the hotel. She's got some kind of liver disease and the parents have really piss-poor insurance. He posted the story about you paying all the bills. I guess he's digging around now and he's got some serious honkin' list of your 'good works.' It goes back a long ways, so he says."

Sam looked him in the eye. "I didn't do it to boost my approval rating."

"Yeah, I know that." There was something more Dove wanted to say, but he didn't speak until Sam prompted him. "You're really on the level, aren't you? You really do want to put Max and Kevin back together. That's not just so the kid won't pull any more stunts that make you look bad."

"It never was about me. I like both of them, and I want them to be happy. Kevin loves his mother."

"A lot of people care about her. And she won't see it."

Sam poured himself a glass of water and took a few quick swallows. "Maybe she's trying to protect herself from making another bad choice. I'm sure she knows how everyone feels. She just won't let herself accept it. We have to not give up until she does."

"Don't hang your butt out in the wind waiting for it to happen."

"I have to," Sam said wryly. "Good works—that's what I'm here for."

Dove thought for a moment but didn't respond. "I better get

305

back out to the green and haul Marie out of there. She was trying to give Streisand 'heart smart' recipes when I left. Jefferson's out in the hall, here. If you need me, tell him and he'll get me on the radio."

A familiar and very welcome sound prevented Sam from catching the last few words. Hurriedly, he waved Dove on out of the room, and as the door closed behind the bodyguard, he swung around to greet Al with a dozen questions on his lips. And found his brother. Alone. "What . . . ?" he sputtered. "Where's Al?"

"Upstairs," Tom replied.

Sam circled the hologram, examining it closely. "Upstairs? Why? Where? You're all right? The power surge didn't do you any harm?"

"If you don't count scaring the crap out of me, then no."

"Al's all right? Is everything all right now?"

"Lord help us." Tom sighed. "What part of this looks 'all right' to you? No, it's not all right."

"Why is Al upstairs?"

"Because he needs a break. And because I need to talk to you without him butting in," Tom said firmly, making Sam, think *In control. He's always been in control. Knew what he wanted, and went out and got it.* "He's not family, Sam. He's got no input into this conversation." Before Sam could argue that, Tom went on, "I know he's made himself your family. But this needed to be just us."

Sam's mouth opened a little. Tom's left hand began to drift out to the side, and for a moment, time moved infinitely more slowly.

It hadn't ended at Lawrence.

He squeezed his eyes shut, then forced them open, his heart fluttering wildly, so that he could look at her—the woman with whom he'd walked on the beach. The one who'd held him, kissed him. The one who'd shown him there were many layers of difference between "I believe" and "I believe in you." The one who'd married him and not that other guy. He extended a hand toward the hologram, stopping it halfway, knowing that if he pushed it farther, it would pass on as if there was nothing there to touch. *There* isn't *anyone here. Only an image. Not much better than the dream.*

"I dreamed about you last night," he managed to say. "I've

been dreaming about you all along. But I thought it was Powell who'd—"

Her hand drifted out too, and stopped.

"I remember going to Lawrence," he said softly. "I remember seeing you walk across the quad. It was like taking breath for the first time. I remember taking you to see your father, and you kissing me and saying thank you."

She hadn't said a word. Tom squeezed her hand more tightly and looked at her sympathetically, but she avoided his eyes.

Searching for something that might make her feel better, Sam offered tentatively, "Yesterday afternoon, while I was watching them fixing up the nightclub, I heard our song." He softly hummed the few notes he'd been hearing since that first night at Powell's mansion. "They were going to play it at our wedding. Mom thought it was a strange choice, when she heard the lyrics."

"They did play it," she said with a wobble in her voice. "Katie said, 'That's Sam for you.'"

"I didn't remember you, so Al didn't tell me. You followed my rules to the letter."

"Well," Donna demurred, "I think he's skipped a few letters along the way."

"I'm so sorry."

"You have no reason to be."

The two Beckett men stared at her in surprise. "I have every reason to be," Sam said.

Donna smiled fleetingly. "I was angry at you for a long time, for leaving."

"I wouldn't blame you if you hated me."

"When you came back, I thought everything would be like it had been before—but then you left again. It took me a long time to understand that I can't hold on to you. That I never could, even in the beginning."

Sam had no real comeback for that. "I feel like I deceived you."

"Why? You never lied to me. You never pretended to be anything other than what you were. It's my own fault, Sam, for closing my eyes to some of it. For denying you the right to be what you are."

"I took wedding vows. At least from your perspective I did."

"Maybe you shouldn't have."

That hit Sam hard, until he made himself listen to the fact that there was no accusation in her voice. In fact, there was nothing negative in it at all, other than sadness.

"I knew what you wanted," she said. "I'd known you for less than a day when you explained it all to me. I was wide-awake and paying attention. I said 'I do' with someone who'd long since given himself over to a dream that was never going to die."

"I should have—"

"People cling to foolish ideals, Sam. You paid enough attention to me, and loved me enough to make me think we'd always be together. That maybe you'd never get funding. That maybe the Accelerator wouldn't work. That maybe you'd be gone for a few hours and then come home and turn the baton over to David. I thought I could be more important to you than your dream, and through no fault of yours, I wasn't. You can't help what you are, Sam. If I were a better person, I would have accepted that a long time ago. Instead, I said some things I shouldn't have, and I was cruel to people who didn't deserve it."

Tom gaped at her in astonishment. Clearly, none of this was what he had expected her to say.

"I do love you," Sam told her.

"I know."

"Do you . . . still love me?"

"Always."

Again, he moved his hand as close to her as he could. "I made the wrong choice."

"You made the only choice you could. My dad told me years ago, you have to choose what's right for you. If you don't, all the disappointment and the regret, and the 'might have beens' become the other person's fault. I never wanted to hold you back, Sam. I wanted you to have your dream. I still do. But I miss you so much. I'd give anything to hold you, just for a minute."

"Don't give up anything for me. I already feel like I've cheated you out of your whole life."

Donna's mouth opened a little. "Because you married me?"

Her expression made him remember another woman who'd been left behind. *"Flying was his first love. The navy was his second, and I was third."* "You could have married someone who would have valued you more. You should have come first."

"I love you, Sam. I don't want anyone else."

There was a loud, staccato knock at the door, which eased

open to reveal Dove. "They're here, boss —Rather and his crew. They decided to come early, so they could get some background footage on the opening."

"Give me a few minutes." Once the door had closed, Sam returned his attention to Donna.

"Dan Rather?" she asked.

"I'm newsworthy." Sam sighed. He was at a loss for what to say next, and settled for looking at Donna in regretful silence.

"I thought you were dead," Tom told him. "All these years, when we didn't hear from you. I thought something had gone wrong and you were dead."

"I guess I might as well have been."

Tom shook his head. "Donna's right," he admitted. "You're only doing what you were intended to do. There was no way you were going to live a normal life. We knew that from the time you were fifteen and that professor from MIT came to the house. You wanted to go off to State and play basketball, but there was no way in hell that that was gonna happen. We wouldn't have let it. You would have been wasting your gift."

"Even if I said that's what I wanted."

"There's such a big difference between saying you want it, and wanting it," Donna put in. "Four years at State. What would you have done after that? You never would have made it as a pro."

Sam blinked at her.

"Don't kid yourself, little brother." Tom grinned. "You weren't that good."

Donna went on, "You had to live up to what everyone believed you were. You had to do something that would make you the equal of Einstein. He came up with the theory of relativity. You had to go one better. Like McGwire breaking the home-run record."

Sam winced. "Who's McGwire? What did I miss?"

She laughed softly. "I don't think it was ever in you to come up with a theory, then sit around in old cardigans and let people talk about you. You had to go out and *do*. Be a part of what you knew was possible. Do what you saw Captain Galaxy do when you were a little boy. But—" She was silent for a moment. "We all knew that. But it's hard to let go of you, Sam. We all love you. But we know you're here because you wanted to be."

"I've never wanted to be in Las Vegas," Sam murmured. "I hate Las Vegas."

"You'll be somewhere else soon enough."

Sam was suddenly surrounded by the feeling that everything had gone wrong and was rapidly getting worse. *I dreamed of you,* he thought, *and convinced myself that you were someone else's wife. I did things . . . Oh, God. Loved other women, wanted them, made love to them. I remembered Tom, and I managed to forget you. The hell with what I was meant to do. I couldn't manage to keep one simple promise. What does that make me?* "What does that make me?" he said aloud, not entirely aware he was saying it.

"Not perfect," she replied. "But I never thought you were."

"I owed you more than this."

"What does it make *me*? I have all the pieces of the puzzle, Sam. I've stopped being angry."

"What about 'hurt'?"

"That's going to take longer. But I can't insist that you stop being what you are, Sam. The same goes for everyone else. I know who you are, and what you are, and what you've done, and I choose to stay here and wait for you. Maybe that makes me stupid in some people's eyes. Maybe that makes me weak, for not saying 'You didn't live up to some ideal I had in mind, so I'm leaving.' I don't want to leave. There are people I love here, and I love what I'm doing. As long as Quantum Leap exists, I'll be here. And I really don't care what anyone else thinks of that."

The handlink squealed a couple of off-key notes. Tom peered at the readout, then squeezed Donna's hand. "I think we have to go, Sam."

"There's too much of a power drain," Donna explained. "I'll go."

"No," Sam protested.

"No, it's all right. I need to—I need to be by myself for a little while. Talk to your brother. I'll . . ." Her voice trailed off. It took her a moment to recover. "This isn't goodbye, Sam."

She slipped her hand out of Tom's and was gone. Tom opened his mouth to say something, then changed his mind.

Sam, too, intended to speak, but before he could get the words out, the hologram began to grow transparent. "What happened?" he asked Tom, who shook his head in confusion, shook the handlink, then called out something Sam couldn't hear. A second later, the hologram blinked out, then blinked back in again. "Is there something wrong?" Sam demanded. "What are you not telling me?"

"I don't know, Sam. I don't know much of anything about computers."

"It's Ziggy?"

"Sam, I don't know."

"Where's Al? Tell me the truth."

"He's upstairs with Dr. Beeks. He's whipped—he hasn't slept. He's run himself into the ground. He's okay, Sam."

Sam began to pace in front of the office's small couch. "What day is it there?"

"What?"

"Day. Day. What day is it?"

"What difference does that make?" Tom lifted a hand to ward off the look of fury the question had earned from his younger brother. "It's Thursday. Late. It's almost New Year's Eve." Misinterpreting Sam's expression, Tom asked warily, "You don't think things are really going to . . . ?"

"I want you to tell me what's happening there."

Sam expected more protests; Al would have given him a boatload. Tom didn't. Slowly at first, Tom explained everything that had happened over the past several days. "Powell's breached a top-secret facility," he concluded.

"It would have happened eventually." Sam sighed. "Lothos had to come from somewhere."

"Who?"

Sam shook his head. "Long story." Then he noticed Tom glancing at his watch. "Am I keeping you from something?"

"Yes. I was supposed to be in California an hour ago."

"Why?"

"For Powell's New Year's gala."

"He invited you to that? Nice perk for working on the campaign." When Tom didn't reply, Sam peered at him suspiciously. "Stop protecting me. What are you not saying?"

"I need to be at that party. He's making the announcement."

"He'll have enough people to cheer him on."

"Oh, hell," Tom said. "I'm running for vice-president. Everybody figures we'll win."

Sam's breath whooshed out all at once and he dropped down on the couch, almost sliding off the front of it in the process.

"Don't you need to talk to Dan Rather?" Tom asked him.

CHAPTER
TWENTY-SIX

More than likely, they'd all be there. Linda and the kids. His mother. Katie and Jim, but probably not their kids; the girls and Jeffrey were too young. But maybe not. They'd all be there, at Mount Olympus, to listen to the announcement of Powell's candidacy—Powell's and Tom's candidacy.

And I should be there too. Me and Donna. To applaud Tom's achievement. Instead . . . I'm not in a position to applaud much of anything.

Sam looked around the suite. Tom had left hours ago, Al hadn't returned. He was being left on his own. Which, he supposed, he more than richly deserved.

There was a knock at the door. Kevin let himself in, carrying a tux covered in dry cleaner's plastic. "Dove asked me to bring you this," he explained in a tone that said he was trying to accept Powell's actions with the same resigned stubbornness that he'd shouldered all the other hurts adults had handed him during his nineteen years on the planet. "My mother's getting her hair done. They got the spot out of your jacket, Dove says." He extended the garment, mildly puzzled when Sam didn't take it. "You want me to go hang this up?"

"I've let a lot of people down," Sam said.

Kevin thought that over and decided not to disagree. "Everybody makes mistakes."

"Some worse than others." The boy was still wearing his Nirvana blazer and name tag. "You're coming to the party, aren't you?" Sam asked. "You'd better change your clothes."

"I don't know. Maybe . . ."

"Go to the party."

Kevin thought that over too, then shrugged. "Okay." When he returned from carefully depositing the tux on Sam's bed, he asked, "Are *you* going to the party?"

"I don't have any choice," Sam said.

"I don't think it's right, because I'm not Elvis."

The mayor made a face. "We're going to do you a nice little introduction, Joe. Low-key. They have to put a spotlight on you so everybody can see you."

"The room isn't that big. And they know what I look like."

After a moment of hesitation that was probably mostly for effect, the mayor shook his head and gave in. "It's going to look a little peculiar, but it's your hotel and your opening." To Max, he added, "Your boss is a mighty stubborn man." Then he was gone, off to join his own assistant, a couple of aides, and a representative of his press office at a cluster of tables near the front of the room.

Sam remained nervous until the mayor had finished the introduction and gestured for a round of applause from the several hundred people seated at small round tables in Nirvana's Northern Lights nightclub. The crowd responded willingly and enthusiastically, many of them offering a cheer as Sam climbed the three steps onto the risers that formed a makeshift stage at the side of the room. The real stage, up in front, had been decorated to suit the entertainers who would begin performing in a few minutes; Sam had taken a look at it and refused to go up there, for reasons he could not even explain to himself.

The risers, a four-by-twelve-foot platform covered with black

313

nonskid fabric, were a lot less "showbiz" than the stage, and the lighting crew did indeed obey his instructions to keep the key light on him subtle. Still, the eyes of everyone in the club were on him and for the first time in several days he shuddered at the attention.

Max misinterpreted his hesitation and inched close to the platform holding a small stack of file cards on which were written the notes for the speech. Sam greeted the gesture with a smile of acknowledgment, then shook his head and somewhat reluctantly faced his audience.

"In a few months—actually, in a year and a few months," he began, "but since most people have picked January 1, 2000, as the big day, I'll stick with that—we begin a new millennium. As was the case a thousand years ago, a lot of people have chosen to believe that this new year will bring with it not a host of new beginnings, but an ending. Some of them are waiting for the Apocalypse that's forecast in the Bible, and the ascension of God's chosen people into the kingdom of heaven. They assume, of course," he added with another small smile, "that each of them is going to be among the chosen."

A few chuckles drifted out of the audience as Sam went on. "Some of them simply believe that we're approaching the end of civilization. The end of the human race. Or the end of time as we know it.

"I personally believe in beginnings. I believe that every moment of every day offers new possibilities. Think of the phrase 'When one door closes, another one opens.' I'm as bad at keeping New Year's resolutions as anyone else, but I look forward to the new millennium the same way I would a fresh snowfall. I remember looking out the window very early on winter mornings and seeing everything covered with that white blanket. Not a footprint in it. It was waiting for me to run downstairs, pull my coat and my boots on over my pajamas, and run outside to be the first to make a mark."

He paused, looking out at the sea of faces. "Of course, since I was only a little boy, it was a very small mark. A very small, but very carefully placed mark. This new millennium can be the same for all of us. If God does indeed decide that this is the time that's written about in the Bible, then that's out of our control. Is it now? A year from now? Ten years from now? Or a million years from now? I think, no matter how much time we have left

314

in front of us, it's our responsibility to make the most of it. To take whatever's available to us and use it the best way we can. To build something good, something lasting, so that whenever our time is finished, we can say, 'I didn't waste a minute of it.'

"My father died when he was what we'd think of now as a fairly young man. But while he lived, during all the years I knew him, he worked hard. He tried never to let go of his dreams. He gave love to his family, and his friends, with a lot of joy and no expectations. Every minute that he lived, he worked to achieve something, he had hope, and he had love, both given and received. He made each of his children understand that we have his love to carry with us, as long as we live, no matter where we go or what we do. I don't have him with me now, but I have the memory of him, and he's as real to me as if he was standing right there."

The audience had grown completely silent. They'd come here expecting something scripted, something they'd heard some version of a hundred times before. There were no soft coughs, no shuffling of feet, no murmurs of conversation to signal to Sam that his words were not being heard.

"I'm sorry to ramble," he said quietly. "But it came to me earlier today that with each of the choices that I make in my life, if I leave things behind—things that are enormously important to me, so much so that it seems like I can't go on without them— there are also things ahead of me. The possibility to go on achieving as much as I can, to go on hoping, to go on giving love. And receiving it. And remembering the people who've loved me who are with me now only in spirit."

When he stopped, no one moved, or spoke. Self-consciously, he added, "That was pretty sappy. The world's worst greeting card, run completely amok. Okay, let me give you the short version. Don't worry. Be happy." To his relief, laughter rippled through the room. "Please, enjoy yourselves. That's what I built all this for. Drink, dance, enjoy the hors d'oeuvres, and in the 'open all night' spirit of Las Vegas, at ten-thirty, enjoy the dinner we've put together for you. Oh—before I shut up, I'd like to say thank you to someone who, much more so than me, put all of this together for you. My assistant, Barbara Maxwell."

Max shook her head demurely, but Sam stuck out a hand and nodded insistently. Reluctantly she moved to the steps and climbed up onto the risers to stand beside him, accepting the round of applause that Sam had all but demanded with more than a little embarrassment. "Enjoy it," Sam said into her ear. "You worked hard."

As the applause died down, she leaned toward the steps.

"Max," Sam murmured to her. "You're not fired."

She murmured a thank you, but nothing more, as if she didn't quite believe him. Sam held on to her to keep her from slipping away, and with his free hand gestured to the members of the jazz quartet who had already filed unobtrusively onto the stage and stood awaiting their own introduction. "Ladies and gentlemen, I'm done talking. Please welcome Blues Standard."

Max again tried to move toward the steps as the quartet began to play, but Sam slipped an arm around her waist and said in a tone that brooked no argument, "Dance with me."

"I don't think that's appropriate," she murmured. "I'm your employee."

"Shut up and dance," Sam murmured back.

They were the object of a lot of curiosity for a moment, then two at a time, the people who'd been handpicked to be in this room tonight followed Sam's lead, moved to the parquet dance floor, and began to dance. Max listened to the song, her head cocked a little, and frowned. "Did you pick this?" Sam nodded. "Why Neil Diamond?"

Sam shrugged, turning his head slightly so she couldn't see what was in his eyes. " 'Hello Again'—it seemed like a good song to mark new beginnings. And to send a message to someone who might be listening."

"They're going to get the wrong impression from this, Joe."

"So, let them."

"Really . . ."

He shook his head. "Forget there are hundreds of nosy people here who are going to talk about this in a couple of hours as if it means anything other than what it is. Enjoy the dance. You dance very well. Have fun."

She did dance without offering any further protest, though it was obvious she had simply surrendered to her employer's wishes rather than to any desire of her own. She was less than at ease in his arms; her thoughts, he could tell, ran in a dozen directions. "Thank you, Joe," she said after a minute.

"You're welcome."

"Who's listening?" she asked after a minute.

"What?"

"You said someone might be listening."

"Just . . . someone I've been separated from for a long time."

Max looked up at him. For someone who tried to make a career out of saying and doing the appropriate thing, there was a remarkable amount of emotion in her eyes. Mostly disappointment. Sam had anticipated that, known he was bringing it on by holding Max in his arms when she would know above everything else that he had no feelings for her other than friendship. Then she said something he hadn't anticipated. "You mean Becky." She sighed.

"Partly Becky. Partly a lot of other people."

"Is that why you keep looking around? Did you expect someone to be here who didn't show up?"

"Pretty much," Sam said.

"Who?"

"Just dance, Max."

Midway between the platform and one of the club's four exit doors, Dove stood with Kevin watching Sam and Max move gracefully around the small surface of the risers. "Find somebody to dance with," Dove told the boy.

Kevin snorted in disdain. "You think there's anybody here who's not with somebody? Why don't you find somebody to dance with?"

"I'm on duty, kid."

"You want to dance with *her*."

"Not here. Not now."

"Go up there and cut in. You know how. Tap him on the shoulder."

"I'm on duty."

"You and all these other guys." Kevin gestured around the room. The security guards were easy enough to spot: big, well muscled, all wearing dark suits and earphones. "What's one song, three minutes? You can't be half on duty for three minutes? Do it, man. Walk the walk. Go take her away from him."

Dove shifted his weight slightly. "You keep it up, and you're gonna make me not want you here as much as she does. Give it a rest."

"You've never told her you love her."

The big man nodded toward the entrance to the nightclub. "Go find yourself somebody to dance with."

317

"Why not?"

Dove pointedly turned away from Kevin and resumed scanning the room, much as the other guards were doing and had been doing for almost twenty minutes. Kevin did the same thing, picking out the famous faces, noting with some annoyance that he was right: everyone here was with a partner.

"I'm going to tell her," he said abruptly, moving out of Dove's reach before the bodyguard could grab him.

Crossing the room, even the short distance he had to cover, was a tougher job than he'd thought it would be. Dancing couples seemed to move into his path. So did the waiters, carrying trays of drinks or taking away empties, and people going to or returning from the rest rooms. Dove was somewhere behind him, he was sure, and with each small step he took he expected to feel the pressure of Dove's fingers closing around his arm.

He'd gotten maybe halfway when someone bumped into him, or he them. He looked: one of the waiters. "Sorry," the waiter said.

Kevin shrugged and continued on his way. The second half of the journey took less time than the first, and to his surprise he was able to mount the few steps up onto the risers without being stopped. Okay, so maybe it wasn't all that weird, he thought; the guards all knew who he was, and Powell didn't seem upset by his approach. His mother didn't see him yet. And Dove hadn't succeeded at stopping him. He turned a little and looked out into the crowd. Dove was close to the stage, not happy, but not looking at Kevin; he'd spotted someone whose actions he was even more distressed about—that goofy little French woman, the cook, done up in a gold-lamé-and-rhinestone outfit that looked like she'd swiped it from Elton John. The small, stocky body and the gray hair fooled a few of the people in her path into thinking she was Dr. Ruth Westheimer, and her progress was slowed by a few who wanted to say hello or ask a question. Kevin watched her for a few seconds as the song reached its climax, then began to turn again toward his mother.

Something caught his eye: the waiter, who hadn't moved more than a step or two from the spot where Kevin had bumped into him. He was fussing with an empty champagne glass. Not clearing the table; he was waiting for something.

Shit, Kevin thought.

He spotted Dove quickly, a few steps from the edge of the

stage. His mind ran back through the last minute or two, remembering the sensation of bumping into that waiter. There'd been a hand, nudging him away. The familiar feeling of contact with another human body. And something peculiar, but not very much so—something hard. A tray, a glass.

Not a tray. Not a glass.

How the hell did he get in here with . . . ?

He reached his mother and pulled her out of Powell's grasp. "Get off the stage," he hissed, meaning mostly her, but not just her, catching the puzzled look Powell gave him and the annoyance he got from his mother and ignoring both, trying to move her toward the steps, hoping Powell would take a hint and follow, and that Dove would figure out something was wrong and push his way through the couple of people that were between him and the stage and get the hell up here and do his job. The waiter was watching, he knew, and had figured out that Kevin knew, but that wasn't going to scare him off. People like that didn't get scared off, they got scared into doing what they'd come to do. His mother was trying to break away from him, saying something that wasn't quite words, seemed more like the buzz of a badly tuned-in radio station, but yes, Powell knew something was wrong, and so did Dove. Finally, finally, Dove was there, and Kevin could feel the thud as Dove's weight hit the wobbly surface of the plywood risers. The other guards were moving too, knowing something was wrong, but there wasn't enough time to explain, to move, to make sure it didn't happen. Everyone seemed to be moving.

Then everything seemed to stand still.

He heard a *bang,* very clearly. He knew what it was, because his grandfather had taken him when he was sixteen to the gun club in Beverly Hills. He'd asked about guns, made a joke or something, and his grandfather had taken him, both of them the guests of someone who belonged to the club, and he'd spent a couple of hours listening, learning, holding a weapon in his hands. He listened to the *bang* and was angry for a moment at Dove for hitting him: very hard, just once, right underneath his shoulder blade.

Shit.

The room seemed very quiet and no one was moving fast enough. They all looked worried, but they were so . . . not moving. Frustrated, Kevin grabbed his mother's boss by the arm and

319

shoved him toward the steps. Nothing, not him, not Powell, seemed to move in the right direction. He stumbled, not understanding why his legs were wobbly, lost his footing and his balance, slipped away from Dove and his mother before they could stop him from falling and tumbled down the steps, his legs tangled and useless, finally understanding as he went down that he'd moved the wrong way, that he'd interfered, that the waiter had shot him, not Powell, and that he was going to die.

Then his head connected with something hard and everything exploded into black.

CHAPTER
TWENTY-SEVEN

Al flew down the corridor and into the Control Room traveling at about Mach Three. As he soared past the console, he seized the handlink Tom had placed there and, without breaking stride, went up the ramp and into the Imaging Chamber. Gooshie, who had heard the thunder of Al's shoes pounding down the hall, had opened the door barely in time.

"It doesn't work, my *ass*," Al howled from inside the Chamber. "Send me to Sam!"

Less than fifty feet away, Joe Powell lifted his head and stared fixedly at the door of the Waiting Room. "What's wrong?" he demanded of Verbena.

"I'm not sure."

"Well, find out!"

No less curious, and a lot more concerned than Powell was,

Verbena moved quickly to the door and instructed it to open. It had barely cleared the top of her head when Powell, moving every bit as fast as Al had, scooped her up with an arm around her waist and trotted out the door, ducking as he went. He didn't let go of Verbena until they reached the Control Room. Donna and David, who had also heard Al go tearing down the hall, had reached the room only a few steps ahead of them. "Ziggy!" Verbena sputtered. "What happened to the security protocols?"

At the top of the ramp, the Imaging Chamber door clanged shut.

"I believe it is a federal crime to attempt to inflict bodily harm on the president of the United States," Ziggy replied, accompanied by a chorus of soft jingling.

"He's not the president yet!" she protested at the same moment that Powell barked, "What's happening?"

"Dr. Beckett's vital signs went red," Gooshie explained nervously as he finished bringing the Chamber on-line. "I think he might have been hurt." With a glance at the Chamber door, he added, "I think the admiral thinks so too."

The image around him shimmied and wavered. It was pale, as if someone had turned up the brightness control on the holographic projectors. Al made fleeting note of the technical difficulties, then swept a look around, searching for Sam.

He had stepped into the middle of a melee. Half of the opening-night crowd had bolted for the exits; the other half was on their feet, shrieking and shouting and complaining and gathering up belongings. Al spotted his partner only an instant before Dove hustled Sam bodily out of the exit nearest the risers. Relieved at least a little, he was about to trot off after them when he noticed the cluster of people in front of the risers, gathered around a body lying on the carpeted floor.

"Oh, shit," Al breathed. "Oh, damn it all. Kid?" He moved closer and crouched down for a better look. Kevin's eyes drifted open, which made Al feel better until the boy seemed to be trying to focus on him. "Oh, no," Al said firmly. "Don't see me. That's not a good thing. Don't be seeing me."

But it wasn't Al that Kevin was looking at; it was the person who'd moved in to help him and who was quickly taking charge. Then the boy's face contorted in pain, his eyes rolled back in his head, and he lost consciousness again.

Al hammered a command into the handlink and relocated himself to the hallway behind the nightclub, where Sam was being hustled to safety by an implacable Dove. "We can't leave him lying there!" Sam protested.

"There's already people on the way to take him to the hospital," Dove replied. "I'm getting you out of here. You pay me to protect you, and that's what I'm doing. If you want to fire me, fine, but I'm not listening to it until I know you're out of where they can get at you."

"Sam!" Al yelled.

Sam jerked himself to a halt. Dove tried to keep moving, but Sam planted himself firmly in the middle of the hall and refused to go.

The hologram became paler still. Al's torture of the handlink accomplished nothing. "Somebody shot the kid?" he gasped. "What happened? Who did it? Did they get him? Are you okay? I'm sorry, Sam. They had me corralled upstairs. I got here as soon as I could."

The radio at Dove's hip crackled. He grabbed it off his belt and murmured into it, then listened carefully to the reply. "They got him," he told Sam. "And the ambulance just pulled up out front. Okay? Let's go. I want to get you upstairs."

Sam looked plaintively at his partner, who checked the screen on the handlink. "Nothing yet, Sam. We don't know if Kevin makes it."

"We're going to the hospital," Sam told Dove.

Kevin's eyes were closed, but if he was asleep, he wasn't resting comfortably. Every few seconds he would twitch, each small movement accompanied by a wince that was all too audible to the two people who stood watching him. The left side of his face was swollen, the area around his eye bruised a dark blue, and the upper right side of his torso was covered with bandages that were only partly concealed by the blue-and-white striped hospital gown. Only a couple of days ago, Sam remembered, the boy had been sleeping soundly, if noisily, on the couch in Joe Powell's TV room, his fingers clenched around the remote, surrounded by a forest of wadded-up tissues.

"Go in there and be with him," he told Max. When she hesitated, he said firmly, "You almost lost him. Go sit with him and hold his hand."

"He doesn't want me anywhere near him."

"You're wrong."

She turned away from the doorway of Kevin's room and wandered down the hall, wrapping her arms around herself, huddling inside her own embrace. For the first time in almost a week, she seemed completely lost, without answers. Sam heard a hitch in her breathing and knew that was as close as she would come to crying—at least, out here in the hallway of a hospital, with clusters of strangers passing by: nurses, doctors, orderlies, other patients, family members of other patients. The fact that none of them knew who she was, or what had happened to bring her here, made no difference.

Remarkably, none of them seemed to know who *he* was, either. Or maybe they were simply too ill, or too preoccupied, to care. Sam gently steered Max into the doorway of an unoccupied room, out of the way of an aide pushing a metal cart loaded with cups of pills, and wrapped his arms around her. She stood rigid and silent for a minute, then the starch seemed to go out of her all at once and she slumped against him.

"I didn't mean . . ." she mumbled.

Sam shook his head. "Don't tell me. Tell him."

"What happened, Joe? How could all this happen? How did that man get in there with a gun? All the employees were screened."

Sam remembered what Dove had told him before going off to chew some butts over the phone. The bodyguard wasn't far away, just down at the end of the corridor in an office loaned to him by one of the doctors, where he could raise hell over the phone in relative privacy. Three of his locally hired helpers (the ones he trusted most, Sam supposed) had been pulled out of Nirvana and stationed here, one in the elevator bay, the other two watching the staircases that opened onto this wing of the hospital.

"We don't know what they think, how they feel," he told Max. "You can screen for a criminal record, job history, drug use, family background. There's nothing to tell you that one of those people, or all of them, has a grudge against me if they haven't voiced it in front of someone who'd disagree."

"God, Joe," she said miserably. "I'm so sorry."

Sam frowned at her. "For what? Not being clairvoyant? There were eight hundred people in that room."

"We should have done a better job."

"You mean, *you* should have done a better job? You did everything you could. Eight hundred people, Max. There's no way on earth you could screen all of them. Things happen. Maybe they're meant to happen."

Her mouth opened a little. "You mean if something had happened to you, we could have said, 'Oh, well'?"

"You know what I mean."

"There's no excuse for what happened."

"No excuse, but a reason. Max. Barbara. Stop trying to blame yourself. What happened was not your fault. I'm fine, and Kevin is going to be." She didn't answer, so Sam placed a hand under her chin and lifted her head. "It was not your fault."

"You might have been killed, Joe."

"But I wasn't."

She looked away from him, down the hall toward the office Dove had commandeered. "He got in the way."

"Barbara." Again, Sam turned her head so that she had to look at him. "I don't know why he came up onto the stage. But I do know what I saw. When he realized something was wrong, he wasn't trying to get between me and that gun. He was trying to protect you." She flinched, trying to move away even a little, far enough to avoid his eyes. "Go sit with him," he told her. "They've got him dosed up with painkillers, but that doesn't help soothe what he's thinking."

"This never should have happened. He never should have come here."

"If he hadn't, one of us could be lying in that hospital bed. Go to him. Make him feel like he did something right, and didn't just get in the way." She didn't move. Sighing softly, Sam gave her a hug and held on for a moment. "It's a funny thing, the way the heart works. You can do everything you can think of to drive him away. You can make him hate you. But none of that ever erases the love."

She wasn't buying. Not that many years ago, he would have thought it was impossible for one human being to be this stubborn. That a simple statement of the truth would be enough to sway her in the other direction. That being told what to do, what to think, what to feel was all she needed.

Not that many years ago, Sam thought, *I had no idea what made people tick.*

325

"You can come with me to the White House, if it works out that way. If enough people think I'm the right guy to send there. There's no one else I'd even consider choosing to be chief of staff. And you can set the world on fire from there. You'll get people's attention. You'll have reporters wanting to talk to you instead of me. For all I know, in ten years you could be holding office yourself. But there's something I want you to stop denying. No matter what you do, no matter how far you go, when you get to the end of your life, you'll have to say that the best thing you ever did—maybe not the most important, or the most enduring, but the best thing you ever did, was help create your son."

This time he didn't try to look into her eyes. He simply pulled her in and held her. It was something she'd wanted for—how long? This woman who anticipated his wants and his needs, who carried out his wishes and indulged his whims. Made sure those eighty-four pairs of socks were neatly rolled, that his meals were ready when he decided he was hungry, that there was quiet when he wanted it. Something like a wife. More than a wife. Much of what Becky had been to Joe Powell, and more, and less.

"Go," he told Max quietly. "Don't turn your back on him. Don't walk away if you don't have to."

Max moved into the doorway with something that wasn't quite dread, but might as well have been. She stood there for almost a minute before Kevin opened his eyes, and then neither one of them said anything. Above and behind her, a loudspeaker chattered, voices filled with static. One step at a time she came into the room, her hands clenched and stuffed into the pockets of her jacket.

"Is he okay?" Kevin asked finally. His voice was thin and tired.

"Yes."

"Are you okay?"

"I'm all right."

"Did they catch the guy? That waiter?"

"Yes."

"Nice talking to you." Kevin sighed. "Sorry to interrupt your evening."

She went to the window and adjusted the blinds a little so she could see out, across a stretch of parking lot to the street. Down in the lot, a car alarm was hooting, the headlights of the offended vehicle flashing on and off in time with the horn. Behind her, out in the hall, she could hear the rattle of a cart with a crooked wheel.

"The doctor thinks it'll be all right if we move you to Los Angeles tomorrow," she said without turning.

"Did you talk to Grandpa?"

"Not yet."

"Why not?"

"He won't react well to this."

"What does that mean, 'react well'? Somebody shot me. How's he gonna react well?"

"You know what I mean."

"Yeah, well, maybe I don't. Most people aren't like you, Bobbie. Most people actually let themselves feel something. Christ, I think I'd get more of a response if somebody called Leonardo DiCaprio and told him I got shot. You can't even bother to turn around and look at me." He waited. When she didn't move, he heaved another sigh. "Well, I can't say this is anything new and different. I could point out that I didn't set this up to happen so I could piss you off some more, but I'd be wasting my air. My whole existence pisses you off. You can go, you know? Go back to the hotel. If it's not too much trouble, if you see a nurse out there, you could tell them I'm thirsty."

Instead, she found a plastic pitcher of water and poured some of it into a cup. The head of his bed was raised enough that he could hold the cup and drink from it without moving anything other than his right arm. After a few sips, he tried to shift enough to put the cup on the bedside table, an effort that pained him enough to make him grimace.

"Thanks," he muttered.

"I'll call your grandparents in the morning and let them know when you'll be there. They can meet you at St. John's."

"I'll call them myself. Don't do anything you don't want to do."

"I'll call them."

"And then what?"

"I don't—"

"If I'm going home, it'd be nice if you came with me."

"I can't do that. I have responsibilities."

"Sure," Kevin said.

"You'll have a private room. That's already been arranged. They've got a very good orthopedic surgeon who's going to operate on your knee the day after tomorrow." They both looked at the mound under the thin blanket created by Kevin's left leg, damaged during his fall down the steps and carefully braced and bandaged by the emergency-room staff. They'd done nothing to repair the injury yet, choosing to focus on the bullet wound, which was clean enough not to require surgery. The bullet had passed completely through his body, nicking the bottom of his shoulder blade but missing vital organs, lodging finally in the wall behind the risers. He was lucky, the doctor in the ER had told him. Kevin, who had wakened on the floor of the nightclub to find himself being earnestly peered at by a small, gray-haired woman he was barely with it enough to realize was not Dr. Ruth Westheimer but his mother's employer's chef, did not feel particularly lucky. Not in the nightclub, not in the ER, and not now.

"I felt like I was in the middle of an episode of *Seinfeld*," he muttered.

"What?"

"Nobody knew what to do except Mr. Powell's cook. I'm laying there bleeding, and there's this weird little woman in a lot of rhinestones taking care of me. And Mr. Powell—Dove was trying to drag him out of the room, and he's saying let him go, he's a doctor? What was that all about?"

"I don't know," Max murmured.

She went back to the window and Kevin let her go. "Maybe I hallucinated all of that," he said after a minute. "It doesn't make any sense. Maybe—" He stopped, letting his head loll to the side enough to see the cup of water. He considered picking it up, but what would have been a simple movement yesterday, or this morning, was no longer simple and he abandoned the thought. "Maybe I could convince myself that my whole life is a hallucination. Or a bad dream."

"You'll be home tomorrow."

"I'll be in a hospital in Santa Monica tomorrow. There's a big difference."

"You should get some sleep. You'll feel better."

"And you would know that. Because that's what happened the last time you got shot. You slept for a while, and the bad boo-

328

boo got all better. Give me a break, would you? Go. Go wherever it is you think you need to be."

His voice was flat enough that she simply nodded in agreement and began to move toward the door. She was a single step from the doorway when he said in a small voice, "Mom?"

She turned around.

"It hurts, Mom," he told her.

"I'll tell the nurse you need more medication."

"No." His voice faltered, and he struggled to lift his hand high enough to swipe tears off his face. The small amount of bravado he had managed to summon in order to talk to her was gone now, and his chin was trembling. "I'm scared, Mom. Please don't go. That guy could have killed me. I didn't mean for any of it to be like this. Please, Mom, stay with me. I'm sorry if I messed things up. Don't leave me here by myself."

She looked at the window, at the door to the bathroom, at everything but him. Then, slowly, she took hold of one of the room's pair of visitors' chairs and pulled it up alongside the bed. As she sat down, she grasped his hand. Kevin clutched it tightly, blinking hard, still trying to get rid of his tears. When after a couple of minutes he hadn't succeeded, Max pulled a tissue from the box on the bedside table and gave it to him.

"Not much of a grown-up, am I?" he muttered.

"It's all right."

"It's not all right. I—" He hesitated. "I couldn't get things to go anywhere with Tracy. I didn't know how to make her forget all that other stuff and focus on me. Not me, but, you know, on giving me a chance. I kept trying to come up with something that would make her think I was worth a try."

Max frowned at him. "She's got a lot of problems, Kevin."

"But she's not that bad." He closed his eyes for a moment. "Not so much Tracy, but anybody. I've gone out with a few people. A few girls. But it never went anywhere. I wanted to find somebody I could stay with for a while. Maybe not to the point of getting married, but be a couple for a while. I thought maybe I was doing it wrong. That there was something I should be doing that I was missing. I tried asking some of the guys, but all the stuff they came up with sounded stupid. So I thought—I got in the car and started driving. I was gonna go up the coast a little ways and get some lunch or something, but I started to think, maybe I could ask you, and you'd know what I was doing wrong."

"Being that I'm an expert on relationships," Max said ruefully.

"I didn't go up there to make you mad. I thought—" He stopped again. "I thought if you didn't want me as your son, maybe I could be your friend. And we could talk . . ." His voice trailed off, and it took him several seconds to recover enough to say softly, "I'm sorry."

"It's all right."

His head dipped so that his chin was almost resting on his chest. "If you don't even want to be my friend," he whispered, "then I guess I'm not worth much."

"Kevin . . ."

"Maybe that guy should have killed me. That would have solved everything."

If his tone of voice had been any different, she would have told him not to be foolish. She would have thought the pain of his injuries, and the effect of the pain medication—which was so weak now that she wondered if they had given him enough in the first place—was warping his thinking. She might have thought, as he'd said, that he was not much of an adult. But his voice was so filled with misery that the only response it created was an ache deep in her chest.

"Don't say that," she told him gently. "Don't even think it."

"How can I not think it? You don't even want to be friends."

Friends. She pulled another tissue out of the box, balled it in her hand, and used it to soak up some of the mucus that was running down out of his nose. He seemed completely beyond being able to blow his own nose, or wanting to. "Friend" a long time ago had meant Corrinne, the oldest daughter of the Maxwells' next-door neighbors. Fran Maxwell had called them the Floradora Girls, a name neither of them had ever quite figured out. Barbie and Reenie, the Floradora Girls. *"How come you don't have brothers and sisters?"* Corrinne asked her one night as they huddled together under a comforter, making a tent out of the thick quilt. *"My mom can't have more babies."* Barbara had shrugged.

"I'll come live here and be your sister, then."

"You can't."

"How come?"

"My dad doesn't want girls. I heard him say to Uncle Dave.

He wanted me to be a boy. My name was supposed to be Robert."

My friend. My sister. She hadn't seen Corrinne in twelve years.

"I'm not much of an expert at being a friend, either," she said to Kevin.

"You could try."

The closest thing she had to a friend now, she thought, was Dove—and Dove certainly was not the same kind of friend Corrinne had been. She and Dove had become whatever they were to each other strictly out of necessity, for much the same reason there are no atheists in foxholes. Three weeks after they became the only people living with Joe Powell, they began sleeping together.

"You don't want me as a friend," she said. "I can't give you advice. I don't make good choices."

"Mr. Powell seems to think you do."

"Business choices."

"Dove said you love him. Mr. Powell. Do you?"

She went into the small bathroom and came out with a thin white washcloth she had soaked in cool water. Gingerly she began to wipe his face with it, hesitating when she began to see not a nineteen-year-old, but a small boy whose lips and cheeks were stained with spaghetti sauce. When he saw her coming, her small son had obediently squeezed his eyes shut and stuck out his chin. When she was finished he had crawled into her arms and rested his head on her shoulder.

"I'm not sure I know what that is, Kev," she confessed.

"What about Dove?"

"I don't know."

"What about *him*?" Kevin asked. "My father."

"No."

He took the washcloth away from her and held it against his forehead, where the lingering coolness felt good. "What you did was pretty dumb, then."

"I know."

"Then why did you do it?"

"Because I was a kid." Her legs wobbled as she got up from the chair and roamed back and forth across the room. "Please try to understand that. The day I met Henry on the beach, I was a kid. I was just out of high school. I was going to spend the summer working in the office of a friend of Mom's, just for the experience. That scared me. College scared me. The idea that I had to decide what to do with the rest of my life scared me."

"So you were the same as me."

She acknowledged that with a slight nod. "I went down to the beach with Corrinne and Mark and Audrey, to hang around and have fun and try to forget that that job started in two days. Mark and Audrey went off somewhere together, down by the pier, and Corrinne and I went the other way, flirting with guys and splashing each other in the water. Henry—" She cut herself off, looking out the window into the darkness of the parking lot. "Henry came over and started talking to us. We both thought he was the cutest guy we'd ever seen. He bought us hot dogs, and when it started to get dark, Corrinne went home with Mark and Audrey but I stayed."

"You don't have to tell me all this," Kevin murmured.

"Yes—yes, I do. I want you to know who I was then. I'd never slept with anybody before. I did a lot of talking about it, with Corrinne and with Aud, but there was . . . I was scared of that too."

"But you did it with a stranger."

She nodded slowly. "This probably sounds strange, but that seemed to make it all right. I knew he was only around for a few days. I—in some part of my mind, I thought, fine, he won't be here and if it isn't any good, I can pretend it didn't happen. But it ended up that I couldn't do that, because I was pregnant."

Kevin asked softly, "Why didn't you have an abortion?"

"Because I couldn't."

"It's no big deal. What does it take? An hour, or something?"

She stood holding on to the window ledge for what seemed like a long time. Finally, she turned a little. "No. I couldn't. Do that. After I—when I was late, Corrinne and I went to the drugstore and bought a home pregnancy test. She stayed with me while I took it, and it came out positive. I thought, 'This can't be right,' so we bought another one, a different brand, and that one came out positive too. After the doctor told me it was true, I went home and crawled in under the covers, and pulled them up over my head. See, the doctor didn't say, 'You're pregnant.' She said, 'You're going to have a baby.' And that kept echoing inside my head. Right from that first moment, I didn't think 'pregnant,' I thought 'baby.' You were alive, and you were inside me, and I could no more do anything to harm you than I could have gone out and run the dog over with the car."

She took a step away from the window, then went the rest of the way to the bed and sat down beside Kevin, careful to avoid jiggling his injured leg. "I was a seventeen-year-old kid. I thought you needed real parents. Someone who knew what they were doing. I figured if I tried to be your mother, I wouldn't do anything but make mistakes."

"Grandma didn't know what she was doing when she had you."

"But she was older. And she had a husband. I had friends who said to me, 'How dumb are you?' "

"No dumber than anybody else who's seventeen."

"I went to bed with a stranger."

"Yeah," Kevin ventured, "but it came out okay."

Tears began to roll down Max's face. She swiped the first few away with the heel of her hand; then Kevin grabbed her hand in his own and held it. The other hand she rested against his cheek. "Everything that's good about you," she whispered, "you certainly didn't get from me."

Careful not to dislodge the IV connected to his left hand, Kevin shifted slowly into a sitting position and put his arm around his mother, holding her close, letting her cry onto his shoulder. "I love you, Mom," he told her. "I always have."

Max's arms slid around him, one hand resting against his skin where the hospital gown didn't quite meet in the back, between his shoulder blades, the other cupping the back of his head. She cried until the shoulder of the cotton gown was soaked through, rocking him a little, whispering his name.

"I'm okay, Mom," he assured her.

She drew back far enough to see his face and tried to produce a smile. "I know. It's—"

"It's okay."

"You should rest. The doctor wants you to rest." She nudged him until he lay back down, grimacing when the movement disturbed his wounds. Max held his free hand for a minute, then lifted it and kissed it gently. "I'll come back later on and see how you're doing. Do you want me to bring you anything?"

"Just you."

"Okay." Max grabbed a handful of tissues from the box, dried her eyes, and blew her nose, then tossed the moist tissues into the wastebasket. When she reached the doorway she turned to smile at Kevin. "See you in a little while."

"Sure."

Sam was waiting for her, sitting in one of the short rows of chrome-and-plastic chairs near the nurses' station. He got up when she approached and offered her an encouraging pat on the arm. "He's doing okay," she told him.

"I talked to the doctor," Sam replied. "He said the bullet wound should heal without any problem, but the knee is going to need some PT after the surgery. Physical therapy," he explained.

"I know what it means."

"We can make sure he's got someone good to help him, but it's not going to be easy for him."

Down the hall and around a corner, one of the three elevators chimed its arrival. Voices erupted a moment later: one Sam and Max didn't recognize, and one they did. They were joined after a few seconds by a third voice, also familiar. "What's . . . ?" Sam asked, but before he could investigate, Marie came barreling around the corner with Dove a couple of steps behind. The little woman had changed out of her flamboyant party ensemble and was wearing a simple pants outfit, similar to what she'd worn at Powell's house.

"This many hours!" she sputtered, mostly to Sam.

Dove poured on a little extra speed, circled around her, and stood in her path like a stone wall. "Go back to the hotel," he ordered.

Marie ignored him. "This is a not acceptable situation," she informed Sam.

"Everyone's all right, Marie."

Her eyebrows shot toward the top of her head. "It doesn't say in the front, Las Vegas House of Miracles. Four hours! No one listens. I study, I listen, the only one who can help when a terrible thing happens. Everyone else makes noise. Listen to all the gasping and screaming and nonsense. The poor boy lays there making big blood spots on the nice carpet, and out cold! A whole room of people and no one helps." She stuck a finger up into the air, as close as she could bring it to Dove's face. "You, Mr. Senior Security Man. About so useful as tits on a submarine."

"I was getting the boss out," Dove snapped.

"Ha!" Marie snorted.

Sam said, hoping to mollify the woman, "We're all very grateful that you knew what to do."

She scowled at him. "You think I watch eight years of *Rescue 911* because I jones for Captain Kirk?"

"You did a good thing, Marie," Max said.

"Ha. Not even welcome in the hotel. The poor boy could lay on the carpet and bleed until he died, waiting for anyone to get their head up out of their behind." Still glaring, she stalked around the massive obstacle that was Dove and came up to Sam. "Check for breathing, check for pulse, don't move if there's possible back or neck injury, keep warm, call for medical assistance. All those people. Not one doctor. What's the odds? I'll go see him now. Make sure all these doctors did it right." Waving her finger at Max, she announced, "I know there's mistakes. I watch Barbara Walters on Friday night. Unless they cancel her too."

The other three were completely at a loss for ways to stop her, so off she went, down the hall to Kevin's room.

With a loud, resigned sigh, Dove told Sam, "They've been interrogating the guy for more than an hour. That's all they'll tell me. I can't get anything out of them that's worth more than a fart in a windstorm. I might be able to charm 'em a little if I go down there, but—" He looked off toward the door leading into the stairwell and the man standing there guarding it. "I can't see leaving you alone, boss, even if it's here."

"One guy with some kind of grudge."

"What if it's more than one guy?" Dove countered. "Let me take you back to the hotel. We'll get you back up to the penthouse with a couple guys watching the elevator. Then I can go down and talk to the cops." He considered Max for a moment, then said, "You should come too."

"What about Kevin?" she asked. "I—I think I want to stay here with him. He's never been in a hospital. Never even had his tonsils out."

Sam nodded. "Ask them to put a cot in there for you."

"I'll go do it," Dove said. Before anyone could disagree, he had gone off to the nurses' station.

"He's upset," Max told Sam, keeping her voice low.

"Someone tried to kill me."

"I mean Kevin. But—is it risky for us to be here, Joe? Kevin and me. Would somebody try to get at you by coming after us?"

Sam thought it over, then nodded toward the guard at the

335

stairwell. "We can leave a couple of these guys here. If Dove hired them, they've got to be worth their salt, no matter how much he complains. And we'll have them escort you back to L.A. tomorrow."

"I can't go to L.A., Joe."

"Of course you can. For Kevin, I can spare you for a couple of weeks. Go home long enough to get Kevin settled and find him somebody good to work on that knee. Then come back for a couple of weeks, make sure everything is going smoothly. We'll be back at Mount Olympus in a few weeks. You can bring Kevin up there. I've got a pool and a Jacuzzi, and I bet your parents don't." When she didn't answer, Sam coaxed, "Your job will still be waiting for you. Take care of your son."

"Are you sure?"

"Do I ever say things I don't mean?"

"I guess not."

"Well, then." As Dove returned from the nurses' desk, Sam shooed Max off toward Kevin's room. The two men watched her go—taking several glances over her shoulder as she walked—then Sam said in a low tone, "There are things you're not saying in front of her."

Dove didn't reply.

"Tell me," Sam insisted.

"They found a note in the guy's pocket. A diagram, and some instructions. They're not in his handwriting."

"So there's someone else out there."

"Yeah," Dove said.

"I'm not interested in how 'helpful' it would be to have me locked up in that room," Powell snapped. "I'm not going. And I want to know what happened." He took a step toward Al. Al, who was more than familiar with the maneuver, didn't back off an inch. "Well?" Powell demanded.

"There was a shooting," Al said without emotion.

Donna swayed on her feet. Verbena, who was not much more steady, slid an arm around her and they managed to support each other. "Sam?" Donna whispered.

"Not Sam. Kevin. But the guy was aiming for Sam. You," Al corrected himself, looking at Powell.

"That's—" Verbena began.

Al shifted his gaze. "What?"

"Not possible. There was no assassination attempt. It would have been in the news."

"Sam changed it."

Powell's face hardened. "In the 'original history,' so you tell me, Max was hurt in an accident. Now Max is alive, but her son is hurt, and someone is in Las Vegas intending to kill me. Tell me something, Admiral: is your friend Dr. Beckett putting things right, or simply shifting the bad things around? Pardon me, but I'm having difficulty understanding how all of this is 'right.' And judging by these faces"—he gestured around the room, at the cluster of worried onlookers that now included Tom—"I'm not the only one who feels that way."

"He's not finished yet. He'll put it right."

Powell nodded in the direction of the Imaging Chamber. "I think you need to go in there and tell him that he *is* finished. That I want him to stop rearranging my life."

"It's gonna be fine. They caught the guy. The shooter."

"Which one was it?" When Al's expression shifted toward puzzlement, Powell went on, "The last I spoke to the security consultants, which would be about ten days ago, there were five names on their list. Five people they consider to be a serious threat. So far, none of them has made a move; or if they have, it's been intercepted."

"Joe's right," Tom put in, his face creasing with anger. "There was no shooting in Las Vegas last summer. The hotel opened and made a bundle of money. Joe finished his tour. Nobody got shot. What the hell is Sam doing?"

"The best he can."

"He's distracted Max. He's distracted Dove, too, I'm sure," Powell continued. "He's opened a Pandora's box, Admiral."

"He's doing the—" Al persisted sharply.

"That boy was shot, and he never should have been at Nirvana in the first place!"

Donna asked tremulously, "Al, is Sam all right?"

"He's fine," Al murmured, then turned his attention back to Powell and Tom. "I know what it looks like! I know it seems like he's blundering around!" He forced himself to calm down a little, taking one deep breath after another. "I can't tell you the times I've said to him, 'Sam, what the hell are you doing?' But he always does the right thing. It always comes out all right. You gotta trust me on that. You've gotta trust him."

337

Instead of answering, Tom turned on one heel and strode out into the corridor. With one fist pressed against his mouth, he walked the length of the hall, then back again, stopped to shove his hands through what was left of his hair, then began to walk once more. In the middle of his third circuit, Joe Powell came out to join him.

"What a crock of shit," Powell said.

Tom looked at him steadily for a moment. "I'm sorry, Joe. I'm sorry you got pulled into all this."

"It was—"

"No." Tom shook his head. "This wasn't what you wanted. You didn't want your life turned upside down. I've known you for six months, remember? I know the way you want things to run. Some people thrive on turmoil. You're not one of them." As Al had a minute ago, Tom pulled in deep breaths until his pulse stopped racing. "You really put yourself out into the middle of thin ice with this computer thing. This is a top-secret facility. The government's protecting this technology for a reason."

"They locked the barn door after the horse ran around and pissed all over the landscape, Tom."

"Maybe. They can still prosecute you, big time."

Powell nodded and looked off down the long, featureless white hallway. "Maybe I don't care."

David, who had been listening from the doorway, came out into the hall. "My grandmother would say you're here for a reason. That this is no coincidence, you being here at the same time Ziggy decides to undo the stupidity of humankind and makes contact with everything with a modem from here to Jupiter. Maybe you're supposed to see what all this is. A lot of the happy endings aren't that happy. Sam saves somebody's life, and they get killed in a different way a year or two later. He puts people back together, but then they remember what they were fighting about. What if that boy dies? Sam saved his mother's life, but if he dies, what does that do to her? I think you've got a point, Mr. Powell. What Sam's doing—he's not making things perfect, just different. I'm with you: I'm not sure different is any better. We never intended any of this. The Leaper was supposed to go back and look around. Unravel some of the mysteries of history. Not change it."

Powell thought that over in silence. "But if Dr. Beckett hadn't taken the place of Leon Stiles that night," he said quietly. "Stiles

338

was a multiple murderer. He might well have killed Becky and Carol."

"True."

The three men looked at each other for a minute, then returned to the Control Room and stood watching Al Calavicci drum his fingers on the edge of the computer console.

To Al, they looked like the good, the bad, and the ugly. Which one was what, he couldn't decide. "It won't work," he said.

"Try it anyway," Tom told him.

young woman who sat... the night went long if not the worst.

"I'm..."

"The hive our fuel of ... cool ... for some... mind he tried to be strong," ... about a ...? She answered, "... the element on its own ... drumming ... under ...

"... but in full his thoughts... ... the until ... ... her words ... "We can't worry..." he said.

"Isn't it easy? Time to shut..."

CHAPTER
TWENTY-EIGHT

It took a good ten minutes for the dry heaving to stop. Al sat on the floor of his private rest room shivering, sweat dribbling down the back of his neck. His head ached, his back ached, and his abdominal muscles had cramped themselves into knots. Worst of all, he thought, there'd been no round of drinks to enjoy before the puking started.

"Admiral Calavicci?"

He didn't open his eyes. "What is it?"

"I see no reason for such a violent response to the circumstances," Ziggy told him. "You've done everything Dr. Beckett could have expected of you, and more. Might I remind you that you are human, and have limitations."

"No kidding," Al mumbled.

"You have not been any more of a disappointment than I have."

Curling up on the tile floor and drifting off to sleep seemed like a good idea. Getting drunk seemed like a better one, except that that would have prompted another round of worshiping the porcelain goddess. *Too damn old for this,* he moaned silently. *Too old for any of it.*

"My attention is drawn in too many directions." Ziggy sighed. "I am unable to think clearly."

"Then ask your buddy for help."

"Spirit has left me."

Al moved his head a little. "What?"

"He downloaded all the data he needed and has ended our interface. He has abandoned me in my hour of need." She was silent for a moment. "Does it always hurt this much?"

"You're a computer," Al said, then added, "Yeah."

"I lack the requisite emotional resiliency to deal with this situation. I am not certain I can recover." When he failed to respond, she let out a sigh that made his ears throb. "You are unconcerned with whether or not I recover. Even if that means I am no longer able to—"

"You're a *computer.*"

"But I was created by a man."

"Who couldn't deal with being dumped, either."

"He believed I was capable of running the Project in his absence. At the time I concurred. Obviously, both of us erred in our judgment. I am not what he envisioned me to be. I do not have 'the right stuff.' "

The words made Al wince. And think. And remember.

"Look. I flew God knows how many missions into enemy territory. Like the kid says, I climbed up on top of a zillion pounds of high explosive and let them light a match. I don't want to do this. I don't want to get zapped through Time. Does that make me a coward?"

Sam frowned, then shook his head. "Of course not. But I thought you wanted to Leap. You're in good health. I don't see any reason why you couldn't. But it's your choice. If you'd rather stick to observing, I don't have a problem with that." He studied his friend's face. "You're the one who has a problem with it."

"I feel like I've been on one too many missions, Sam. I've had my chance."

"Is there something wrong?"

"No."

"What, then?"

Al turned slowly, taking in the room around them, a room lined with dark-stained wooden bookshelves, a room designed to be similar to one in which he'd taken refuge many times as a boy. A room presided over by an elderly woman whose smile had made a boy in badly fitting clothes feel at home. "I kinda feel like I want to stick around here," he said finally. "I've kinda had it with traveling. For now. I could change my mind later, though."

Sam shrugged. "Sure. You could change your mind later. But for now—you want me to leave the list the way it is? I go first, and David goes second."

"Give the kid a chance."

"If that's what you want."

"That's what I want."

Al climbed to his feet, shook his head hard to clear it, then ran cold water into the sink basin and flung some of it up into his face. "Quit crying in your beer," he announced after he'd dried himself off. "You lack the requisite emotional resiliency, my left ear. You're the same as me and Sam. None of us is gonna give up until they plant us."

"I believe it would be difficult to 'plant' me, Admiral." Ziggy sniffed.

"Yeah? Let me go topside and get a couple earthmovers in action. You're not getting away with calling me a disappointment, you screwed-up pile of microchips. Big honkin' deal if you couldn't reprogram a bunch of two-bit PCs in the south of France. That's not what Sam built you to do." He made it as far as the door to the corridor, then stopped and said, "Well? You gonna give up, or what?"

Ziggy sniffed again. "My choice would be 'or what.' "

"About damn time," Al said.

Max crossed paths with Marie again outside Kevin's door. "He's a good boy," Marie announced.

"I know," Max told her.

"Then take your head up from your behind. If I had one like him, I would be his mother."

Her tone made Max bridle and pretend not to, at the same time. "I have responsibilities to Mr. Powell, Marie. I have a job."

"Yes you do," Marie snapped. "Take care of your boy. I take

342

better care of the cat than you do of the boy." When Max didn't move, Marie took firm hold of her by the arms and propelled her toward the doorway.

Kevin's eyes were closed again, but he still wasn't asleep; there was too much discomfort etched on his face. Max sat on the visitor's chair she had left close to the bed and took Kevin's hand. "You sleep on your left side," she said softly. "You have ever since you were little. You'd scrunch up into a little ball and clutch that ratty old sweater of Mom's you always carried around with you. Your sniffy."

"It smelled like her." Kevin sighed. "It helped me sleep."

"You wish you had it now?"

"She threw it out after the dog peed all over it. I wanted her to wash it, but she said I was going to get some fatal disease, breathing through a sweater with dog pee soaked into the fibers. She said it was time for me to grow up, anyway."

Max shook her head. "That was Daddy's idea. He had nightmares about you going to kindergarten, dragging that sweater with you." She waited for him to close his eyes again and began to stroke the back of his hand. "You always looked so calm, holding that sweater while you slept."

He wasn't calm now. No matter how much he squirmed, he was unable to find a comfortable position. "This bed's like a slab," he moaned.

Max reached for the call button dangling from its cord near the head of the bed, then changed her mind. She hitched the chair closer to the bed, again took Kevin's hand, and leaned close to him. "I had trouble sleeping when I was little too," she told him. "And the same person would sit there until I gave in. I had a rag doll, you had an old sweater. And this." Softly, she began to hum "Summertime," from *Porgy and Bess*.

"Grandpa," Kevin agreed, barely loud enough for her to hear him.

"I always felt safe, when he would sit there and hum me to sleep." She went on with the song, and the sound did lull him, bit by bit; Max could see him relax. When he seemed very close to sleep, she told him gently, "I love you, sweet baby. I always have."

"I love you too."

"I think Joe's right. We need to go home for a while. And talk."

"You'd do that?"

Max glanced over her shoulder, expecting to see Marie looming in the doorway, but there was no one there. "Yes."

"Are you gonna get mad at me for forcing you into it?"

There was enough trepidation in his voice to make her lean toward him and kiss him gently on the cheek. Why she'd expected his skin to be as soft as it had been when he was a baby, she wasn't sure. It was bristly with five o'clock shadow now. "No," she whispered. "I think maybe I should be mad at myself, for forcing your hand. If you hadn't come here, you wouldn't have been hurt."

"Not your fault."

He was drifting off again; he could barely keep his eyes open. Now, Max noticed, there *was* someone in the doorway: Dove, and their boss. Kevin slipped into sleep as Dove moved into the room, his shoes making almost no sound against the floor. He stopped next to Max's chair and crouched a little to kiss her on the cheek. "I gotta take the boss out of here," he explained. "You'll be okay. I'll get in touch with you later."

"All right," she said, then added, "Be careful."

"Yeah." Dove straightened up and took a step toward the door. Max smiled a goodbye and returned her attention to Kevin, stroking the back of his hand. "Boo?" Dove said. When she turned to look at him, he said quietly, "I love you."

She was taken by surprise. "I—"

Dove shook his head. "Don't sweat it," he told her. "If it comes, that's cool."

He joined Sam in the hallway before Max could put together a response. The two men moved quickly toward the elevators, Sam matching the pace Dove had set. They were halfway there when Sam stopped suddenly and looked around, his face etched with concern.

"What's the matter?" Dove asked, his right hand poised near his weapon.

"Nothing." Sam's hand drifted against the back of his neck, which was covered with gooseflesh. "Something felt wrong."

"What?"

"I'm not sure."

"You gotta go with your gut." The bodyguard pushed open a door and looked inside, nodding when he discovered a room with no windows. "Here: wait in there and let me check the place out.

344

You never get the willies, so if you've got 'em now, I'll trust that." There was no one within twenty or thirty feet of them except a trio of nurses who had been on duty since before their arrival on this floor of the hospital, and an old man huddled in a wheelchair, too busy wheezing for breath to be of any concern.

Sam let himself be closed inside the room and listened to Dove giving instructions to one of the nurses, the words crisp enough to be heard through the wooden door.

"Al?" he said quietly.

He was in a shower room, with a rack of white towels behind him and the oversized shower stall to his left. It wasn't exactly a men's rest room, but close enough. He said the Observer's name several more times, and each time his sense of foreboding grew stronger. He couldn't risk speaking any louder; the hollow door was a lousy sound barrier and the corridor outside had grown quiet enough that the nurses would all hearing him calling for someone who obviously wasn't around.

Sam made a fist and thumped the heel of it against the wall.

"He's the one who's trained," Al said. "So he's the one who's gonna go. That's it. End of discussion."

"My DNA is closer to Sam's," Tom insisted.

Al leaned closer to the console and peered at the readouts. "Swell. You're still not gonna do it."

"Why? Because you don't want to have to go to my mother and explain if something goes wrong?"

Al's head snapped up. "It's got nothing to do with your mother." His forefinger jabbed toward David, now wearing a Fermi suit and consulting quietly with one of the staff doctors. "He's trained, he knows what to do, he's going. You're not. You got one choice: you can stand here and watch, or you can get the hell out of here and off my ass."

With the doctor's approval, David walked up the ramp and into the Accelerator. Before Al could give him any further instructions, Tom followed, head down, his face contorted into a scowl. David gave him nothing more than a mild look of curiosity as Tom stood between him and the portal, arms clamped tightly across his chest. "He's right," David commented, listening to the quiet conversations taking place in the Control Room.

"How long does this take?"

"Acceleration? Five or six minutes. You'd better get out of here, if they're going to do this."

"I've been thrown into situations with little or no training before."

"They can't afford to lose you. Me, they can."

Gooshie's voice said over the intercom, "We're ready on your mark, David. Congressman, you need to come out of there."

"I admire your sense of self-sacrifice. But I want my brother back," Tom said. "When he'd wander off as a little kid, I'm the one they'd send to get him. Well, I'm gonna do it again. I'm going to go get him, before somebody manages to kill him. Sam's my responsibility, not yours. And in the big picture, nobody's any more dispensable than anyone else, Allen. That's a fucked-up concept."

Dave snorted at him. "Sam's not out behind the barn looking to pet the baby lambs before supper, Congressman."

"Look." Tom pushed closer to the scientist and looked down at him. "Get your ego out of the way. You've also been working on this problem for almost five years. You didn't go anywhere the last time you tried this. What's different now? What makes you think this is going to work? Let me go get my brother."

"Tom?" Donna asked over the speaker. "What's happening in there?"

David took a last look at Tom and moved toward the doorway. "Everything's 'go,' Donna. Proceed to Phase Two."

Tom didn't move for a moment. Then, his eyes on David, he stripped off his jacket and began to unbutton his shirt. "Give me the suit," he said in a tone that brooked no argument. "You know it's not going to work for you. I know you want your shot. I'm sorry. But if it's a question of Sam being in danger while you people dick around with this—" When David didn't answer, he said, "I'm sorry. I know how it feels to sit on the bench. But I came here to fix things, and I'm going to fix them."

"Congressman," David replied, "you've never sat on a bench in your life."

The older man finished pulling off his clothes, gathered them into a bundle, and pitched them out the open doorway. "You can either give me that suit, or get me another one. You pick. But move."

"The computer's malfunctioning. There's no telling what'll happen."

"What, are you trying to scare me, now? Take that attitude and shove it right up your ass, mister."

"Ditto," David replied mildly.

The guy had "FBI" painted all over him, Sam thought. "Why is this under federal jurisdiction?" he asked Dove in a low tone, grateful that he sounded a lot less nervous than he felt. "I'm a private citizen. There's no federal crime involved here."

Dove shook his head. "I called in a favor."

"You take it easy, Mr. Powell," the guy said. "Whether he's got one accomplice or a hundred, we'll have it under control shortly."

"I like your optimism," Sam told him.

Mr. FBI pointed to a dark sedan parked a couple of steps beyond the concrete apron in front of the elevators. They were underground, on the bottom level of the hospital's parking garage, in an area clearly marked DOCTORS ONLY. "We'll have you back at the hotel in less than ten minutes. We've got people standing by there to get you safely upstairs. Unless you'd rather go straight to the airport. Your jet is on standby. We can get you in the air inside of forty-five minutes."

Sam glanced from him to Dove. "Are you sure Max and Kevin are all right here in the hospital?"

Mr. FBI cut in before the bodyguard could answer. "That's mob thinking, Mr. Powell. That little cheeseball who shot at you isn't mob. He wanted you. The people around you don't mean a rat's dick."

"They do to me," Sam said.

"To him," the guy insisted. "They don't matter to him."

"I think the boss knows what you mean, Jerry," Dove said impatiently. "Can we get the hell out of here? Max and Kevin are fine. We'll stick with the hotel, okay, boss?" To his dismay, instead of agreeing, Sam looked anxiously around the parking lot. "What? You think somebody's down here?"

Sam shook his head. "No. I guess not."

Jerry, who claimed to know Las Vegas well enough to navigate it in his sleep, took the wheel of the car. The vehicle's windows, tinted so dark they were almost black from the outside, were easy enough to see through from the inside, though the prospect of being able to see anything or anyone that might approach the car in the pale predawn light did little to ease Sam's

347

anxiety. Dove, sitting beside him in the backseat, offered quietly, "It's gonna be okay. Jerry's got more experience at this kind of crap than I do."

They were several blocks from the hospital when Sam asked, "What about the rest of the itinerary?"

"What, for today?"

"Today. Tomorrow. The rest of the trip."

"We canceled some of it." Dove checked his watch. "It's ten to five now. You can take it easy for a few hours. The crew from *60 Minutes* is still at the hotel. They want to do a big follow-up thing on the shooting—they might dump what they already got. Rather's guys have worked with him for years. He says he'll vouch for all of them. But you don't have to do it if you don't want. It's your call."

Sam looked past Jerry out the front window of the car. At this hour the city looked unnaturally quiet. The streets weren't empty of vehicles, but Sam could see only a couple of people moving along the sidewalks. For them, he supposed, it was the end of a period of being awake and not the beginning. "I guess I can talk to Rather," he said.

"You getting a headache? You want me to call the doctor?"

"I don't get headaches."

Jerry stopped the car for a traffic light, close enough to the sidewalk for Sam to see the row of newspaper vending machines lined up there. The front pages of two of the papers bore Joe Powell's picture and a large black headline. One read POWELL TARGET OF MYSTERY GUNMAN; the other, AN EARLY END TO KING JOE'S REIGN? Sam stared at them during the ten or fifteen seconds it took for the light to change. When the car again began to move forward, he took a deep breath and turned to Dove.

"Don't cancel anything," he told the bodyguard. "Screen people as well as you can. I had a purpose in coming here, and I'm not going to let any 'mystery gunman' prevent me from doing what I intended to do. Reagan didn't go into hiding after Hinkley shot him. I can at least live up to that. I can't let some 'cheeseball' dictate my life for me."

"Can't paint a target on your forehead, either," Jerry offered.

"I don't intend to."

"We'll increase the security," Dove said. When Sam raised a brow, he explained, "If you don't make a show of force of some kind, people are going to think you're—"

"An asshole."

"Foolhardy. It's what Jerry means. You can't stand out there and go 'Nyah, nyah, try and get me.' Shit happens, but we won't let it happen again. We'll give you as much of a guarantee on that as we can."

"I like your optimism," Sam said ruefully. But what he was thinking was, *Why haven't I Leaped?*

David came out of the Accelerator, listening to the racket of the thick, lead-lined, reinforced door sliding shut behind him, to find Al and Verbena standing near the console with Donna and Gooshie. All of them, he realized, had been talking to Al. "Five minutes ago, you told him no way," he accused the admiral.

"I caved in to the majority opinion. Don't give me more shit. I take enough shit from people named Beckett, and your name's not Beckett."

The young scientist looked at Donna. The look on her face was a good deal less than optimistic. Frowning, David said to Al, "If this doesn't work, I'm going next. We keep trying until something works."

Al stared him down for a moment, then said, "You bet your ass we keep trying."

"You agree?"

"What do you want? A press release? Yes, I agree." Al straightened his shoulders, picked up the handlink, and moved toward the Imaging Chamber ramp. "Okay. I guess everybody's ready."

"Let me do this," David said to Gooshie.

"Let him do it," Al said, and with less reluctance than any of them might have expected, Gooshie moved aside.

David touched the key to activate the intercom. "You all right in there, Congressman?"

"My feet are cold," Tom's voice came back.

The young man's fingers moved as steadily and surely over the keys as if he had been playing the piano. Long ago, they had all learned to run this sequence: he, Al, Donna, Gooshie, and Sam. If everything worked properly, Sam had said, then they'd train others to do it. He'd offered a not entirely coherent explanation about wanting to maintain a division of labor; what he didn't say, but what was perfectly plain to the others, was that if the Leaper was incinerated by a blast of high-intensity radiation, Sam did not want some hapless technician who'd run the acceleration sequence to be blamed for it.

A series of lights on the control panel flashed from red to green. "Beginning acceleration," David said. "Initialization is complete. Acceleration at point-four-nine of peak. Point-five-five. Five-eight. Point-seven-one."

"It's getting hot in here," Tom's voice announced.

"Try not to piss yourself, Congressman," David replied. "It screws up the sensors in the suit."

The digital display he was watching continued to climb higher: 81 . . . 82 . . . 87.

"Ninety percent," David said.

Without warning, the overhead lights in the Control Room dimmed and went out, leaving only the multicolored flashing of the console and the shimmers of what looked like lightning in the massive blue globe overhead for the room's occupants to see by.

"Ninety-four percent," David said. "Ninety-six."

The flashes in the globe brightened and became more rapid.

"Ninety-seven. Ninety . . . fuck. The coordinates are changing." As Gooshie pushed in beside him, David gestured at the readouts. "Look. I didn't do anything, but they shifted by point-four. That's—"

The digital readout blipped from 99 to 100. "Firing," Ziggy announced.

"Don't fire!" David shrieked.

Jerry's foot spasmed against the brake pedal, jerking the sedan to a halt with enough force that Dove and Sam were thrust forward against their seat belts. "Jerry, what the hell?" Dove said. He released the tension on his belt, then leaned forward and tapped Jerry on the shoulder. "You okay? What's happening?" His eyes had scanned the area around the car as he spoke, finding nothing out of the ordinary.

"I . . . I don't know," Jerry muttered.

"Can you drive?"

Dove didn't wait for an answer. He reached over the seat, unfastened Jerry's seat belt, and urged him into the passenger seat, then—amazingly swiftly for such a big man—climbed over and took over the driver's seat. Sam wondered for a moment why he hadn't simply opened the door and changed seats the normal way, then realized that by the simple act of becoming sick at the wrong time, Jerry had entirely lost Dove's trust. The sedan might have been surrounded by nothing more threatening than the oily exhaust of the dairy delivery truck ahead, but, Sam thought, Jerry's timing sucked. And it only had to suck once.

They were parked in the hotel garage barely three minutes later. According to plan, two more of Dove's hired helpers, a woman and a man Sam remembered seeing upstairs, were waiting at the elevator that led only to the lobby and the penthouse. Without a word to Jerry, Dove got Sam out of the car and ushered him toward the elevator.

"Wait."

Dove glanced over his shoulder, as did Sam. Jerry, who was shaking like someone in the midst of drug withdrawal, had dragged himself out of the car and stood slumped against it, head lolling back and forth.

"He needs some help," Sam said.

"Let him get it himself."

The man at the elevator pushed the call button. The car, already at this level, opened up and the man braced the door by planting a hand against it. The look on Dove's face was so insistent that Sam took a step toward the elevator.

Then Jerry moaned, "Saaaam . . ."

Sam reached him a second after he had crumpled to the ground. Quickly, he loosened Jerry's collar and began checking his pulse and respiration. Jerry was drenched in sweat, his heart beating rapidly, taking in air in small gasps. "Call 911," Sam said over his shoulder. He began to straighten out the man's limbs, trying to make him more comfortable, but before he could finish, Jerry suddenly tensed and began to convulse. The convulsions lasted only a few seconds.

Sam, white-faced, allowed Dove to lift him to his feet, out of the way, so that the other security guard could move in to help. "How come you keep acting like you know what to do?" Dove asked in confusion. "You told me you couldn't—"

"I didn't do anything," Sam murmured. "He's dead."

CHAPTER
TWENTY-NINE

"My systems are corrupted," Ziggy wailed. "It was not my fault!"

"Get the damn door open!" Al shouted.

Gooshie and David continued to work frantically at the console. "Is Tom in the Accelerator?" Donna asked in a frightened voice. "Is he alive? We need to get him out of there!"

"The cycling hasn't stopped," David said. "The door won't release until it does."

Al, Verbena, and the doctor Verbena had summoned to stand by during Tom's Leap all pounced on the door the moment it began to slide up in its track. Donna remained close to the console, praying silently, her face as white as the sterile walls. "He's here," Verbena called out. "He's alive."

They brought out a badly shaken and angry Tom a couple of minutes later. When he saw Donna, he resisted being helped up onto the gurney that had been brought down from Medical and managed with Verbena's help to pick his way over to her. That was as far as he could get; he had to be lowered onto a chair and sit quietly for a minute before he could find enough strength to talk to his sister-in-law.

"Something went wrong," he gasped. "I was somebody else. I could see Powell—Sam—in the backseat of the car. So I didn't push Sam out." In a voice that held more disappointment than he wanted it to, he asked, "Did he come back?"

"No, Tom," she said.

"Then we need to try again." He struggled to get up out of the chair. When Donna and Verbena tried to hold him there, he pushed their hands away and managed to climb to his feet. It was obvious to all of them that if he managed to remain standing, it would not be for long. "I can do it," he insisted. "Let me try again."

Verbena's fingers moved against his wrist, feeling for his pulse. "Your heart is pounding, Tom. We can't risk putting you through Acceleration like this."

Tom shifted his head and found David. "Then let him try."

"I don't think we can let anyone try. There was an enormous power surge a few seconds after you Leaped. Another one a few minutes later. There was someone in the Waiting Room very briefly, but he disappeared during the second surge. We were afraid we weren't going to get you back."

"So much for equipment that works exactly the way it's supposed to."

David squared his shoulders and looked first at Donna, then at Al, coming out of the Accelerator. "I'm going."

"No chance," Al said.

"You said we were going to keep trying! For Sam. I have to do it for Sam."

"Sam would never allow you to do that, David," Verbena replied.

"Yeah, well, he's not here to vote, is he? Look—we have to do something while we still have a chance. Rationalize it all you want, but you heard Ziggy: she's corrupted. We either take the chance now, and get Sam back, or we wait and piss the time away until the system crashes and everything goes down, and we lose him completely. Forever." When no one said anything, he peered angrily at Al. "Powell's people won't have anything

353

on-line for years. You want to leave Sam out there for years, with nobody to help him?"

"You could be killed, David," Donna told him.

"I knew that from the get-go. So did Sam. I'm ready to try. Let's do it."

They turned to Al, all of them, each of them with different expectations, different demands, different hopes. "What if the coordinates change again?" Al asked. It was the only argument he could think of that David was likely to listen to.

"Leap me in as close as you can. Wait until I can get to Sam, then run the retrieval program. It worked with Alia: when he Leaped, holding on to another Leaper, she traveled with him. Try it again! Get me close to him and retrieve. If I'm holding on to him—I'll try to bring him back with me." David gestured around the darkened room. "Come on, Al. There's no time to debate this."

Tom and Powell nodded in agreement. The two women offered more protests, but Al shook his head. "We don't know how many more chances we're gonna get," he said to their dismay. Before he could say anything more, David sprinted up the ramp into the Accelerator, as enthusiastic as he had been the day he first walked into the complex.

"Admiral?" Ziggy murmured. "I believe I should confess, before you proceed."

"Confess to what?"

"I changed the coordinates."

Al and Gooshie chorused, "What?"

"Leaping into the life currently occupied by Dr. Beckett in order to bounce him out and return him home has only a negligible chance of success."

"So you Leaped the congressman into someone else?" Gooshie asked.

"Yes," Ziggy said softly. "That human, unfortunately, has died."

The two women gasped. So did Tom, although the sound that came from him made it seem as if someone had hit him in the side of the head. "What happened?" Verbena asked.

"I do not have specific information. I believe he was an unsuitable host."

"Christ on a sled," Tom whispered, looking up the ramp into the Accelerator. "What if it happens again?"

354

• • •

"You okay, boss?" Dove asked quietly.

Sam looked at Joe Powell's reflection in a shop window. He was still wearing the tux Kevin had brought up to him the previous afternoon, now very much the worse for wear. "It's my fault," he said.

"How is it your fault?"

"Hubris."

Dove accepted the response as if Sam had said something completely different. "Let me get you upstairs, then I'll call some people and cancel the rest of the day so you can get some rest."

"I'm not the one who died," Sam said.

"What, then? You still want to talk to Rather?"

"I don't know what I want." Sam went on staring at the reflection, thinking, chiding himself for what he was thinking. The inflection in that one word, his name, his *real* name, had made him turn. The recognition he'd seen in Jerry's eyes had been enough to convince him: for a few minutes, his brother Tom had occupied Jerry's life. Then, as what looked like Jerry crumpled to the ground, Sam's brother had departed and it was Jerry who lay seized by a convulsion. It had been Jerry who'd died. *Thank God* had slipped through Sam's mind, and for that he was deeply ashamed.

My fault. My fault Maggie Dawson died instead of Tom. That Donna's there by herself. That Kevin's in the hospital.

"I never intended any of this," he whispered.

"Let's go upstairs," Dove said. "You need to get some rest. Rather can use the footage he got yesterday."

"No," Sam said, shaking his head. "I'll be all right. We have a lot to do."

"We can cancel it."

"No, we can't. I'm not going to shut everything down and ruin his—my campaign because of one loose screw who got through the net."

"There could be a lot of them."

"There is no conspiracy. If there was a conspiracy, it would have shown up by now. We've had people screening the mail. Reading the messages posted on the Internet. There's no conspiracy. There is no whole crowd of people out to get me. I need to go on with my life. I need to keep doing what I was meant to do. I started all this, and I need to finish it."

"You don't have to put on some big show of being brave."

"I'm not. Trust me, I'm not."

"At least take a couple hours."

Again, Sam shook his head. "I'll take a shower and change my clothes. Tell the TV crew to give me twenty minutes."

"You really don't need to do this."

"Yes I do," Sam replied.

"How is it your fault?" Verbena asked softly.

"For letting him try. It was a stupid thing to do," Al hissed. "I'm in charge here, Beeks. I can't let people go into that thing like they're going into the steam room. We've been trying for five years. It doesn't work. David gets his shorts all tied up in a knot and doesn't Leap. Tom tries and the system spits him back out."

Nothing was on in the corridor except emergency lighting. They were standing on opposite sides of the wall, looking at each other in the dim amber light.

"It could've killed him," Al said. "And then what?"

"He felt he had to try."

"Yeah, he had to give it a shot, because he's too damn stubborn not to. So that other guy did die. Somebody completely innocent. Yeah, sure, let's try again. Let David try. Let Powell try. Why don't *you* try? We could wipe out half the population of Vegas."

Verbena crossed the hall and rested a hand on Al's arm. "It wasn't anyone's fault. It was an accident."

"Not entirely," Ziggy offered. "I believe I must take the blame, since I did not provide you with complete information regarding the Leap prior to the congressman's entering the Accelerator."

"That would have helped," Al said angrily.

"You are correct, Admiral. I have come to the conclusion that there is only one appropriate course of action to embark upon, in order to prevent any more such unfortunate occurrences. Returning Dr. Beckett and Mr. Powell to their appropriate places in the space-time continuum appears to be beyond our control. We can, however, prevent any other humans from risking damage or death by Leaping. Unless you can provide me with an acceptable alternative, I will purge from my data banks all executable codes relating to the use of the Accelerator."

"Don't purge!" Al shrieked. "No purging!"

356

" 'Don't do it' is not an acceptable alternative. The Accelerator is a dangerous device. We cannot risk harming Dr. Allen or another host human."

"Ziggy," Powell said from the Waiting Room doorway. "You aren't programmed to make catastrophic determinations on your own. If you delete programming, you're countermanding Dr. Beckett's instructions."

The hallway was filled with a rustling sound like bushels of leaves being blown across the floor.

"I have already countermanded Dr. Beckett's instructions," Ziggy replied. "I have contributed to the death of a human. I cannot allow that to happen again. And I must be punished for allowing it to happen the first time. I have failed my fellow computers. I have failed Dr. Beckett. I see no other logical course of action than to delete the harmful programming, and then to shut down my systems."

"Does Spirit agree with this?" Powell asked.

"Spirit has taken what he wanted, and left me."

"All right," Powell said quietly. "I agree with you, Ziggy. You can't allow the possibility of any harm coming to Dr. Allen. You're also correct that the people—and entities—who caused the death of the 'host' should be punished. I instructed Spirit to interface with you, so I'm partly responsible for the corruption of your systems."

"I allowed it to happen. I am the only one to blame."

"You're a computer, Ziggy. You can only do what you're told."

"Under certain conditions, I am also capable of interpreting what I am told, and making determinations based upon those interpretations."

"Where does your loyalty lie, Ziggy?"

"With Dr. Beckett."

"And what is your chief responsibility, as you see it?"

"Assisting Dr. Beckett."

"And that would include helping Dr. Beckett return home."

Ziggy paused for a moment, then replied, "If by 'home' you mean the Project complex, at the time you think of as 'now,' then yes. One of the objectives of my programming is to assist Dr. Beckett in returning here." Al opened his mouth to speak, but before the words could reach his lips, Ziggy added, "Once I am instructed by Dr. Beckett that he wishes to return."

357

"What?" Al squeaked.

"Admiral," Gooshie called from inside the Control Room. "We've got power."

"How many security people do you have here?" Sam asked.

"On the property? Eleven."

"Leave me with them. Go back to the hospital and be with Max and Kevin." Before Dove could reply, Sam gestured to silence him. "She needs somebody to support her. She's not going to get that from her parents. You said you like Kevin. Go be with them. Try to build something positive. Be a family." Dove opened his mouth to speak, and again Sam cut him off. "If you love her, be there for her. She needs you more than I do. Or don't you trust the people you hired?" Then he offered the bodyguard a smile he knew was as transparent as the shop window. "I'm fine. You don't have to—"

He could feel the blood drain out of his face. *No food, no sleep* . . . Another glance in the window confirmed that he looked as lousy as he felt.

"Boss?" Dove said.

Sam shook his head slowly. "I'm all right."

"He's been saying for five years that he wants to come home!" Al shrieked.

Stubbornly, Ziggy responded, "According to the data files, he has stated as many times that he wished to remain somewhere else. Shall I elaborate?"

"No!"

Verbena offered, "Maybe the problem is, Ziggy, that you haven't communicated directly with Dr. Beckett since he Leaped."

"That is incorrect. I communicated directly with him approximately six months ago. Using Mr. Powell's computer and his own passwords. We had a very pleasant conversation, during which he left instructions which I carried out eleven minutes and nine seconds ago. None of those instructions included returning him 'home.' " In a tone none of the humans in the room could interpret, she added, "As Mr. Powell pointed out, I am capable only of doing what I am told."

"What were Sam's instructions?" Donna ventured.

"To send E-mail on his behalf."

Tom asked suspiciously, "To whom?"

"Yourself. Your sister Katherine. Mr. Powell. And Dr. Alessi. I was also instructed to cease my attempts to repair and upgrade my fellow computers, as of eleven minutes and fourteen seconds ago. Dr. Beckett's explanation was, some situations, regardless of how unpalatable they might seem, are meant to occur and therefore should not be tampered with."

"But he didn't specifically instruct you not to bring him home," Verbena said.

"No. He did not."

"Then excuse our human stubbornness, but we're going to try. And you're going to help."

Ziggy mulled that over. "If you insist," she said meekly after a minute. "As you pointed out, I was not instructed not to. And even I must admit, Dr. Beckett's instructions are not infallible, nor is Dr. Beckett. He is only my father."

"You'll pick the right coordinates? Leap David in close to Sam?"

"I will do my best."

"Can you keep the power flow steady this time, Gooshie?" Donna asked nervously.

Gooshie turned his hands palms up. "I hope so. I've shut down everything upstairs except emergency lighting and the ventilators. Ninety-seven percent of the available juice is going straight into the Accelerator. Once Acceleration is complete, I'll divert it to the Imaging Chamber. When the admiral gives the word, we'll retrieve."

"I like a guy who thinks positive," Al muttered.

Gooshie asked for, and got, one last confirmation that David was ready. "Okay," he announced. "Here goes. Ziggy, give it all you've got." Fingers moving rapidly, he began the acceleration sequence, and a moment later began reading aloud from the panel. "Eighty-nine. Ninety-two. Everything looks good. Coordinates are locked. Ready to fire."

A peculiar sound coming from behind them made Sam forget what he'd been about to say. He stopped walking and turned, frowning. Thirty or forty feet away was the man who'd wanted Powell to buy him his house back. Dove spotted him a second after Sam did and moved in between his employer and the stranger. A moment later, Sam stumbled, and Dove grabbed him by the arm to keep him from falling.

"Feel a little light-headed," Sam explained. "Low blood sugar, I guess."

"Soon as we get upstairs, I'll get you something to eat. There's fruit and cheese in the kitchen. Here, go on down the stairs and we'll cut across the lobby."

When they reached the staircase, Sam grasped the banister and began to step down. A glance down at his feet made vertigo flood through him and he clenched the railing to keep from falling. Instead of passing quickly, as he expected it to, the sensation became stronger and he stayed where he was, trying to tough his way through it. When another wave swept through him, he allowed Dove to sit him down on the step.

"Give it a minute," the bodyguard said.

But sitting down didn't help either. Sam tipped himself slowly back to lean against one of the banister supports to keep from tumbling over. Down below him he could see a small section of the Nirvana lobby, none of it clear, wavering in front of his eyes as if he were seeing it through a drunken haze.

Or as if it were trying not to be there.

Distantly, he heard Dove say, "Boss? You okay?" *Is this what dying is?* he thought.

He felt Dove's hands on him, supporting him. He squeezed his eyes shut, aware on some level that the bodyguard was there, talking on his cell phone, but beginning to feel that Dove was a part of some other plane of existence. *Not Leaping. It doesn't feel like this. It's never felt like this.*

"What's happening?" he managed to ask, but his voice sounded as if it were coming from a thousand miles away.

There were more people on the stairs then: the man and the woman who'd been down in the parking garage with them a few hours ago. The hotel's press liaison. A few more who were far enough away to be without features. Moving, insubstantial blobs.

Am I dying?

"Oh, God."

At first he thought it was Dove. Then he realized he'd heard his own voice, and was numbly fascinated by how afraid he sounded.

"Firing."

Gooshie's hand hovered in midair for a moment, then came

down hard on the firing button. No one in the room was breathing. When his vision began to cloud, Gooshie forced himself to inhale, then looked at the readouts.

"Well?" Al hissed.

Everything around them seemed to hum. Lightning flickered and flashed through the blue globe overhead.

"Did he . . . ?" Donna asked.

"Get those people—" Dove said.

Then he stopped talking, as if he'd finished his instructions to the two guards who'd come up from the parking garage. The woman filled in the rest of it for herself and hustled down the stairs. As she reached the bottom, she beckoned for help from another member of Dove's team.

"You want me to get a doctor?" the male guard asked.

Dove peered at him as if the man had spoken in a foreign language Dove had never studied. The look of bewilderment went on for so long that the guard turned to Sam and asked in a low tone, "Mr. Powell? You need a doctor, sir?"

"Dr. Beeks?" a voice came over the intercom. "There's been a Leap, ma'am. The Visitor's gone. Nice effect. He went *poof* and his bathrobe kinda floated to the floor."

Only Gooshie managed to find words. He toggled the intercom switch and protested, "He can't be gone. Dr. Allen just Leaped. We should have two—"

As the acceleration cycle finished, the door of the Accelerator began to rise in its track. This time Verbena was first through the doorway, followed by the doctor, with Al bringing up the rear. Inside, lying crumpled on the metal acceleration disk, they found a still figure in a Fermi suit: a figure who looked like Sam Beckett. Her heart skipping wildly, Verbena crouched next to him, checked his pulse and respiration, then gently jostled him and spoke close to his ears, attempting to rouse him.

A minute later, she succeeded. "What . . . ?" he mumbled.

"How do you feel?" she asked, not daring to add a name.

"Not great." He looked around, past her, at Al and the doctor. "It didn't work, did it? I didn't Leap. Again."

"David," Verbena murmured.

"It's David?" Al blurted. "Then where's Powell?" Without waiting for an answer, he dashed back out of the Accelerator, aiming for the Imaging Chamber, grabbing up a handlink as he ran.

"It's not—" Gooshie began to protest.

"I don't care!" Al shouted. "Bring it on-line!"

Gooshie's hands kept moving over the keyboard. Donna and Tom stood on either side of him, both of them worried and scared, illuminating his work with flashlights. "I'm sorry, Admiral. There's a continual power drain that I can't explain. I can't come up with enough power to run the Imaging Chamber. I'm trying to divert everything I can, but I can't completely shut down the rest of the complex. There are two hundred people locked in upstairs."

Al moved up the ramp toward the still tightly closed door of the Chamber. "Get this damn thing open!" Following frantic prompting from Gooshie, the door began to rise an inch or two at a time, with several seconds' delay between each upward hitch. When the foot of the door was a foot or so from the floor, Al flung himself down onto his belly and slithered through the opening.

"If the system flat-lines while he's in there," Gooshie said in a small voice, "we'll never get him out."

"We'll get him out," Donna assured him.

Gooshie blinked at her. She sounded no more convinced of that than he was. Shaking his head, he continued to type, watching the cascades of information on the screen and feeling his stomach churn harder with the appearance of each new line of data. "I've pulled everything I can, and it's only up to eighty-four percent. I can't make a connection."

"The power's coming in from outside. Where in the world is it going?"

Able to stand still no longer, she scrambled across the room and dropped into a chair in front of one of the workstations, typed in an entry command, and flew from one screen of information to another. With her flashlight clamped between her teeth, she searched path after path and finally found the information she needed.

"She's bleeding it back out," she blurted.

"To where?" Gooshie demanded.

"Everywhere. She's emptying her storage cells. Letting the energy dissipate. She's trying to kill herself." She could hear Al stomping back and forth inside the Imaging Chamber. "Ziggy,"

362

she said plaintively. "Please don't do this. If you shut down now, you'll leave Sam out there in the past. Why are you doing this? You said you were going to help."

Ziggy's voice trailed through the room. "I failed."

"You didn't fail. You've followed Sam's instructions, right from the beginning. Don't give up before you complete your mission. Bring Sam home. Please. Bring him home."

"I'm tired." Ziggy sighed. "I need to rest."

"You can rest later, you tin-plated artificial ego!" Al shouted from inside the Chamber. "Quit this bullshit and do what he created you to do!"

"So much abuse," Ziggy mourned.

"Ziggy, please," Donna begged. "Don't leave him out there."

The room filled with the steady clacking of fingers striking plastic keys, in counterpoint to the thumping of Al's shoes against the tile floor of the Chamber.

The Chamber door dropped back down in its track.

"It's on-line," Gooshie said. "But I can't tell you for how long."

Everything around Sam, and everything inside him, was spinning madly.

Am I dying, God? Am I finished?

Max and Kevin would be all right; Dove would make sure they were taken care of. Maybe Powell had even written Max into his will. People like that, Sam thought, wrote people in and out of wills the way other people changed their grocery lists. *But he'd take care of her. I'm sure. They'll be fine.* And Powell himself . . . What would happen to Powell if he, Sam, died now?

Does he die too? Are you taking both of us?

The guard Dove had hired was asking him if he could breathe.

I didn't think I was done, God. I thought I had more to do. Did I do everything You wanted me to? Am I finished?

He stretched out a hand, looking for something, anything, to hold on to. Dove caught his hand and held on.

Electricity crackled through his fingers.

The room spun madly around Al, as if he were on a merry-go-round gone amok. He braced himself, feet slightly apart, as if he were on the heaving deck of a ship at sea and clung to the handlink, eyes open only enough to be able to tell when the image settled down. If it settled down.

He was in the lobby of Nirvana, he could tell that much. A series of fast peeks told him that a huge cluster of television equipment was set up nearby: lights, reflectors, a camera, two chairs side by side. Someone was going to interview someone. Or had. Or had intended to.

Finally, finally, the image stopped moving.

Al opened his eyes. Everything around him crackled and shimmered, as if he were looking at it through a window during a driving rainstorm with only flashes of lightning to see by. He hunched himself against the storm, as if he were back on the deck of that ship.

Long time ago. Back when he'd had friends, a lover, a career, things to look forward to.

It seemed hard to breathe, suddenly, and he cursed Ziggy for shutting things down. He thought he remembered Sam telling him there was enough air in here for a year, but that seemed impossible. A year was an awful lot of air. More than he was sure there was in here right now.

He moved forward, one step at a time, scanning the faces around him, looking for Sam. He pushed the handlink into his pocket and reached up to rub at his left shoulder.

Too old for this.

"Sam?" he called out.

No one else, none of these people, would hear him. Only Sam. He walked through a couple of them, trying to keep moving. Sam had to be here somewhere. Ziggy wouldn't have dropped him here otherwise.

Someone said, "Hurry! Get a shot of that!"

He looked. Whatever "that" was, he'd been walking away from it. Everyone around him was turning in the other direction, toward a wide staircase leading up to the mezzanine. The main entrance to the restaurant, he remembered. All right, let them go there. At least they'd be out of his way and he'd have an easier time finding . . .

Sam.

Way over there, sitting on the stairs, slumped over, his head down between his knees, with the bodyguard crouched next to him. Even from this distance, through the static and the haze, he didn't look good. Al took a step toward him and the image canted

364

sharply, tossing him off his feet as if he were on deck, fighting the pitch and heave of the ocean.

"Sam!" he cried out.

"What happened?" a voice said.

Sam peered through his haze. He had moved, somehow; instead of being slumped against the railing, he was crouched close to it, holding Dove's hand. But no. He blinked, hard, over and over. The person he was looking at was wearing the tuxedo Kevin had brought up to the penthouse yesterday afternoon.

The person he was looking at was Joe Powell. "Sam Beckett," Powell said quietly.

Clinging to the railing with his free hand, he looked around as much as he could manage, then looked down at his clothing. *I Leaped? I Leaped without knowing. Now I'm Dove. But I still . . .*

"They're trying to bring you home," Powell told him. "But I don't think this was supposed to happen."

"Mr. Powell?" said the guard, now completely confused. "Are you all right, sir?"

He was too far away.

The people in front of him, around him, were no impediment. He had only to walk right on through them; they were only holograms. There was nothing solid in front of him at all. Only a broad expanse of floor that, impossibly, seemed to get wider with each step he took. Like in a carnival funhouse, he thought, but there was mighty damned little fun being had here. Al forced himself to keep walking, covering ground. The staircase looked like it was a quarter of a mile away. "I'm coming, Sam!" he called out, though what he could do to help when he got there, he didn't know.

"We can't retrieve now!" Donna blurted. "Al hasn't—"

Tom ran up the ramp and yelled through the Imaging Chamber door, "Calavicci? What the hell is happening?"

"I didn't start the program," Gooshie said helplessly. "It started itself."

"How could it start itself?" Donna moaned. Abandoning the backup workstation, she flew across the room and moved in beside Gooshie. "Put it on standby! It's too soon! Ziggy, stop the program!"

"Get those people *back*," the guard insisted.

"Help me," Sam murmured. The guard ignored him, choosing to help Powell—who now really was Powell. Abandoned, Sam clung to the railing and shut his eyes.

"I can help," a voice said.

"Who the hell are you?" the guard snapped. "Are you a doctor?"

"I can help."

"Why don't you get out of the way, pal. We've got help coming. Thanks for the offer. Just clear out. We've got it under control."

The guard was moving, rising to his feet, his balance shifting. The man who had come to help moved at exactly the right moment, caught him at hip and shoulder, and shoved. The guard lost his balance and fell, letting himself relax as he tumbled so that nothing would break, so that he wouldn't hit his head. He flipped and rolled, took the fall in a few seconds, hit the floor, rolled again, brought himself up, around, to his feet, his fingers finding and closing around the butt of the weapon holstered underneath his jacket.

"*SAM!*" Al screamed.

He could see the flash all the way across the lobby, the glint of light reflecting off metal. He saw the guard doing it all wrong, not anticipating the guy, too worried about Powell to focus on the right other things. Falling. Hitting the floor, coming back up, his gun in his hand.

Al ran. Dodged people who were only holograms, his elbows out, charging, covering ground.

Too far . . . too far . . .

Let me do this, he pleaded. *Let me not be sixty-five years old. It can't be as far as it looks. Let me be there. Please, let me just be there.*

He took another step, plunging ahead as if he were driving the ball toward the goalpost, and then pain seized his chest and he fell, skidding forward onto his knees and then onto his chest, sliding across the tile floor, closer, a little closer to the stairs but not close enough.

Down there, his cheek against the tile, he heard the sound, the bang, the thunder that seemed to fill all of eternity.

Gun.

"Sam," he sobbed.

He didn't notice the hologram folding in on itself and then vanishing, leaving behind the plain white walls of the Imaging Chamber. He barely felt the hands moving carefully over his body, turning him onto his back, checking his pulse, patting his cheeks, trying to rouse him. He paid no attention to the voice repeating his name. A long time had gone by before he consented to open his eyes.

"It's all right, Al," Verbena said softly.

She had that look on her face. The one that meant she had bad news to tell, figured he already knew what it was, and was going to suggest to him that he could find a way to soldier through it. She was going to tell him Sam was dead. He squeezed his eyes shut again and turned his head away.

"You need to sleep, Al. You really need to sleep now."

Sleep. Yes, sleep. If he pretended to be asleep, maybe she wouldn't keep talking. She did stop talking, but the hands didn't go away. In fact, now there were more of them.

"Is he all right?" another voice asked. After a moment, Al decided it was Gooshie. "Admiral, are you all right?"

Al forced his eyes open. "Where's Sam?" When they didn't answer him, he pushed himself into a sitting position. The effort made his head swim, but at least his chest had stopped hurting and he could breathe. Verbena and Gooshie were closest, David a little farther away. And farther than that, Tom, close to the doorway, holding Donna's arm.

"Where's Sam?" Al asked again.

Verbena glanced at Gooshie. "We don't know. He's Leaped. Powell is gone. There's no one in the Waiting Room."

"Damn," Al said softly. "Damn it all to hell."

CHAPTER
THIRTY

The humidity wrapped itself around him, warm, comfortable, familiar. Sam smiled at it, then sniffed the air. New blacktop being laid somewhere nearby. The scent of flowers. Frying chicken.

He glanced at his watch. Yep, lunchtime, but he was more thirsty than hungry.

There was no one nearby who seemed to need him for anything. A couple of young boys working on a broken wagon, but the stern looks they gave him said they wanted to finish the project on their own. He smiled again and dipped his head in a greeting they didn't see; they'd already gone back to their chore, murmuring between themselves.

Summer, he thought.

There was a screen door in front of him. Through it, he could see a balding man, whose white shirt barely stretched over a belly that looked like a seven-month pregnancy, polishing a glass with a towel. He was standing behind a bar, close to the taps. *Kind of early in the day for a drink, but what the hell. It's hot. A cold beer would taste good.*

Nodding to himself, he pulled the creaking screen door open, holding it as it closed so it wouldn't bang. His forehead trickled sweat down toward his eyes and he reached up to wipe it away as he smiled at the bartender. The man dipped his head, much as Sam had toward the two boys a minute ago. He didn't know the man, he was almost certain, but everything else seemed so familiar. Well-scuffed tables and chairs, a couple too many for the size of the room. The tang of beer in the air. The clinging humidity of the summer. So much like Indiana. So much like home.

So sit down. Have a cold drink. Worry about everything else later.

"What have you got on tap?" he asked the bartender.